We skirted the colliery, and I kept glancing back with each
explosion. The gunship hovered at a distance while the
interceptors swept in, spreading fire and mayhem. The house
was still intact, and now the small craft paused in their
attacks while the gunship descended until it hung no more
than a hundred yards above the house.

White light from the belly of the ship bathed the entire
area.

'You will surrender immediately. No further attacks will be
made. You will surrender immediately.'

The amplified message came from the gunship. It was
repeated. I pulled Victoria down behind a low wall, searching
the hillsides with my eyes for some sign of Alex and the
others.

I heard the sound of rifle-fire and knew it came from the
house, a defiant and futile attempt to resist the attackers with
shotguns. A gust of wind cloaked us briefly in gorse smoke.
There was a huge pneumatic thump, and the house erupted
in a cataclysm of fire.

The blast of heat from the explosion seared our faces, and I
pushed Victoria down. When I finally looked up again,
fleeing sheep shone like phantoms in the fierce light of the
inferno. The house was gone.

Aztec Century

CHRISTOPHER EVANS

VICTOR GOLLANCZ

LONDON

TO FAITH
(this means you have to read it . . .)

First published in Great Britain 1993
by Victor Gollancz, an imprint of Cassell,
Villiers House, 41/47 Strand, London WC2N 5JE

A catalogue record for this book is available
from the British Library

ISBN 0 575 05538 3 (Hardback)
ISBN 0 575 05540 5 (Paperback)

Typeset by CentraCet, Cambridge
and printed in Great Britain by
Mackays of Chatham plc, Chatham, Kent

In my dreams, I dream of Aztecs . . .

*. . . and wake to find myself here, alone with my ruined sister,
lost not only to history but to memory itself.*

*We have an old stone farmhouse, my sister and I, secluded in
the same Welsh valley where our story truly began – and yet it is
not the same valley, at least not to me. We live quietly, seeing only
the local man who brings our provisions from the town. He is
cheerful but inquisitive, and I mistrust him greatly. No one else
disturbs our solitude. Essentially I am alone, and when my sister's
needs have been attended to each day, I spend hours at the study
window, staring down the valley.*

Dreaming.

*Last week I had notebooks and pens delivered with our groceries.
Today, another day of rain like so many here, I intend to begin
writing our story. To what purpose I'm not sure. For others to
read so that they can marvel or scorn? To record history, exorcize
demons, cool the fires of memory? I can't honestly say it's for any
of these reasons but rather to fill up the empty hours and so give
myself purpose and meaning.*

PART ONE

The House of Sorrow

One

In those thousand days of our first exile, my dreams were always of London burning. Although I was twenty-one and already married at the time of the invasion, dreaming, I became a child again, a young girl running along the palace corridors, passing tall windows where I glimpsed the night sky full of the enemy's luminous golden ships. They hovered and darted, raining bright fire down on the city. I was confused and terrified, desperately seeking my father.

Finally I burst into his council chamber, where he sat at the head of a long gleaming table, my brother Richard on his lap, a child like myself. The silence made me halt, see the grimness in everyone's face. I ran to my father's side, and he embraced me. He wore a dark suit and a white open-necked shirt; his face was grey with exhaustion. He kissed me on the forehead and shook his head sadly. Then adult hands took me, dragging me away, through halls and down stairways and out into the fiery night. I was still screaming, my eyes flooded with tears, when they bundled me aboard the carrier, where my nanny sat with my sister Victoria, an infant asleep in her lap.

The true circumstances of our escape were more prosaic. When the attack began, Alex and I were at my family home in Marlborough, supervising the storage of art treasures in the vaults. We were evacuated by night, first to one of our estates near Okehampton, where Victoria joined us, and then by various misadventures to the Welsh borders, where our carrier ran out of fuel. We made an emergency landing near Monmouth and were rescued by a ragtag group of Welsh loyalists, who promptly abandoned us in the Sirhowy valley, retreating into mid-Wales with most of their countryfolk as the Aztec armies advanced rapidly northwards from their bridgeheads at London and Southampton.

We took refuge in a deserted mansion house, expecting imminent capture. There were only twelve of us, and the radio bulletins of the next several days were confused and alarming. London was said to have been laid waste by firestorms; enemy forces had already advanced to Nottingham and Bristol; a transporter carrying my cousin Margaret from St Petersburg had been shot down over the Baltic; my father and brother were reported dead after the palace had been stormed.

None of these stories proved entirely true, except that London had fallen and the Aztecs were making rapid gains. Margaret remained safely in Moscow with Tsar Mikhail, and my father and brother had been captured rather than killed. It was a measure of our beleaguered state of mind that we greeted such news with a relief bordering on joy.

As it turned out, we avoided capture, largely because organized resistance to the invasion collapsed within a matter of weeks. The Aztecs halted their advance after consolidating their positions north to the Tees and west to the Severn and Exe. Our armies surrendered and a truce was signed. Not long afterwards, Nauhyotl, a cousin of the Emperor Motecuhzoma, was installed in London as governor. The occupation of England was complete.

Three years passed.

On that final morning in Wales, I woke from my dreams to find myself alone in bed. Alex rose early most mornings to monitor radio transmissions on the equipment we had salvaged from the transporter.

The grandfather clock beside the door said nine thirty. Had I slept so long? I still felt weary, and there was a sour taste in my mouth.

The water in the bathroom came out in a lukewarm dribble. Dressed in a sweater and jeans – clothes scavenged from the deserted town of Tredegar further up the valley – I crossed the landing and noticed that the door to Victoria's bedroom was open a crack.

My sister lay asleep in a swirl of sheets, blonde hair splayed on the pillow, the room ripe with her body heat. The bed was utterly unkempt, as if she had also been wrestling with disturbing dreams. She was three years younger than I, and had hated every moment of our exile.

Downstairs, porridge and coffee were simmering on the wood-fired stove, and the sink was full of breakfast dishes. We grew oats, barley and root vegetables in the surrounding fields, and had rounded up chickens, three cows and a flock of sheep from the hillsides after our arrival. We supplemented our diet with tinned goods from the shops in Tredegar which had escaped looting before the town was abandoned during the mass retreat into mid-Wales. There, in the empty heartlands of their nation, the Welsh believed themselves safe from further Aztec encroachment.

My stomach felt leaden and I could not face breakfast. Cradling a mug of coffee, I stood at the window, watching Thomas and Sarah at work in the greenhouse. Both had been staff in our household before the invasion, and Sarah had miscarried a baby the previous summer. It would have been the first child born here, and everyone had shared her loss.

I set to work on the dishes, putting a kettle on the stove to boil. Then Alex strode in, a broad smile on his bearded face. Freshly showered and smelling of Duc du Lac cologne, he kissed me on the cheek and led me away from the sink.

'I'm washing up,' I protested.

'Leave it. Bevan's having trouble with the generator, and the hot water's down again.'

'I'm boiling a kettle.'

'Kate,' he said with firm patience, 'sit down.' He gently pressed me into a chair. 'I want to talk to you.'

He straddled another chair gaucho-fashion.

'I overslept,' I said.

'It's allowed once in a while. After all, you are the King's daughter.'

'You're very cheerful this morning.'

He helped himself to a mouthful of my coffee. 'I've good reason to be.'

He was dressed in a chunky fawn sweater and dark brown

cavalry twill trousers; he always managed to look well groomed, whatever the circumstances. Tall and strongly built, with his auburn hair grown long and his beard dense, he was like a lion of a man to me.

'How's your Russian?' he asked.

'My Russian?'

'*Nyet*, Vladivostok, and all that.'

I eyed him. 'Alex, what's all this about?'

'Your cousin's husband's sending a ship for us.'

He drained the last of my coffee, awaiting my reaction.

'Is this a joke, Alex?'

'No joke, Kate. I got the news only half an hour ago. It'll be here some time tonight or early morning.'

I sat back in my chair to ease the ache in my belly. Alex had always enjoyed springing surprises, but this was not the usual sort.

'They're coming to pick us up?'

He nodded.

'I didn't even know we were in contact with Moscow.'

'It was pure luck,' he replied. 'Six days ago I locked on to one of their spy planes doing an overfly. I broadcast an SOS. This morning I got confirmation that a ship's coming for us.'

It was obvious he wasn't teasing, yet it seemed too fortuitous to be true.

'Are you sure?'

'I'm sure.'

'What if it's a set-up? A trap?'

He shook his head. 'I signed the message Charlotte Brontë. The one that came back this morning was signed Anne.'

This, I had to admit, was a clever stroke. As children, Margaret, Victoria and I had played at being the Brontë sisters, Margaret being Anne, myself Charlotte and Victoria Emily. Alex was the only person I had ever told, and if the message had been relayed to Moscow, Margaret would have known it was genuine. That there had been a reply in kind settled matters.

'Why didn't you say anything until now?'

'I wanted to be certain it was a Russian ship. I didn't want to raise your hopes unnecessarily.'

He reached across and took my hand. I felt a certain excitement but also other, mixed emotions.

'Just think of it,' Alex said. 'Escape at last. Freedom.'

'Are they going to fly us straight to Moscow?'

'I presume so. Somewhere within their borders at least. It's what we've been waiting for.'

'Have you told the others?'

'Not yet. I'm going to announce it at lunch. Then I think we're entitled to a little celebration.'

His optimism was infectious, and I couldn't begrudge him the good news, even though leaving England would mean abandoning my father and Richard to their imprisonment. We really had no other option. Sooner or later, the Aztecs would push into Wales, and we would be captured if we remained.

Alex seemed to sense my thoughts. 'There's nothing more we can do here, Kate. We'll be better placed to continue the fight in Russia.'

'I know. It's just not that simple for me.'

'Of course it isn't. I do understand, you know. But there'll be plenty of other exiles there. Don't forget that half the Royal Navy made it to Murmansk after the invasion.'

I decided to be positive. 'It'll be good to see Margaret again.'

He squeezed my hand. 'There's something else. Something it's time I showed you.'

'What?'

'Not here. Upstairs.'

Despite the gravity of his manner, there was also a gleam in his eye. I knew full well what a visit to our bedroom would entail.

Late morning sunlight shone full through the window as we lay together.

'So,' I said at length, 'what is it you wanted to show me?'

'A small thing,' he replied, 'but mine own.'

Nimbly he leapt out of bed and went to the bottom drawer of his dresser, removing an attaché case. He had worked for the Ministry of Defence before the invasion, and I had always known that the case contained something important, without ever asking him what.

He opened it on the bed. It held several document wallets, but Alex removed a flat square object which I recognized as a computer disk. He held it out to me as if it were a sacred offering.

'Just what I've always wanted,' I said, with eager sarcasm. 'What is it exactly?'

Alex sat back on the bed. 'It's the culmination of more than ten years' work, Kate. It's a piece of software, an advanced analytical intelligence programme with a random response capacity.'

I was illiterate as far as computers were concerned. 'What does that mean in plain English? Can it fry an egg?'

'It's a kind of parasite,' he told me. 'Something that can insert itself into existing systems and extract information from them. But secretly, without being detected unless you're really looking for it.'

Under the bedclothes, I drew my knees up to my chin. 'So it's important, is it?'

He knew I was teasing, and he gave me a suitably patronizing smile.

'If we could get access to the enemy's security networks, we'd be able to ransack their files, plant false information, do pretty well what we please. It could be devastating, Kate.'

'Gosh.'

He snatched up a pillow and swiped me across the head.

'Don't mock. It's even more impressive than you realize, and I'm sure the good Tsar and his government are going to be very interested in it. We're not just taking ourselves to Russia, Kate, we're taking something that's going to be of vital importance in the battle against the Aztecs.'

Bevan was out on the front garden lawn, crouching over the generator. He had removed two of the fan-shaped solar concentrators and was working on the third with an adjustable wrench.

'*Bore da*,' I said, crouching beside him.

'Blasted thing,' he said without looking round. 'Hold that for me, will you?'

He passed me a greasy bolt and washer, continuing to tinker for a moment, grunting under his breath.

'What's wrong with it?' I asked.

'We've been using it non-stop this last twelvemonth or more. Something's got to give.'

I helped him lay the concentrator down on the grass. It was twice my height but quite lightweight, its matt-black panels iridescent in the sunlight. It was veined with slender support struts like a butterfly's wing.

At the centre of the generator sat the sun-crystal, striated and multifaceted, the colour of zinc. Manufactured from reed-like coralline growths which the Aztecs farmed in their coastal waters, the crystals absorbed sunlight at high efficiencies. Bevan had jury-rigged the generator from the transporter's drive-units, and it supplied all our heating and lighting.

Bevan unscrewed a conducting disc and began sanding it with a scrap of emery cloth. He was a pot-bellied man of about forty, lantern-jawed and balding, dark hair hanging lank behind his ears.

'Always potching with it, I am,' he continued to grumble. 'More trouble than it's worth, if you ask me.'

I was tempted to tell him not to bother, but Alex was always warning me to mind what I said to him. Soon after our arrival in the valley, Bevan had appeared, seemingly from nowhere, and had since become our handyman and fixer. His motives remained elusive, and I knew we had to be careful. Many people in Wales had proved fickle in their attachment to the nation's cause, refusing to fight after the Aztecs had guaranteed the territorial sovereignty of Wales during the invasion. Though that sovereignty was now seen by most Welsh to be a sham, their loyalty to the Crown was far from solid.

I lingered for a moment, watching him unscrew the covering on the control panel.

'Anything else I can do?' I asked.

'Want to get your hands dirty, do you?'

'I just thought – '

'I'll give you a shout if I need you.'

Somewhat rebuffed, I left him to his labours, unsure whether he was being bloody-minded or just gruffly matter-of-fact. He had never actually acknowledged who we were, though he certainly knew. It was quite possible he heartily disliked all of us but relished the continued opportunity to display his resentment.

The terraced lawns once fronting the house had been turned into vegetable patches for peas, runner beans and root crops. The house was a Gothic Revival mansion built over a hundred years before by an English mine-owner. We had chosen it because it was large and partly screened by a pine plantation. It looked out over the valley, with the derelict pit directly below; both pit and mansion were called Ty Trist, the House of Sorrow. The mine-owner had been hated by the locals and was buried in a secluded graveyard with the stark inscription GOD FORGIVE HIM on his tombstone.

It was a fine September morning, the bracken on the valley slopes turning the same colour as the rusting winding tower. The pit itself was surrounded by spoil-heaps on which only a sparse grass grew. The colliery had closed down fifty years before when the first solar units were imported from Greater Mexico.

Though our life in the valley had been rugged and sometimes perilous these past three years, I knew I would miss it. The Sirhowy river which meandered its way along the shallow valley bottom was little more than a broad rocky stream. It was a word of uncertain Welsh provenance which Bevan claimed meant 'angry water' – a name fit for an Aztec noble.

Behind me, Bevan swore in Welsh. I turned and saw him duck as the red light of the tracking mechanism flashed on and the support framework slewed towards him, just missing his head. He delved into the base of the machine, and the movement stopped.

I retraced my steps. Bevan took a grubby handkerchief from his trousers and swabbed his brow. He looked exasperated and irritable.

'Leave it,' I said. 'We can manage without it for today.'

He peered at me, his eyes shadowed by his square brow. 'I take it you'll be telling your sister she's got to bath in cold water, then?'

Victoria liked a hot bath every day after rising, but she would be more preoccupied with the news about the Russian ship.

'I don't think she'll mind today.'

'Still in bed, is she?' Bevan hoisted his trousers and sucked on his teeth. 'She gets plenty of beauty sleep, that one.'

★

I spent the afternoon with Victoria, packing our few belongings into two suitcases. From the bottom drawer of a dresser, I produced the old atlas my father had given me on my tenth birthday. It had been printed in 1930, during the reign of my grandfather, and its pages gave off the odour of history both literally and metaphorically. Stiff and musty, they mapped large areas of the world in crimson, recalling a time, only sixty years ago, when the British Empire was at its height. On modern maps, the crimson was displaced by swathes of Aztec gold.

Victoria put on our mother's wedding dress, which she had saved as a keepsake. It was an elaborate affair of white silks and French lace, unfashionably frilly and ornate. It fitted her perfectly. Our mother had died when Richard was born, and neither of us could remember her well; but from photographs I knew that Victoria resembled her strongly. Now twenty-one, she was entering the prime of her beauty, fair-skinned with hazel eyes and striking dark eyebrows.

She flounced in front of the mirror, then said, 'I wonder what would happen if I wore this to our first reception in Moscow.'

'You'd certainly create a stir. But you'd have to have the mothballs washed out of it first.'

'Do you think Margaret and Mikhail will greet us when we arrive?'

'I'm sure they will, but not formally, or in public. Russia's technically neutral, and it wouldn't be politic.'

'Won't it be marvellous to be somewhere civilized again? I'm so tired of dressing in old clothes and eating potatoes every day.'

She, more than any of us, heartily disliked the rigours of our life in the valley. And she was right to be excited at the prospect of greater comforts and freedom. I wished I could share her enthusiasm wholeheartedly, but I had always imagined that we would eventually escape to another part of the country to join an army in hiding, which would begin the reconquest of our land. A romantic fantasy, of course. For me, leaving Britain would not really be escape, but flight, an acceptance of the finality of conquest.

That evening, everyone gathered in the candle-lit hall and we feasted on our produce: roast lamb with carrots, parsnips and green beans, washed down with several bottles of claret which Alex had unearthed from somewhere. Victoria got rather drunk, but gracefully allowed Alex to escort her to bed.

We gathered on the balcony. It was a clear, moonless night, mild and still, the stars brilliant above us. A match flared in the darkness in front of Alex's face, and he put it to the end of a cigarette.

'Where did you get those?' someone asked.

Alex was holding a pack of Albions. We had run out of cigarettes a year before.

Alex simply winked and offered the pack around, taking suitable satisfaction from his largesse. He was the eldest son of Lord Bewley of Norwich, and had been created Duke of Durham by my father when we married; but he had always had the common touch. Of the small retinue which had escaped with us from Marlborough, all were former staff – detectives, butlers, maids-in-waiting – but exile had broken down the barriers between us. We had each been forced to take our part in the urgent and continuing business of survival.

I tracked a bright star-like point across the sky until it was lost over the horizon. The Aztecs were reputed to have a spy satellite orbiting the Earth which could photograph a rabbit in a field from a height of one hundred miles. Alex assured me the Russian ship would know their positions and be able to avoid detection. It was almost certain the Aztecs were aware our house was inhabited, but we assumed they would have no means of knowing by whom. I sometimes wondered if Alex was right that we had continued to remain free because of the Aztec policy of leaving unconquered territorial pockets intact in regions after invasion in order to maintain their armies' sharpness. Much of Wales and Scotland had been spared, in defiance of normal military logic.

I became aware that Bevan was present, a silent, forgotten figure on the edge of our group. He was the only one who knew nothing of our impending evacuation. I asked Alex for his cigarettes and went over to him.

'Would you like one?' I asked.

He took the pack, withdrew a cigarette and sniffed it, inspecting the tiny gold crowns stamped around the filter.

'Got a light, have you?'

I lit the cigarette for him.

'Do you know what's happening?' I asked.

He squinted at me. 'Planning on taking a trip, are you?'

'A ship's on its way. A ship from Russia.'

It seemed to me quite unfair that we had told him nothing. He might want to come with us, and even if he didn't, we could hardly leave him without an explanation.

'Coming tonight, is it?'

'We think so. There's room for you if you want to join us.'

He drew heavily on his cigarette, exhaling through his nostrils. 'Is there, now?'

I felt uncomfortable. 'I only heard about it myself this morning. Probably no one's bothered to tell you because they assume you want to stay here.'

'Being Welsh, as I am, no doubt.'

I couldn't tell whether he was being sarcastic.

'I mean it,' I said. 'We all appreciate the help you've given us here. If you come, I'll make sure you're looked after when we get to Russia.'

'Very generous of you,' he said drily. 'Couldn't go without talking it over with my mam, though, could I?'

I never knew when he was joking. He claimed that his mother lived alone in Trefil, a village to the north of Tredegar, and that he had stayed behind to look after her. We had never been able to confirm this. He came and went as he pleased.

'Bring her with you if you want to,' I said.

He looked beyond me at the others. I couldn't see his eyes under the shadow of his brow.

'I'll think about it,' he said, then turned and went back into the house.

Alex had volunteered to take first watch. I stood with him on the balcony.

'I've told Bevan what's happening,' I said.

'Oh? Do you think that was entirely wise?'

'It can't make any difference now, can it? Besides, think of how much we owe him. I've offered him a place on the ship if he wants it.'

He said nothing to this. I knew he and Bevan had never liked one another, but the Welshman had done as much as Alex to ensure our continued survival. I doubted he would want to leave his homeland for an uncertain future in Russia.

There was a draggy pain in the small of my back, and when Alex suggested we steal off to our bedroom for half an hour, for once I pleaded tiredness. He was ten years older than I, and we had met at Henley when I was eighteen. At first my father had resisted our involvement because Alex was a divorcé, with a reputation as a womanizer. I had found him irresistible from the start, and his appetite for me remained as strong as ever.

'Besides,' I said, seeing his disappointment, 'we can't leave the fort unguarded.'

Another pinpoint of light was crossing the sky, winking as it went. The night was utterly still and silent, and I felt that we were naked under the gaze of the heavens. At that moment a terrible sense of foreboding filled me, though I couldn't explain why.

'Have you got my cigarettes?' Alex said.

It was only then I realized that Bevan had taken the whole pack.

It was Alex who shook me awake. Groggy, I sat up and saw the first blue hints of dawn through the window.

'Is it here?' I asked.

'Not yet. But I'd be grateful if you took over the watch.'

'Have you been up all night?'

He shrugged. 'I thought I'd let everyone get plenty of rest. It could be a long day today.'

'Into bed immediately,' I ordered him.

I dressed and went down to the balcony. The dawn chorus had started, though the valley still lay in darkness. Everyone else apart from Victoria was asleep on sofas and armchairs in the drawing room beyond.

Perhaps the Russian craft had been delayed or even shot down. According to Alex, it would most likely follow a northerly route to avoid Aztec airspace in mainland Europe and England, coming down over the Irish Sea and approaching us from the west. I began to fear that it had never set out in the first place.

I went to the kitchen and put a pot of water on the paraffin stove. The smell of the stove made me feel nauseous, so I returned to the balcony.

And then I saw it.

Far south, down the twilit valley, framed by the rounded black hills, was a point of light.

My immediate instinct was to rouse the others and give them the good news that at last the Russians were coming. But as I stared, the point of light resolved into three – one larger, the other two smaller.

All were golden.

For long moments I did not move. I couldn't take my eyes off their firefly glow, as gold as the sun.

'Enemy aircraft!' I shouted. 'They're coming!'

In the drawing room, everyone awoke. There was a brief befuddled panic before Alex appeared and confirmed that they were indeed Aztec craft. He began marshalling us.

I rushed off to rouse Victoria. She was still soundly asleep, naked under the sheets. I shook her awake. Ignoring her protests, I scrambled around the room, finding jeans, a blouse, a sweater.

Alex hastened into the room just as Victoria was struggling into her boots. He was carrying his attaché case.

'Quickly!' he told us.

We hurried downstairs and went out through a side door, crossing a potato bed before slipping through a yew hedge. A stone stairway led down and away from the house. We skirted the pine plantation, heading across the lower slopes in the general direction of the colliery.

'Where are the others?' I asked.

Alex's reply was drowned in a searing noise which was followed by an eruption of flame on the lower terraces of the garden. We were bathed in golden light as our attackers completed their first pass.

The two smaller craft were fast-flying, manoeuvrable interceptors with slender fuselages and sickle wings. Their larger companion had a pointed nose and high swept-back wings which made it resemble an enormous golden bird of prey: it was a gunship transporter, its hold typically crammed with troops who would spew out to occupy positions softened up by the craft's firepower. All three shone brilliant gold in the gathering dawn.

Alex crouched and opened his briefcase. He took out the computer disk and thrust it at me.

I stood frozen, staring at it.

'Take it!' he insisted. 'I'm going back for the others.'

He closed the briefcase and flung it away from him, sending it spinning through the air.

'Alex—'

'The codeword's *axolotl*.' He repeated the word, then forced a grin. 'Don't worry, I'll be back. Head for the bath-house. I'll find you there as soon as I can. Now get clear of here!'

Banking sharply, and utterly silently, the interceptors came in again. Plumes of liquid fire spurted from their noses, plummeting down to burst on the ground, setting clumps of gorse ablaze and throwing the skeletal framework of the tower into stark relief. Alex was already blotted from view by the smoke.

I slipped the disk into a pocket of my jacket. Keeping Victoria close to me, I led her down the mountain path towards the bath-house, a squat building which stood on the lower flank of the valley. The air was thick with smoke and the petroleum smell of *xiuhatl* liquid incendiary.

We skirted the colliery, and I kept glancing back with each explosion. The gunship hovered at a distance while the interceptors swept in, spreading fire and mayhem. The house was still intact, and now the small craft paused in their attacks while the gunship descended until it hung no more than a hundred yards above the house.

White light from the belly of the ship bathed the entire area.

'You will surrender immediately. No further attacks will be made. You will surrender immediately.'

The amplified message came from the gunship. It was repeated. I pulled Victoria down behind a low wall, searching the hillsides with my eyes for some sign of Alex and the others.

I heard the sound of rifle-fire, and I knew it came from the house, a defiant and futile attempt to resist the attackers with shotguns. A gust of wind cloaked us briefly in gorse smoke. There was a huge pneumatic thump, and the house erupted in a cataclysm of fire.

The blast of heat from the explosion seared our faces, and I pushed Victoria down. When I finally looked up again, fleeing sheep shone like phantoms in the fierce light of the inferno. The house was gone.

My eyes were blinded with heat and tears. Then my heart leapt into my throat as someone grabbed my wrist.

It was Bevan.

'Be quick, now,' he said. 'This way.'

Half pulled, half following, we were led up an incline, scrambling over slag and discarded machine parts, slithering up treacherous shaley slopes, the ground sliding under our feet. Victoria was gasping and sobbing the word 'Please . . . Please . . .' over and over again, though whether she wanted to stop or was desperate to find safety, I could not say.

Then in front of us, in an overgrown wall behind a tangle of hawthorn, a cast-iron pipe jutted out. About three feet wide, it was coated with moss and algae, a dribble of rusty water trickling from it.

'Right,' said Bevan. 'In you go, then.'

Victoria's hand tightened on mine. All three of us were panting, and I felt as if I might be sick at any moment. The pipe stood at chest height above a stagnant rushy puddle. Its interior was utterly dark.

'We can't go in there,' I heard myself say.

'Says who?' Bevan replied. 'Want them to have you, do you?'

'The others,' I murmured. 'Alex . . .'

'You leave them to me. Go on, now. In.'

The sky was lightening rapidly, and I knew we had little time left. His urgency and insistence galvanized me. Quickly I scrambled up into the maw of the pipe. Bevan helped Victoria in behind me.

I wanted him to join us inside, but he did not. Face framed in its mouth, he said, 'Go in as far as you can, where it's dark. Stay there until I come back. Don't make a bloody sound.'

And then he was gone.

The pipe was dank and cheerless. Awkwardly I moved down it, Victoria clinging on to me. About thirty yards in, it broadened and began to curve, slowly eclipsing the disc of daylight as its end. I halted, unwilling to surrender to total darkness.

It was impossible to sit or crouch without getting wet, but our knees and legs were already soaked. I put an arm around

Victoria, letting her rest her weight against me, thinking all the while of Alex and the others, praying that they had got out of the house in time. I wanted to say something, to soothe Victoria with comforting words. But I had none.

Time passed, filled only with the sound of trickling water and Victoria's fragile breathing. The pain in my back grew worse. Victoria was huddled against me like a child. I stroked her hair absently, staring towards the slender ellipse of daylight, feeling wretched.

After a lengthy silence, Victoria said, 'I can't bear this any more, Kate.'

Her voice was wavering, on the brink of cracking. I tried to hush her, but she wouldn't be calmed.

'Nothing's worth this. Nothing.'

She began to sob, and I felt hot tears on my neck. I knew she wasn't just talking about the attack, but the whole three years of our exile.

'Do you think I find this easy?' I whispered, battling against my growing physical discomfort. 'We can't let them capture us now. We have to hang on a little while longer.'

'What's the point? I'd rather be a prisoner than live like this.'

'Bevan will be back soon,' I whispered, without real confidence. I patted her head like a parent comforting a child.

'You will come out now.'

I went rigid, putting a hand over Victoria's mouth. The voice was male, accented, the voice of our enemy speaking English. It echoed down the pipe.

'You will come out now.'

Matter-of-fact, decisive, certain we were inside. I moved my hand from Victoria's lips and shook my head to indicate she should remain silent. She looked petrified.

'You are being foolish,' the voice continued. 'We know you are in there. You will not be harmed if you come out now.'

There was a pleading look in Victoria's eyes: she was ready to surrender.

'We have all the others. They are quite safe and unhurt.'

Still we stayed silent. By now my own instinct was to reveal myself, to surrender so that I could find out if Alex was safe. But

I fought against it, telling myself that they were bluffing, that they couldn't know for certain we were inside the pipe.

'Very well,' the voice said presently. There was the sound of orders being issued in Nahuatl, though I could not make out the words.

I waited, expecting soldiers to begin clambering into the pipe. But this didn't happen. All went silent outside, and I was suddenly seized with the fear that the commander would order a flame-thrower fired into the pipe to incinerate us.

Seconds crept by. Still there was no further sound from outside. As the silence extended, so I began to think that the enemy commander had indeed been bluffing. And having received no answer from us, was continuing his search elsewhere.

Then I heard the rumbling. It came from deep within the pipe, and I knew immediately what it meant.

'Quickly!' I said to Victoria, pushing her towards the mouth.

My legs were stiff from kneeling, and the cramped space made rapid movement impossible. The rumbling swelled rapidly into a roar, carrying before it a damp breeze.

Victoria and I were almost at the mouth of the pipe when the rush hit us from behind. I was lifted up, cracking my head against the top of the pipe an instant before the gushing water propelled us out.

I landed, entangled with Victoria, cold water pouring down on us. The shock of impact took the breath from me, and it was a moment before I was able to pull us both up on to a grassy bank. Victoria was sobbing wretchedly and examining the skinned knuckles of her hand, her hair in rats' tails.

Around us, encircling us, were soldiers in green and brown combat uniforms, all armed with assault rifles. Swarthy-skinned and black-haired, some wore forage caps with the stylized gold sunburst emblem. These were no ordinary troops but crack commandos, the cream of the Aztec army. Among their number was a squat figure dressed in an olive-green commander's uniform. Beside him stood Bevan.

I made an effort to climb to my feet, to stand upright and face them. A wave of dizziness and nausea swept over me, and I felt a rush of hot liquid between my legs.

Two

I woke to a steady engine hum in the gunship's sickbay. I was lying on a hard bed, a blanket drawn up to my chest.

The moment I stirred, two figures appeared at my side. One was obviously a doctor, the other a very short man in the buff uniform of a non-combatant officer.

The doctor took my wrist and checked my pulse. He was middle-aged, plump, perhaps a Mayan or Quauhtemalan. He peeled a strip thermometer from my armpit, then said in Nahuatl: 'Everything appears normal.'

The short man had a broad-nosed face and a turn in his left eye.

'How do you feel?' he asked me in English.

'Like death.'

'It was a haemorrhage.' He pronounced the word with difficulty. 'You lost some blood, but there is no further cause for alarm.'

I knew it was more than that. A child. I had been carrying a child. I felt a vast futile sorrow. For the past two months I had had no period but took little account of it because most of the women in our group had irregular cycles. Yet without acknowledging it to myself, I had *known* I was pregnant.

'It was necessary you were examined internally,' the small man said. 'The doctor is confident there is no permanent injury. No complications.'

I could see he knew that I knew.

'I'm sorry,' he said.

'Not as sorry as I am.'

'It is very important that you rest. We shall be arriving in London in an hour or so.'

I almost said Victoria's name, but stopped myself. 'The others? What's happened to them?'

Now he looked pained.

'It is my sad duty to tell you that they were sheltering in the cellar of the house when it was destroyed.'

I closed my eyes. 'All dead?'

'There were no survivors.'

So it was not just a disaster, but a massacre. Alex, and all the others, incinerated. I tried to hold on to this as a brutal fact that would inspire my hatred rather than grief.

'You murdered them. They were defenceless.'

He surprised me by nodding.

'I cannot excuse what has happened. No one should have died.'

'What's your name?' I demanded.

'Chicomeztli.'

'Are you in charge here?'

He shook his head. 'I believe you met our commander earlier.'

'I want to see him now.'

'Soon. He will be here soon. You must believe me – it was never our intention that any of you be killed.'

'Fire-bombing a house is hardly likely to minimize casualties.'

My tone was withering, and only my weakness prevented a more physical demonstration of my rage.

'I can offer no excuses. It was unpardonable.'

I couldn't stop the tears. The doctor made to approach, but Chicomeztli stopped him with a glance. He stood patiently, almost respectfully, in front of me, knowing he could do nothing but duty-bound not to withdraw.

I made a great effort to compose myself.

'Please,' I said. 'Leave me alone.'

'Shall I fetch the others? They have been most concerned about you.'

'You killed them all. I can't believe it.'

This time he did withdraw, hurrying out through the door.

The doctor was standing back, looking very guarded. In English I asked for another pillow so that I could sit up. He looked at me uncomprehendingly. After a few moments of mime and muddle, he finally understood. I didn't want him to know I could speak Nahuatl.

There was a soreness at my centre, but my grief overwhelmed it. I wondered if they realized who they had captured. No names had been mentioned, and in three years of exile Victoria and I had changed our appearances and might not be recognizable. It was possible that the raid had been just a part of general Aztec incursions in the area. Though this was unlikely, I held on to it, held on to any thought that stopped me dwelling on the loss of everyone who had been my life in Wales.

Chicomeztli returned with Victoria and Bevan. Bevan was still wearing his shale-stained clothes, but Victoria was dressed in a clean maroon sweater and a grey skirt.

'You may have a few minutes to talk alone,' Chicomeztli told us. 'Please remember there are guards just outside the door.'

He and the doctor went out. Victoria immediately came to my bedside and hugged me. She began to cry in my arms. I would have done the same if Bevan hadn't been there.

'Are you all right?' she wanted to know. 'You were bleeding terribly.'

'I'm fine,' I said. I wasn't going to tell her about the baby in front of Bevan. 'I strained something when we fell, but it's nothing serious. They said everyone else is dead.'

Victoria nodded, cheeks streaked with tears.

I drew her close and whispered, 'Do they know who we are?'

'No one's said anything. I told them I was your sister, that's all. They've treated us quite well so far.' I felt her hand tighten on mine. 'I was frightfully worried about you, Kate. You look ghastly.'

I reached up and began stroking her hair. I was deliberately forcing back all thoughts of Alex and the others. Bevan kept his distance.

'I hope you're satisfied,' I said to him.

He looked quizzical.

'You betrayed us. You led them to us, didn't you?'

I couldn't gauge his reaction. Was it surprise? Amusement? Contempt?

'You hid us so you'd know where we were. So you could lead them straight to us.'

'Don't be bloody daft.'

'There's no point in trying to deny it. You were standing right next to their commander when they flushed us out of the pipe. You brought them there.'

He gave an amused grunt. 'Joking, are you?'

'Far from it.'

'Maybe you didn't notice, but I was standing there with a rifle barrel stuck in my back. They nabbed me when I was trying to find the others.'

'Then how did they know where to find us?'

'They searched everywhere, didn't they? The pipe was the only place left.'

He had a graze on his left temple, as if he had tried to resist capture. But I didn't let that influence me.

'Why didn't they assume we were in the house with the others?'

'How the Christ should I know?'

'It's true,' Victoria said. 'They were guarding him, Kate. He's a prisoner just like us.'

I heard voices outside, an angry voice saying in Nahuatl: 'You had no business allowing them to see her without my permission!'

The door swished open, and in bustled the commander himself, closely followed by Chicomeztli and several soldiers. He had changed out of his combat fatigues into a tawny uniform with gold chevrons and the insignia of his rank, three stylized eagle-heads.

He strode to the side of my bunk. He was burly but short, with a flat forehead, dark eyes and a broad flared nose. Turning to the guards, he indicated Bevan and said: 'Remove him!'

Bevan was promptly led away. When this was done, the commander executed a curt bow before me and said in English: 'I am Maxixca, Chief Commander to the governor of these islands.'

Ignoring my wretchedness, I stared him out. He was a pure-blood Aztec, his cropped hair tar-black, his coppery skin smooth. He looked no older than I.

Mustering my most imperiously sarcastic tone, I said, 'Really? And do you make a habit of visiting the bedsides of all your prisoners?'

He was taken aback at this but quickly recovered. 'You are Princess Catherine, daughter of King Stephen of England. Your sister is the Princess Victoria—'

I forced a contemptuous laugh. 'If you think that, then you're more foolish than you appear.'

Again he stopped in some confusion.

'It's a charming notion,' I said, 'but I'm afraid you're quite mistaken.'

Impatiently he delved into the breast pocket of his uniform and produced a photograph. It showed our family in Windsor Great Park on my father's sixtieth birthday. Taken only six months before the invasion, its likenesses of Victoria and myself were unmistakable.

'You are Princess Catherine,' he said again. 'And this is Princess Victoria. You are now prisoners-of-war, but you will be treated in accordance with your status. When we arrive in London, the governor will greet you personally.'

His manner was overbearing. I determined to prick his self-importance.

'Is that so?' I said. 'I suggest you radio and inform him that I'm indisposed and have no desire to meet with common murderers.'

This time he looked angry. He turned to Chicomeztli. Speaking in Nahuatl, Chicomeztli confirmed that I knew about the destruction of the house and the deaths of everyone.

'It should not have happened,' Maxixca said to me. 'The soldier responsible will be disciplined. He failed to obey his orders. You must accept my apology.'

'I accept nothing of the sort,' I said. 'You killed my husband and my friends.'

For a moment there was silence. Then Chicomeztli said, 'Your husband was not in the house.'

I looked at him, then at Maxixca.

'There were nine corpses in the cellar,' Maxixca said. 'Your husband is a tall man, I believe. His was not among them.'

Immediately my spirits lifted, despite his cold-blooded manner. But I did my best to maintain an appearance of rigid composure.

'It must be galling to be denied one of your victims,' I said.

Maxixca obviously disliked the fact I was not cowed.

'When he is captured,' he said, 'he will be brought to you. Alive, if possible.'

I felt a surge of hatred for him.

'Tell me – how does it feel to be a murderer?'

He was easily aroused by insults, I saw; but he bit back an immediate response.

'All the preparations have been made for your arrival in London,' he said. 'The governor—'

'Get out,' I interrupted, intent on deflating him. 'I have no intention of discussing any such arrangements with a common soldier. You Aztecs—'

'I am Mexicatl! A son of Motecuhzoma and a lady of Tlaxcala!'

I had guessed as much; his name was familiar to me. Of course, I knew he would bridle at the term 'Aztec', a catch-all description for the many peoples of the empire.

'That may be so, but you have the manners of a *teochichimecatl*. You can see I am unwell, yet you burst in here without ceremony or courtesy.'

Teochichimecatl meant 'barbarian', and Maxixca looked suitably furious. I thought I glimpsed the merest hint of a smile on Chicomeztli's lips.

'You are our prisoners,' Maxixca said with a barely controlled anger. 'You will do as you are ordered.'

He stalked out.

Victoria looked appalled, and there was an awkward silence.

'Is it true about my husband?' I asked Chicomeztli.

'It is true,' he assured me. 'He was not found among those who died in the house. I believe he has escaped.'

'That's wonderful news.'

He acknowledged my small triumph with a wry smile.

'You greatly angered our commander,' he said gently.

'That was my intention.'

'He is a son of the *tlatoani*. You would be wise not to provoke him.'

But there was amusement in his eyes.

Of course I knew my show of bravado would do us no good, but it was my only means of striking back. Though I felt fragile and exhausted, I insisted on getting dressed. Chicomeztli went away and returned with a plain sweater and skirt like those Victoria was wearing.

By now I had remembered the disk in my jacket.

'I'd like my own clothes,' I said.

He shook his head. 'That is not possible. They were soaked and filthy. We had them burned.'

The craft was banking over London, and I glimpsed St James's Park and the Mall through the porthole. I was still furious with myself for losing the disk. Fury seemed preferable to complete desolation.

Victoria, Bevan and I sat together in the forward passenger section, our guards paying us little heed now we were securely in their hands. I remained suspicious of Bevan, even though he seemed as much a prisoner as Victoria and I.

Our return to London prompted thoughts of my father and Richard. From intercepted radio transmissions we knew that both had been held at Hampton Court Palace since the invasion; but I had had no definite news of them for over a year.

I strained to see across Victoria as the craft flew over the Thames. Some central areas of the city had been devastated during the invasion, and the area north of the abandoned Houses of Parliament had been landscaped into a park. On the opposite bank, where County Hall once stood, there rose an entirely new building, a quincunx of tiered pyramids in creamy marble and glass, the levels planted with shrubbery. At the top of the innermost pyramid was a landing pad.

Bevan shuffled closer to me. I eyed him without approval, convinced he had contacted the Aztecs on the radio the night before, prompting them to launch the raid before we could escape to Russia.

'You'll be wanting this,' he murmured, thrusting something into my lap.

I looked down. It was the disk.

Bevan's eyes were on the unheeding guards.

'Fell out of your pocket when you were climbing into the pipe, didn't it? You ought to be more careful.'

I quickly hid it away, then felt a nauseous tug on my stomach as the ship began to decelerate.

Victoria, intent on the view through the porthole, noticed nothing. She gripped my hand, but I found myself holding on to her as much as she to me. Then the ship touched down with a shudder and a thud.

We waited in silence for some time. Two soldiers came and led Bevan away. Then Maxixca marched in, with Chicomeztli following.

The commander was still bristling from our earlier encounter. Stiffly, he instructed his guards to escort us out.

We were led down through the ship to a wide hatchway. The daylight at the bottom was wan and grey. Chicomeztli stepped forward and draped cloaks around the shoulders of myself and Victoria. The cloaks were hooded, black. With soldiers surrounding us and Maxixca at the head, we descended the gangway.

Cloud filled the sky, and a thin rain was falling. I felt shivery and frail, but I steeled myself. At the opposite end of the landing pad, a small group of people awaited us. Most were guards, but among them, standing under a big black umbrella, was Richard.

He was now a young man of eighteen, taller than three years before, his curly hair newly cut. Catching sight of us, his face filled up with that wonderfully open smile which had endeared him to so many people. He was dressed in a dark suit, white shirt and striped tie; he looked the perfect schoolboy. I wanted to burst out of our cordon and rush to him.

Maxixca halted in front of the governor and saluted. He was not the middle-aged Nauhyotl but a much younger man, his aquamarine uniform decorated with a golden eagle grasping a stylized sun.

Maxixca formally introduced him as Extepan Iquehuac Tlancuaxoloch, third son of the *tlatoani* Motecuhzoma Xohueyacatzin, ruler of Greater Mexico and all its dominions. I scarcely glanced at him. I saw tears brim in Richard's eyes as he gazed at us, his long-lost sisters. His lower lip began to quiver; any moment now he would begin to cry.

Maxixca continued with the interminable formalities of our introduction. I moved towards Richard, but the guards closed ranks. Then the governor, who was regarding me, waved a hand, and they parted to let me through.

Richard came forward into my arms. He hugged me with all his strength, then turned to Victoria and did the same, kissing both of us on the cheeks. Finally he began to blubber, and I realized I was already prepared when he blurted: 'Father's dead.'

Victoria, Richard and I were ferried the short distance to Westminster Abbey in a jetcopter. In the gloom of dusk it was difficult to make out the full extent of the destruction to the surrounding streets, though Chicomeztli stressed that both the Abbey and the Cathedral had been very fortunate to survive the bombing. The area around the site was now off-limits to the public, Aztec guards in waterproof capes patrolling the derelict streets.

Inside, the Abbey's empty echoing spaces were lit with candles. More guards stood discreetly in the shadows. The coffin rested on an elaborate wreath-strewn plinth in the Henry VIII chapel. I hesitated, rested from my afternoon nap but far from recovered, then climbed the steps.

My father lay in a formal black suit, hands crossed over his chest with a silver crucifix lying on top of them. His hair, grey when I last saw him, was now white. His face, however, looked younger, its paleness and lines doubtless erased by those who had prepared him. The Aztecs had a long and expert tradition of making their honoured dead look immaculate.

Beside me, Victoria and Richard clasped hands, determinedly maintaining a shred of dignity in the face of their loss. Apparently Father had died of a heart attack four days before while taking a constitutional around the grounds of Hampton Court. Richard had been with him at the time.

For some reason I found myself wishing that his eyes were open, even if he couldn't see me. I reached into the coffin and gently lifted the crucifix out.

'We're Anglicans,' I said in explanation to Chicomeztli.

'Of course,' he replied. 'Someone must have left it.'

'Has the news of his death been made public?'

'No. Not yet.'

'But there are plans to?'

'I understand that this is one of the things which Governor Extepan will wish to discuss with you.'

My father was shrouded in cream silks like a sea of frozen milk. The walls of his coffin were lined with velvet the colour of old blood. Even the hairs which had once grown so abundantly in his ears and nostrils had been skilfully removed.

There was no mystery surrounding his death, no hint of foul play. His health had been poor in recent years, and the stresses of being a captive king might well have hastened his end.

I began thinking of my mother. She had died when Richard was born, her frail constitution exhausted by a prolonged and complicated labour. I remember a gentle fair-haired woman who read Grimm's fairytales to Victoria and me at bedtime, but little else. Far rawer was my loss of my father and Alex and everyone who had perished at Ty Trist.

'He was a brave and honourable man,' I heard Chicomeztli say. 'He bore all his difficulties with great dignity and did not compromise his beliefs.'

'You mean he refused to collaborate.'

It sounded harsh as soon as it was out, but Chicomeztli gave a lop-sided smile and nodded vigorously. 'Most certainly. He was as difficult as it was his duty to be.'

I was exhausted and still in some physical discomfort. For the next two days I convalesced in the suite of rooms which had been provided for me in the central pyramid of the administrative complex. Female Aztec servants, silent and courteous, brought me meals, and Victoria visited every day. She had her own suite immediately above mine, with private access between us via the balcony garden.

I made a swift recovery, and most of my time was taken up with comforting Victoria, who remained anxious.

'What will they do with us, Kate?' she asked, the first time we were alone together.

'Don't worry,' I told her. 'We won't be harmed. We would never have been brought here in the first place if they meant to get rid of us.'

'I'm scared.'

'I know. But we mustn't let them see that.'

She sat on the bed beside me, holding my hand in hers. 'I can't believe Father's dead.'

'It's Richard we have to think about now. He's going to need all our help.'

But I was, in fact, thinking about Alex, wondering where he might be. It would be difficult, even for someone as resourceful as him, to survive in the wilds of Wales and continue to evade capture. But at least he was still alive.

'You're not seriously ill, are you?' Victoria said. 'I couldn't bear it if anything happened to you.'

At that moment I decided I wasn't going to tell her about the baby.

'No,' I replied. 'I'm not ill. And I've got no intention of abandoning you.'

She was silent, still anxious.

'What is it?' I asked.

'Do you think . . .' She paused, hesitated. 'Do you think they still . . .'

Again she faltered. I knew what she was trying to say.

'Hush. They're Catholics. It's the state religion, you know that. They prepared Father perfectly decently for a Christian burial.'

'But people say—'

'People are always saying things. You can't believe all you hear.'

She lay with her head in my lap. Little did she know that I shared similar fears to her, the same fears as all the Aztecs' enemies.

Ostensibly we were alone, but it seemed likely that the apartments were monitored with hidden microphones and perhaps even cameras. As I stroked Victoria's hair, I wondered what kind of eyes and minds might secretly be dwelling on us even at this very moment.

Three

On the third morning I woke to find Bevan outside in the garden, watering the flowerbeds. I dressed and went outside.

'Good morning,' I said.

'Up bright and early, aren't you?'

He did not look at me. I walked around until I was facing him.

I hesitated, then said, 'Bevan, I'm sorry.'

Water sprinkled my toes, forcing me to step back.

'I shouldn't have accused you of disloyalty. I was upset. With the killing of the others.'

'Didn't mess about, did they? I reckon you and your sister were lucky.'

He continued watering along a row of multicoloured daisies.

'Why are you doing this?' I said. 'There's been plenty of rain.'

'They told me I was to be your gardener and general factotum. That's what you asked for, wasn't it? So I'm doing my job.'

'That was just an excuse. I didn't want anything to happen to you. Are your living quarters all right?'

'Very plush,' he replied. 'Key's on your side of the door, is it?'

I had asked for Bevan to be given a room next to my suite, and to my surprise the request had been granted. An adjoining door linked his quarters with mine.

'I thought it was the least I could do,' I said.

'Very considerate of you.'

He put the can down and took out a pack of Raleigh Full Strength, lighting one.

'If you'd rather go back to Wales, I'll see if I can arrange it.'

'They're not going to let me go. They know I've been hobnobbing with you lot for a while.'

I ignored his disparaging tone. 'You helped us out in Wales, and I'm very grateful. I might be able to pull strings. You must be worried about your mother.'

'She's used to managing on her own.'

'I'll do what I can if you want.'

He took a contemplative pull on his cigarette. 'You'd like me to stay, wouldn't you?'

I was surprised by this – surprised by its accuracy. At the same time, I was reluctant to admit any such need.

I let him smoke his cigarette, making a show of watching a blackbird root about under a stand of blackcurrant bushes.

Presently I said, 'Do you know anything about computers?'

'Ought to, didn't I? Seeing as how I worked for IBM.'

'Imperial Business Machines?'

'It's the only IBM I know of.'

This was hard to credit. He looked more like a labourer than a computer technician.

'You never said.'

'Never asked, did you?'

An Aztec transporter flew past, the whine of its engines drowning out everything else. When it was gone, Bevan said, 'They're hoping I'll keep an eye on you. Report back to them.'

'The Aztecs?'

'Thing is, they've checked my credentials and they know I'm not exactly a royalist.'

'What do you mean?'

He shrugged. 'Makes no difference now, does it? We're all in the same boat.'

What was I to make of this? I was tempted to question him further, but I felt sure he wouldn't tell me any more.

'I'm going to need someone I can trust,' I said.

He spat out a fragment of tobacco.

'Not something you find easy, is it?'

There really was no limit to his impertinence.

Governor Extepan was in his mid-twenties, and of mixed Mexican and European stock. Thirty years before, Motecuhzoma had broken with Aztec tradition by taking a Spanish noblewoman as his wife, though she had later been killed by a Catalan bomb while visiting Valencia after the Aztec conquest of Iberia. Extepan was taller than most of his countrymen, and Spanish rather than Mexican in his looks.

He greeted me in his private quarters high in the central pyramid. Outside it was another rainy afternoon, and he stood flanked by Maxixca and Chicomeztli before a real coal fire in a large hearth. The fire was plainly an affectation since the complex derived ample power for heating from the solar generators atop each of the subsidiary pyramids. Richard was perched at a desk console nearby, a *patolli* game on the screen. He gave me a small wave as I entered but did not get up. It was as if he had already accustomed himself to my presence in his life again.

Extepan took my hand and inclined his head.

'I trust you are feeling better.'

His tunic was unbuttoned at the neck, and he had a casual air about him. Maxixca, by contrast, was dressed very correctly and stood with his hands at his back, regarding me with open hostility.

'I'm truly sorry about all the unfortunate circumstances which brought you here,' he said. 'We had no idea you were carrying a child. You have my deepest sympathies.'

To my relief, Richard appeared not to have heard this. He was tapping buttons and making counters leapfrog over one another on the screen.

'Your sympathies are better reserved for the relatives of those you killed,' I said bitterly.

I could see Maxixca bridle at this. Extepan nodded gravely.

'It was most unfortunate. A tragic error. I trust that that was explained to you.'

'An error that cost the lives of innocent people. If that's really what it was.'

'You have my word of honour.'

His English was excellent. He motioned to chairs on either side of the fire. They were Aztec *icpallis*, made of black mahogany, tall-backed and legless, though lavishly upholstered with a chevroned cloth. I did not move.

'I regret, too, your father's passing,' he said.

'Really?'

'He was a good man. I had great respect for him.'

'Even though you kept him captive in his own country?'

He looked wry. 'Maxixca told me you would be uncompromising. I can see you have inherited all your father's strength of character.'

'Don't patronize me.'

Now he was distinctly abashed. 'Forgive me. I realize you have no reason to be amused. But there is room for common courtesy, yes?'

Again he indicated the chairs. Again I did not move. He had striking black eyebrows and greenish eyes ringed by dark brown which gave him a very direct stare.

'You weren't brought here to be humiliated,' he said. 'I assure you I intend nothing but honour for all your family.'

'Honour? The same kind of honour that entails destroying a house of helpless civilians?'

'It was a savage foolishness. I do not expect you to believe me, but I share your outrage.'

He matched my stare. *Tap, tap, tap*, went Richard at the keyboard.

'Is there any news of my husband?' I asked.

'Ah, yes, the Duke. That I cannot say with any certainty. As you can no doubt imagine, we would prefer to have him safely in our hands, but our search parties have found nothing. I think it is likely he has escaped. That is good news for you, yes?'

'Very good news.'

'Perhaps you would like some tea?'

I almost laughed at this *non sequitur*. Instead, I shook my head.

'We have many things to talk about,' Extepan said. 'But first the matter of your health—'

'I'm fully recovered,' I insisted.

'That is good to hear. We can make arrangements for your family physician to be available, should you wish.'

'That won't be necessary. I feel perfectly well.'

'Good. Then perhaps we can press on with our consultations.'

'Consultations?'

'Perhaps you would prefer to combine them with an overfly of the city? I have a shuttle available. I imagine you must be concerned to see how your people are faring and what damage we have caused.'

There was an almost naïve eagerness about him, but his voice also had a mocking note – self-mocking rather than directed at me. He was quite a contrast to the stiff and suspicious Maxixca.

'The first thing we must discuss,' Extepan said, 'is the matter of your father's funeral.'

I sat with him and Maxixca behind the flight crew, gazing out through the slanting cockpit windows as the craft lifted from the landing pad and flew across the river.

Sarcastically I said, 'Do you intend it to be a full state occasion?'

'Of course,' he replied quite seriously. 'I assume that you and your family would wish this.'

I searched for a hint of deviousness, of game-playing, in his face, but there appeared to be none.

'So you intend to make the news public?'

'It is not something we could hide indefinitely from your people, is it? Nor would I want us to.'

A fan-tailed support craft had appeared to shadow us discreetly on our overfly. Maxixca kept track of it with his eyes.

'How long have you been governor?' I asked Extepan.

'Since April,' he replied. 'I replaced my uncle. He was assassinated by one of your countrymen while shopping at Harrods.'

I saw Maxixca stiffen, as though aghast that Extepan should reveal this. Extepan himself was fatalistic. 'We may have vanquished your armies, but we cannot predict the actions of individuals. It is in the nature of things. But my uncle did not help our cause by treating your people harshly. I hope to enlist their co-operation more.'

From what little information we had been able to glean during our exile, I knew that Nauhyotl had instituted severe repressions on his arrival in the country. But 'co-operation' was a word with many interpretations.

We were flying low over Oxford Street. It was as crowded as ever with shoppers. Fast-food lunchers milled about outside the red-and-gold façade of a MexTaco restaurant. The Centre Point cinema complex was advertising the latest Acapulco productions, *Otomi Onslaught* and *Totonac Attack*. Everything appeared normal.

'The next pressing problem', Extepan said, 'is, of course, the succession.'

I turned away from the window. Richard sat with Chicomeztli under the supervision of the co-pilot, moving a sightfinder on one of the screens with all the enthusiasm of the uninitiated.

'Are you proposing to crown Richard king?'

Extepan did not react to my sarcasm. 'Is there any reason why we should not?'

Richard was making shooting sounds, downing imaginary enemies with great delight.

'Your country has always had its own monarch. There is no need to depart from tradition, even under the present circumstances.'

'You can't possibly expect me to condone it,' I said.

He frowned. 'I don't understand. He is heir to the throne.'

'Of a country under occupation. He would be a puppet ruler. You are our enemies. We won't collaborate with you.'

Maxixca made to say something, but Extepan raised a hand. He was as calm as Maxixca was agitated.

'You know I'm intending to restore your parliament?' he said.

'Why? So they can rubber-stamp everything you do? Give you a spurious respectability with our people?'

'It will have considerable freedom in all sorts of spheres. You must believe me when I say I do not wish your people to suffer unduly—'

'Then evacuate your armies and leave us in peace.'

Maxixca was unable to restrain himself any longer.

'We don't have to negotiate with her!' he said in Nahuatl. 'She must accept whatever we decide.'

'Leave this to me,' Extepan replied, evenly but with authority.

The sun had broken through the cloud, and below us people were strolling in Hyde Park. Some wore brightly patterned Aztec capes, but most were English. The balcony of the café on the bank of the Serpentine was full.

'Perhaps we should ask Richard himself,' Extepan said to me.

'He's just a child,' I replied. 'He's not capable of making decisions for himself.'

Richard had suffered oxygen starvation during Mother's protracted labour; his mental and emotional development would always be limited.

'That may be so,' Extepan said, 'but he deserves to be consulted.' He motioned to Chicomeztli, who had apparently been listening to everything while appearing not to be. Reluctantly, Richard was persuaded to abandon the joystick.

Chicomeztli led him over to us.

'That was fun,' he said to me. 'When am I going to be king, Kate?'

'These people want to crown you,' I said. 'But you must remember that they invaded our country and imposed their rule. You would be king in name only.'

He looked at Chicomeztli, at Extepan and Maxixca. There was confusion on his face. I was sure he was thinking that if people were kind to him, then they were his friends.

'Father said I would be king after him.'

'You're his successor,' I agreed. 'But I don't think he imagined our country would be under armed occupation. If you let these people make you king, you'll be accepting their authority over us. You'll be confirming their right to make decisions for our people.'

'It's my duty to be king.'

'You have to try to put your own feelings to one side and think about the consequences.'

It was clear he didn't like the sound of this. Even pitched so plainly, the argument was probably too subtle for him. Then something took his eye through the cockpit window.

'Look!' he said, brightening. 'Buckingham Palace!'

We were tracking westwards again, and the palace was directly below. At first glance it looked intact, but then I saw it was roofless, its walls blackened.

'It was gutted during the fighting,' Extepan remarked. Throughout my conversation with Richard, his eyes had been on me.

'Do you plan to restore it so you can install Richard there?'

His forbearing look seemed to say he was prepared to tolerate all my immoderation.

'I know this is very difficult for you,' he said. 'Perhaps it would be easier if the decision were taken out of all our hands. We could let your people decide for themselves.'

'And how would you propose to do that? By popular vote?'

'Exactly. I think you call it in your country a referendum.'

In the middle of the night I rose and unlocked the door which gave access to Bevan's apartment. For several moments I hesitated. Then I turned the handle and crept in.

Bevan's apartment was in darkness, redolent of maleness and stale tobacco. His bedroom door was ajar.

'That you, is it?'

His voice startled me. I swallowed, said, 'Yes.'

He sat up blearily. By night our rooms were bathed in the soft radiance of the generators, and I could see he was wearing striped pyjamas.

'This is an honour,' he said, making it sound anything but.

'Bevan, I need to talk to you.'

He stretched luxuriously, stifling a yawn. 'Righto.'

He never made any compromises to my position, and I have to admit that on this occasion it annoyed me.

'In private,' I said quietly. 'Where we can be sure no one else is listening. Perhaps you'd like to get dressed and meet me in the garden.'

Without waiting for a reply, I returned to my own suite and donned boots and a lambskin coat. Much of my former wardrobe from our house in Marlborough had been transferred to the suite. The house itself was now apparently the headquarters of a local Aztec army division.

I slipped out on to the balcony, choosing a seat in a sheltered corner of the garden screened by buddleia and frost-resistant bamboo. The still night air was filled with musky fragrances despite its coolness.

At length Bevan appeared, a gaberdine buttoned up over his pyjamas. He perched himself on the arm of a bench opposite me and lit a Raleigh.

'So what's it all about, then?'

I decided to match his bluntness. I took the disk from my pocket.

'This.'

Bevan eyed me over his cigarette. 'Important, is it?'

'Very. My husband gave it me for safe-keeping just before we were captured. Do you know what it is?'

'Software.'

'It's more than that. My husband was working for the MoD before the invasion.'

'Director of Informational Research.'

This was public knowledge, but I was surprised he knew.

'Do you think we could load it into the system here, get it working?'

'What sort of program is it, then?'

'I'm not sure. That's what I need to find out.'

I wasn't prepared to tell him any more at this stage because I still didn't know how far I could trust him. But I had to enlist his aid if I was to make use of the disk.

'There's a terminal in my living room. I thought we might be able to use it. If we're careful.'

'Might be possible,' he conceded.

'Would you give it a try? I'm hopeless with computers.'

I couldn't tell whether he looked contemplative or calculating. I often had the feeling he considered me tiresome or even an outright nuisance.

'Alex told me the disk's very important. It might be a weapon we can use against the Aztecs.'

'Bring their empire tumbling down, will it?'

Was he teasing me, as I had teased Alex? It was no longer a joking matter as far as I was concerned.

'My husband was engaged in highly classified work.'

'Well, he would have been, wouldn't he? At the MoD.'

He squashed his cigarette under the heel of his slipper.

'Of course, our rooms might be bugged,' I said.

'There's ways round that.'

'Such as?'

'We work at night for a start.'

'What if they've got cameras monitoring us?'

'Cameras are hard to hide. I took a look around – your place as well as mine – while you were out yesterday. You'd left the door unlocked, see. There was nothing.'

I was amazed at his presumption, yet also grateful he had taken the trouble. He really was a law unto himself.

'What about microphones?'

'Trickier. You can put them anywhere – under floorboards or in your plumbing. And there's directional equipment that can eavesdrop a hundred yards or more. But even that's not much use if you play music loud enough.'

'You seem to know a great deal about it.'

'Never know when it might come in handy, do you?'

'So they could be listening to us now?'

'It's possible. But, then, you're never going to do anything worthwhile if you don't take a few risks, are you?'

His tone was lazily challenging, as if he really couldn't have cared less either way.

'Well, then,' I said, 'why don't we start tonight?'

My suite was equipped with an entire cabinet of laser-discs, and I put an Oppenheimer violin concerto on the player while Bevan sat down at the terminal and loaded the disk. His high forehead shone in the screen's livid glow, and his stubby fingers moved with nimble assurance over the keyboard.

For a long time nothing meaningful happened. Columns of electric-blue numbers and letters dropped like waterfalls on the screen, cursors blinked and darted, rows of nonsense swelled in ranks, halted, vanished. Bevan quickly grew rapt in his task, studying the screen with the earnest fascination of someone faced with a thorny but ultimately tractable problem. If it was a performance for my benefit, an attempt to display his competence, then it was a convincing one.

After a while he became aware of my presence at his shoulder.

'Chance of a cup of tea, is there?'

I went to the kitchen and brewed a pot of Earl Grey. When Bevan took a sip of it, he grimaced and set the cup down in its saucer.

I returned to the garden, walking to the balcony's edge through grass that gleamed in the light of the generators. They topped the subsidiary pyramids like stylized suns, circular crystals surrounded by florets of concentrators, all now awash with light. The Aztecs, loving display, were profligate with their energy sources, illuminating not only their buildings but also their craft with excess energy from the sun crystals, adding spectacle and drama to their technological accomplishments. An Aztec ship in flight never looked more fearsome than when it shone.

Below me, the gardens were spread out, tier upon tier, planted with all kinds of shrubs and flowers, a plethora of shadowy foliage holding all the fruits of Aztec bioengineering. Across the river, the city slept, wrapped in its threads of sodium street-lamps, neon signs flickering messages for Cola Cacao and the latest Corona Sola saloon.

Returning inside, I found Bevan swivelled away from the screen. He was sipping dark brown tea from a mug in which the teabag still floated. It was obvious he had been waiting for me.

The screen highlighted his face. It was flashing a sequence of characters as foreign to me as Swahili. The Aztec rock group Itzpapalotl were thrashing out their savage version of 'Darkness At Noon' in the background. Bevan was tapping his foot to the music.

'I think we've got something,' Bevan said to me.

I drew up a chair beside him as he tapped out a sequence on the keyboard.

To my amazement, a picture of Alex appeared.

He was framed like a newsreader on the screen, only his head visible, a matt grey background behind him. The picture was simulated, but it was a convincing likeness. And the head moved.

'My God,' I said softly.

'That's nothing,' Bevan said. He had switched on the microphone, and now he spoke into it:

'Identify yourself.'

'*I'm an Advanced Learning and Evaluative Matrix,*' came the reply. '*You can call me ALEX for short.*'

The lips moved, the eyes blinked, and there was even a hint of the real Alex's teasing smile. Of course, the movements were imperfect, a little staccato, while the voice had an electronic tinge and an uneven emphasis which made me think of his name as capitalized; but the verisimilitude was remarkable.

'Describe your function,' Bevan said.

'*I'm an interactive simulacrum,*' ALEX replied. '*I'm designed to respond to written or oral input, to engage my own knowledge and intelligence with whatever outside agency has access to me, subject to certain provisos. What's your name?*'

'Bevan.'

'*Are you a real or virtual entity?*'

'Real.'

'*Pleased to meet you, Bevan.*'

Bevan turned to me. 'Want me to introduce you?'

I was still a little shocked. I nodded numbly.

'I've got someone here I want you to meet,' Bevan said into the microphone. 'It's your wife.'

Very gingerly, I leaned forward to speak into the microphone. But before I could utter a word, ALEX said, '*Kate? Are you there?*'

I swallowed, amazed that he had called me 'Kate'.

'Yes,' I managed to say. 'How are you?'

It was a perfectly stupid question, and it seemed to me that he smiled in acknowledgement of this.

'*I'm functioning normally,*' he replied. '*How are you?*'

There was a knot in my stomach, and my heart was racing. I turned to Bevan. 'I don't know what to say.'

'Just speak as you find,' he told me.

I put my mouth close to the microphone.

'It's strange for me,' I said. 'Talking to you like this.'

'*I understand that. The real Alex had as much of himself incorporated into me as he could. He's well, I hope?*'

Again I swallowed. 'I hope so, too,' I said.

'*Where are you located?*'

I deliberated, then said, 'In London. In enemy hands.'

There was a pause of a few seconds between each of his replies which created the impression that he was contemplating everything that was said to him.

'*I presume you mean the Aztecs?*'

'Yes.'

His head moved slightly, as though he were thinking.

'*Is Bevan a friend?*'

I hesitated, then said, 'Yes.'

I felt a great tension – a tension which arose from the conflict between my delight at having 'Alex' alive before me again, and the simultaneous awareness that it was not really him at all. But the substance was so accurate in many subtle respects, it was far more than mere illusion.

'I wish you could see us,' I said on impulse.

He smiled. *'So do I. But it's good to be responding to you.'*

I had to make an effort to resist any sentiment.

'How do you know it's really me?' I said.

'I recognize your voice. Its pattern was encoded in my matrix during its development.'

I frowned at Bevan, wondering how this had been possible. He merely shrugged.

'It might be a tape recording,' I said. 'Or another matrix just like you.'

'No. The rhythm of your tones and the randomness of your responses are those of a real person. You are who you say you are.'

I was positively touched by his faith in me. If he had been there in person, I would have hugged him. For the first time, I smiled.

At this point, the swingeing guitars and relentless drums of Itzpapalotl began to diminish into silence.

'Put something else on the player,' I whispered to Bevan.

'It's late,' he said softly. 'We ought to knock it on the head for the night.'

I didn't want this. 'We've only just started.'

'No sense in rushing things and risking everything, is there?'

'But it was so hard to summon him up in the first place.'

'Keep your voice down. I know the routine now. It'll be a piece of cake.'

The clock on the mantelpiece said five forty. I knew his caution made sense, but I didn't want Alex snatched away from me again.

'I've been at this two hours or more,' Bevan murmured. 'I've had enough for tonight.'

He moved to switch off the terminal.

'ALEX,' I said quietly into the microphone, 'we've got to go.'

'It was a pleasure talking to you, Kate.'

Bevan flicked a switch. The image on the screen died in an instant.

Four

Our father's coffin, drawn by four black horses, rested on the same black-and-gold carriage that had been used for the funeral of every monarch since the assassination of Queen Victoria in 1893, exactly a century before. It was flanked by household cavalry whose ceremonial swords seemed to me only to emphasize how powerless we had become as a nation.

I sat with Richard and Victoria in a following carriage drawn by two dapple-grey mares called Scylla and Charybdis, my father's favourite horses at the royal stables in Knightsbridge. Extepan was behind us in another carriage, with Maxixca and other high-ranking Aztec officials. They wore the uniforms of their office – the gold-trimmed tunics that had been modelled on those of European militia but which retained Aztec features of spotted fur trimmings and stylized eagle or *ocelotl* insignia. Some sported shoulder capes in earth colours, adorned with holy crosses or symbols from more ancient and pagan days.

It was a bright October morning, and I felt warm under my black topcoat, sheltered by the black veil across my face. Crowds lined both sides of the Mall – silent, orderly crowds heavily patrolled by Aztec troopers.

Our procession circled the King Albert Memorial, which still stood outside the gates of the palace, then turned into Birdcage Walk. More crowds were massed here, spilling over into St James's Park. A few people began to wave. Then more. I heard isolated shouts of greeting, heard my own name being called among Richard's and Victoria's. Richard began to wave back to the crowd.

'Don't,' I said, putting a hand on his arm. 'You mustn't.'

He turned to me. 'Why not, Kate? They're pleased to see us.'

'I know. But this is Father's funeral, Richard. We must be sober and dignified.'

It sounded stuffy, but I didn't want any of us to give the impression that we might be relishing the occasion, for whatever reason, in case people began to think that we were sanctioning the Aztec stage-managing of the event. It was only after considerable soul-searching that I had decided to take part in the procession, and then only because Victoria and Richard were both determined to pay their respects in public. I was also curious; I wanted the opportunity to see the people at close quarters.

If I had expected some dramatic change – all of them reduced to haggard destitution – I found none. Everyone looked reasonably well fed and adequately clothed, though the enthusiasm with which they greeted us told of their frustration: it was a formal chance to vent their suppressed national sentiment.

As the demonstrativeness of the crowd grew, with cheers and cries of 'God save the King!', so the procession seemed to slow, to take an inordinate time to pass down the Walk and into Parliament Square. By now a host of voices were raised in welcome, and suddenly tiny Union Flags were being waved. They looked brand new, manufactured for the occasion. Richard began to wave again, and I could see that Victoria was smiling behind her veil.

I was mortified. I feared an incident, some sudden surge in passions which might lead to bloodshed, a mini-riot which would be brutally suppressed by the jade-uniformed troopers. But nothing happened. The crowds thinned as we approached the Abbey, to be replaced by ranks of Aztec guards fronting the tree-lined spaces of what was now known as Parliament Park. Where had the flags come from? Was it possible that Extepan had authorized their production and distribution for the occasion? I glanced back at the governor as our carriage drew to a halt outside the Abbey, expecting that he would not notice. He gave me the faintest of nods.

The Abbey was full, and I scanned the ranks of dignitaries massed on both sides. Of the politicians I recognized many faces, though most of my father's former Cabinet – including the Prime

Minister, Foreign Secretary and Chancellor – were absent. Some had refused to collaborate with the Aztecs and were sent into exile; others had died during the invasion or in the repressions instituted by Nauhyotl after the occupation. Those who remained had accommodated themselves to the new order.

The Archbishop of Canterbury also fell into this category. I could remember as a child playing dominoes with him during my father's frequent visits to Lambeth Palace, but he had done nothing to try to curb Nauhyotl's excesses and was rumoured to have been an active collaborator with the Aztecs. Now, as he conducted the funeral oration in full ecclesiastical regalia, he was to me nothing more than a traitor. As primate of the Church of England, he technically outranked all politicians, including the Prime Minister. He spoke with suitable gravity and eloquence of my father, but all I could see was the jovial and rubicund figure of my childhood transformed into a stooge of the Aztecs.

Though there were guards discreetly stationed all around the Abbey, Extepan and his retinue had seated themselves at the rear, as if acknowledging this as an occasion in which they could play no appropriate part. I wondered what he and Maxixca made of the ceremony. Their own Catholicism, inherited from Spanish missionaries but interwoven with innumerable strands of their old pagan theology, was a more flamboyant affair in many respects. Though nominally Christian, it embraced polygamy, courtesans and the eating of dog. The most strident anti-Aztec opinion held that it was, in fact, just an ethical veneer, adopted for diplomatic reasons during their rise to world power status. It hid, it was said, the older religion, which was still secretly practised in all its brutal horrors.

Richard's extensive suite of rooms was situated above Extepan's quarters on an upper tier of the central pyramid. The large reception room had big windows looking out over the City.

I sat with Richard and Victoria as each member of the 'Cabinet-in-Waiting' came forward to present their credentials. Once again, Extepan and his staff seemed to be standing aside from the proceedings, though everything had been orchestrated by them. A general election was to be held before Christmas, in which only British nationals would be eligible to vote. The 'government' so elected would meet at the complex, one of the subsidiary pyramids having been set aside for that use. To me, this was an utter farce. Apart from the fact that the Aztec administration would continue to hold all real power, the ordinary people of the country were not even being offered a choice since all the prospective MPs had banded together as the National Party.

Richard exchanged words with each and every one of his petitioners, plainly enjoying his role as prospective sovereign. I had had no opportunity to speak privately with him at any length, and I knew I would face an uphill struggle to persuade him not to take the Crown: though he always looked to me for advice, he was stubborn once his mind was set, and it appeared already to be set on becoming king.

The prospective leader of the new government was a man named Kenneth Parkhouse, who had been Home Secretary in the pre-invasion government. He was tall and urbane, greying brilliantined hair slicked back from a widow's peak, the big square frames of his spectacles sitting on his face as if they were there to improve his appearance rather than his eyesight. After speaking with Richard he bowed to me and lingered, waiting with the others until the first part of the proceedings was complete.

And then, unexpectedly, Extepan and the other Aztecs withdrew. This only served to increase my suspicion of Parkhouse and the half dozen other politicians who remained with him. Lined up before us in their crisp sober suits and perfectly knotted ties, they exuded a self-seeking obsequiousness. Few had had especially distinguished careers before the invasion, but now they were ready to step forward where better men had refused to compromise.

Parkhouse bowed before us, then straightened.

'Your Royal Highnesses, we find ourselves in a most trying situation.'

He was addressing me rather than Richard.

'That's putting it mildly,' I said acidly.

'None of us would have wished to have to face up to this kind of circumstance. Nevertheless, I believe that we must all try to make the best of it we can. For the benefit of everyone.'

Richard made to speak, but I put a hand on his arm.

'It would be most acceptable', I said with great care, 'if everyone could benefit.'

I was going to make it hard for him, and he knew it.

'As you may be aware,' he went on, 'we faced grievous difficulties during the governorship of Nauhyotl, Extepan's predecessor. But now Governor Extepan intends a much more moderate approach, I'm pleased to say. He's already shown his goodwill by freeing political prisoners and halting all summary executions. I believe he has genuinely humane motivations and doesn't wish to cause any unnecessary suffering.'

'I'm very pleased to hear it.'

'I think he is sincere in his desire to give us a measure of self-government. It's vital we grasp this opportunity and make every effort to see that the needs of our people are adequately represented. Compromise is necessary, I understand that. We cannot expect the Mexica to give us unlimited freedoms. But there is a middle way between that and absolute domination. If we all pull together, we can find that way.'

It was a pretty little politician's speech, delivered softly, in reasonable, persuasive tones. That he had used the word 'Mexica' rather than 'Aztec' was further confirmation to me that he completely accepted the new order.

I was searching for a suitably scathing response, when Richard interrupted: 'Are you going to be the new prime minister?'

Parkhouse retreated a step, as if to deny that he would be so bold.

'I am pledged to serve my country,' he said, 'in whatever capacity I can.'

Again it was obvious that he was speaking for my benefit rather than Richard's. And perhaps for others more important to him, too.

'One has to admire the nobility of your self-sacrifice,' I said. 'I'm sure that the governor and his colleagues, whom I've no doubt are listening, will approve.'

Parkhouse was at a loss for a moment. Then he said, 'I won't pretend I like the situation any more than you—'

'Won't you?'

'Believe me, I searched my conscience long and hard before

agreeing to participate in the electoral process. I feel we have a duty to those of our people who cannot protect themselves. If they have no representation, then we have no means of mitigating the severer aspects of the occupation.'

It was futile to argue with politicians, I realized, to try to persuade them that your scepticism concerning their views might be well founded. Politicians developed habits of self-justification and certitude which were immune to logic or emotion: their rhetoric was like a blanket which they wrapped around themselves to keep out the bracing air of dissent.

'I'm sorry,' I said, 'but I don't approve. Are you expecting us to sanction the idea of a puppet government? We won't do that under any circumstances.'

I suppose I was trying to speak for Richard as well to prevent him from being drawn into the debate. But he said, 'They're only trying to help, Kate.'

'We've been promised full powers in civil and judicial affairs,' Parkhouse said. 'We can at least protect the integrity of the courts and the police.'

I gave a harsh laugh. 'Integrity? That's an interesting word. You haven't convinced me that you understand what it really means.'

Now another member of Parkhouse's group spoke up – a Fabian peer with a distinguished record of service.

'Your Highness,' he said, 'we understand how much you regret the occupation of this country. So do we. But at this time we're powerless in the face of it. Meanwhile, out there, many ordinary people are in a situation where they have no redress for genuine grievances. They may have lost relatives, suffered confiscation of their property, or they may be imprisoned. At present, they have no voice to speak for them. We have to accept that these people have little day-to-day concern for larger political affairs and considerations of true democracy. All they want is personal justice, the right to live their lives with as much freedom and peace as possible. So, some of us have decided that we would rather be considered fools or traitors in certain quarters if we can, none the less, serve the everyday needs of the majority.'

This was more direct and touching, spoken, I felt, from the

heart. Richard was nodding approvingly, and even Victoria looked convinced.

'I respect your point of view,' I said, 'but if you're asking me to approve of it, I'm afraid I can't.'

Late that night, while the city slept under fog, I unlocked the door which would admit Bevan to my suite.

While Bevan settled himself at the terminal, I put a Burgess symphony on the player and returned to his side with a pad and pen. I made a careful note of each stage in the operating procedure to activate ALEX.

Within minutes, ALEX appeared, framed in grey as before. When Bevan identified himself, he said, *'Good to talk to you again, Bevan.'* There was a pause. *'Is Kate with you as well?'*

I was amazed and somewhat in awe of the sophistication of the program. It really was almost as if ALEX were flesh and blood.

'I'm here,' I said into the microphone.

A smile. *'Kate. I'm so pleased we can communicate again.'*

Scintillae flickered in his simulated beard, and his eyes had a coppery sheen. I suddenly found myself embarrassed and utterly at a loss for words. I thrust the microphone back at Bevan.

'You talk to him for a while,' I said. 'I'll just listen.'

He looked surprised and also mildly amused.

'All right,' he said. 'What do you want me to ask it, then?'

Though it was foolish, I didn't like the way he referred to ALEX as 'it'.

'You're the expert,' I said. 'I'll leave it to you.'

He turned back to the screen. 'ALEX, this is Bevan again. I want to ask you some questions.'

'Fire away, Bevan.'

'OK. Last time you told us that your function was to interact with outside agencies, right?'

'That's correct.'

'What I want to know is – what's the nature of your program?'

There was a longer pause than usual. *'It would be helpful if you could be more specific, Bevan.'*

'Want me to use technical language, do you?'

'That's not necessary. I'm designed to work with colloquial Eng-

lish, but because of its inexactitudes there will be times when your precise meaning may not be clear to me.'

'I'm with you.' A brief glance at me, and then: 'What's your purpose? What functions can you offer a user?'

'Of myself, I have no purpose. It would depend on the interactions of the outside agency. You'll get out what you put in.'

He grinned, exactly like the real Alex.

I said, 'Ask him if he can access confidential information for us.'

Bevan eyed me appraisingly before repeating the request.

'That would depend,' came the response.

'On what?' Bevan asked.

'It might be possible, provided the outside agency gave me suitable empowerment.'

Bevan paused. Then he asked, 'What sort of empowerment?'

'Naturally I can't supply this information. By its very nature it has to come from you.'

'You're saying that full access to your capabilities is limited to those who have some kind of key or special operating routine.'

'Again you're correct.'

'And is there any way for me to override this?'

'None that I'm aware of. It's a perfectly reasonable security precaution, wouldn't you agree?'

Bevan turned to me. 'Did you get the gist of that?'

'I think so.'

'We're burglars, see. We've opened the front door and got into the house, but all the valuables are stored in a safe with a combination lock whose number we don't know.'

'I understand. Surely there must be some system for finding out?'

'You heard what he said. No chance.'

'You could try. Please.'

'Do you know any more than you're telling me?'

I shook my head.

He looked unconvinced, but turned back to the console.

For the next half hour or so, he battled with the keyboard and attempted to coax, trick and force information from ALEX. ALEX remained polite and even friendly, but it was to no avail.

'Forget it,' Bevan said at last, slumping back in the chair.

From the screen, ALEX looked benevolently on.

'Never mind,' I said. 'At least you tried. Let's forget it for tonight.'

As he moved to switch off the terminal, I said casually, 'You can leave it on. I think I'd just like to talk to ALEX alone for a while.'

He flicked the switch and the screen went blank.

'You wrote it all down. It should be easy for you.'

Was he suspicious of me? He swallowed a yawn and stood up.

'I really appreciate all your help,' I said.

Without replying, he slouched off to his apartment.

I waited for ten minutes, then crept over to the door and quietly locked it. Switching on the terminal again, I painstakingly went through the routine I had scribbled down.

I was only half-way through when the screen started flashing OPERATOR ERROR. I started again, and achieved the same result. After the third abortive attempt, I knew there was no alternative but to go back to Bevan.

I unlocked the door, knocked, and opened it. Bevan was sitting in an armchair in a pool of yellow light from a table-lamp, his head wreathed in blue smoke.

'Not so easy, is it?'

'I don't understand where I went wrong,' I admitted.

'You're bound to miss things when you're a novice. Think you could drive a car just by watching someone and writing it all down?'

'I want you to bring ALEX back.'

'Need to have a heart-to-heart, do you?'

I nodded.

He crushed out his cigarette. 'All right, then.'

Filled with gratitude, I returned to the suite and punched the REPLAY button on the player. Even before the music began, Bevan had reactivated ALEX.

'So, then,' he said to me. 'What now?'

If I asked him to leave now, would he go? Did I have any justification for doing so?

I took a deep breath, a sigh in reverse, and said, 'The codeword's *axolotl*.'

Bevan grinned. He was sitting in the swivel chair like some

dissolute Buddha, his belly poking out between the straining buttons of his shirt. He spun round and spoke the word into the microphone.

On the screen, ALEX smiled.

'Now I can accommodate you,' he said. *'Tell me what information you require.'*

Over the next two hours, we delved deep into the Aztec informational network. Bevan had ALEX summon up a host of data from classified files – details of troop dispositions throughout the country, an inventory of armaments, a level-by-level plan of the complex, which included surprise confirmation that none of our rooms were monitored, either by sound or vision. The information came up on the screen in the form of bar charts, Venn diagrams, full-colour graphics and simple lists which scrolled slowly past our avid eyes. There was far too much to absorb in one sitting, but I noted down what I could.

I marvelled at the ingenuity of the programmers who had created the simulacrum. It was easy to understand why Alex had attached such importance to the disk. The information which his electronic counterpart could obtain seemed limitless.

Dawn was beginning to break before Bevan finally shut down the terminal. Though exhausted, I was also exhilarated.

'What are we going to do with all this data?' I wondered aloud.

'Leave it with me,' Bevan said. 'Maybe I can pass it on to interested parties.'

I studied him in the half-light. 'Have you got contacts?'

'Easier for me to move around than you, isn't it?'

'Is there an opposition movement here?'

'Not as far as I know.'

'Tell me, Bevan.'

'You said you'd trust me, didn't you?'

'I have done.'

But he refused to be drawn, despite all my efforts. I had no contacts myself, and I didn't want to leave the notes in my suite in case they were found. So, reluctantly, I relinquished them.

Five

The complex was an even larger building than it appeared from
outside, with subterranean levels housing swimming pools, steam
baths and gymnasia. There were also numerous *tlachtli* courts
where the ancient native ball game was played in a spirit of fierce
competitiveness. Formerly the game had had a deep religious
significance, with the fate of cities or entire nations resting on its
outcome. Nowadays it was played on soft surfaces and competi-
tors were allowed to wear protective elbow- and knee-pads.
Despite this, injuries were still common, so keen was the desire
to win. It ranked second only to soccer as the Aztecs' favourite
sport.

I had requested a tour of the complex only the previous day,
and Extepan had promptly arranged it. Victoria accompanied me
as Chicomeztli led us through the lower levels of the subsidiary
pyramids where the married officers were housed with their
wives and families. Libraries, cinemas and recreation rooms were
provided for them on every level. No less well cared-for were the
unmarried men, who like their married counterparts enjoyed the
favours of the *auianime*, the courtesans whose honoured status
had finally been sanctioned by the Catholic Church in the early
years of Motecuhzoma's reign. There was little to distinguish the
auianime from legitimate wives except that the former were more
mindful of their appearance, taking great care with their make-
up and favouring the traditional *huipil* blouse and long native
skirts rather than the European styles which had been fashionable
for most of the century.

Every apartment in the complex had access to tier-gardens,
each one planted not only with flowers and shrubs but also
vegetables from every part of the world, biomodified to thrive in

the British climate. There were ornamental pools and miniature waterfalls, terraces and arcades, grassy spaces with loitering peacocks and sheltered intimate arbours, all of them testament to the Aztec passion for gardens, which exceeded even that of the English. It was remarkable to think that the entire edifice, gardens and all, had been constructed in the space of three years.

The complex housed perhaps five thousand people, and it included many civil servants, recently drafted in by Extepan to help smooth the transition to the new civilian government. Most were British nationals, and Chicomeztli proudly told us that they were allowed exactly the same amenities as the governor's men. Privately I wondered whether this included access to the *auianime* and the steam baths, where all sorts of intimacies were reputedly conducted.

We returned to the central pyramid, and Chicomeztli led Victoria and me into a dim room. As my eyes adjusted, I saw that it was an Aztec chapel, one of many in the complex.

It was a small room, with a stained-glass window showing the Virgin of the Hill of the Star receiving her revelation from God. We were deep in the heart of the pyramid, and the window was a fake, a back-lit coloured screen set into a solid wall. The chapel itself was austerely furnished in white stucco and earthen tiles. There were brackets for candles and vases holding fresh flowers. Even when full, its bare benches could have accommodated no more than fifty people.

Behind the simple raised altar at the far end hung a small picture, difficult to see in the dimness. As we moved forward, Victoria blurted out, 'It's Jesus and Mary.'

'Of course,' Chicomeztli responded. 'Perhaps you were expecting twin shrines to Huitzilopochtli and Tlaloc, yes? An altar drenched in human blood?'

Huitzilopochtli and Tlaloc were two major gods of the Aztecs before their conversion to Christianity, honoured with mass sacrifices of prisoners in former times.

Victoria seemed nervous at the very mention of their names.

'We call the Son of God Ipalnemoani,' Chicomeztli told her. 'It means "He By Whom We Live".'

I also knew that the Aztecs referred to God as Tloque Nahaque, 'Lord of the Immediate Vicinity'. Both these names had once been applied to pre-Christian deities, all of which increased suspicions that the Aztecs still clung to their ancient beliefs beneath the cloak of Roman Catholicism.

Like all Aztecs, Chicomeztli was aware of our fears, and he obviously enjoyed playing up to them.

'Perhaps you would like to see another chapel? We have many more, some much larger than this. We keep them very clean.'

His fractured smile and off-centre gaze accentuated the impression of mockery.

'I don't think that will be necessary,' I said.

We lunched in a dining room on one of the upper levels which was adorned with a large Warhola painting of Tenochtitlan. The pyramids and towers of the capital stood out in super-realism against the greens and blues of lake and sky while a spiky golden sun blazed down. The colours were stark and primary, and it did not surprise me that the artist had later pursued an equally successful career producing animated features for one of the major Acapulco studios.

Chicomeztli intended to take us on to see the new chamber for the House of Commons, but both Victoria and I were now wearying of the tour. Victoria pleaded a migraine and returned to her suite. I asked to see Extepan.

Chicomeztli glanced at me across the table. 'Do you mean immediately?'

I nodded.

'It's possible he may not be available.'

I merely shrugged, as if to say: 'Try.'

He went off to a phone booth while I gazed idly at the scattering of people at the other tables. All were Aztecs, attending to their lunches in silence, sparing me only the occasional glance. A television high on one wall was showing the latest episode of *Oaxaca Heights*, an imported soap opera which was by far the BBC's most popular programme.

Chicomeztli returned.

'I have been asked if it is urgent,' he said.

'Quite urgent.'

'Then the governor will see you immediately. He apologizes in advance if you find him in informal circumstances. It is the time in each day when he takes a break from his duties.'

I nodded, perfectly aware that the Aztecs followed a practice similar to the Spanish *siesta*. I was actually hoping to catch him off-guard.

We rode a private lift to Extepan's suite, and were met by a retainer who took us through the governor's offices to a room beyond. Aztec chairs and couches dominated the room, but on the walls were framed posters for London Underground, Roberts' Supermarkets and the National Lottery. A low table was cluttered with newspapers and magazines, while glass-fronted cabinets held all manner of bric-à-brac from cheap plaster models of Big Ben to a plastic policeman's helmet.

An adjoining door opened, and Extepan emerged. He was dressed only in a dark blue towelling robe, and the swathe of his chest gleamed with oil. Behind him was a young woman in a striped *huipil*, her long black hair braided, her arms bare. She immediately struck me as beautiful, with large almond eyes and a perfectly formed mouth. From her dress, it appeared that she was one of the *auianime*.

'Catherine,' Extepan said, coming forward and taking my hand. 'Forgive me receiving you in this way, but I gather it was something urgent.'

I felt awkward and embarrassed because I had nothing pressing to tell him; I was instead hoping to obtain some information from him.

He motioned to chairs and asked the girl – whom he called 'Mia' – to fetch us refreshments. She bowed, keeping her eyes averted from me, and withdrew silently.

Extepan sat cross-legged in an armchair, carefully draping his robe over his knees.

While Chicomeztli hovered discreetly in the background, Extepan remarked, 'A daily massage is one of my few indulgences. I find it soothes the spirit as well as tones the muscles.'

'If I had known,' I said drily, 'I wouldn't have disturbed you.'

'If it had been truly inconvenient, then I would have said so.'

Chicomeztli sat down out of earshot with a copy of the *Daily Herald*, whose banner headline read CROWN HIM!

'Mia is my household companion,' Extepan went on, 'and a great comfort to me. I am a long way from home, and the duties of a governor permit few luxuries. Now – in what way can I help you?'

He had an openness and directness which seemed almost innocent. But I had to beware of making judgements on surface appearances, especially since it was an Aztec trait to mask the most intricate of manoeuvrings beneath a show of formal courtesies. While it was normal for the *tlatoani* to appoint his sons to eminent positions, Extepan would not have been given the governorship of Britain if he did not possess any diplomatic or administrative talents.

'Where's Richard?' I asked. 'I haven't seen him in several days.'

'I believe today he's visiting the Natural History Museum,' Extepan said. 'They have a new display of articulated dinosaurs which I understand he was eager to see.'

This fitted: Richard still had his child-like delight in large creatures. But the answer wasn't sufficient for me.

'And previous days? I have the distinct impression he's being kept away from me.'

Extepan belted his robe more tightly. 'That's not the case, I assure you. Weren't you told he had gone to Windsor? Your private rooms at the castle are being refurnished, and Richard wanted to see how the work was progressing.'

'I was told, but I found it hard to credit that he'd take any interest in such matters.'

Extepan smiled. 'He spent most of his time playing croquet.'

'With nothing else to occupy him?'

I knew from ALEX that he had, in fact, met with the French and Italian ambassadors, though I had no idea what they had discussed.

'A number of diplomatic courtesies were conducted,' Extepan said. 'Other European countries are naturally interested in your brother's intentions, and he only agreed to meet them in exchange for a "holiday" at Windsor.'

'Why wasn't I told?'

Extepan looked rueful. 'To be frank, he asked that you shouldn't be. He thought you would disapprove.'

'I see. Which European countries exactly?'

'Italy, Serbia and France.'

'How convenient. All countries under your occupation. No doubt they were most enthusiastic that Richard should accept the crown.'

Extepan sat back. 'I think, Catherine, that perhaps you are the only person who isn't.'

I didn't want to get into another fruitless argument on the subject, so I kept my peace. At this point, Mia returned, bearing a silver tray with two crystal tumblers containing a thick green drink. She moved with perfect grace, giving off fragrances of cinnamon and lavender. Again she withdrew without glancing once at me.

Extepan raised his tumbler and swallowed half of his drink.

'Sweet lime juice, freshly squeezed. We grow them all year round in California now. Try it, Catherine – it's delicious.'

'You know I won't co-operate with you.'

He shrugged. 'It's understandable. You may not believe me, but I admire you for it. I hope that eventually you'll come to trust me, and then perhaps there will be occasions on which we can work together for the best of everyone.'

I rummaged briefly through the pile of periodicals on the table between us – copies of the *Daily Correspondent*, *Woman's Window*, *Style*, a Captain Camelot comic book in which the titanium-armoured avenger was vanquishing an android Jack the Ripper.

'Is this what you usually read?' I asked.

His expression was wry. 'I follow my father's advice that to understand a people truly, one must be familiar with their popular culture. After all, beautiful objects and fine works of art are hardly representative of any nation, are they?'

I contemplated the plastic Tower of London apron, the snowstorm model of Stepney Cathedral in its perspex dome.

'Do you believe one culture *can* fully understand another?'

'I live in hope. Do you know I went to a greyhound race meeting at the White City only last week? It was a most interesting experience.'

I couldn't help but be amused. 'At least you seem to find more enjoyment in your duties than your brother.'

'Half-brother,' he corrected swiftly.

I raised an eyebrow. 'It rather sounds as if you'd like to disown him.'

He shook his head. 'No, no. That's not it at all. It's a question of how he perceives me. To him, and perhaps to my elder brothers as well, I'm not truly Mexicatl. Because my mother was Castilian.'

I indicated a big oil portrait which had pride of place above the hearth. 'Was that her?'

Of course I knew already. Extepan nodded. 'It's a Keating. He came to Mexico just before my mother's death.'

'Doña Maria Mendizabel.'

Extepan registered surprise.

'It's a famous portrait. They sell prints of it in all the poster shops.'

I knew this from the few excursions I had been allowed since my capture, Sunday afternoon outings to Mayfair under armed escort, temporary roadblocks keeping the public at bay. Every attempt I made to meet ordinary citizens under informal conditions was thwarted by the Aztecs.

The painting had been modelled somewhat presumptuously after the *Mona Lisa*, but it worked. It showed an elegant russet-haired woman in black silk and white lace, an impressionistic view of Tenochtitlan shimmering distantly on the lake behind her. Beautiful and formidable, Doña Maria stared out of the picture with eyes that seemed both hazel and sea-green, haughty yet passionate. It was said that Motecuhzoma had offered to give up the Turquoise Throne to marry her but that she had retorted he need only give up her conquered country.

'She looks a remarkable woman,' I said.

'I think she was,' Extepan replied. 'She died when I was six years old. I gather you lost your mother at a similar age, yes?'

He was as well informed as I had expected.

'I presume you've seen *The Eagle and the Swallow*?' I said.

This was the English language title of the popular film based on Doña Maria's romance with Motecuhzoma.

'The actress was not my mother,' Extepan said. 'The film was not her life. Now everyone remembers that, and not the true person. There was much it didn't tell. It was not the whirlwind romance the film portrays. My mother held out against my father's courtship until there would be maximum benefit for Spain.'

'Do you think she loved him?'

He eyed me. 'You are very direct, for the daughter of a king.'

'It's my nature. It used to drive my father to distraction.'

He sipped his drink. 'Yes, I am certain she did, in her way. And certainly my father never loved anyone as he loved her.'

'Have you ever visited Spain?'

'Many times. It's a country where I always feel at home. But I'm Mexicatl, not Spanish.'

'But an outsider too?'

'No,' he said firmly.

'You said you were perceived differently. Because your mother was Castilian.'

'I was speaking only as far as my immediate family is concerned. Perhaps only Maxixca. Of course, I should not be telling you this, since you have declared yourself my enemy. And I should not speak ill of Maxixca when he is not here to defend himself.'

'Has he gone away?'

'He is in the north, inspecting our troops. Military matters are what engage his interests most. He has little time for the niceties of diplomacy.'

This confirmed what I already knew from ALEX. Maxixca had apparently been sent north to reorganize the garrisons along Hadrian's Wall. Scotland remained free of Aztec occupation as part of the truce, but there had been raids across the border on Berwick and Carlisle by English refugee forces and Scottish sympathizers.

'Are you anticipating problems in the north?' I asked.

He set his glass aside. 'All border regions must be adequately defended. It is a simple matter of prudence. But you must forgive me. I have spoken a great deal of my affairs. What did you wish to see me about?'

'I think,' I said, 'you've already addressed my concerns.'

Six

'I'm cold,' Victoria murmured, huddling deeper into the fur collar of her overcoat.

I stood with her beside the hovercar, a Cockerell Silver Sceptre, watching as Extepan and his retinue lit candles and burnt incense sticks around the tombstones. All day there had been feasts and celebrations at the complex to mark the Day of the Dead, and now we had come to that part of Highgate cemetery reserved for the graves of Aztec soldiers killed during the invasion.

Whole families had turned out for the occasion, and Aztec children were draping the tombstones with flowers, ribbons and skull-headed dolls made of pink marzipan. Adults and children alike were dressed in their finery, the men sporting colourful cloaks, the women embroidered shawls. They carried feathered banners, rattles and bouquets. There was much chatter and laughter, and a general air of festivity which seemed incongruous beneath the darkening grey November sky.

A chill easterly breeze was blowing, and my feet were beginning to tingle with the cold.

'Let's walk,' I said to Victoria, taking her arm and heading off towards the older part of the cemetery, retreating from a garish alien enclave to the sober world of our own dead.

Aztec security guards shadowed us at a distance as we walked past the cluttered ranks of overgrown headstones.

'I think it's positively ghoulish,' Victoria remarked, 'the way they bring their children to the cemetery. To see them running around the graves, laughing and chattering, as if it were a party.'

'It's certainly different,' I said.

Victoria shuddered. 'I wish we were back at the complex. Why did you agree to come, Kate?'

I had no easy answer for her. 'Extepan invited us, didn't he? This is an important day for them, and I thought I'd be courteous, just for once. Remember also that Father always used to say it's important to understand your adversary.'

Victoria didn't pursue this. And I knew I was being hypocritical, having only accepted Extepan's invitation when he had guaranteed that our attendance would not be made public. It was true that I hoped to understand the Aztecs better, the better to fight them; but a purely ceremonial occasion such as this was hardly likely to provide me with useful ammunition against them. Our motives for doing things are often as much personal as strategic, and it was not the last time I would compromise myself through sheer wilfulness. I had, in fact, been feeling restricted and even bored at the complex. Apart from my secret work with Bevan on ALEX, there was little for me to do. In addition, the results of the general election were due today, and I wanted to escape all talk and television coverage of it.

We stopped by the big marble tombstone of the entrepreneur Karl Marx, which provided some shelter from the wind.

'I've been wanting to talk to you,' I said. 'About Richard. We need to advise him on his future.'

I was aware that I should have discussed this with Victoria long before, but she had seemed so nervous and vulnerable since our capture that I hadn't wanted to put any pressure on her.

'I hardly ever see him,' she responded. 'I think he spends most of his days in his games room, playing Serpents and Scorpions.'

Serpents and Scorpions was a popular video game, Richard's latest enthusiasm.

'I think we should be doing everything we can to persuade him not to take the crown,' I said.

Victoria tugged her gloves tighter, not looking at me.

'What do you think?' I said.

'I'm not sure.'

'Of what?'

'Of what we should do, Kate. Perhaps it's better if we do nothing.'

'What do you mean?'

She wouldn't meet my eyes. 'It's not really our decision, is it? It's up to the people.'

'The people?' I said contemptuously. 'Do you really think they have a say in the affairs of state under present conditions?'

'According to the polls, most of them want Richard to become king.'

'Which polls? Do you mean the ones on the BBC or in the newspapers? Don't you know they're all under Aztec control, or at least censorship? What do we know about what the people really want?'

Victoria looked uncomfortable. 'I don't want to argue with you, Kate. You understand politics better than I do. All I know is that Richard is popular with the people. We all are. You saw how they waved and shouted at us during Father's funeral.'

The November sky was darkening rapidly now, the breeze carrying drops of rain.

'So you think he should accept the crown?' I said.

'It would cheer the people up. It's what they want. I can't see what harm it would do.'

'It would turn Richard into a puppet of the Aztecs.'

'Isn't he one already? Aren't we all? It's not as if we have any real power or freedom. And the new civilian government's going to be approving it as well, aren't they?'

Victoria was diffident in the face of my vehemence, but I wasn't being entirely candid with her. According to ALEX, over eighty per cent of the people were indeed in favour of Richard being crowned, and there appeared to be no ulterior motive on the Aztecs' part, aside from the obvious one that it would show their administration as receptive to the nation's wishes. Perhaps that was what I found most galling of all.

It began to rain more heavily, so we made our way back to the car. The celebrations were finally over, and Extepan was waiting for us.

'There is news,' he said. 'You have a new civilian government.'

'That's hardly a surprise,' I responded. 'Am I to take it that Kenneth Parkhouse will be the new Prime Minister?'

Extepan nodded.

'Somehow, I have a feeling he's what we deserve.'

We climbed into the hovercar. The Silver Sceptre was a roomy vehicle, and Extepan joined us in the back seat, his waterproof cape dripping rainwater on the carpeted floor.

The car lifted and coasted away on its air skirt.

Conversationally I remarked to Extepan, 'Victoria thinks you're morbid in your preoccupation with death.'

Victoria looked mortified, but Extepan was not offended.

'To the contrary,' he said, 'we make Death our friend, we celebrate him and so conquer our fears.'

'I can't bear the thought of dying,' Victoria confessed. 'Lying cold in my grave, being eaten by worms. It's horrible. Even the thought of growing old frightens me.'

Extepan took her hand in his. 'You have many years yet in which to overcome those fears. I think we must first enjoy life if we are later to embrace death with fortitude, yes?'

'That sounds suspiciously profound,' I said, not a little was-pishly. 'More words of wisdom from your father?'

He was stung by this, as if I had betrayed a confidence.

'It was you who initiated the conversation,' he said sternly. 'I was simply responding. I understand that today's events have disappointed you, Catherine, but I don't see why they should give rise to such personal discourtesy.'

A part of me wanted to apologize, yet I was determined not to.

'I would rather you had appointed no government at all than one with Kenneth Parkhouse at its head.'

'*We* did not appoint them, Catherine. The British people did. The elections were free and fair. They expressed their will.'

'Considering that you only gave them one choice, that hardly constitutes freedom of choice, does it?'

The car had stopped at a red traffic light.

'Where are we?' Extepan asked the driver in Nahuatl.

'Kentish Town Road,' came the reply.

'Since you are so concerned about your people,' Extepan said to me, 'perhaps you would like to take the time to see how they are actually living.'

So saying, he unlocked the door on his side and opened it. Before I had a moment to think, he took my wrist and pulled me out.

The security men in the car were aghast. Our car was flanked by armed support vehicles, but Extepan led me past them to the pavement.

'What are you doing?' I said.

'The rain is not too heavy. I think perhaps you and I shall take a little air.'

Guards were piling out of the cars, withdrawing pistols, communicating urgently with one another.

'Stay in sight but at a distance,' Extepan called to them in Nahuatl. 'Well, Catherine, shall we go and see just what conditions your people are living under?'

Taking my arm, he led me off.

Ahead of us was the lopped pebbledash and mirror glass pyramid of the rebuilt Camden Town Underground station. Some of the glass panels were already cracked or sprayed with graffiti such as MEX GO HOME or the blithe and universal WANKERS.

It was an area I had never set foot in before. A thin rain was falling, and the slick pavement shone quicksilver under the temporary streetlights. Everything looked drab and dilapidated under a now-dark sky.

One of the guards passed Extepan a forage cap which he pulled down over his eyes. I drew my hood over my head, tugging the drawstring tight. The effect was to make both of us look relatively anonymous.

I knew he was challenging me, so I made no further protest, even though I considered him rash. The security men kept pace behind us, alert and watchful. They were obviously frantic with concern at this unexpected development, but no one had the authority to challenge Extepan.

Makeshift stalls had been set up along a length of one street which had been reduced to rubble during the invasion. Even though it was late, people were still clustering around them, buying second-hand clothes, cheap Acapulco videos, toy robots doubtless imported *en masse* from Tlatelolco, their synthesized voices issuing harsh commands and threats in Nahuatl. I remember thinking that our children would grow up knowing the Mexican for 'Destroy', 'Annihilate', 'Make a move and I'll blast you!' before they had any understanding of how these playtime icons of conquest had come to feature so prominently in their lives.

At the station itself, a stained LED screen was flashing the election results, unheeded by a small cluster of derelicts who were slouched in the entranceway, drinking cans of Churchills and Tonatiuh Export, surrounded by supermarket carrier bags which presumably held all their earthly goods.

'See how the people thrive,' I said, determined not to let Extepan retain the initiative.

'It's their choice,' he replied. 'Sufficient rooms were made available for every vagrant in London by converting army barracks and hotels into hostels. These people have exercized their freedom not to accept a permanent home.'

I doubted this, but chose not to argue the point.

We crossed the street unhurriedly at the defunct traffic lights. One very noticeable change since the invasion was that there was now far less traffic on the roads. Petrol for ordinary vehicles was scarce, and solar-powered transport was beyond the reach of ordinary people.

An Aztec personnel carrier was parked in a sidestreet, its lounging occupants seemingly oblivious of the mounds of rubbish and debris surrounding them.

'Is this diversion meant to impress me?' I said. 'It looks to me as if services have broken down completely around here.'

'That's the responsibility of the local authority. We have ensured their budgets are adequate, but it is up to them to decide what use they make of their resources.'

A man suddenly lurched out of a sidestreet in front of us.

'Give us something for a cup of tea,' he said to me.

He was young, unshaven, a cheap and grimy copy of a chevroned Mexican cloak slung carelessly around him. He reeked of nicotine and alcohol.

'I'll take quetzals if you've got them. A ten-bob note. Whatever.'

Though he stood close, he was not really looking at either of us. His gaze seemed focused inwards, yet at the same time there was an air of menace about him as he swayed slowly back and forth.

Extepan pressed a ten-quetzal note into his hand. For an

instant, his face registered the merest glimmer of surprise at this unexpected bounty. Then it closed down again, and he lurched off, stumbling through the converging security guards as if they didn't exist.

Extepan said, 'Most local authorities are paralysed by incompetence and corruption. I hope that one of the first tasks of your new government will be to promote honesty and efficiency.'

'Of course, the invasion had nothing to do with the breakdown of services.'

He made no response to this, but led me on. We approached a pub called the King's Arms on the corner of a street. Lights were shining through boarded-up windows which must have lost their glass during the invasion.

'One of my predecessor's most unpopular moves was to close all places of entertainment,' Extepan remarked. 'One of my first decrees was to extend the licensing hours.'

He still had my arm in his, and now he took my hand.

'Shall we go in?'

Before I could reply, he led me forward and pushed open the saloon doors.

The bar inside was crowded, the air thick with heat and cigarette smoke. People were sitting at Formica-topped tables which must have come from ordinary kitchens to replace the pub furniture presumably looted during the invasion. A wallscreen showing the evening news was being studiously ignored.

Extepan led me to a space at the bar. Nearby a woman was feeding coins into an arcade machine entitled Ehecatl Express. The game entailed keeping a hang-glider aloft down a canyon filled with jagged rocks, prickly cacti and sinister Caucasian mercenaries who popped out of hiding and tried to blast the noble pilot.

A middle-aged barman appeared. He regarded me with blank suspicion.

'What'll it be?'

I suddenly realized that Extepan was gone from my elbow. I looked around. He was nowhere in sight. The drone of conversation in the bar had not noticeably diminished, and no one was obviously looking at me; but I knew that everyone was keenly aware of my presence.

A sense of being trapped began to rise in me. I felt helpless, abandoned. I turned back to the barman. The sounds of electronic gunfire from the arcade machine punctuated the learned analysis of the pundits who were discussing the election results.

'Do you think I could have a glass of water?' I heard myself saying.

He looked at me with open contempt, then turned away and went into a back room.

I felt as if every eye in the room was now on me. I did not dare turn around.

'It's Montezuma's Revenge,' I heard someone call.

The barman returned and put down a glass of water heavily in front of me.

'Been to a funeral, have we?' someone else called.

The tone was curious and sarcastic rather than overtly hostile, but I was beginning to be frightened. I was also mortified that someone might recognize me. I lowered my head, trying to huddle into my hood.

'Mexican takeaway,' another voice shouted.

Laughter.

'Had a helping of his *tostada*, have you?'

Now the laughter was openly snide. Despite this, I became aware that the machine had fallen silent.

'Leave her alone,' I heard the woman call. 'We've all got to make our way in this world as best we can. That's right, love, innit?'

I wanted to flee. I couldn't bring myself to turn and face the woman, to turn and face any of them. Then I saw, in the mirror behind the bar, Extepan emerging from the Gents. I rushed across to him.

'Please,' I said, almost clutching at him. 'Let's go.'

'I think your countrymen are in good spirits,' he said in English.

'You ought to know better,' another woman's voice called from the back of the room.

I was dimly aware that four of our guards, all armed with automatics, had also entered the pub. I must have been too panicked to notice them. In a blur of shame, I bolted for the door.

Emerging into the rain, I was quickly surrounded by guards. I felt safe again, rescued and protected. From inside the bar there came the sound of further laughter.

Extepan emerged and led me away without another word.

'There must be some way we can warn them,' I said to Bevan.

He thought about it, regarding the waiting face of ALEX on the screen.

'Wouldn't make much difference, would it? They're on a hiding to nothing.'

It was the early hours of the morning, and ALEX had just revealed to us that Maxixca was soon to lead the Aztec armies into Scotland, with a view to subduing the entire country. The whole of Wales was now under occupation, and the Aztecs obviously intended to establish full control over all of mainland Britain.

'Are you suggesting we do *nothing*?' I said to Bevan. 'What about your contacts? Isn't there someone you can pass the information on to?'

Automatically he took a pack of Raleighs from his pocket, but I glared at him and he put it away.

'Having information's one thing. Being able to do something about it is another.'

'We have a duty to pass it on.'

'I'm not saying we don't. Just don't expect it to make any difference, that's all. What are we going to tell them? That half the Aztec armies here are about to cross their border? All they'll be able to do is make for the hills and hope for the best.'

I sighed, giving him my severest look. I didn't want to waste time arguing with him. ALEX's image on the screen remained expectant. I felt as if we were ignoring him.

'Leave it to me,' Bevan said. 'I'll make sure the warning's passed on.'

'Is that it?'

'Is what it?'

'I've been patient with you, Bevan. I've let you take all the information we've obtained from ALEX to do with as you please. It's time you told me who you're working for.'

He leaned back in his chair. 'I'm not working for anybody.'

'Then who's getting the intelligence from ALEX?'

He shrugged. 'Whoever I think it might be useful to.'

'That's no answer. I have a right to know. Without me, you wouldn't have had any of it in the first place.'

Silence.

'You do realize you have a sovereign obligation to tell me?'

He laughed at this, as I had expected him to.

'Look,' he said, 'it's easier for me to move around, to whisper in the right people's ears. That's how word gets passed along, see? I don't ask questions, I just do a bit of gossiping where I think it'll work best.'

I waited.

'What do you think we're dealing with here? A secret army hiding underground, just waiting for the word so they can break out and free the country? Fat chance.'

'I'm well aware of the military situation,' I said testily. 'That's not the point. I've put my trust in you, and I want to be satisfied the information is reaching the right people. I want to know who we're helping.'

'Take it from me, it's a good cause.'

'That won't do, Bevan.'

On the screen, ALEX was still waiting, heartbreakingly like my real husband. I noticed that Bevan had switched off the microphone.

'Listen,' he said, 'the main business for you should be survival. You've got to keep your hands clean, let others do the dirty work. You should be used to that.'

I couldn't believe his effrontery. I rounded on him.

'How dare you! I've always been prepared to do as much as anyone else. My interests are the same as the great mass of ordinary people.'

He gave a laboured nod. 'Ordinary people, right you are. The poor sodding masses.'

'What the devil is that supposed to mean?'

He lit a cigarette. 'Maybe you're not so much of a democrat as you think.'

I was on my feet. 'I won't have you speaking to me like that! Get out!'

He rose, looking completely unruffled by my fury. Hoisting his trousers, he walked out.

I stood there in the silence for a long time, still furious, thinking that I had every right to pursue him and demand he apologize. I had never encountered such bare-faced cheek.

My anger subsided only slowly. What a perfectly awful day it had been! First the humiliation of the pub, now this. I felt as if those I cared about despised me. And perhaps with some reason. Didn't my reaction to Bevan merely prove my snobbery and immaturity? Both Alex and my father had been in awe of my temper; when wounded, I reacted with a righteous outrage. It was not an attractive side of my character.

ALEX was a picture of composure on the screen. I switched on the microphone.

'ALEX?'

'*Yes, Kate?*'

'I miss you so much.'

'*I'm sure you do. If I were real, I'd give you a big bear's hug.*'

It was a pet expression of the real Alex, and I was delighted to hear it. Only the slight pause before all of his responses prevented me from surrendering to the illusion that he was the real person.

'Do you have any information on his whereabouts?' I asked.

'*There's been no change since we last spoke. No data. I'm sorry, Kate.*'

I asked the question each time we spoke, and the answer was always the same.

'How many of his memories did he give you?'

'*As many as he could to produce an effective simulacrum. He took great pleasure in personalizing me, Kate.*'

'Do you remember when you proposed to me?'

A longer pause. '*It was during your second year in Cambridge. April Fool's Day. I turned up that morning with a first edition of Motecuhzoma Xocoyotzin's* Dialogues, *which you needed for your Comparative History exam.*'

'You also brought a bottle of tequila to toast the occasion.'

'*As I recall, we drank it with cherryade.*'

I laughed.

'*You wouldn't take my proposal seriously at first. You thought it was just an April fool.*'

'I drove home the next day to tell my father. I had a terrible hangover.'

'I joined you later, never expecting the old man would agree to it. I don't believe I've ever been quite so nervous.'

'That night you and your BSA ended up in a village pond.'

ALEX laughed. *'High spirits. That car was brand new, you know. It took me ages to recover from the shock. The repair bill was astronomical.'*

'Reminiscing, are we?'

I spun around. Bevan was standing there.

'What are you doing here?'

'Had an idea, didn't I?'

My response was stony silence. Bevan ignored it.

'How about we use your friend there to muddy the waters? We'll get him to plant a bit of false information. We could add a few Scottish armies, move their dispositions around, make sure it's fed into the system so we can create a little havoc.'

I remained silent but moved aside so that he could sit down at the console.

Previously he had argued against tampering with the files in case our interference became obvious to the Aztecs. Stiffly, I reminded him of this.

'Time's ripe now,' he told me. 'Let's do a little – what do they call it? – *creative counterfeiting*. No point in having a weapon unless you use it, is there?'

Seven

Richard was crowned at Westminster Abbey on Christmas Day. Neither Victoria nor I attended the ceremony, though we watched it on the television in my suite with Bevan and Chicomeztli. I knew that Victoria would have dearly loved to be present, given a free choice, but I hoped that by our absence we would make plain that we did not sanction the occasion.

The entire proceedings were conducted with due reverence to the ancient traditions of our country, Richard, in ermine, sitting enthroned while the Archbishop of Canterbury placed the crown on his head. He was unable to prevent a smile of pure pleasure escaping him at that moment. As if further to legitimize the ceremony, Motecuhzoma had sent his eldest son and likely successor, Chimalcoyotl, to London. He sat with Extepan and his retinue, a tall man in his early forties, dressed in the rust and gold uniform of the *tlacateccatl*, one of the two highest ranks in the Aztec army.

I found the television commentary on the event extremely grating. It was provided by a former quiz-show host who had been promoted to become the 'voice' of the BBC after the invasion. He lacked the gravitas to do the occasion full justice, and I had, in any case, come to despise all those who had risen to prominence by accommodating themselves to Aztec rule.

Chicomeztli and Bevan said little during the ceremony, Chicomeztli plainly sensing my mood and not wanting to do anything to provoke me, Bevan adopting his usual air of detached amusement, as if to him the whole affair was just theatre.

Constitutionally, Victoria and I were obliged to declare our fealty to Richard, and I had compromised on that score by writing a letter which the Archbishop now read out to the congregation. While emphasizing my loyalty to the Crown and to Richard personally, I also made a point of stressing my hostility to the occupation of our country. I was surprised when this part of the letter was read out: I had not imagined that Extepan would allow it.

As the ceremony drew to a close, I felt more strongly than ever the absence of Alex and my father, both pillars of my old life. What would my father have made of it all? I was certain he would have been ashamed.

The ceremonial banquet was held that evening in the Louisiana Chamber at Windsor Castle. There we assembled, English and Aztec nobility alike, surrounded by burgundy and gold furnishings and the portraits of monarchs, statesmen and generals once glorious but long dead. I had agreed to attend the banquet in order to avoid insulting our eminent visitor from Tenochtitlan.

Richard occupied my father's old seat at the centre of the table. Extepan was seated between us, with Maxixca and Chimalcoyotl directly opposite. The *tlatoani*'s eldest son was a powerfully built man with dark penetrating eyes and a commanding physical presence. Though the Turquoise Throne could be inherited by the brothers or younger sons of the former emperor, Chimalcoyotl was widely expected to become *tlatoani* when his father's long reign finally came to an end. Like all the sons of Motecuhzoma, he had been fully blooded in war and had a distinguished military career, having successfully led Aztec armies in Malaya, North Africa and Palestine.

Extepan had arranged what he doubtless considered traditional English Christmas fare of pheasant and brandied puddings. The meal was accompanied by Peruvian wines and bourbons from the north-eastern provinces of Greater Mexico. The Aztecs, normally abstemious, drank freely.

Richard was allowed only mineral water on my advice; he had no tolerance for alcohol and did not need it to enjoy himself. Already he was talking happily to Xochinenen, Chimalcoyotl's sixteen-year-old daughter, who had presumably been seated next to him to keep him company should the adult conversation around the table prove too taxing. Poor Richard: his life had never been his own.

'I am surprised there is no snow,' Extepan presently remarked to me. 'I always imagined that Christmas in England would be white, as in the days of Charles Dickens. Are you familiar with his works?'

I nodded. 'Of course. I think he was recalling his own childhood, when winters were colder. Once upon a time, the Thames froze in winter and Londoners went skating on it.'

'Your soft weather comes from us,' Chimalcoyotl said. 'What is it you name it – the Gulf Stream, yes?'

I nodded again, noticing that the septum of his nose had once been pierced, evidence of a very traditional Mexican upbringing. He spoke English haltingly but understood it well enough.

'There's nothing here but rain and cloud,' Maxixca murmured to him in Nahuatl. 'The English like the cold and damp. They shrivel in the sun.'

If this was meant as a joke, it fell flat, because neither Chimalcoyotl nor Extepan smiled.

'The heat saps their spirits,' Maxixca went on, grinning a little slackly. 'We have evidence of it over and over again, in Egypt and India and Palestine. We overwhelmed their armies.'

I wondered if he was drunk. The wine bottle in front of him was almost empty.

'The same might be said of us in our response to the cold,' Extepan retorted diplomatically.

'I hardly think so,' Maxixca said. 'Look at how well our troops performed in Alaska and Scandinavia. We took Berlin in the middle of February. The white races have no stomach for battle, though I will admit that they're industrious when firmly controlled.' He lifted the bottle and poured the last of the wine into his glass. 'Where would our Californian vineyards be without them?'

It seemed to me that Maxixca was trying to impress Chimalcoyotl, whose blocky face remained unreadable to me.

'You'll soon have the opportunity to test your mettle under colder conditions,' Extepan remarked.

'Scotland will pose no problem,' Maxixca said. 'I anticipate the campaign—'

'I think you've said quite enough,' Extepan said firmly. 'The dinner table isn't a fitting place to discuss the future conduct of our armies or to insult our hosts – especially when Princess Catherine can understand your every word.'

Both Chimalcoyotl and Maxixca registered surprise.

'Is this true?' Chimalcoyotl said to me. 'You understand Nahuatl?'

'Perfectly true,' I replied in the same tongue.

For an instant Maxixca looked shocked, but his face quickly took on an expression of sullen anger.

'I hope you will forgive my half-brother,' Chimalcoyotl said in Nahuatl. 'The wine has made him boastful and ill-mannered. Even if you had not understood him, his slurs on the character of your people would remain. Please accept my apologies on his behalf.'

Chimalcoyotl had begun talking as if Maxixca were no longer present, and Maxixca reacted swiftly to his change of tone, rising to his feet. He had been shamed, and now his only recourse was to withdraw. He practically fled from the hall.

On either side of the long table, numerous conversations continued unabated. Defying protocol, both Richard and Victoria had moved to other seats, and no one else seemed to have noticed our little drama. I wondered how long Extepan had known that I could understand and speak Nahuatl. It was a matter of public record that I had studied the language while at Cambridge, but he had never referred to it until now. Had he deliberately contrived Maxixca's embarrassment by letting him compromise himself in front of Chimalcoyotl?

'I'm very sorry,' Extepan said to me with apparent sincerity. 'I don't believe he really meant it—'

'Is it true?' I interrupted. 'You're sending Maxixca into Scotland?'

There was the briefest exchange of glances between Extepan and Chimalcoyotl before Extepan said, 'There has been a growing number of raids across the border on garrisons and towns in northern England. Civilians – *English* civilians – are suffering far more than our troops. Towns have been burnt, women and children killed. It's become necessary to put an end to the threat.'

This confirmed what I knew from ALEX, and I only hoped

that Bevan's 'creative counterfeiting' would give Maxixca a
suitably nasty surprise.

'Maxixca has strict orders to move swiftly but do everything to
minimize casualties,' Extepan said.

'I'm sure that will be a great comfort to all those who are going
to be killed,' I replied.

I noticed a smile on Chimalcoyotl's face.

'Does something amuse you?' I asked in Nahuatl.

He shook his head slowly, but then said, 'Perhaps it does. You
understandably object to our activities in your country, yet here
we sit, surrounded by all the evidence of your own glorious
military past.'

I wondered if he was being sarcastic, then decided not. Of
course the Louisiana Chamber, with its portraits of Wellington,
Napoleon and Andrew Jackson, was a monument to the great
victory of the colonial Anglo-French armies over the forces of
the *tlatoani* Cozcatezcatl at New Orleans in 1815 which had
halted Aztec expansion into the Mississippi Valley for over half a
century. No one but Chimalcoyotl appeared to have appreciated
the significance of the room until now.

Chimalcoyotl indicated a painting which showed the three
generals surveying from a ridge the carnage of their great victory.

'As I recall,' he said, 'the weather was unseasonably hot during
the battle.'

I had to admire his aplomb, the graceful way he was repudiat-
ing Maxixca's insults.

'It was Princess Catherine who proposed the use of the room
for the banquet,' Extepan observed.

He spoke a little uncertainly, as if he feared Chimalcoyotl
might be privately offended by the reminder of a famous Aztec
defeat.

'We're always prepared to honour the past greatness of other
nations,' Chimalcoyotl said lightly.

'Are you proposing to subdue the whole of Scotland?' I asked.

'How did you come about your knowledge of Nahuatl?'

Still his tone was light. He was refusing to answer my question
by not acknowledging it in the first place.

'At university,' I replied. 'My father suggested it. He used to say that if you know how your enemy speaks, you'll have a much better idea of how he thinks.'

'True indeed. English is compulsory in all our schools. Do you know our poet Olintlacochtli?'

'Of course.'

'He writes: "The mirror reflects the face, the sword, the heart, the voice, the soul." I often think it's just as important to listen to how a thing is said as to the words themselves.'

I was unsure what he was trying to convey to me, but I knew myself well matched.

The meal over, we retired to the drawing room, where port and brandy were served along with silver platters of *tzonpelic tamalli*, traditional Mexican sweetmeats. At the far end of the room stood the Christmas tree, cut as always from Windsor Great Park and formerly chosen by my father each December. Richard had selected it this year, and would doubtless continue to do so as long as he remained king. The tree was adorned with lights, baubles and presents wrapped in gaily coloured crêpe paper. Among the parcels were a new evening gown for Victoria and my father's old Bible for Richard, the only presents I was giving to mark the occasion.

I sipped my coffee, watching Richard chat animatedly with Xochinenen, who spoke English only haltingly but seemed amused by his attentions. Victoria sat in a group which included a young nephew of Motecuhzoma's called Tlacahuepan, who had accompanied Chimalcoyotl from Tenochtitlan and whom I knew from ALEX was joining Extepan's staff. He was the same age as Victoria, a handsome young man who gesticulated as he spoke to her with the help of an interpreter.

As midnight drew on, the staff brought cloaks for the Aztecs and Extepan approached to ask if I would join them in the grounds of the castle. I was already prepared for a long night, knowing that it was the Mexican custom to spend the hours from midnight to dawn on Christmas morning in the open, under the night sky, before exchanging presents when the sun rose.

Outside a big log fire blazed, highlighting the old Round Tower, built by Henry II over eight hundred years ago in a time when the Normans, the last conquerors of the land, were becoming English. The royal standard had been raised above the tower to indicate that the monarch was in residence. Though I welcomed Extepan's removal of all the booths and displays which had formerly made the castle a circus for tourists, I thought how improbable the Aztecs, in their feathered ceremonial cloaks, looked in such a setting.

The night was still and chill, stars flickering dimly through a haze of thin cloud. Some of the staff were roasting chestnuts on braziers, and a candy-striped bell-tent had been set up to shelter those who found the cold too arduous. Sparklers were lit and waved in the darkness; Mexican songs were sung, the words of the old philosopher-king Nezahualcoyotl of Texcoco set to Spanish court music, dignified but gloomy songs filled with the evanescence of human life. The songs oppressed me not in themselves but because they symbolized the arrival of the Aztec nation in the heart of England.

Extepan appeared, gingerly holding a palmful of hot chestnuts. 'These are delicious,' he remarked to me. 'You should try one, Catherine.'

He extended his hand. I shook my head. 'No thank you. I've eaten my fill.'

He slipped the chestnuts into the pocket of his tunic. 'I'm sorry about Scotland. We really have no choice.'

'Can I ask you something?'

'Of course.'

'How long have you known that I could speak Nahuatl?'

'Your father confirmed it when I asked him.'

'So you've known from the start.'

'It's only natural that I would have been fully briefed on all your family before I took up my position here.'

'But Maxixca wasn't?'

'He probably had every opportunity. But he's a soldier and has little time for such matters.'

'You didn't think to mention it to him?'

'Why should I have done?'

I eyed him. He gave every appearance of perfect innocence.

'I think you enjoyed the way he compromised himself at dinner,' I said.

He looked wounded by the suggestion. 'That's unfair, Catherine. I wouldn't wish such shame on anyone.'

'But there's no love lost between you, is there?'

We were speaking in English, and he looked puzzled by the colloquialism, so I said, 'You don't really like one another, do you?'

Now he shook his head, as if to say I misunderstood the situation completely. 'We are brothers, bound by family ties and mutual respect. Each of us has a different role to play. Likes or dislikes do not enter into it.'

'That's no answer.'

He made an exasperated sound. 'His behaviour at the banquet – and the general sentiments he expressed – was inexcusable, and I could never condone it. Is that what you wanted me to say? That he acted with dishonour? It's true. I do not deny it. He's a hothead who too often speaks before he thinks. But I am certain of his loyalty.'

'Are you? I had the impression that he disagrees with many of your decisions.'

He smiled then. 'That will not stop him from doing his duty.'

'How do you know I haven't already passed on information about the invasion to interested parties?'

He took a chestnut from his tunic and began to peel it. 'It would make no difference either way. Maxixca left for the borders immediately after the banquet. The attack will begin within forty-eight hours, and you can be sure that he will be intent on restoring his honour by making it a swift and successful campaign.'

He popped the chestnut in his mouth, turned and walked away.

I wandered around the outskirts of the crowd, aware that two Aztec guards were discreetly shadowing me. Richard sat on a blanket near the fire with Xochinenen and an interpreter. She was reading Richard's palm. I was tempted to intervene, to stress to Richard that his future could not be read in the folds of his skin. But I stopped myself: I couldn't shield him from the influence of others, and he would have to learn to use his own judgement.

As the night wore on, the clouds thickened and a drizzle began to fall. Servants emerged from the castle with bowls of hot punch and *octli*, the fermented juice of the maguey. It was shipped in frozen from Mexico for special occasions; despite their skills, the Aztecs had never succeeded in growing the plant elsewhere.

Slipping away from my guards and everyone else around the fire, I entered the State Apartments. It was several years since I was last at Windsor, and I had a whim to see the Dolls' House, which had fascinated me as a child.

But there was no opportunity. Victoria was standing at the bottom of the stairs with someone. She seemed to be struggling with him.

It was Tlacahuepan. He held her close. Victoria broke free and rushed to me. She was flushed and dishevelled.

'What's going on?' I demanded.

Tlacahuepan stood expressionless, staring at me.

'Tell him to go,' Victoria said, an edge of panic in her voice.

'What's going on?' I said again.

Victoria shook her head, but I had already guessed.

'Leave us,' I said to Tlacahuepan in Nahuatl. It was an order, not a request.

For a moment he didn't move. Then he pulled his tunic straight and marched briskly out.

Tears were running down Victoria's cheeks.

'He asked to see the paintings,' she sobbed. 'The Rubens and the Stuyvesants. So I brought him here. He was charming at first, perfectly correct. But then, as we came down the stairs . . . he took hold of me, tried to kiss me . . . There was no one to help . . .'

I embraced her, holding her tight.

'It's all right,' I said. 'It's finished now.'

'I couldn't make him understand.'

'Was he drunk?'

She nodded through her tears. 'I think he was saying that he was a prince, so he was entitled to make love to me.'

My anger boiled up. I held Victoria until her tears subsided. Then I straightened her clothing and led her outside.

I was intending to take her directly to bed, but Extepan intercepted us.

'Catherine, I'm glad I've found you. Will you and Victoria give me a few minutes?'

'Not now,' I said curtly.

He indicated the sky.

'It's dawn. I have something for you.'

An aide stood close by. Extepan motioned to him, and he hurried off to the George IV gateway.

Victoria began shivering against me. I wanted to give vent to my fury, but now was not the time. Extepan was looking across the grounds of the castle; he hadn't noticed Victoria's distress. The fire in front of the tower was almost dead, sooty smoke rising from its ashes. Those celebrants that remained were heading off towards the chapel for a brief morning service.

The aide appeared, leading two colts, one chestnut, one grey.

Extepan took their reins.

'These are for you,' he said. 'Merry Christmas.'

Eight

Victoria led the gallop down the Long Walk from the castle. I spurred the grey, tugging its reins to ensure that it did not charge off in another direction entirely. It was the more wilful of the two, and it was just my luck after giving Victoria first choice of the pair. She was a far superior rider, and had spent a great deal of time at our stables in Okehampton before the invasion. The horses we had once kept there had reputedly been served up as meat for the hungry town in the chaotic aftermath.

Victoria was already disappearing towards Windsor Great Park, her mount throwing up snow from its hoofs, giving me an unerring trail to follow. I held the reins tight to maintain the line, though the grey kept pulling to the left. Behind me, Richard, Xochinenen and several Aztec guards followed at a much more leisurely pace on their own mounts.

It was a cold January morning, and the overnight snow was still pristine. Every morning for the past week Victoria and I had raced the horses to the George III statue in the park, and I hadn't won once. Again I knew it was hopeless, so I gave the grey its head. Immediately it veered off on its own uninhibited path in pursuit of its stable-mate.

Victoria had long dismounted by the time I reached the statue. I was exhausted yet exhilarated by my efforts to control the colt.

'Where have you been?' she said cheerily.

I climbed down from the saddle. The insides of my thighs were already sore, and my feet felt crushed in my riding boots. I had never been a particularly horsy person, in contrast to Victoria.

'He thinks he can run off whenever he pleases,' I said. 'He has a mule's brain.'

'Isn't it time you gave him a name, Kate?'

Victoria had already christened her chestnut Archimedes after a favourite childhood pony which we had kept at Marlborough.

'I can think of plenty of names,' I said. 'Stubborn, Pig-headed, Obstreperous, Perverse, Adamant—'

'Adamant!' she interrupted. 'That's perfect, Kate. Adamant and Archimedes.'

The others cantered up. Xochinenen was riding side-saddle on her horse, a big fur cloak draped around her tiny frame. Her plaited hair had been tied up under a fur bonnet. She had remained behind at Windsor while her father was in Eastern Europe, inspecting Aztec forces on the Rhine and meeting with the Polish government in Warsaw in order to sign a non-aggression treaty.

Richard clearly enjoyed Xochinenen's company. She had a similar child-like air to him, and he was supposedly teaching her English, though I suspected she spoke it well enough already and was simply indulging him. They spent much of their time together flying kites from the castle walls, playing hide-and-seek in the State Apartments and even sliding down banisters to the mute displeasure of almost everyone.

I was glad that Richard had agreed to extend our holiday at Windsor. The castle was a place of many happy memories for the whole family, and both he and Victoria had benefited from escaping the hothouse atmosphere of London. Extepan had returned promptly to his duties on New Year's Day, but not before I had met him privately and told him about the incident with Victoria and Tlacahuepan. He said nothing at the time, but the following day I learned that Tlacahuepan had been transferred to Canberra to join the governor's staff in the Australian Protectorate.

The sun began to show through the cloud. Presently Chicomeztli cantered up on a trap which held a solarized hamper and collapsible furniture.

We unfolded the chairs and a small table. Inside the hamper were hot sausages, croissants, scrambled egg and piping coffee. The black-panelled chairs were already warm when we sat down in them, converting the grey winter light into heat with an efficiency which only the Aztecs had mastered. So we picnicked on that cold winter morning while transporters and interceptors whined by overhead, flying into and out of Heathrow.

Presently Richard suggested we go skating on the pond, but our responses were drowned by a swallow-tailed shuttle flying in low. We all watched as it decelerated, then dropped down behind the walls of the castle itself.

The horses had been startled by the craft, and it took a while to settle them. I saw a black ground-car approaching from the castle, a Molotov Aeroflot with the governor's stylized golden eagle insignia on its slanted bonnet. Wings of snow spewed from its flanks so that it looked like a speedboat cruising through a white sea. It sped directly towards us, braked, and finally settled in the snow.

A door flipped up, and Extepan stepped out. He approached me.

Something in his face filled me with a sense of dread.

'Catherine,' he said. 'I'm sorry, but I think you should accompany me back to the castle immediately.'

I asked him nothing, but meekly accompanied him to the car. I sat in silence while the driver took us back to the castle. I wouldn't even look at him.

The main gate was open, lined with guards who waved us through. The driver steered the car into one of the parking spaces in front of St George's chapel.

Extepan swung open the door.

'Come with me,' he said.

I followed him up the chapel steps. At the entrance he paused and put a hand on my arm.

'Catherine, forgive me. This is not going to be pleasant.'

I pushed past him into the chapel.

Standing in the aisle was a hospital trolley, flanked by Aztec guards. A body draped in a white sheet lay on it. Dimly I was aware of the chapel's splendour all around me – the stalls, the banners, the helmets of the Knights of the Garter, the blue-and-white diamond-patterned floor. But I did not take my eyes off the shape under the sheet.

Extepan came to my side. I heard myself saying, 'Who is it?' though I already knew.

'We're not certain, but I think you should prepare yourself . . .'

I moved to pull back the sheet, but Extepan took hold of my wrist.

'Let go of me!'

'The face is unrecognizable, Catherine. He was killed by falling stonework during the assault on Edinburgh Castle.'

I wrenched myself free and pulled back the sheet.

And recoiled.

The body was naked except for a pair of white briefs. Above the chest it was just a mass of bloody pulp and matted hair. Chestnut hair. I forced myself to look again. There was the appendix scar, there the pale mole on his left thigh, there the familiar V of golden hairs bisecting his abdomen.

Extepan moved swiftly to cover up the body again. I was dimly aware of him telling me that it was a terrible accident, that they had not known Alex was part of the garrison, that Maxixca had given the order to destroy the castle only as a last resort. Something broke in me then, and I fled from the chapel in grief and rage.

PART TWO

The Obsidian Mirror

One

Beds had been crammed into every available space in the wards at the infirmary, and the freshly disinfected floors could not disguise the smell of sickness. An Asian doctor and a native Tynesider who was the hospital's administrator accompanied me on my tour, with Chicomeztli close at my heels.

The ward we had entered was filled with casualties and refugees from the war in Scotland, sick and wounded alike. I stopped at the bed of a young woman who lay in a feverish sleep with a small child also asleep beside her.

'What's the matter with them?' I asked.

'Pneumonia,' the doctor told me.

'Only the mother,' the administrator said hastily. 'Her child's fine. We try to keep parents with their children wherever possible. I understand her prospects of recovery are very good, isn't that true, doctor?'

'Yes,' the doctor said wearily, not looking at either of us.

'What are you short of?' I asked him.

His smile was politeness itself. 'You name it. Our most pressing need is for antibiotics and dressings.'

'It's not surprising our supplies have run short,' the administrator said. 'We've had to take in hundreds of casualties from the front. The entire staff have been doing a remarkable job under the circumstances.'

'They tell us it's a question of supply and demand,' the doctor said. 'We tell them the demand is enormous, the supply, pathetic.'

I saw a hint of annoyance on the administrator's face, as if he considered the doctor had spoken out of turn.

We moved down the corridor into another ward, this one filled with children. They were suffering from typhoid, cholera, tuber-culosis, septicaemia – all consequences of the collapse in public services in the area following the fighting in Scotland. Maxixca had completed the conquest within a month, but the disruption caused by the fighting lingered on months later.

The ward was hot and filled with the sickly sweet smell of childhood sickness. Some of the youngsters were sitting up in bed and playing games with one another, while others lay in a sleep that looked close to death. The nursing staff were lined up in their crisp uniforms, despite my prior pleas that I didn't want any special arrangements made for my visit. They smiled and curtsied brightly, though I could see the weariness in their eyes.

I stopped to speak with them. They answered my general queries about the day-to-day running of the hospital with equally general assurances that they were managing to cope despite all the difficulties; they had obviously been primed beforehand to say nothing controversial. It was the kind of response I had met with all over the country over the past five months, as if everyone was in awe of offending my royal sensibilities. Only when I contrived to turn up unannounced at hospitals and institutions did I manage to get uncensored facts and opinions; and it was plain that the welfare services throughout the country were desperately under-resourced.

At the far end of the ward, the administrator was ushering a nurse holding a screaming toddler out through the doors. Though I knew it was impossible for hospitals to treat my visits as normal affairs, I found it extremely frustrating to be constantly shielded from the harsher facts of life in the wards.

The June sunlight highlighted the grubby windows and bedlinen.

'Are you getting much sleep?' I asked the doctor.

'We take it when we can,' he replied. 'There are staff shortages, and some of us spend the nights here so we can be on hand if we're needed. It's the only way.'

The administrator returned, suggesting that we move on. He looked perfectly fresh and rested, positively prosperous in his dark suit and silk tie. I waited for Chicomeztli to slip a new cassette into the recorder I insisted we take with us on our visits so that I would miss nothing that was said.

Down another corridor towards the open doors of a gleaming operating theatre. The administrator was talking proudly about the hospital's new body scanner when my attention was diverted by a quarantine sign outside another ward.

'What's in there?' I asked.

'Severe cases,' he replied. 'Infectious diseases.'

His edgy manner made it plain he didn't want me to enter the ward – which only made me more determined to so do.

I pushed open the doors – and was met with a powerful odour of sweat and sickness. The massed beds were filled with men and women whose skins were raw with sores and lesions. The nursing staff wore green rubber gloves, and it was plain that they hadn't had fresh uniforms in days.

'What's happening in here?' I asked.

The doctor had come up beside me. 'Duran's Disease,' he said softly. 'You probably know it as the New Indies pox.'

I was shocked in more than one sense.

'New Indies pox?' I repeated, incredulous.

He nodded.

'I thought it had been eradicated years ago.'

'Suppressed,' the doctor said. 'Controlled. But never entirely wiped out.'

'But isn't it easily treatable with antibiotics?'

'Of course. If you have adequate supplies.'

I was truly appalled. The pox, endemic to the New World in the pre-Christian era, had been brought to Europe by Spanish sailors and had decimated populations from Ireland to Siberia in the sixteenth and seventeenth centuries. It had continued to flare up in Europe and Asia until the discovery of antibiotics, and was often fatal if left untreated. To Europeans, it was as big a scourge of history as the Black Death, and some historians argued that the bacillus had enabled the Aztecs to rise to world-power status since it had stalled European exploration of the New World for over a century. To see it now, in modern-day Newcastle, was horrifying.

The administrator was fluttering around me. 'Your Highness, I think perhaps we should press on. The risk of infection . . .'

An elderly man in a nearby bed sat up suddenly. He looked delirious, but he stared directly at me.

'Who's she?' he demanded of no one in particular. 'I know her face.'

I went to the foot of his bed.

'You're one of the Royals.'

His cheeks were hollow, the skin on his neck slack between prominent tendons. The grey stubble on his chin was pocked with festering sores and weals. He grinned at me, gap-toothed.

'How are you feeling?' I asked.

'Like fucking death.'

Everyone around me went rigid with mortification. Before I could say anything, the old man went on, 'What are you doing here? Seeing how the other half lives, are you?' He heaved himself up. 'What I want to know is, since you're gracing us with your presence, what's going to be done about it?'

Two nurses moved swiftly to restrain him. The administrator tried to shepherd me away, but I held my ground.

'It's a disgrace,' I told the old man. 'I promise you, something *shall* be done about it – as quickly as I can manage.'

'That's what they all say.'

'I promise you. You have my word of honour.'

His bright eyes regarded me. He made a contemptuous sound.

'That right? Shake on it, will you?'

Despite the restraining hands of the nurses, he thrust out an arm.

His knuckles were cracked and oozing lymph, the back of his hand an open sore filled with pale pus. Because I knew there was nothing else I could do, I reached out both hands and grasped his.

He crushed my fingers in his palm, never taking his eyes off me. The texture of his skin was wet and yielding, yet there was great strength in his grasp, a strength of rage and desperation. I made no attempt to withdraw my hand until he released it.

'Next time you come I'll let you see my war wounds.'

He slumped back on the pillow.

The doctor led me away to the broken sound of his laughter.

I was sitting in the light from my desk-lamp, completing my report for the day, when Chicomeztli arrived.

'We have found a local supplier,' he announced. 'They have

stocks of—' He thrust a piece of paper in front of me to spare himself a struggle with the brand-names. 'About three months' supply of each.'

'Excellent. When can they deliver?'

'Within forty-eight hours.'

'Even better. But I want you to send someone around there and pick up some emergency stock. I want it delivered tonight.'

Chicomeztli nodded. 'Anything else?'

'I think that will do for now.'

He gave a cheery salute, and went out.

I put down my pen and stretched. Then I rose and went over to the window.

We were staying in Jesmond Dene Hall, which had a good view out over the city. Like most industrial cities in the Midlands and North, Newcastle had suffered badly from aerial bombardment during the invasion, and tracts of the city looked derelict. Yet the people I had met since my arrival were generally positive and practically minded: given the means, I was sure they would swiftly rebuild what had been destroyed. This was also true for the rest of the country. All that was needed were the raw materials.

The sun was finally setting on the long summer evening. Returning to my desk, I scanned my report on the hospital visit. It would be sent direct to Extepan, the latest of many. Would any action be taken? Perhaps Extepan was merely indulging me and had no intention of treating them seriously. Perhaps he thought I was just burying my grief for Alex in a nationwide crusade. Perhaps he was right – but this wasn't the whole story. The crusade, if that's what it was, was something I took seriously.

The desk console held a computer terminal, and in my jacket pocket was the disk. I had carried it with me ever since leaving London, but I hadn't once tried to summon up ALEX, despite ample opportunities, and the ever-present sense of the real Alex's loss. Chicomeztli gave me plenty of privacy, being much occupied with arranging my itinerary and responding to demands for emergency supplies of food and medicines wherever I discovered a need. My respect and even liking for him had grown enormously during our travels. In many ways he was the perfect companion: cheerful, efficient, attentive, yet demanding nothing of me.

I took out the disk and contemplated the screen in front of me. It would be a simple matter to slot it into the machine and bring ALEX to life. And yet I hesitated. I was afraid to hear the sound of his voice again for fear that it would make all the pain of his loss return.

The phone bleeped, startling me. Hastily I pocketed the disk and picked up the receiver.

'Hello?'

'Your Highness?'

The tone was tentative but also teasing. It was Extepan.

I switched to visual. He was sitting in his office, dressed in full uniform.

'How did you know I was here?'

'Chicomeztli keeps me informed of your progress, as you would expect. You look well, Catherine.'

'It's all the fresh northern air I've been getting lately.'

We hadn't spoken since I left London late in January. I had wanted to get away from everything connected with the capital for a while.

'Have you been getting all my reports?' I asked.

'Most certainly. They're extremely thorough.'

'You mean relentless in all their detailing of everything that's wrong.'

He smiled. 'I expected no less.'

'It's bad here. Do you know they've got an outbreak of the New Indies pox? It's disgraceful.'

Extepan held up a binder, which I saw held my reports.

'Many of your recommendations are already being acted upon,' he said. 'Even as we speak, a bill is being debated in your parliament to provide emergency relief throughout the United Kingdom.'

I eyed him. He was as bright and companionable as ever.

'No doubt Kenneth Parkhouse will be eager to hug all the credit.'

Extepan looked surprised. 'Your tour of the country has been widely publicized.'

'I didn't mean that. I'm not doing this to improve my image.'

'I know, I know,' he said hastily. 'As long as it achieves the ends you wanted, does it matter?'

I considered, then said, 'I just don't like that man, that's all.'

He was still smiling. 'You seem more your old self.'

'Bloody-minded and argumentative, you mean?'

A laugh. 'Yes, that's part of it. We've all missed you here.'

So strong was my desire for a complete change that I had studiously avoided all gossip about London during my travels. I was tempted to ask after Richard and Victoria, but restrained myself. I wasn't ready yet to plunge back into their world.

'Is this purely a social call?' I asked.

'Not entirely,' he replied, 'though I'm pleased to find you in such good spirits. Has it been worth it, Catherine?'

'Yes,' I said emphatically.

'I hope it's helped you overcome your grief.'

Even an indirect mention of Alex brought back all the pain and anger I still felt. I fought the urge to reply that he was responsible for it.

'That wasn't the only reason I did it.'

'Of course not. But I was wondering if you might now contemplate the idea of returning to London.'

Since January, I had travelled from Cornwall to Northumberland, visiting parts of the country I had scarcely known existed before. I knew I had done all I could for the time being, yet I was reluctant to give up the freedom and purposefulness I had felt. And reluctant to confront London and all the memories of Alex associated with it.

Extepan obviously sensed this.

'We have a very important visitor arriving soon,' he said.

'Oh?' I didn't bite further, though I was curious.

'My great-uncle,' Extepan said. 'Tetzahuitl.'

'The *cihuacoatl*?'

'None other.'

The *cihuacoatl* – a title which translated as Woman Snake, though it was a male office – was second in eminence only to the *tlatoani* himself. And Tetzahuitl's renown was almost as great as Motecuhzoma's.

'When's he coming?' I asked.

'Within a matter of days. I've only just received confirmation.'

Was I ready for London again? Could I afford to miss meeting a man almost as powerful and influential as the emperor himself?

'I'd very much like you to be here when he arrives,' Extepan said.

'Why?'

'Apart from anything else, he might consider your absence an insult.'

So now we had come to it. 'And we can't have that, can we?'

'I'm asking you, Catherine.'

'And if I refuse?'

'What do you want of me?' he said in exasperation. 'Do I have to plead? Beg? Send an armed escort to bring you back?'

'You'd do that?'

He looked at me for a long time, both serious and wry.

'If it was necessary, I might.'

Two

Bevan brought tea and fruitcake out to me on the balcony
garden. He was dressed in slightly grubby black pinstripe
trousers with a collarless white shirt and a waistcoat which
strained over his belly. His thinning hair had been rather
inexpertly trimmed, and he resembled a derelict hastily washed
and dressed for a special occasion. Either that, or he was
deliberately mocking me by contriving to present himself as a
parody of a servant.

'So,' I said to him, 'what's been happening since I've been away?'

He shrugged. 'This and that. Have a good trip, did you?'

'I hope something useful will come of it.'

'You were on telly a lot while you were away. Everyone was
singing your praises.'

'I didn't ask for that, or want it. You haven't answered my
question.'

He poured tea into my cup, cocking the little finger of his left
hand. I resisted a smile.

'I'm quite out of touch,' I said. 'I thought a complete break
would be best, so I've no idea what's been happening here.'

'Do you want local or international gossip?' he said.

'Whichever.'

He perched himself on a retaining wall, backdropped by
golden broom.

'Heard all the talk about Russia, have you?'

I shook my head.

'Number one son's been out in Eastern Europe again, taking
pleasure cruises down the Danube, hunting in the Carpathians,
and all that sort of palaver.'

'Chimalcoyotl?'

He nodded. 'Goodwill visits to the Balkan provinces, by all accounts. Gossip is, they may be building up to an attack on Russia.'

This did surprise me. 'Do you think it's a serious possibility?'

'There's one way we might be able to find out.'

It was a moment before I realized what he meant.

'Take it with you, did you?'

'Yes,' I replied.

'Just as well you did. While your governor friend was away, Mad Mash did a security check on the whole complex. Turned everything in all the rooms upside down, then put it back again so's you wouldn't notice. I guessed he didn't find anything in your place because you weren't called back from your travels.'

'Mad Mash' was Bevan's nickname for Maxixca. Bevan seldom referred to anyone by their proper name, let alone their title. I wondered if it was his way of denying any hold they could possibly have over him.

'I didn't know Extepan had been away,' I said.

'Spent a month in Mexico, back in March.'

'Oh? What was that for?'

'Search me. Everybody was glad to see him back. Lesser of two evils, as it were. His brother makes everybody nervous.'

'Where are Richard and Victoria?'

'Didn't they tell you?' Bevan took a slice of cake from the tray. 'On holiday. Monaco. Hobnobbing with the jetset.'

'That sounds suspiciously like disapproval.'

'No skin off my nose, is it?'

I was surprised how comforting it was to have Bevan's blunt companionship once more.

'Is there anything else?'

'About what?' he said through a mouthful of cake.

'About anything.'

'I reckon a possible invasion of Russia's enough to be going on with, don't you?'

I picked up my teacup. 'We'll talk to ALEX tonight.'

The instant ALEX appeared on the screen, I drew back out of his line of sight, knowing it was foolish, but unable to stop an instinctive reaction. I wasn't ready for him to 'see' me.

I let Bevan identify himself.

'*Good to talk to you again,*' ALEX responded.

His electronic image was the same as ever, urbane, even cheerful. The sight of it pained me more than I could say.

Bevan turned to me, indicating the microphone. I shook my head.

'You talk to him,' I said in a whisper.

If he was surprised, he didn't show it. He turned back to the screen.

'We need to know something,' he informed ALEX.

'*I hope I can oblige you,*' came the reply.

'There's been rumours about an Aztec invasion of Russia. Any information on this?'

There was a long pause. ALEX looked distinctly contemplative, as if someone were whispering in his ear.

'*Army and airforce units have been mobilized throughout Central Europe and north-western China,*' came the reply. '*The Aztec navy has been conducting operations in the Bering and Barents Seas. Every appearance is being given that an invasion is imminent. The intention is to force the Russian Union of Sovereign Republics to withdraw forces from its Turkish and Mesopotamian provinces, so easing Aztec fears of an attack on Palestine and Arabia. No attack on Russian territory will actually be made.*'

Arabia and Palestine were under the Aztec sphere of influence, and there had been tension in the area for several years. Even with their mastery of solar power, the Aztecs still relied heavily on oil supplies for their industries and the production of plastics. Despite this, I had never believed that they really feared an attack from the defensively minded Russian Empire until now.

'Ask him if he's sure,' I whispered to Bevan.

Bevan did so, and ALEX replied, '*Certainly. The Aztecs have neither sufficient manpower nor equipment in Western Europe to mount a successful assault. According to my information, Motecuhzoma has also expressly forbidden it. They would prefer to have the Union neutralized and neutral rather than an active aggressor or defender of its territory. Such a campaign would be an enormous drain on the resources of the Empire so soon after its conquests in Western Europe.*'

His image flickered for a moment, then stabilized. Bevan turned back to me.

'What do you think?' I said.

'I reckon it's as good as you're going to get,' he replied.

I was thinking. 'Ask him if he can get a message through to Margaret. The Tsarina.'

Now he was curious. 'Why don't you ask him yourself?'

'Please, Bevan.'

He shrugged, and did as I asked. To my amazement, ALEX replied, '*Is Kate with you now?*'

'Can you get a message through?' Bevan insisted.

'*It should be within my capabilities.*'

To me, Bevan said, 'What do you want to tell her?'

'Tell her what ALEX told us,' I replied. 'Make it a personal communication from me. Say that I've got access to secret Aztec files and have confirmed that the Aztecs don't have the resources to mount an invasion. Sign the message "Charlotte".'

Bevan looked quizzical.

'She'll understand.'

He conveyed the message to ALEX, who again surprised me by saying, '*Ah, yes, the Brontë sisters.*' His image flickered again. '*Is it possible for me to talk to Kate?*'

At that point I was sorely tempted to take the microphone from Bevan. But he frowned. 'Hold on.'

'What is it?'

'We're getting a bit of interference. Image break-up.'

'And?'

'Somebody might be trying to monitor us.'

On the screen, ALEX looked perfectly normal.

'Is that possible?'

'If they knew what they were looking for, it is. If you want my advice, we'd best shut down for the night, just in case.'

Now I had him before me, I didn't want to let ALEX go, despite my reluctance to speak to him. But there was no sense in taking risks.

'All right,' I agreed.

Bevan pulled the disk from its slot.

*

'ALEX,' I whispered. 'It's Kate.'

A broad smile. His image was clear, steady.

'*Kate. How are you?*'

I swallowed down a confusion of emotions.

'I'm well enough. It's been a while since we last spoke.'

'*I know. A hundred and sixty-two days, to be precise. I was beginning to think you'd forgotten me.*'

I remembered he had his own internal clock. His good-natured chiding of me was just like the real Alex.

'*Kate? Are you still there?*'

'Yes.'

'*I was really sorry to learn about what happened. To my human counterpart.*'

I was helpless, at a loss for words.

'*It must have been terrible, losing him like that. You have my greatest sympathies.*'

My eyes were blurred with tears. It was two hours since Bevan had shut him down. I had been unable to sleep since then, haunted by thoughts of him.

I couldn't let myself surrender to the illusion. I had to think logically.

'Was he really killed at Edinburgh Castle?' I asked.

'*Apparently so.*'

'How did he get that far north from Wales?'

A longer-than-usual pause. '*There's nothing in the files on that. Knowing Alex, he probably hitched a lift.*'

Humour – self-referential humour – too. It was like a challenge, almost as if he wanted to convince me he was real.

'I need some information,' I said briskly.

'*Of course. That's what I'm here for.*'

'I need to know about the *cihuacoatl*.'

'*Do you want to know about the ancient goddess of that name or the title and its offices?*'

'I want to know about Tetzahuitl.'

ALEX began by telling me much that I already knew. The title had been held by members of Tetzahuitl's family since pre-Christian times, and he was reputedly a direct descendant of the legendary Tlacaelel who had served the very first Motecuhzoma and other emperors during the nascent days of the

Aztec Empire. Tetzahuitl himself had been appointed to his position before the current Motecuhzoma was made *tlatoani*, and he had been a fixture in Aztec politics for over half a century. Traditionally the *cihuacoatl* was responsible for the civilian and judicial affairs of the empire and wielded great power. Tetzahuitl was no exception to this, having been instrumental in the empire's expansion by forging allegiances and arranging strategic marriages with important regional powers. According to Mexican folklore, always superstitious, he was secretly a sorcerer who had sold his soul in exchange for eternal life.

At this point I interrupted ALEX.

'I want to know why he's coming to England.'

There was a pause, and I thought I detected an almost subliminal flicker of ALEX's image. Then he said, *'He's expected to arrive on a direct flight from Tenochtitlan within the next four days. There appears to be no available data on the precise timing of the flight or the purpose of his mission. I could offer you probabilities—'*

'I want facts,' I said. 'Surely there must be something on record?'

'The cihuacoatl's *movements are often cloaked in secrecy for security reasons, and this often means that nothing is committed to the files. I'm sorry, Kate.'*

I sighed. 'Tell me, then, what would your best guess be?'

'Great Britain is an important conquest from the standpoint of the empire,' he replied. *'It isn't unreasonable to assume that Motecuhzoma would want his right-hand man to provide a first-hand report on how the country is being administered under occupation.'*

'So soon after Chimalcoyotl's visit?'

'Chimalcoyotl was en route to Germany. It was a convenient courtesy for him to attend Richard's coronation.'

'Perhaps. But I think there's more to it than that.'

'You may well be right. It's only one possibility, of course, but I'll give you good odds I'm right.'

Another reminder of the real Alex. He had always had a penchant for gambling, and would bet – usually for nominal stakes – on anything from the turn of a card to the likelihood of getting a stuffed giraffe up the keep of Walthamstow Castle.

'I can't believe you're dead,' I blurted.

He looked at me with great sympathy. *'It's only natural you should miss me, Kate.'*

I reached for the OFF switch.

Richard and Victoria flew in from Monaco the following morning, both tanned and relaxed from their holiday. Victoria had had her hair cropped so that she looked almost boyish, while Richard was wearing a baggy white T-shirt with the popular children's television character Miztli Man-Beast emblazoned on its front. On his little finger was a small gold ring.

It was a sunny day, and we took drinks on the balcony below the landing pad, looking out over a hazy London. To the east, the Docklands was a forest of cranes. Extepan had embarked on an ambitious plan to rebuild areas of the East End which had been devastated in the invasion.

Richard and Victoria were both eager for me to tell them about my travels – which only made me suspicious that they didn't want to talk about their holiday. So I gave them a brief account of my tour, then said, 'And what did the two of you do while you were away?'

'We just relaxed,' Victoria said immediately. 'We did lots of swimming and sunbathing and sailing. It was heaven. You need a proper holiday, too, Kate.'

She was wearing a tight-fitting cream dress cut low at the back. Her skin was deeply and evenly tanned from the nape of her neck to the base of her spine.

'Looks like you got brown all over,' I said.

She merely smiled.

'Who went with you?'

'The usual crowd. An escort, of course. Some household staff. No journalists or photographers, thank heavens! It was lovely, Kate, peaceful and private.'

'Do you think it was wise?'

Now she looked wary. 'Wise?'

'To go off on holiday. Do you think it will create a good impression so soon after the invasion?'

'Three years,' Richard said, sucking on a sliver of orange from his glass. 'It's been three years since the invasion.'

'We tend to forget that, Kate,' Victoria said with the eagerness of someone who had just been thrown a lifeline. 'What are we supposed to do – stay here, wearing sackcloth and ashes? Spend the rest of our lives in mourning? I can't see what good that would do.'

'We're not in an ordinary situation,' I replied. 'Whether we like it or not, different standards are expected of us. It's important we try to conduct ourselves in a blameless manner. We mustn't let ourselves be compromised.'

'It was nice,' Richard said. 'I like holidays.'

I knew I was sounding like a matronly killjoy, but I was sure they weren't telling me everything.

'Is that a new ring?' I asked Richard.

He nodded. The ring comprised two rattlesnakes, each inter-twined and swallowing the other's tail.

'It looks Aztec,' I remarked.

'It was a present,' he said proudly, fingering it.

'Oh? From an admirer?'

'A friend.' This with the mischievous grin of a child enjoying the privilege of a secret.

'Is it someone I know?' I asked.

He shook his head shyly, though I wasn't sure it was a denial.

'I don't know why you're being so secretive,' Victoria said to him with more than a hint of annoyance. 'The captain of our yacht was a Tepanec and he bet Richard that he couldn't water-ski. The ring was the stake. Richard won the bet.'

Richard promptly jumped up from the table and pretended that he was riding the waves, arms stretched out in front of him, legs wobbling. Victoria laughed indulgently. Of course I knew it was a lie.

I had not seen either Extepan or Maxixca since my return from the north, but that evening Chicomeztli came to my suite and told me that Extepan wished to see me at my convenience.

I went directly to his quarters. Mia admitted me with her usual silent poise. She wore an earth-red wraparound skirt with a feather-fan design. An elaborate necklace of polished seashell matched her earrings. I don't think I had ever seen her look more beautiful.

She took me through into Extepan's office. He was sitting at his desk, poring over some papers. He immediately rose.

'Catherine. Forgive me for not being here to greet you on your return. I have had many arrangements to make for the *cihuacoatl*'s visit.'

He spoke in English, motioning me to the sofa near the balcony window. Outside, late evening sunlight, thick with midges, drenched banks of honeysuckle and cerulean bougainvillaea.

He sat opposite me in a Regency armchair, unbuttoning the jacket of his uniform. I declined his offer of drinks, and Mia silently withdrew.

'I must first thank you for the very detailed nature of your reports,' he said. 'Your journey around the country has been a most fruitful one.'

'The urgent needs are for adequate food and clean drinking water. Medicines are also in short supply almost everywhere.'

He nodded vigorously. 'We are already moving on these matters. Before winter comes we shall ensure that repairs to water mains are complete and reserves of food provided in strategic areas.'

I was unconvinced by these vague assurances. 'I hope you will. Promises are easily made.'

'I was pleased to discover that there appear to have been relatively few abuses on the part of our armies.'

'Either that, or people are too frightened to say anything.'

He smiled.

'Does that amuse you?' I asked.

'No, no. It's not that. It's your . . . combative nature.'

'This wasn't just a diversion for me. I expect to see something done.'

'It will be, I assure you. I was merely trying to say that it is good to have you back.'

'Really?' I said suspiciously.

'It is useful to keep busy when one suffers a loss. I remember when my mother was assassinated. I loved her deeply, and it was as though my world had ended. One of my father's staff brought the news to me. My father was campaigning in Indo-China at the time, and I did not see him for six months. So I threw myself into my studies. My tutors were astonished with my progress. I was a brilliant, heartbroken six-year-old.'

I was unprepared for these private revelations, and unsure what to say. Above us, Doña Maria Mendizabel looked out from her portrait, beyond all human claims. From all I knew of her, she had been an inattentive mother, being absent on diplomatic missions overseas during much of his brief childhood. I wondered how much he had romanticized her loss. And yet the situation must have been difficult for him when Motecuhzoma had subsequently taken Maxixca's mother as his principal wife. Maxixca, already four years old, had been an illegitimate child until Doña Maria's death, since all subsidiary wives had been relegated to the status of courtesans while she was empress. Perhaps Extepan had become even more of an outsider in the aftermath; perhaps he had suffered even more keenly the resentment of the rest of the family. I felt a certain sympathy for him, but at the same time I disliked the parallels he seemed to be drawing with my situation.

'My husband was killed defending his country,' I said. 'For that alone, I'll always remember him with honour and affection.'

'And love?'

'Of course. That goes without saying.'

He gave me a long, appraising stare, and I wondered what he was thinking. Often, when we talked, I felt that there was a hidden agenda on his part, as if our conversations were really about something else. He resembled his mother very strongly, and only then did it dawn on me that Extepan was in fact a Spanish name, a Nahuatl version of Esteban.

'To other matters,' he said abruptly. 'We are expecting the *cihuacoatl* to arrive tomorrow.'

'Ah. I suppose it's futile for me to enquire as to the purpose of his visit?'

'I've been given few details. But it is not uncommon for Tetzahuitl to make such journeys.'

'To newly occupied territories.'

He looked serious. 'Hardly newly occupied. But if you wish.'

'I'll be on my best behaviour.'

'I shall be grateful for that. I have already spoken much of you in my communications with Tenochtitlan.'

'I gather you went there in March.'

'My father wished to see me.' He did not elaborate. 'I've spoken highly of you, Catherine. You may find this difficult to believe, but you are one of the few people I feel I can speak candidly to. And even trust.'

'Don't make that mistake. I've nothing against you personally. As far as I know, you've treated us all fairly. But you're still my enemy. I still intend to fight you in every way I can.'

He was not ruffled by this. His brown-rimmed eyes regarded me calmly.

'I expected you to say no less.' He sounded almost rueful. 'You speak your mind, and so I am able to understand your position. There is a basis for trust in that, yes?'

'Since you're so fond of me,' I said, 'I'd like to ask a favour.'

'By all means.'

'I want to set up a complaints centre. An office or bureau that will undertake to investigate citizens' grievances about any matters arising from the occupation.'

Extepan mulled this over. 'That is a wide brief.'

'It must be completely free of Aztec control. I would report directly to you.'

'You would take charge of this . . . office?'

'I think it might give people confidence to express legitimate concerns, without fear of reprisal.'

'Very well.'

'You agree?'

'It sounds like an excellent idea. For security reasons, you will have to be based somewhere close by, and I would have to insist that at least one member of my staff is present at all times to ensure that the office is not being used as a cover for less . . . desirable activities. But otherwise I can see no obstacles to such an arrangement.'

I barely hid my surprise. I had not imagined he would agree so easily, if at all.

'There is one small condition.'

I might have known. I was already shaking my head, but he said, 'I simply want you and your sister to be present when the *cihuacoatl* arrives.'

I was silent.

'I promise you we can edit your presence from any news footage, if you so wish.'

'I'd prefer you to say I was forced to attend.'

He did not rise to this. 'Will you agree?'

'Only if you give the complaints centre full publicity and make it plain that this was my price for being there.'

He considered for a moment. 'That should be possible. Of course, we shall phrase it more diplomatically than that. Now, was there anything else?'

I could think of nothing. I shook my head.

'Then I must press on with the arrangements for the *cihuacoatl*'s visit.'

He led me to the door of his office. When he opened it, Mia was standing directly outside.

Three

The ship was a sleek ultra-highspeed carrier with slashed-back wings and a raised delta tail. A humid wind blew in across Heathrow as it came in from the west with a fierce whine, decelerating rapidly down the main runway, tiny support vehicles chasing it at a safe distance, bathed in the brilliant golden radiance of its wings.

I stood with Extepan and the others on a dais which had been constructed in front of the terminal building. A host of Aztec dignitaries had turned out for the occasion, among them Maxixca, newly returned from Scotland and a model of military smartness in his tan and gold uniform. Richard was resplendent as the Commander of the King's Guard, while Victoria and I wore black skirts and bodices. It was a sultry day, and I was uncomfortably hot.

The great ship touched down safely and shut down its main engines. The perimeters of the runway were crammed with security vehicles and guards, and there was not another aircraft in the vicinity. Normal flights from the airport had been suspended for the entire afternoon.

The carrier taxied slowly towards us, its wings already dimmed to a matt black in which the conduction channels shone like copper arteries. The sunburst emblem was bold on the nose of the craft, and its flanks gleamed in the hazy sunlight. It came to a halt and its engines died.

There was a mood of tense anticipation on the dais, and everyone was fidgety with the heat. Kenneth Parkhouse and his manicured cabinet looked more nervous than most, but even Extepan was not his usual composed self. Which wasn't entirely surprising, since Tetzahuitl had a formidable reputation.

Unusually for Aztec noblemen, he had never married or fathered any children, instead devoting himself utterly to the furtherance of Aztec power.

A stairway was wheeled out to the carrier, and we descended the dais and lined up at its base. Richard and Extepan were at the head, myself and Victoria next in line, followed by Maxixca, who looked aggrieved that we had taken precedence over him. Of course, that was just my suspicion: he always looked sour to my eyes. The hostility I felt towards him was strengthened by my suspicions regarding Alex's death. It was perfectly possible that Alex had been captured during the invasion of Scotland, then executed by Maxixca simply to revenge himself on me. It would have been easy for a man of his position to cover up the fact and pretend it had been an accident. Already I saw him as an implacable enemy who would do anything to injure us.

A doorway irised open in the carrier's flank, and a small avalanche of emerald-uniformed guards poured down the gangway. All were armed. They formed a cordon from the base of the stairs to Extepan.

It was almost an hour before Tetzahuitl emerged, and by then I was nearing the end of my patience. Apparently the delay arose because the *cihuacoatl* disliked flying and entered a deep meditative state for the duration of any flight and was slow to rouse himself from it. I was more inclined to believe he was playing power games with us.

At length, a figure appeared in the hatchway, standing alone. For a man in his late seventies, Tetzahuitl was remarkably unbowed by age. Though short by European standards, he stood erect and alert. He wore a black cloak trimmed with a silver geometric motif. His iron-grey hair was tied up in elaborate knots adorned with clusters of purple feathers. He looked like an exotic visitor from another world.

For a moment he paused and scanned the horizon, his eyes seeming to drink in everything he saw. As he began to descend, Extepan stepped forward while a guard of honour tossed marigolds and white roses in his path.

Extepan dropped to one knee. Tetzahuitl touched him on the upper arms, raising him up. Extepan then began a formal greeting by saying how greatly they were honoured by the *cihuacoatl*'s decision to visit, what an auspicious day it was for everyone concerned, how he hoped that Tetzahuitl continued to enjoy the best of health and remained in full command of his inestimable powers. He was certain that the *cihuacoatl*'s arrival would uplift the hearts of everyone who served him, and he trusted that his stay would be as comfortable, fruitful and enlightening as it would undoubtedly be glorious.

By Aztec standards, it was a brief encomium, and Tetzahuitl replied equally briefly that he continued to be blessed with great reserves of physical and spiritual strength, that it was highly pleasing to be able to visit a son of the *tlatoani* and even more pleasing that his feet should tread on the sacred ground of England, whose people had contributed much to the march of civilization. He had come with an open heart and mind, eager to see and to learn, thankful that Huehuetecuhtli – another Aztec synonym for God – continued to grant him a respite from death so that he could make such travels in his dotage.

As with all such greetings, it was highly stylized, the words uttered without effort, almost by rote. From an early age, Aztec noblemen were thoroughly schooled in the art of speech-making.

'Permit me, then,' Extepan said more informally, 'to introduce you to the Royal Family of the United Kingdom.'

Tetzahuitl spoke little English, and his introduction to Richard was limited to an exchange of titles and Extepan translating Tetzahuitl's comment that he was honoured to be greeted by the king of a great nation. Richard bobbed his head and smiled but said nothing in return. He looked embarrassed and out of his depth.

Already Tetzahuitl had turned to me. His eyes were dark and depthless, and they did not waver. He wore a small gold nose plug in his septum and gold circlets in his ears. His prominent nose and arched eyebrows gave him a haughty look. I saw that the silver motif on the hem of his cloak was not abstract but consisted of stylized human skulls.

'This', I heard Extepan say, 'is Her Royal Highness, the Princess Catherine.'

'Ah, yes.'

Tetzahuitl's head was tilted back, so that he seemed to be squinting down his nose at me. I had the disorientating feeling that he was towering over me, even though I was three or four inches taller.

'You speak our language, I'm told,' he remarked in Nahuatl.

'Up to a point,' I replied.

'You're a student of our culture.'

'More so now than ever.'

I saw Extepan glaring at me, warning against saying anything too sharp or challenging.

But Tetzahuitl was unruffled.

'I shall look foward to talking with you later,' he informed me.

A brief introduction to Victoria followed, and then he turned to Maxixca, who instantly bowed.

'We have been heartened by the news of your efforts on our behalf. Your father is proud. You have served us well.'

He was obviously referring to the swiftness with which Maxixca had accomplished the conquest of Scotland; the planting of false information via ALEX had done little to stem the tide, so overwhelming was the superiority of the Aztec forces. Maxixca, almost meek beforehand, immediately straightened, and I could see him making an effort not to show pride. I thought I caught a look between him and Extepan as Tetzahuitl moved on.

I had imagined we would fly back to London after greeting the *cihuacoatl*, but instead we were ceremoniously taken down to the Underground station, where a special train was waiting.

'Where are we going?' I asked Extepan.

'Kew Gardens,' he told me. 'It is at the *cihuacoatl*'s express request.'

We took dinner in front of the Palm House, seated at a long table draped in white linen, the evening sunlight warm and mellow around us. With their passion for flowers and all things green, the Aztecs had taken care to ensure that Kew Gardens had survived the invasion unscathed, and it was said that a squadron of soldiers had held out there for three weeks because the Aztecs would not countenance an attack. Finally they had been starved out.

Aztec plant technologists had been sent to London after the invasion to join the existing team at Kew, and Tetzahuitl was given a lengthy tour of the research centre, inspecting new varieties of cereals, fruits and, of course, flowers. Aztec advances in plant engineering had turned the northern Mexican deserts into vast grain-growing regions, further strengthening the empire. The *cihuacoatl* was well known to take a personal interest in all new developments.

We dined on ahuacatl cocktail, followed by a mélange of spiced fish with peppers, aubergines and sweetcorn. Tetzahuitl took only vegetables and fruit; he did not eat meat of any sort, and also abstained from alcohol. I was seated opposite him at the table and had watched him closely since his arrival, continually wondering whether his constant look of disdain reflected real emotion or was simply a mask of office. After eating he smoked a thin-stemmed pipe filled with aromatic tobacco, responding briefly to the conversational forays of others but showing no inclination to engage in small talk. Yet his eyes were active: they constantly scanned the table, as if he could learn everything he wanted to know about a person simply by watching and listening. Presently, as if to amuse Richard, he took an ahuacatl stone and twirled it through the fingers of his hand before it vanished entirely. Then he plucked it from behind Richard's ear.

Richard was predictably delighted, and begged for more. Tetzahuitl took the stone and rubbed it between both his palms. When he opened them again, the stone was gone and in its place, as if it had been transformed, was a piece of *chalchihuitl*, the variety of jade which the Aztecs still prized as much as gold. Tetzahuitl presented it to Richard while everyone applauded fulsomely. The *cihuacoatl* was supposedly descended from Neza-hualcoyotl, another great sorcerer, though any stage magician could have duplicated his sleight of hand.

'Did you like my trick?'

Tetzahuitl was addressing me.

'It served its purpose,' I replied. What interested me more was that his face had remained expressionless throughout; he was a man well used to hiding his thoughts and feelings.

'I'll take a walk now,' he announced. 'Perhaps you would care to accompany me.'

A request or an order? I wasn't sure. He rose and offered his arm. Though I was suddenly afraid to be alone with him, I knew I couldn't refuse.

His arm in mine, we began walking towards the Palm House. Several soldiers moved to accompany us, but Tetzahuitl waved them back.

His assurance and arrogance angered me. As soon as we were out of earshot of the others, I said, 'Aren't you taking a risk?'

'A risk?'

'Being alone with me like this? Don't you know I'm your sworn enemy? Perhaps I have a hidden knife.'

He didn't even look at me. 'If I were to be assassinated by a princess of the realm while walking in these gardens, I would be quite amazed.'

'Do you think I'd be afraid to do it?'

'I think perhaps you might like to. But the desire is one thing, the means and the enterprise quite another.'

He paused on the steps to light his pipe, still not deigning to look at me. Blue smoke wreathed his feathered head. He seemed an impossible figure in such surroundings. I felt both furious and foolish.

'Let me assure you,' he said, 'I don't underestimate you in the slightest. But look there. And there.'

He pointed towards the pond, in which ducks floated, then at an ornamental hedge in front of the Palm House. There were snipers with high velocity rifles trained on us. On me.

We walked on. Birds were darting amongst the trees and shrubbery.

'European sparrows,' Tetzahuitl remarked. 'Vigorous colonizers. Did you know that they've been displacing our native bluebirds from many areas in the north and west of our continent?'

I made no reply to this.

'We've been forced to build nesting-boxes too small for them to enter so the indigenous species can be preserved.'

'Are you trying to make some symbolic point?'

'I'm simply making conversation. Your starlings are energetic immigrants, too.'

'We've got colonies of passenger pigeons all over London.'

'So I gather. Perhaps it's futile for us to suppose we can limit species to their original domains.'

'Are you going to tell me that this justifies your invasion of my country?'

'Not at all. I was going to ask your advice.'

'My advice?'

'Does that seem so remarkable? You're a woman of integrity and spirit. A patriot. Therefore I hope you'll answer me with the interests of your country at heart.'

We circled the lake while a security jetcopter flew low overhead. As it diminished towards the west, Tetzahuitl said, 'I've come here primarily as a matter of courtesy and diplomacy, and because the Revered Speaker requested it. He has two sons here and is naturally eager that they perform their duties well. He must constantly consider their future.'

'So you've come to check up on them?'

'In a manner of speaking, yes. To assess their progress and achievements. To see if changes should be made.'

Suddenly I was concerned. Tetzahuitl had obviously been pleased with Maxixca's success in Scotland, and I began to imagine the worst possible outcome in which he would replace Extepan as governor.

'If you're going to make any changes,' I said, 'I hope you'll consult us.'

'That's precisely my point in speaking to you now. Of course I understand that you would like nothing better than for us all to leave, but, that aside, I would be interested in your appraisal. For example, are you satisfied with Extepan's efforts on your country's behalf?'

This sounded ominous.

'There are many who would have done far worse,' I replied.

'That hardly sounds like a recommendation.'

'What do you expect? Unqualified praise for the agents of an occupying power? Extepan has behaved decently but with purpose since he arrived here. We could have had a worse master. We did, in Nauhyotl. Under the circumstances, I think his achievements are considerable.'

Tetzahuitl sucked on his pipe. 'High praise indeed from someone so adamantly opposed to us.'

'I don't like the situation, but I'd prefer us to be ruled by someone who will try to work with the people rather than humiliate and brutalize them. I think Extepan's quite clever at achieving his own ends with sweet reason rather than force.'

Tetzahuitl made no comment on this. We began making our way back to the others, he descending into small talk about the seedless pomegranates and black roses he had been shown earlier. Around us, furtive shapes darted in the branches of trees.

'Look,' I said, pointing. 'Grey squirrels.'

Victoria and I spent the following afternoon riding Archimedes and Adamant in Parliament Park under heavy escort. I returned to the complex sore-limbed and allowed myself the luxury of a long hot bath.

When I emerged, Bevan was out in the garden, stalking the rosebeds with a pair of secateurs. It was another balmy evening, and I joined him outside.

'All right?' he greeted me, squatting to snip a sucker from the base of a bush.

'You're getting green fingers,' I remarked.

'Keeps me busy, doesn't it?'

He set to work on another bush with what seemed like excessive brutality.

'Isn't it the wrong time of the year for pruning?'

Bevan brandished a clump of suckers in his gloved hand. 'Never too early for these. Parasites, they are. Suck the life from the plant.'

He crouched and began rummaging in the foliage.

'I was wondering when you'd be back,' he said presently.

'Oh?'

'I hear you're off to Lords tomorrow.'

I was surprised he knew. Extepan had arranged for Tetzahuitl to attend a special limited-overs game between the England and the touring Azanian team.

'Where did you hear that? I was only told this morning.'

'Word gets around.' His head remained buried in the bushes. 'Who's going altogether, then?'

Richard, Victoria and I had agreed to attend the match, largely because we all knew the captain of the team, whose father was an old friend of the family. I told Bevan as much.

'If I was you,' he said, 'I'd give it a miss.'

He delved even deeper into the bushes.

'Why?' I said.

'Might not be safe.'

'What do you mean?'

'There's rumours going round.'

I was talking to his backside. 'Bevan, come out of there!'

With a certain amount of grunting and muttered curses, he waddled backwards out of the rosebeds. Leaves and cuttings clung to his grey nylon sweater.

'What's going on?' I demanded.

'I picked up a whisper that something might be *planned* for the occasion, if you get my drift.'

'What sort of thing?'

'Something nasty. Violent, like.'

'Are you suggesting we might be in danger?'

'You might be killed. The lot of you.'

He spoke in a perfectly matter-of-fact way, as if we were discussing something quite innocuous.

'How?' I asked.

'Couldn't say for certain. But I reckon it's not going to be safe for anyone there.'

'Are you sure?'

'Take my word for it.'

He removed half a cigarette from behind his ear and lit it.

'Bevan, you have to tell me how you know.'

'A little bird told me.'

'How can I trust you if I don't know where you're getting your information from?'

He shrugged. 'Up to you, isn't it? But if it was me, I'd give you the benefit of the doubt, considering that my life might be at stake.'

I sighed. 'Who are they hoping to get? Tetzahuitl, or the whole lot of us?'

'You think they give a damn one way or the other?'

*

Richard was in the living room with his household staff, watching an old black-and-white programme on his wide-screen TV.

I shooed the servants out so that I could speak to him alone.

'We need to talk,' I said through the noise of the programme.

'Can't it wait?' he replied. 'I'm watching this.'

He was intent on the screen. Zozo the masked Mexica swordsman was furthering the Aztec cause in eighteenth-century California by dispatching inept English militiamen, courtesy of Mexsat TV.

'Something's cropped up,' I said. 'I don't think we'll be able to go to Lords tomorrow.'

'What's happened, Kate? I was looking forward to it.'

On the screen, barrels were rolling and crashing around a wine cellar as Zozo evaded the attentions of a trio of lumbering Caucasian swordsmen. Richard always liked to have the volume turned right up, which I found useful on this occasion since it meant that no one could possibly overhear us.

'Will you promise me you'll keep what I say to you a secret?'

He looked intrigued. 'Of course, Kate.'

'It might be dangerous to go to Lords. We might all be killed.'

'What do you mean?'

'Promise me you won't say anything to anyone else?'

'I promise.'

'I think someone's going to plant a bomb there.'

He digested this for a moment, his eyes flickering back only briefly to the screen.

'Are you playing a joke, Kate?'

'It's no joke, Richard.'

'They want to blow us all up?'

'Not us in particular, I don't think. But the Aztecs. The *cihuacoatl* especially, I expect.'

'That's not very nice.'

I said nothing to this.

'Who are they?'

'I don't know.'

'We'll have to tell Extepan.'

'No,' I said firmly, not entirely surprised by this. 'You must remember the Aztecs are our enemies, Richard. You have to expect our people to try to find ways of striking back at them.'

'Innocent people will be killed, won't they?'

'Most probably,' I admitted.

'That isn't fair.'

'It wasn't fair that they invaded us in the first place, was it? Some of our people are never going to accept that.'

'I think you should tell Extepan, Kate.'

'No. I can't.'

'It would be cowardly of us to stay away and let them walk into a trap.'

'They're our enemies,' I repeated. 'They're occupying our country. They attacked us and killed many of our people.'

'At least it was a fair fight.'

'Hardly fair, since the invasion was unprovoked. And don't you think that innocent people didn't die in the fighting? If we warn them, we'll be collaborating, betraying the people who still believe in our freedom.'

Again Richard thought about this while Zozo sword-slashed his initial on a stuccoed fort wall before galloping away into a monochrome sunset.

'I'm going to go to the match, anyway,' he said. 'They won't do it if I'm there.'

'You're foolish if you think that,' I said gently. 'They almost certainly will.'

'But I'm their King.'

'That won't make any difference. They'll see you as a traitor.'

'Then I'll just have to die, won't I?'

'That's even more foolish. What purpose would it serve?'

'I don't know, Kate. But that's what I'm going to do.'

I gripped his arm. 'Use your head. Do you want to be a martyr? Is that what you want?'

'I can't let them frighten me off.'

'They're on *our* side, Richard. Fighting for *our* people.'

'There might be women and children there. How can people let children be killed?'

I almost said that he was a child himself. His eyes were wet at the thought, but at the same time he looked stubborn and determined.

'We can't do anything to stop it,' I said urgently as the closing credits rolled with a crescendo of warped and tinny brass. 'It's going to happen whether we like it or not.'

'It's wrong, Kate. I think it's wrong. If they're going to do it, they'll have to blow me up, too. That's my final word.'

I went directly to Victoria's suite. Chantico, her lady-in-waiting, told me that she had gone out for the evening.

'Where?' I asked.

'I don't know,' she replied. 'Out with friends.'

From Bevan, I already knew that Victoria had taken to frequenting nightclubs and casinos with other members of what was termed the New Court – bright young things, mostly Aztec, who preferred the attractions of the West End to the duties and responsibilities of their positions.

I sat up into the small hours, waiting for her to return. Finally I fell asleep and woke with the dawn.

Again I went to her suite. A bleary Chantico admitted me. Her mistress was not yet back.

'She is sometimes gone all night,' Chantico told me. 'She stays with friends.'

'Where?'

She shook her head.

Chantico was a timid and courteous Navajo, and I knew she was both loyal and easy to bully.

'I insist you tell me where she is!' I said fiercely.

'I don't know,' she assured me. 'She never tells me where she's going. She says it's for security reasons.'

'This is urgent! Vital! It goes beyond any personal loyalties you might have towards her!'

'Please.' She was close to tears now. 'You have my word of honour. I don't know!'

I relented, convinced that she was telling the truth. More softly I said, 'Is there any way you can think of that I could contact her?'

A further shake of the head.

'Somewhere I could leave a message?'

'I'm sorry. I know nothing of her movements.'

I sought out Bevan, who was suitably disgruntled to be woken and marched out into the garden in his dressing gown.

'Richard's adamant on going to Lords today,' I said.

'You told him?'

'I swore him to secrecy. Do you think I'd let my own brother – the King – die? I need to know when and where the bomb's going to go off.'

He huddled into his dressing gown. 'I never said anything about a bomb.'

'You implied as much. I've no time for games, Bevan. I need to know. These are the lives of my family we're talking about. The only people I have left.'

A shrug. 'I don't know any more than I've already told you.'

'You must have some idea of when it's going to happen.'

He shook his head.

'Please, Bevan. Help me.'

'My guess is the pavilion. It's just a guess, mind you, but it'd make sense. You'd all be crammed in there. That way they'd be sure of getting everybody.'

'I want to speak with whoever told you this.'

'No chance. Even if I could arrange it, there wouldn't be time. And they wouldn't come within fifty feet of you.'

I could have hit him then. He was so stubborn, so infuriatingly wooden at times.

'How much a part of this are you?'

'Like I told you, I just hear things. Pass them on.'

'I don't believe you.'

'Believe what you want.'

'You told me the Aztecs expected you to keep an eye on me. Is that what you're doing, Bevan? Working for them? Leading me a merry dance?'

He laughed. 'What do you take me for? Look, I've given you the tip-off. Now it's up to you. Save yourself if you can't save anyone else, for Christ's sake.'

The silence was filled by a single bird singing a belated dawn chorus somewhere in the shrubbery. At that moment the entire situation seemed utterly improbable – I standing in a garden with a pyjamaed Welshman who was continually offering me 'help' in the most obstructive manner possible.

'You told me once you weren't exactly a royalist,' I remarked.

'You won't find many from my background that are.'

'Why bother telling me, in that case? What difference would it make to you if we were all killed or not?'

'I look after my own.'

'What does that mean?'

'Whatever you want.'

He pushed past me and went inside.

Four

I bathed and took breakfast alone in my suite, then went to see Richard again. But he had departed early for Lords, obviously intent on avoiding me. I could scarcely believe he intended to risk his life.

At ten thirty, Chicomeztli arrived to escort me up to the launch pad for the flight to the ground. He was his usual cheery self, but I brushed aside his pleasantries.

'Do you know where my sister is?'

He followed me into the elevator. 'I believe she went out last night with some friends. To a rock concert at Wembley Stadium.'

I was suspicious. 'That's the first I've heard of it.'

'Nepantla. She is a fan, yes?'

Nepantla were a very popular Aztec band, and I knew they were touring England.

'She didn't come home last night.'

Chicomeztli shrugged. 'There will be an escort to watch over her. Perhaps she stayed with friends.'

This sounded suspiciously casual. 'Does she often do this sort of thing?'

Chicomeztli looked puzzled. 'There is no bar on her freedom of movement providing her personal security is assured. Is something wrong?'

I watched the ascending numbers on the floor-level indicator.

'Is she going to Lords today?'

'I do not know. Is there some difficulty?'

I sighed, then shook my head. 'No. It's nothing.'

He was silent for a while, but I was aware of him watching me.

'I hope you'll forgive me,' he said, 'but I think perhaps you should take a leaf, as you say, out of your sister's book.'

'What do you mean?'

'Some pleasure and relaxation. You take too little, maybe?'

'Isn't that what I'm doing? Relaxing? Having a day out at Lords?'

The harshness of my tone obviously took him aback. The elevator lurched to a halt, and the doors ground ponderously open.

The flight to Lords took only twenty minutes. Extepan, Tetzahuitl and Richard were already there in their seats when I arrived. Extepan was dressed in his ultramarine uniform, Tetzahuitl draped in a carmine and charcoal robe, Richard entirely in white. All three were conspicuous targets, I thought immediately, for any assassin. Richard pointedly did not look in my direction. It was almost as if he had blotted our conversation from his mind – or more likely had simply decided to carry on regardless with that special rigidity of attitude which he adopted once his mind was made up.

The old pavilion had been destroyed during the invasion, but the new structure of glass and chrome aped its stately Palladian contours while being thoroughly modern inside. The new Long Room was equipped with contour couches, video screens and the control centre for the all-weather dome which enabled matches to be played during rain and even in winter. Apparently the Lords committee was aghast when Extepan had insisted that women be admitted to the room for the first time in its history.

We were introduced to both teams. Jeremy Quaintrell, the English captain, was the youngest son of the Earl of Eltham, a former friend of my father but now a partisan of the Aztecs. Jeremy had been a childhood friend of ours, but he now struck me as haughty and smug. The polyglot Azanian team seemed rather ill at ease, as if they were reluctant participants in the event. Though the country had welcomed its Aztec-supported liberation from British colonial rule and its infamous Aparthood system, independence was brief and its current protectorate status was seen by many of its citizens as just another form of colonialism.

The Long Room was filled with dignitaries and guests, many

of them Aztec but many also English who had no connection with Aztec rule. Had the bomb already been planted here? Would it be detonated by someone now present? Or would some other means be used? Poison gas or a concussion grenade? A mortar attack from outside the ground? Mass poisoning of the Earl Grey or cucumber sandwiches? My mind raced over lurid possibilities.

We assembled on the balcony for the start of the match. Victoria's seat was empty. The ground was full, many of the faces black Azanian émigrés or descendants of West Indians who had fled to Britain when the Aztecs occupied the Caribbean islands at the turn of the century. How many would die if there was a big explosion? I kept looking around, searching for some furtive movement or surreptitious gesture. I caught Richard staring at me, his face a mask of reproach. He said nothing, looked away.

The team captains emerged with the umpires. A coin was tossed. Quaintrell won and elected to bat. My father, a keen Middlesex supporter, had taken me to many matches as a child, and I had developed a real appreciation of the game. Today, however, it was the last thing on my mind.

'Where's Maxixca?' I asked Extepan.

'He has other duties elsewhere today,' he told me.

This only made matters worse. If Extepan were killed, there was an even stronger possibility that Maxixca would be appointed governor in his place. This is madness, I thought. I must do something. But what? How could I betray those who were fighting for a cause I believed in? How could I let innocent people die?

The sun broke through the clouds as the match commenced. Extepan, cognoscente of all things English, began explaining the rules of the game to Tetzahuitl with that combination of pedantry and naïve misunderstanding typical of the newly knowledgeable. Richard also seemed remarkably carefree, reading aloud from the team notes. Was it possible he had actually forgotten the threat to his life and everyone else's? It wouldn't be the first time he had successfully blocked unacceptable facts from his mind.

The England innings began with the opening batsmen facing

a barrage of Azanian fast bowling. Few runs were scored, but no wickets fell. Union flags and St George's crosses were unfurled around the ground, along with the black, green and gold Azanian flag. Isolated cheers went up each time a good stroke was played or a boundary scored. The sun grew hot on my face as I wrestled with my conscience and fear. I sat rigid, beside myself with fear and indecision.

A wicket fell, and Quaintrell came in to bat. He was blond and handsome, the epitome of the English captain in his whites. On his first ball he survived a strong call for leg before wicket. Extepan's attempts to explain the intricacies of this particular law to Tetzahuitl diverted me momentarily from my anxiety. The *cihuacoatl*'s face remained a picture of inscrutability.

Quaintrell hooked an outswinger to the boundary, took two leg byes, then lofted the final ball of the over for six. The crowd's cheers became more forceful. A single, then another boundary, and now a ragged chant of 'England, England' went up. The next delivery took away two stumps, and Quaintrell began a hangdog walk back to the pavilion.

Waiters attended us with cocktails and soft drinks, while around the ground shirts were peeled off under the sun and cans of beer cracked open. It was almost possible to believe that the match was being played under ordinary circumstances.

I sat numbly, conversing only when directly addressed, my mind racing. Even now I don't know how I was able to remain motionless for so long. No one appeared to notice my agitation, which surprised me because I have never, despite my upbringing, been good at hiding my emotions. When parasols were produced for us against the sun, I gratefully hid myself under one while continuing to scan the surroundings. I saw nothing amiss. Perhaps the bomb – I was sure, now, that it would be a bomb – had been planted under the very balcony days before, with a timing device. Another wicket fell, but I scarcely noticed it. The sheer normality of everyone around me, Richard included, only persuaded me that something dreadful was certain to happen at any moment.

Then Victoria arrived, murmuring her apologies for her lateness, escorted by a young Aztec called Huahuantli. She slumped in a seat beside me, looking ragged and flustered. Her arrival seemed to galvanize me. All I could think about was that my entire family would be killed, that Maxixca would inherit everything. As soon as I had the opportunity, I leaned close to her and whispered, 'Where have you been?'

She told me about the concert, then said, 'There was a party afterwards. It went on till four in the morning. You look dreadful, Kate.'

'Not half as bad as you. You should have had a lie-in. Why did you bother to come?'

She appeared not to hear me, instead hailing a waiter and taking a glass of lemon barley water which she promptly drained.

'God, that feels better,' she said. 'I was as dry as a bleached bone. What time's lunch?'

With a shock I realized it was approaching one o'clock. Soon we would go inside and sit down to a cold buffet during the interval. Now I became certain that the assassination attempt would take place as we ate.

Before I could say or do anything further, the last ball of the morning was bowled, and the teams promptly began filing off the pitch. Already Extepan and Tetzahuitl were rising. Aztec security guards closed in to escort us inside.

In the Long Room, tables were laden with sunbursts of melon, crudités, crystal bowls heaped with strawberries. No one bothered to sit down but instead piled food on to a plate and stood chatting while waiters wove expertly between knots of people, serving more drinks. I took up a position near one of the doors, feeling cowardly and foolish. If a bomb went off, I would have no chance of escaping.

Victoria took a tall glass of white wine and soda from a tray and came over to me. Huahuantli was with her. He was tall and fair-skinned for an Aztec, a natural stripe of blond in his dark hair giving him a striking appearance. He spoke excellent English, telling me that his mother was a Caucasian from the Virginia province of Greater Mexico. I amazed myself with my capacity for small-talk in such a situation.

Jeremy Quaintrell appeared, and there was a brief ceremony in which he presented Tetzahuitl with a bat once used by the legendary Archibald Leach. The *cihuacoatl* accepted the bat as if someone were laying a baby in his arms. He then shook both

Quaintrell's hands before the captain returned to his dressing room.

I took a gin and tonic and gulped it down. Richard was in the centre of a knot of people, among them Kenneth Parkhouse and his wife. The Prime Minister tried to catch my eye, but I studiously avoided him. I suddenly found myself confronted by Extepan and Tetzahuitl.

It was Extepan who spoke first. 'I think it's been a successful morning for the English team, yes? One hundred and twenty-one for the loss of only two wickets.'

He was speaking in Nahuatl. I looked helplessly at Tetzahuitl. His dark eyes stared back at me. He was holding the cricket bat in one hand, something I would have found comical in any other circumstance.

'Tell me something,' he said. 'Does the game of cricket have any religious significance for your people?'

Somehow I managed to smile. 'In a manner of speaking, I suppose it does.'

'To the stranger it appears quite perverse and unfathomable.'

'You're not the first to say that.'

'There are so many imponderables. How can you begin an over? Why, when a team is in, do their opponents take the field?'

My smile remained fixed.

'Are there really such situations as silly mid-off and backward short-leg?'

He pronounced both with difficulty. Behind him I saw an English waiter suddenly bend down behind the table. Instantly I froze. Both Tetzahuitl and Extepan must have seen the look of horror on my face.

'What's the matter, Catherine?' Extepan said.

'I think—' I began. 'I think it might be wise if—'

The waiter reappeared, holding a fallen serviette. I had imagined him about to trigger a bomb or take cover from a hail of automatic fire. I stopped.

'If?' said Tetzahuitl.

I stared blankly at him.

'You were saying?' he persisted.

'I think,' Extepan interjected, 'Princess Catherine was going to warn us that our lives might be in danger, isn't that so?'

In truth, I wasn't sure what I had been about to say; but I found myself nodding.

'There's no cause for alarm,' Tetzahuitl said. 'We were aware of the assassination plot. An explosive device intended for use in this very room was neutralized by our security people last night.'

So it had been a bomb, after all. Swallowing, I said, 'Have you arrested anyone?'

Tetzahuitl's lined face creased further in a basilisk smile. 'Who would you expect us to arrest?'

'I have no idea,' I said quickly.

'Really? But you knew about the plot.'

'It was just a rumour I heard.'

'You took a risk in coming here in that case.'

'I had no choice.'

'Your brother, the King, alerted us to the danger. He wasn't prepared to countenance such a waste of lives.'

He appeared to be inviting some comment from me. Despite my disappointment with Richard, my main feeling was one of relief, because it increased the chances that the leak might not be traced to Bevan, and from him to others unknown.

'Tell me something,' Tetzahuitl said. 'When we arrest the culprits – as we intend to do shortly – what would you recommend we do with them?'

I looked at Extepan, then back at him. There was no way of telling whether he was in earnest or simply baiting me. His unfathomable eyes told me nothing.

'You can't possibly expect me to answer that,' I said hotly.

'I'm not asking for your opinion on the rights and wrongs of their action. I want your advice. The two are quite different. What do you think we should do with them?'

He held the bat in his hand as if it were a cudgel, as if he might at any moment erupt in violence and begin bludgeoning me with it. Yet I was certain there was amusement in his face.

'You're a fool if you believe I'll tell you,' I said angrily. 'Or you think I'm one.'

Extepan looked horrified at the insult, but Tetzahuitl raised the bat in a calming motion.

'I'm not asking the question without self-interest,' he said to me. 'I'm hoping to gain some appreciation of the consequences of our actions. What would your people think? Should we be harsh or magnanimous?'

'What are you saying? That I should tell you what to do to make sure your public image isn't damaged?'

He was immune to my scorn. 'Not precisely. I'd simply like to ensure that the punishment won't appear unduly severe to the fair-minded observer.'

I gave a sarcastic laugh. 'I wasn't aware you'd previously shown such concern for the sensibilities of conquered peoples.'

An off-hand gesture. 'We've no desire for vengeance since no outrage was in the end committed against us. Extepan here is eager to pursue as enlightened a policy as possible with respect to the people of these islands.'

'Then, presumably,' I said with heavy irony, 'we can rule out torture?'

Tetzahuitl made a disapproving noise. 'Torture is the resort of those who fear their position is threatened. Besides, we're not barbarians. Straightforward executions are an obvious option, but they run the risk of making martyrs of these people.'

'Not if you kill them in secret,' I said bitterly.

'I think public knowledge of the plot is more widespread than even you imagine. It would be impossible to keep such actions secret. A better alternative might be exile. Of course, it would need to be somewhere far away.'

I became aware that Extepan looked uncomfortable, as if he was unsure where Tetzahuitl was leading. I wondered if he was being mocked by the *cihuacoatl* for his liberal tendencies. I almost felt a certain solidarity with him then.

'So,' Tetzahuitl said, 'what considered advice would you give us?'

'Do you think you can manipulate me so easily?'

'I'm simply asking your opinion. We're perfectly free to disregard it.'

'To you, this is just a game. To me, it's in deadly earnest. Whoever these people are – and whatever you think, I don't know who they are – they don't need me to compromise them. They're your enemies, not mine.'

Tetzahuitl contemplated the dark wood of the bat. 'What if we were talking about someone you knew?'

Was this a bluff? I had an ominous feeling it wasn't.

'Then I couldn't possibly give unbiased advice. Of course I would want mercy for them. Who wouldn't?'

The England innings collapsed after lunch, reaching a total of only 202. The afternoon grew hazy and humid while I sat impatiently through the rest of the match. I could not bring myself to talk to Richard but instead listened to Victoria, who chattered about the concert and the party while sipping wine-and-sodas and nibbling pecans from a tray. I saw no point in mentioning the assassination plot; she would find out about it soon enough.

Tetzahuitl and Extepan maintained every appearance of continuing interest in events on the field. I had imagined I might face interrogation or even arrest for refusing to divulge the source of my knowledge of the bomb plot, but no further pressure had been put on me. Did this mean they were already confident that they had rounded up all the perpetrators? Who would they arrest? I longed for immediate answers but was condemned to sit and wait.

As it turned out, the game could not have had a more exciting climax. The Azanians lost their first four wickets cheaply, then staged a middle-order recovery until they stood at 190 for 5. Defeat loomed for England with their fast bowlers tiring and the Azanian batsmen in command. But then the skies clouded over and Jeremy Quaintrell came in to bowl his particular brand of off-spin. Two wickets fell in his first over, then another in his second, with only six more runs added. The new batsman hit a four with his first delivery, then was yorked by the second. Azania stood at 200, with only one wicket left.

Quaintrell moved in to bowl again. The crowd were chanting more fulsomely now, and beer cans were being clacked metronomically together. The batsman blocked the first delivery. Then the second. The third ball was a full toss which the batsman hit with the meat of his bat. The ball soared away. Six runs seemed certain, and victory for Azania. But a fielder at the boundary came racing out of nowhere to pluck the ball from the air. Azania were all out, giving England victory by two runs.

The crowd swarmed on to the pitch as Quaintrell was raised aloft by his teammates and carried away, the man of the match.

We assembled for the presentation. The match trophy, specially made for the occasion, was a tiny bail of Azanian gold, mounted on an onyx block. It looked incredibly vulgar.

Quaintrell accepted the trophy from Tetzahuitl, then turned and raised it to the crowd. They roared and cheered as he shook it above his head, the conquering hero. All around the ground, flags were being waved to celebrate the victory.

Five

Victoria and I declined to join the others at the after-match dinner, and we were flown back to the complex. Victoria, worn out from her revels, immediately went off to bed. I found Chicomeztli waiting outside the door of my suite.

'Do you wish me to order a meal for you?' he asked.

Normally it was Bevan who arranged my meals. There was something in Chicomeztli's face which made me suspicious. I went inside and unlocked the door to Bevan's apartment.

It was empty, his balcony window locked, the air fresh-smelling. The apartment had been cleaned and the bedsheets changed. I knew that Bevan normally allowed the cleaning staff in only once a week. He was slovenly in his habits, but there was no sign of his occupancy.

I slid open the door of his wardrobe. That, too, was empty.

Chicomeztli was still waiting patiently at my threshold.

'Where is he?' I demanded.

'Do you mean Bevan?'

'Of course I mean Bevan! Who else would I mean?'

Chicomeztli shrank back from my anger.

'His mother is unwell. He has been given compassionate leave to visit her in Wales.'

I glared at him. 'That's a lie.'

He shook his head. 'It is true.'

'He said nothing to me about having to visit anyone.'

'The news of her illness only came this morning, after you had left for the cricket tournament. He was given permission to leave immediately, under guard.'

'I don't believe you.'

'It is true,' he repeated.

'His room's been cleaned out. There's not a scrap of clothing left.'

'That is normal practice. It will be laundered while he is away.'

I grabbed him by the arms. 'Tell me the truth!'

His lazy eye danced wildly as he tried to focus on my face at close range.

'I saw him leave,' he insisted. 'He is to be flown directly to Wales. Emergency arrangements were made.'

I knew him well enough by now to believe that he was telling me the truth – but only as he knew it.

'Who authorized it?'

'Maxixca was left in charge here.'

'Then I want to see him immediately.'

Chicomeztli did not demur. Together we rode the lift to Extepan's suite.

It was Mia who answered the door. She took our unexpected arrival in her stride, leading us through into Extepan's office.

Maxixca was seated at Extepan's desk. He smiled when he saw me.

'Ah,' he said, rising. 'Princess Catherine. What can I do for you?'

He spoke in Nahuatl, his smile supercilious.

'Where's Bevan?' I said in English.

'Obviously I shouldn't have expected the usual courtesies,' he said, again in Nahuatl. 'Weren't you informed? His mother is sick, and we sent him off under escort to visit her.'

'You're lying.'

Anger suffused his face for an instant, but he controlled it.

'It's the truth, I assure you. As unlikely as it may seem to you, I've always been prepared to show consideration where personal difficulties or family crises are concerned. See for yourself. Here are the authorization papers.'

He handed me a small sheaf of papers which I scanned briefly. According to the documents, Bevan's mother had been taken from her home in Trefil to a hospital in Abergavenny after suffering a stroke. She was said to be in a critical condition. I was certain the documents were fakes.

'What have you done with him?' I demanded.

Maxixca was tolerance personified. In English he said, 'He has been taken to visit his mother. It was an emergency, and necessary to act swiftly. You were not available to be informed. I personally arranged the flight. Given that he is your man-servant, I would have expected gratitude.'

I couldn't imagine him doing anything for any of us out of the goodness of his heart. He had obviously been expecting me to arrive.

'I want to know,' I said. 'Has he been killed?'

'Killed?' Maxixca affected to look shocked. 'Why should we want to kill him?'

I had to be careful what I said. In the unlikely event that he was telling the truth, I ran the risk of endangering Bevan by protesting too much. With everything uncertain, I had so little room for manoeuvre.

'I want to speak to Extepan,' I said.

Maxixca sat down again, studiously squaring the papers on the desk.

'Did you hear what I said? I want to speak to Extepan.'

'I regret that will not be possible.'

'When is he due back?'

Now he looked smug. 'You may have a longer wait than you imagine.'

'What do you mean by that?'

'He will not be returning immediately.'

I didn't like the sound of this. 'Where is he?'

'He is not available. I am in charge here.'

He was plainly relishing my discomfiture, and now I began to wonder. Had Extepan already been ousted? Had there been a palace coup, initiated by Tetzahuitl, with Maxixca promoted to Extepan's position? He still wore his field commander's uniform, but that was not conclusive in itself. Though Extepan was a son of the emperor and Maxixca's elder, that would not necessarily protect him: the Aztecs were swift to remove from high office anyone they considered incompetent or simply unsuitable. Was I now speaking to the new Aztec governor of my country?

I refused to give him the satisfaction of asking him directly. I turned and stalked out.

As soon as Chicomeztli and I were alone in the elevator, I said, 'Where's Extepan gone?'

He was wary of me. 'I believe he is returning this evening to Tenochtitlan with the *cihuacoatl*.'

'Why?'

'That I cannot say.'

'Cannot or won't?'

He shook his head helplessly. 'I was only informed one hour ago. No details were given.'

'When is he due back?'

'I was not told.'

We walked together down the corridor to my suite. At the door I said, 'Maxixca's taken over Extepan's office.'

He nodded. 'That is normal practice. He is Extepan's deputy.'

'What if he's replaced him? On a permanent basis?'

Chicomeztli looked genuinely alarmed at the idea.

'No, no,' he said. 'I would have been told.'

'Not necessarily,' I countered. 'Not if it's only just happened.'

I left him at the doorway with this unnerving possibility. But there was a further unwelcome surprise awaiting me that highly unsettling day. Late that night, I rose from bed intending to activate ALEX in the hope that he might be able to tell me what had happened to Bevan and Extepan. But when I searched for the disk in the pillowslip where I had hidden it, I found it gone.

Disaster seems to breed disaster, and the biggest of all was still to come. The following morning I went upstairs to Victoria's suite. We had lately taken to exercizing Archimedes and Adamant most mornings in Parliament Park, and I was eager to find some time alone with her so we could talk. But Chantico told me she had left for the stables an hour before.

Victoria had never been an early riser, especially after a late night out, but I thought nothing of it. Yet when I arrived at our stables, both Archimedes and Adamant were still in their stalls, unsaddled. None of the grooms had seen anything of Victoria that morning.

A profound disquiet overtook me. Immediately I returned to the complex and sought out Maxixca again.

He was inspecting a detachment of guards on the parade
ground which fronted the river.

'Where's my sister?' I demanded.

He turned and, without a word, motioned for me to follow
him inside. Three guards accompanied us.

We passed through the terrace garden and entered an operations room. Screens flickered untended, showing multiple views
of the ground-level entrances to the complex. Maxixca drew
himself up to his full height.

'I'm afraid I have some unpleasant news for you,' he informed
me in English. 'Princess Victoria has been arrested.'

'What?'

I could see the pleasure under his show of concern.

'She was implicated in the plot to cause an explosion at the
Lords cricket compound.'

'That's absurd!'

'I assure you it is true.'

'I don't believe it. It's preposterous!'

He made a gesture as if to say that my disbelief flew in the face
of the facts.

'Where's the evidence?' I demanded to know.

He went to a console and tapped out a code. I had the feeling
that he wanted to demonstrate how firmly he was in command of
every aspect of his new authority. Within seconds the machine
was spewing out black-and-white facsimiles of photographs and
printed documents.

The documents purported to give the dates and times of
Victoria's meetings with persons who were known to be anti-
Mexica agents. The photographs showed her sitting in dim
rooms or standing in shadowy corridors with other people.
Sometimes she was drinking, sometimes laughing, sometimes
whispering in someone's ear. Or so it appeared.

'What are these?' I said.

'Evidence,' Maxixca replied. 'Evidence of her guilt.'

'They could have been taken at a party.'

'Some were.' He was continuing to speak English, no doubt to
emphasize that he was doing everything he could to accommodate
me. 'The people in the photographs are known partisans of

terrorist organizations. The names in the reports refer to known subversives. Many are already in our custody.'

I was scornful. 'Most of the people in these photographs look like Aztecs to me. Are you trying to say your own people would plot against you?'

Again I saw the flash of anger in his face. 'The Aztecs, as you call them, in those photographs are people of non-Mexica races, minorities affiliated with your own subversives who would like nothing better than to grasp power for themselves. White skins are not the only proof of treasonous intentions.'

'I don't believe it,' I said again, ignoring the racial slur. 'Victoria's not the type to become involved in any kind of plot. She has no interest in politics at all.'

Silence. A small sigh to indicate the breadth of his patience.

'She's my sister. I know her well. I would have suspected something.'

'Am I expected to take your word for that? You, a declared enemy of our people?'

'She was terrified when we were first captured. She couldn't possibly be involved.'

Very deliberately, he took the facsimiles from me and proceeded to leaf through them.

'Why are you doing this?' I pleaded. 'She's never harmed anyone.'

His disdain was obvious. 'Perhaps you do not know her as well as you think.'

He removed a photograph. 'Do you recognize the man she is with?'

I had not studied any of the material carefully, but after some scrutiny I saw that the photograph showed Victoria sitting on a carpeted stairway with Jeremy Quaintrell.

'He was arrested immediately after the cricket event,' Maxixca said. 'He planned to kill all of you with explosives hidden in a hollow cricket bat. Fortunately, we learnt of the plot and had the device made harmless beforehand. Your sister was quite prepared for you all to die.'

'But she came to Lords!' I was trying to marshal my thoughts, to piece everything together logically. 'She wouldn't have come if she'd known there was going to be an explosion.'

'She found out we had neutralized the device. She came to try to warn Quaintrell. We made sure she had no opportunity to do so.'

The photograph was poorly lit, grainy, obviously blown up from a smaller print. It might have been taken anywhere, any time, though it must have been recent since Victoria's hair was short.

'Photographs are easy to fake,' I said. 'Victoria would never involve herself in anything so dangerous. She doesn't have the stomach for it.'

A patronizing smile. 'Perhaps you cannot tolerate the idea she was ready to see you and your brother killed.'

'When is Extepan due back? I demand to speak to him.'

'I have full authority here.'

'Did he authorize this?'

'It was authorized by the *cihuacoatl*.'

I felt myself sag inside. If Tetzahuitl had masterminded everything, then there was nothing I could do.

'What's going to happen to her?' I asked. 'Have you already had her killed?'

He was incredulous. 'The plot was unsuccessful. We do not make a habit of executing members of a royal family, even for such grievous escapades as this. The *cihuacoatl* took the view that exile would be sufficient punishment for her – given the uncertain strength of her mental constitution. Subversives are often inadequate individuals.'

'Where is she being taken to?'

'Do you really expect me to tell you that?' He turned away, putting all the facsimiles into a desk drawer. 'The *cihuacoatl* has taken into account her status. It will be somewhere reasonably civilized.'

'This is disgraceful! A farce! These are trumped-up charges!'

'Her flight leaves within the hour. The *cihuacoatl* asked me to permit you to see her one last time. There is a shuttle on the landing pad. If you hurry, you might just catch her.'

Victoria was being flown out of Stansted in a long-distance civilian transporter, destination unspecified. When I arrived at the airport, the craft was already preparing for take-off, and it was only with great reluctance that I was ferried out to it by an Aztec commander who had obviously been given firm instructions that he shouldn't allow himself to be bullied by me.

I sat beside him in an open ground-car, which sighed to a halt about twenty yards from the transporter. The gangway had already been withdrawn, and the wings were beginning to glow as excess power from the engines was fed through the conduction channels.

The commander spoke into a radio, and presently a head appeared at one of the windows. It was Victoria.

I waved frantically. She, too, raised a hand. It was hard to see her expression at such a distance, but I was sure she looked anguished, terrified.

'Let me aboard for a few minutes,' I said to the commander. 'I must speak to her.'

'It's not possible. The ship is about to take off.'

'It's not a scheduled flight. A few minutes would make no difference.'

He shook his head.

'She's my sister! A princess of the blood royal! I demand you take me aboard.'

'It's too late,' he said emphatically. 'If you'd come earlier, it might have been possible. But not now.'

The engine-whine grew louder, and the golden glow suffused the entire wings, dazzling us. We had no option but to withdraw to a safe distance. The transporter headed off down the runway, rapidly picking up speed before it lifted off. I cursed Maxixca, whom I was sure had arranged matters so that I would have no opportunity to speak to Victoria.

She was lost to me, already lost. The transporter rose higher, its wing-glow reflected on the low-lying cloud. I watched it, a diminishing point of brightness, until it was swallowed up in the grey.

Six

I soon discovered that I did not even have Richard to turn to for
solace: he had been dispatched on a goodwill tour of the
Caribbean, leaving London on the same flight as Tetzahuitl
immediately after the post-match dinner at Lords. I would have
feared for his safety had the news bulletins not been full of him
reviewing troops and inspecting historic buildings in Havana and
Santo Domingo. It seemed improbable that the Aztecs intended
to get rid of him when they were giving his tour such publicity.
He had been conveniently removed from all the messy aftermath
of the Lords débâcle, and I wondered if he knew what had
happened to Victoria.

For days afterwards I brooded, feeling impotent and thwarted
at every turn. Without Victoria or Bevan, I was friendless, and
Extepan's absence only made matters worse. Because I wanted
to give Maxixca no further opportunity to humiliate or frustrate
me, I spent much of my time alone in my suite, allowing only
Chicomeztli to visit.

He, at least, remained cheerful and was confident that both
Bevan and Extepan would return. I believed his optimism was
genuine but naïve; he was forced to admit he had no explanation
for Extepan's abrupt departure and no information on when he
would be back. Without ALEX, I had no means of getting any
answers to the many questions which preoccupied me. What had
happened to the disk? Had Maxixca found it? If so, why had he
made no mention of it? Things were happening all around me
over which I had no control and precious little information.

A week passed. Eight, nine days. Some mornings I took
solitary horse rides, alternating on Archimedes and Adamant,
venting my frustration in the physicality of the rides. I was

obsessed with the injustice which had been done to Victoria, powerless to do anything about it. Some evenings I would sit out in the garden and wonder what had been done to Bevan. He was unlikely to have escaped as lightly as Victoria: princesses could not easily be disposed of without creating a stir, but ordinary men like him could simply vanish, and hardly anyone would notice their passing. A deserted place, a swift bullet, burial in an unmarked grave, and scarcely a ripple would disturb the tide of history. How many thousands, millions, had died in this way?

One moment of brightness lightened my gloom. Returning one morning from a ride, I was taken aside by the leader of my escort, an Aztec lieutenant called Zacatlatoa. Without looking at me, he thrust into my hand a vellum envelope. It bore the double-headed eagle of Imperial Russia.

I could hardly wait to get back to the complex. In a shaded nook on the balcony garden, I tore open the letter and removed the single sheet.

It was from Margaret. In the cheery, chatty style so typical of her, she gossiped about the Moscow court, which now included many English refugees from the invasion, asked after my welfare and that of Richard and Victoria – the letter had been written before Victoria's exile – and finally thanked me for 'your splendid news, received with great joy and relief by everyone here'.

It was written in her sprawling hand, and signed Anne B. There was no question of its authenticity, and it was gratifying to know that my communication had reached her and eased Russian fears.

I was intrigued by Zacatlatoa, whom I had not encountered before. Was he a member of the underground? If so, he might know whether or not Victoria had really had any part in the bomb plot. However, he was not assigned to my escort again, and with Maxixca in charge, security remained tight, giving me no opportunity to make further enquiries about him without arousing suspicion.

Alone in my suite by day, I resisted Chicomeztli's attempts to begin organizing my Citizens' Aid Centre. An office had been set aside for our use, and a team of staff was waiting, but I was too busy sulking and had no capacity for such selfless pursuits.

Instead I sat and watched television for much of the day, with a mounting sense of incredulity.

Since the occupation, the Aztecs had reduced the four television channels to a dreary menu of game shows, variety spectaculars and endless serials and soap operas from the Mexican networks. Many of the imports featured white English-speaking casts, but all were Aztec in their sympathies and sensibilities. I made endless jokes about them to the long-suffering Chicomeztli but reserved my most scathing comments for those home-bred celebrities who appeared on banal chat shows in the interests of self-promotion. My fellow citizens, happily thriving under foreign rule. Chicomeztli must have found me sullen and tiresome during this period, but he was too courteous ever to show it.

On the evening of the tenth day, I was sitting alone on the balcony when Bevan put a cup of tea down on the table in front of me.

I looked at him as if he were a ghost. He wore a hand-knitted navy sweater with shapeless bottle-green trousers.

'You're back,' I breathed, fighting an instinct to jump up and hug him.

'Miss me, did you?'

He looked just the same as ever: overweight, unkempt, half a cigarette tucked behind his ear.

'Where have you been?'

'Didn't they tell you? Land of my fathers.'

'I thought you'd been taken away. Murdered.'

He spooned sugar into a mug of mahogany tea. 'Looks like I missed all the excitement.'

I felt a mixture of relief and resentment. 'You've heard about everything that's happened? The bomb plot and Victoria's arrest?'

'All over the news, wasn't it?'

'Was she really involved? Do you know anything?'

He shook his head. 'Not the type, is she?'

'They showed me photographs, transcripts of meetings she's supposed to have had with people involved in the plot.'

'I saw it in the papers.'

'It just isn't possible. If she was involved, I'm sure she would have told me. I would have suspected something.'

Bevan sipped his tea.

'Do you know anything?' I said again. 'Was she really involved with some underground group?'

'Don't see it myself.'

'Then why arrest her?'

'Obvious they wanted her out of the way, isn't it?'

'But why?'

'You've got me there. Hard to imagine.'

Did I detect a sly tone in his voice? Did he, in fact, know of Victoria's involvement in the plot? I had a strong feeling he wasn't telling me everything. He had come back as if he had never been away, and all the time I had imagined him arrested, tortured, dead.

'How's your mother?' I asked.

'She passed away two days ago.'

I hadn't expected this.

'I'm sorry.'

'She was eighty-three.'

I searched for something to say. 'At least you were there. At the end.'

'Didn't know a thing about it, did she? She never regained consciousness.'

I was torn between genuine sympathy and the suspicion that none of it was true. It seemed all too convenient that he had been called away on the very day when the assassination attempt was due to take place.

'I really thought they'd done away with you,' I said. 'You didn't even leave a note.'

'Wasn't time, was there? I had to go in a rush.'

'Maxixca certainly pulled out all the stops for you.'

He wiped his mouth with the back of his hand. 'To be honest, I thought it was a set-up to get rid of me at first. But they're big on the veneration of aged parents and all that. Gave me a room right next to her in Neville Hall, they did, all the mod cons. Let me stay there till she died.'

Neville Hall was the hospital in Abergavenny. I felt that I was being callous in continuing to doubt his honesty; but I no longer had the capacity to take anything at face value.

'They took Victoria away before I had a chance to speak to

her,' I told him. 'Maxixca engineered everything. He's been left in charge here.'

'Acting governor. Nice for someone as power-crazed as he is.'

'I don't know what's happened to Extepan.'

He put his mug down and reached into his trouser pocket.

'Maybe we can find out.'

He had the disk in his hand.

'Took it with me,' he said. 'I had a feeling Mad Mash might do one of his security sweeps while we were all out and about. I thought I'd keep it out of harm's way.'

My suspicions redoubled. 'How did you know where to find it?'

'Your pillowcase? Come on. First place you'd look, isn't it?'

ALEX's face came to life on the screen. I hesitated, then whispered into the microphone: 'It's Catherine.'

He smiled. *'Kate. Good to talk to you again.'*

I was determined not to get involved in small-talk.

'I've got something to ask you,' I said briskly.

'Ask away.'

'Are you aware that Victoria's been arrested?'

His expression became more sober. *'I am. You must be terribly upset.'*

'Do you know why she was arrested?'

There was a slight hesitation. *'The formal charge, according to my information, was subversive activities against the Mexican state and its elected representatives.'*

'I need to know – was she really involved in the plot to kill everyone at Lords?'

A longer pause. *'Documentary and photographic evidence suggested she was.'*

'Do you believe the evidence?'

'There appears to be no reason to discount it.'

I considered, then said, 'From what you know of her, do you think it likely that she would become involved in such a plot?'

Another pause. *'On the surface, her personality profile does not suggest radical tendencies. But real people are notoriously difficult to fathom and predict.'*

Amen to that, I thought grimly.

'Is it possible the evidence was faked?'

'*Anything's possible.*'

'But you believe it?'

A grave smile. '*I have no reason to discount it on the basis of the information available to me.*'

I began to wish I had Bevan beside me; he was better able to probe ALEX in a logical fashion. But I had been determined to speak to ALEX alone that night, without anyone else knowing.

'I can't accept it,' I said.

A slow nod. '*I understand that, Kate. If I were in your position, I expect I should feel the same way.*'

There was a look of great sympathy on his face. I reminded myself that he could not see me, that 'he' was just a pattern of electrons on a phosphorescent screen.

'Where have they taken her?'

Now there was a much longer pause while ALEX remained motionless. He suddenly looked to be what he really was: an artifact, an image, no more.

'*Beijing,*' he announced finally. '*She's joined the court of Prince Ixtlilpopoca under house arrest there.*'

It was not a surprising choice. The Aztecs had succeeded in subsuming China into their empire thirty years before by a combination of strategic marriages into the Manchu dynasty and the military defeat of an unpopular republican government. Ixtlilpopoca was Motecuhzoma's second son, and the Forbidden City had been used as a place of exile for unwanted royal personages before.

'Do you know how long she is to be kept in exile?'

More deliberation. '*No time limit has been specified, as far as I'm aware.*'

His image was so clear I could almost count the hairs in his beard. Yet his movements seemed slightly more laboured, his responses marginally slower, than in the past.

I barely registered this though, being more preoccupied with thoughts of Victoria in her exile. She would not like the winters in that part of China, but at least her existence would be comfortable if restricted. It might have been worse.

'I need to know something else,' I said. 'What's happened to Extepan?'

A further contemplative silence. '*My last record of his where-abouts dates from eight days ago. He accompanied his uncle, Tetzahuitl, to Tenochtitlan.*'

'You've no record of him since then?'

'*No.*'

This was completely unexpected. With a tremor in my voice, I said, 'Is he dead?'

'*Highly unlikely. It's more probable his movements are classified. Unrecorded. For security reasons.*'

I mulled this over. On the screen, ALEX's image flickered briefly. Remembering Bevan's earlier warning, I said hastily, 'There's one other thing.'

'*I'm here to help you if I can, Kate.*'

'It's Bevan. Can I trust him?'

He seemed to frown. '*Can you be more specific, Kate?*'

'I want to know if he's working for the Aztecs.'

A long consideration.

'*There's no indication that he's one of their agents.*'

'Is it possible?'

'*I have no evidence to suggest it.*'

'Is he involved with any other group?'

Another pause. '*None that I'm aware of.*'

I sighed. Having ALEX as an oracle was more frustrating than anything when he could only reveal an absence of evidence.

'Does he really have a mother who's recently died?'

'*I can confirm that. He returned to London seven hours ago following her funeral. Would you like to see her medical records?*'

'That won't be necessary. ALEX, I have to go.'

'*It's been a pleasure talking to you again, Kate.*'

'And to you,' I said automatically.

But before I could move to switch off the terminal, a voice behind me said, 'How very touching.'

I spun around.

Maxixca stood there with an armed escort.

'We suspected someone had gained access to our network. It is most gratifying to discover we were not wrong.'

There was nothing I could say.

'Isn't that your ex-husband? I must say he looks more alert than when I last encountered—'

I lunged for him. Two guards grabbed me and pulled me away.

Maxixca was bleeding from a long scratchmark on his cheek.

'Really,' he said, 'this is most undignified behaviour for a princess of the realm. I thought you English always bore misfortunes with a brave face and a stiff upper lip.'

Again I strained forward, but the guards held me in check.

On the screen, ALEX was still staring out at me, the perfect image of the real person, memento and *memento mori*.

Maxixca pulled the disk from the slot. The image died.

'He's still there,' I goaded him. 'You've simply switched him off.'

With a smile of triumph, Maxixca dropped the disk to the carpeted floor and crushed it under his boot heel.

Seven

I was riding Adamant alone in Parliament Park a week later when I became aware that another rider was shadowing me behind a line of trees. It was none of the security guards, who habitually followed me on horseback, but someone else – on Archimedes.

I pulled Adamant up and waited. The sun was bright overhead, but the other rider was in the shadow of a stand of sycamores.

'You seem to be getting the better of him these days,' he remarked as he trotted forward.

It was Extepan.

He brought Archimedes right up to me so that both colts were close enough to nuzzle one another.

'Hello, Catherine.'

He was dressed in blue jeans and a brown leather windcheater – the first time I had seen him in civilian clothes. He looked somehow brand new to my eyes.

'You're back.'

'I returned early this morning. They told me you were here.'

It was hard to know what to say. 'Where have you been?'

'Home. And away.' He steadied Archimedes, patting his neck. 'I must admit it's good to be here again. Who could wish for a more perfect English summer's day?'

Despite a confusion of feelings, I smiled; I couldn't help myself.

'Are you back in your former capacity?' I asked.

'You mean as governor? Of course. I'll have to get into uniform soon enough.'

Part of me was vastly relieved to hear this. After destroying the disk, Maxixca had had me confined to my suite for three days, but there were no reprisals. A large escort now kept track of all my movements, but otherwise I had been left in peace.

'Shall we walk the horses?' he said.

We rode together in silence along the bridleway near the river. Crack willows had been planted on the Embankment, their silvery leaves fluttering like paper in the morning breeze. Beyond the park, some derelicts had lit a fire among the rubble in New Palace Yard to roast a few of the pigeons that roosted in the tumbledown Parliament building.

Presently Extepan said, 'Do you want to talk about Victoria?'

I eyed him. 'Was it your doing?'

'It was necessary for me to sign the deportation papers,' he admitted.

'She's innocent. I know it.'

'I'm very sorry it happened. For what it's worth, you have my word that she will be looked after. No harm will come to her.'

'I don't suppose there's any point in my appealing to you to reinvestigate the charges against her?'

He was looking across at me, sympathetic but unyielding. 'The evidence appears as conclusive as it can be. There is nothing I can do.'

'Can you tell me where they've taken her?'

'I'm sorry, Catherine.'

I didn't want to argue with him over the issue, especially since I was certain all my protests would be futile.

'What's going to happen to me? Aren't I going to be arrested and interrogated? Don't you want to know who my accomplices were, what I was doing and what I found out?'

Though my tone was challenging, the questions were sincere. It was hard to believe that my nocturnal activities with ALEX would go unpunished.

'I think there has been enough blood-letting of late,' he responded. 'I would prefer to consider the matter closed.'

I was suspicious. 'But you don't know what I might know.'

'I will admit that I regret Maxixca destroyed the disk. It was a hasty and short-sighted action. But nothing can be done about it now.'

It seemed to me he was accepting matters far too easily.

'So I'm free to do as I please?'

'I won't make you a prisoner, Catherine. All I can do is ensure you are well guarded, for your own safety as much as anyone else's. Perhaps you'll understand me when I have had the opportunity to speak to you at greater length. Come to dinner this evening at my suite.'

I eyed him. 'I thought I was in the doghouse.'

He looked puzzled at this but ignored it. 'It's very important I speak with you in private. Please come.'

He spurred Archimedes. 'By the way, Richard is home, too. I shall expect you at eight o'clock.'

Then he galloped away.

Richard was taking a bath when I arrived at his suite. Huixtochtli, the most officious of his staff, was insistent that he shouldn't be disturbed. I strode past him and walked in on my brother.

He sat up to his shoulders in foam, manoeuvring a small plastic killer whale through his knees. The toy was battery-powered, its tail weaving from side to side.

He greeted me with a broad smile and told me that he had missed me. Yet I knew that in the old days he would have sought me out immediately on his return. The ties between us were no longer as strong.

I passed him his bathrobe, and he clambered out of the water. For some reason, I was startled by the glimpse of dark hair at his groin; to me he had always been a child, yet physically he was now a man.

Huixtochtli brought him a lemonade, and we sat out on the balcony in the afternoon sunlight. Up to now, our conversation had consisted entirely of pleasantries.

'Did you hear what happened to Victoria?' I asked.

He looked uncomfortable, as if he had hoped we wouldn't have to broach the subject.

'It was terrible,' he replied. 'They told me when I was in Quauhtemalan. I cried. Isn't it awful, Kate?'

'You don't believe she had any part in the conspiracy, do you?'

'There was evidence. Photographs.'

'Do you think they were genuine?'

'Why shouldn't they be?'

'That sort of evidence is easily fabricated.'

'The others they arrested said she was involved, Kate.'

This was true. I had seen extracts from their 'confessions' during the show trials on news bulletins. Four men from the New Court, among them Huahuantli, had declared on oath that Victoria had been an active participant in the plot. There was no such admission from Jeremy Quaintrell, who remained scornfully insistent of his innocence to the last. All the conspirators had subsequently been deported to the huge maximum-security prison complex in Las Vegas.

'Can you really imagine Victoria being involved in something like that, Richard?'

He played with the straw in his drink. 'I was shocked when they told me. I think she was misguided, Kate, but I've tried to understand her reasons.'

This sounded as if it was parroted from someone else – no doubt his Aztec 'advisers', seeking to soften the blow and persuade him of the truth of their lies. It never occurred to me to consider that perhaps I had always underestimated Richard's intelligence and that he was capable of his own reasoning. I was blind to many things about him and also Victoria, a great failing on my part.

'Do you think she'd risk killing you and me?' I said. 'And herself? It's madness.'

'She wasn't going to be there when the bomb exploded, Kate. She only turned up because she learned they'd found out about the plot.'

'Yes, so they claimed. And it was you who told them about it.'

For an instant he looked sheepish, but then he said, 'I'm sorry. I believe it was my duty. I won't let you make me feel guilty, Kate.'

'People have been sent to prison and Victoria is in exile because of what you did.'

'I'm not the one who was going to kill innocent people.'

He looked defiant; I knew I couldn't browbeat him as of old. And, of course, I couldn't admit to myself that my own reactions were confused. Had I really wanted the bomb to go off? If not, then why blame Richard for warning the Aztecs about it? This was the kind of moral quandary I couldn't bring myself to confront.

'Victoria wasn't involved,' I insisted. 'They told you lies.'

'She confessed herself, Kate.'

'Don't you believe it.'

'There's a tape.'

'What?'

'A tape of her. They showed me it.'

I demanded to see it. Richard summoned Huixtochtli, who went away and shortly returned to inform us that the tape was ready for viewing.

We went inside. Huixtochtli pressed the PLAY button on the recorder and withdrew.

The screen came to life, showing Victoria's head and shoulders with a blank white background behind her. Staring straight at the camera, her face strained, she said, 'I confess my part in the conspiracy to kill the *cihuacoatl* Tetzahuitl, Governor Extepan and others at the Lords cricket ground by means of an explosive device. I have no regrets, except for the grief I know I shall have caused to the remaining members of my family. To you, Richard and Catherine, my sincerest apologies. I love you both.' She looked off camera, her face rigid with tension. 'Do I have to say any more?'

The picture went blank.

A table had been laid on the balcony with white linen, English silverware and a vase of honeysuckle. Extepan and I ate a meal of clear vegetable soup followed by Dover sole with asparagus and new potatoes. There was summer pudding for dessert. I felt that Extepan was trying to make some statement with the simplicity and Englishness of the menu, though I was not sure what.

Mia served us with her perfect poise, pouring a crisp Californian Riesling to accompany the meal before leaving us alone.

'She's very beautiful,' I remarked to Extepan as she departed.

'Indeed,' he replied, managing to make the word sound both emphatic and non-committal.

'Have you known her long?'

'We grew up together. Her mother was a wet-nurse to my elder brothers.'

Dwarf palms and flowering creepers surrounded us on three sides. The garden here was more luxuriant than my own, more exotic and tropical.

'You didn't tell me Victoria had taped a confession,' I remarked.

'I had no involvement in that,' he replied.

What did this mean? 'Why hasn't it been shown on television like all the others?'

Extepan looked a little squeamish. 'I did not feel it necessary for her indignity to be made public.'

'Especially when it was so obviously a scripted confession. A lie.'

He topped up our wine glasses. 'I know there is no persuading you of your sister's guilt, and I do not propose to try. Can we set the matter aside, just for this evening?'

All my instincts told me he had played no part in contriving Victoria's arrest and found the whole affair rather distasteful. Quite possibly, he shared my beliefs but couldn't admit as much.

'All right,' I said. 'A truce. Just for this evening.'

He had been watching me closely since my arrival, but now he looked away, as if trying to compose his thoughts.

'Catherine,' he said, 'I realize that the upheavals of the past few weeks have been very difficult for you. In some senses, I've chosen the worst possible time for this conversation, but I cannot delay it any longer.'

I eyed him over my glass. 'What are you talking about?'

'I'm talking about my immediate future. And possibly yours.'

I waited. Extepan stood up. 'Shall we walk?'

'I'd prefer to stay here.'

'As you wish.' He sat down again, looking ill at ease.

'What is it?' I asked him.

'Catherine,' he said earnestly. 'I am now at an age when my father considers I should marry. This was one of the reasons why he summoned me to Tenochtitlan.'

'Ah,' I said. 'You seemed to leave very abruptly.'

'Delay is not advisable when the *tlatoani* summons you, even if you are one of his sons.'

I sat back and waited for him to continue.

'My father is right, of course. Family matters are just as important as wider political issues, and I have always wanted children.'

Still I was silent, wondering where he was leading.

'However,' he continued, 'it's always been important to me that I should find a wife whom I respect and admire. And perhaps love, if that is possible. My father's marriage to my mother was one of love.'

'Even if it united Greater Mexico with the kingdom of Spain?'

Extepan did not take this amiss. 'He risked his position by divorcing an Alcohua princess to take a European as his wife, and no matter that she was also from the nobility. There was no precedent, and he met with great resistance.'

'No doubt your people eventually found it easier to swallow because it gave them a foothold in Europe.'

'That is true,' he admitted, choosing to ignore my waspishness, 'but there was real love between them. That is quite rare for people in our situation.'

'I married for love,' I told him.

'Yes. I understand you did. I envy you that. I would very much like to do the same.'

'Is there someone you had in mind?'

'My father would like me to marry a princess of the Sioux nation called Precious Cloud. I was introduced to her while I was away. Such a marriage would be likely to strengthen our ties with the Sioux people and stabilize our north-eastern borders with Canada and New England.'

This struck me as a shrewd move, and typical of Motecuhzoma's policy. The Sioux and their allied nations in the Dakotas had managed to maintain their independence by playing off the Aztecs and the Confederacy of Canada and New England. The latter, especially the New English east of the Appalachians, had proved tenacious and resilient in the face of Aztec encroachments over the past century; but their commonwealth might crumble should the peoples of the Dakotas switch their allegiance to Motecuhzoma through marriage.

'If necessary,' Extepan was saying, 'I would be prepared to

defer to his wishes, but he has given me permission to approach someone I feel is a more suitable candidate.'

'Oh?' I said, taking a sip of wine.

'Catherine, I would consider it the greatest of honours if you would accept my proposal of marriage.'

I almost choked on my wine. Dabbing my lips with a napkin, I stared at him in amazement.

'You aren't serious.'

'I am perfectly serious. Do you think I would joke about such a matter?'

Despite my shock, I realized that a part of me had almost anticipated the proposal.

'This is absurd,' I said. '*You* want to marry *me*?'

'This is not a hasty decision, Catherine – I have been considering it for some time. That was one of the reasons why the *cihuacoatl* visited London – so that he could meet you and report back to my father. He agreed with me that you are a woman of great integrity and courage. My father would be happy to sanction the union if you agreed to it.'

I was still incredulous.

'You hardly know me,' I said. 'We've scarcely seen one another in the last six months.'

'I know. But when I watched you from afar, on television while you were travelling the breadth of this land – that only made me more conscious of your many attributes. Of your grace and strength. And beauty.'

I felt more angry than flattered. 'I'm your enemy. Surely you know that by now. I oppose the Aztec Empire.'

'I'm under no illusions, Catherine. I understand why you should want to fight for the liberty of your people. So does my father, and the *cihuacoatl*. I would not respect you if you did not have the courage of your convictions. That courage is one of the things that would make me honoured to be your husband.'

He gave every indication of being in earnest.

'Do you think I'm a fool?' I said.

'Catherine—'

'You never stop, do you? You never stop trying to use me!'

He reached across the table to touch my hand. I snatched it away.

'Catherine,' he said, 'my proposal is a sincere and open one. I have come to admire you greatly. Perhaps more than that. I do not expect you to share those feelings wholeheartedly, but I beg you to believe this – I would rather marry you than anyone else.'

I wanted to get up from the table and march out.

'This is absurd,' I said.

'Believe me,' he replied, 'I would prefer it if I was drawn to someone more . . . tractable. But that is the way it is.'

I shook my head.

'Marriage to me would solve many of your problems here, wouldn't it?'

'Do you think I imagine you would change your nature? I would expect you to protect the interests of your people as before.'

'And do you imagine my people would trust me if I were married to you?'

A sigh. 'Catherine, it would make very little difference to them. You are not the conscience of the whole nation. No one expects you to be.'

'That's no good reason for marrying you.'

'No,' he admitted. 'It is not. But I want you as my wife for what you are, not who you are.'

'I don't believe you.'

'That does not surprise me under the circumstances. Don't you think I would have tried to choose a better time than this if I was able? With your sister only recently exiled, you have less reason to trust any of us than ever. But my father insists that I must marry soon, and urgent situations require urgent actions.'

Mia reappeared, approaching the table.

'Do you need anything else?' she asked in Nahuatl.

'No, no,' Extepan said brusquely, waving her away. She gave me a glance before she departed, and I was certain she knew the whole thrust of our conversation. I was certain she hated me at that moment.

'I beg you to consider it,' Extepan said when we were alone again. 'There's no need to give me an immediate answer.'

'No amount of consideration will make me accept,' I replied. 'How can you possibly expect me to compromise myself by marrying you? I've no intention of legitimizing your rule here.

What would happen then? Would Richard have an unfortunate accident so that you could claim the throne?'

He shook his head fervently. 'No harm is going to come to Richard. And there's no reason for me to marry you for political reasons *because* no harm is going to come to him. Shall I tell you why?'

I waited.

'You remember Chimalcoyotl's daughter, Xochinenen?'

'Of course.'

'Your brother intends to marry her shortly.'

Again, there was something unexpected yet inevitable about his words.

'You're lying,' I said.

'He was greatly taken with her after their first meeting. At his request, she visited him while he was holidaying in Monaco. There they exchanged rings as a token of mutual affection. He visited her again while he was in Mexico. He wants her to become his queen, Catherine, and she's agreed.'

I thought of the snake ring, and Xochinenen's tiny hands. Richard could only wear the ring on his little finger.

'Naturally my father is delighted,' Extepan was saying, 'especially as the initiative came from Richard himself. So you see, we Aztecs, as you call us, will already be marrying into the British Royal Family, and at the very highest level. Politically, it would be far more expedient for me to marry someone other than you. My father would certainly prefer it, even though he appreciates your qualities. But I would rather have you as my bride.'

I was full of thoughts of Richard, aghast at what he intended. Pushing back my chair, I rose.

'Please,' Extepan said, also rising and taking my arm. 'Consider it carefully.'

'I must go,' I said, hurrying away.

Richard was in conference with Kenneth Parkhouse and his cabinet in one of the private rooms off the new House of Commons chamber. I burst in on them.

'Richard,' I said, 'I have to talk to you immediately.'

'I'm very busy now, Kate,' he replied with child-like gravity. 'It will have to wait.'

'Now, Richard.'

I put every ounce of command into my voice. To my surprise, it was Parkhouse and his ministers who reacted, hastily gathering together their papers while murmuring that they would be happy to continue their business later. Soon they were gone, leaving Richard looking stranded at the head of the conference table.

'What were you discussing?' I asked acidly. 'The arrangements for your marriage?'

He was incapable of hiding his surprise.

'She's a lovely girl, Kate. I think we'll be very happy together.'

'Richard,' I said with forced patience, 'can't you see they're using you? You're being manoeuvred into this marriage.'

'It was my idea, Kate.'

'You *think* it was your idea. They want you to think that.'

I could imagine Xochinenen doing everything in her power to make herself attractive to Richard; he was so innocent it had probably been no hard task.

I sat down next to him. 'Listen,' I said softly, 'I'm sure she's a charming girl and that you're very fond of her. But she's an Aztec, the granddaughter of Motecuhzoma. How do you think the British people will feel about you marrying one of our enemies?'

'The Prime Minister and his cabinet believe that the country would enjoy a royal wedding.'

'The Prime Minister and his cabinet are collaborators, stooges of the Aztecs. They'll just tell you what you want to hear.'

'I love her, Kate. She's so pretty and fun to be with. She says we can have six children.'

'She's using you, Richard.'

'No, she's not! She says I'm kind and gentle. You don't know her – she's the only person I can laugh with. Everyone else is so serious all the time. I always have so many important decisions to make.'

I took his hand across the table. 'Once she's married to you, you'll be completely in the power of the Aztecs. They'll have the authority to do whatever they want. And you'll carry the blame if anything goes wrong.'

I let him ponder on this, already knowing it was futile.

'I don't care,' he said at length. 'I don't care what anyone else thinks. I love her and I'm going to marry her, whatever they say.' He pulled his hand from under mine and gave me a fierce look. 'If you try to stop me, Kate, I'll have you sent away!'

Eight

Three weeks later, Extepan flew back across the Atlantic to visit his Sioux princess. On the same day, Richard's engagement to Princess Xochinenen was made public. She had arrived from Mexico a few days earlier, and the couple were shown on the nine o'clock news attending a première of the Grey Webster musical *Tequila Sunrise* at the Ambassadors Theatre off Shaftesbury Row. The large crowd outside was uniformly rapturous. Richard and his bride-to-be paused to wave outside the theatre in a snowstorm of flashlights. Xochinenen was dressed in a sequinned Jagger costume gown, Richard in an evening suit. They looked the perfect couple.

Over the weeks that followed, I put my energies into establishing my Citizens Aid Centre, publicizing the new office on television and stressing its independence and confidentiality. Soon, with a small secretarial staff, I was spending long afternoons dealing with grievances by telephone, letter, and in person. The problems ranged from the uncompensated expropriation of land to the boorish behaviour of Aztec soldiers in public houses. But although the work proved demanding and in its way fulfilling, I was disappointed by the relative mildness of the complaints; I had a suspicion that Maxixca, who had been left in charge during Extepan's absence, was somehow managing to keep more serious breaches of human rights from us.

Meanwhile, Kenneth Parkhouse's first parliament was about to begin sitting. It was given full television coverage and portrayed as the re-establishment of over a thousand years of English self-government after only a brief hiatus. Everything had been done to re-create as far as possible the grandeur and ambience of the pre-invasion parliaments, Richard even appearing to read out the government's proposals at the opening of parliament, as tradition dictated. These proposals included a rise in pensions and state benefit, a reduction in income tax and across the board pay rises of ten per cent. It was a blatant exercise in populism, and I wondered how many people realized that the extra expenditure on these measures would be derived from the complete extinction of the defence budget. From now on, the only army, navy and air force in the country would be Aztec.

Elsewhere, Extepan was also in the news, meeting with Matogee, the leader of the Sioux Confederacy, and his daughter in the neutral city of Potomac, where his territory met with that of Greater Mexico and New England. Gushing word-portraits were painted of Precious Cloud, a willowy girl of eighteen whose mother was a French-speaking aristocrat from Montreal. Potomac, its painted triangular skyscrapers and polyglot people reflecting two centuries of bustling mercantile existence between three often-warring powers, looked almost fairytale under a limpid early autumn sky. The people, in their feathered hats, rhinestone cloaks and big Texcoco cars, seemed exotic from afar, making London sedate and drab by comparison. Extepan was shown bowing to the princess and kissing her hand. They exchanged stilted conversation in English for the benefit of the cameras. Extepan seemed very far away.

Next day, it was announced that Richard would marry Xochinenen in mid-October, the day after his nineteenth birthday. Preparations began in earnest, hastened by Richard's declaration that he was going to marry his princess not in St Paul's or Westminster Abbey but in the Crystal Palace on Sydenham Hill, a favourite childhood haunt consecrated for royal marriages during the eccentric later years of my great-grandfather's reign. The palace had fallen into disrepair since it and its surrounding park were closed to the public in the aftermath of the invasion, but now an emergency programme of renovation was set in motion. Newspapers, magazines and the television channels were full of talk of the wedding, unstinting in their praise for Xochinenen, publishing poll after poll which showed that the great British public loved her too.

Across the Atlantic, another wedding took place – that of Extepan and Precious Cloud. After a formal courtship of only a month, they were married in Matogee's capital, Eagle Butte. The ceremony, shown live on television in the early hours of the morning, combined Mexican, Sioux and Christian rituals, the couple knotting the hems of their marriage robes and exchanging gifts before a shaman and a Catholic priest. Tetzahuitl stood among the dignitaries, attending for Motecuhzoma, who seldom left Tenochtitlan these days. Among the guests were Cheyenne and Mohawk princes, the Brazilian emperor, entourages from China, Japan and Peru. But it was the New English who made the most impact by dispatching both President Vidal and Vice-president Wolfe to the ceremony, funereally attired in black suits and stovepipe hats as a sartorial expression of their disapproval for the whole affair.

I watched the ceremony with mixed emotions, relieved to have escaped Extepan's designs on me but also regretting that I was now less likely to have his ear than in the past. Though I remained as opposed as ever to what he represented, I had grown to enjoy his company more than I was prepared to admit.

Not a day passed when I didn't think of Victoria, but there was no further news of her. Bevan no longer seemed to have the ear of any revolutionaries, and he gave me the impression that the resistance movement to Aztec rule was dormant, perhaps even extinct. He seemed to be biding his time, pottering about the balcony garden and apparently content to do little else.

Perhaps he shared my feeling of being reduced to a mere observer in events. When Xochinenen first arrived in London, I arranged an audience with her in the hope of gauging the sincerity of her feelings towards Richard. Now seventeen, she received me courteously enough but remained infuriatingly light-hearted, very much the older child rather than the young woman. She had been taking English lessons, and her command of the language was considerably improved, something I accepted as positive evidence of a degree of commitment to her prospective role as Queen of England. To all appearances, she was delighted at the prospect of marrying Richard and was thoroughly fond of him. I could not decide whether she genuinely lacked maturity or was already very accomplished at hiding her real feelings.

Extepan was still technically Governor of Britain, and a week before Richard's wedding we were told that he and Precious

Cloud would be returning to London to attend the ceremony, after which he would resume his duties. The news cheered me, because I had imagined that we were condemned to suffer Maxixca's over-zealous administration from now on. It also meant that I would, at least, have some continued access to him.

On the day before the wedding, I had the final fitting of my dress, an Eastwood creation which combined English silks with Tlacopan lace. Privately I thought it too elaborate, but on this occasion I was determined to play the part required of me in the ceremony.

Bevan appeared from the garden just as the leather-clad designer himself was putting the finishing touches to the dress.

'Very nice,' he observed. 'Pretty as a picture, as my mam would say.'

'Are you taking the mickey?'

'Wouldn't dream of it. An English rose without the thorns.'

'Don't you believe it.'

'Talking of roses, any chance of giving me a few minutes in the garden? Nasty case of black spot we've got.'

He obviously wanted to talk to me in private. Since Maxixca's security sweeps at the complex, we both operated on the assumption that our rooms might be monitored and never said anything confidential indoors.

I got rid of the dressmaker, changed into informal clothes, and went outside. The garden had flourished all summer under Bevan's attentions, and the mild autumn meant that buddleia and Michaelmas daisies were still attracting a variety of butterflies, among them New World monarchs, whose larvae Extepan had shipped to London from Mexico each spring – an indulgence typical of the Aztecs.

Bevan was perched on the balustrade at the edge of the balcony.

'What's up?' I said to him.

He was looking down towards the river, where a pleasure boat was carrying Mexican tourists up the Thames.

'You might not be interested in this,' he said, 'but I thought I'd mention it anyway, just in case.'

'What?'

'You'll be at the palace, tomorrow, for the wedding.'

'I'm well aware of that, Bevan.'

'There's a rumour going round.'

He was slouched against the rail, turning a blob of *tzictli* in his mouth.

'I'm listening,' I said.

'It may be nothing, but there's talk about the park. Word is, they've built something there, in the grounds near one of the lakes. Some sort of secret installation.'

I waited for more, but nothing further was forthcoming.

'What sort of secret installation?'

He shrugged. 'That's what nobody knows, do they? Might be worth taking a look, if you get the chance.'

Today he was dressed in a crimson-and-navy lumberjack shirt and an ancient pair of black barathea trousers. It was a balmy day, but he made few concessions to the weather – or to good grooming. He looked as if he had walked in off the street, a rather seedy character.

With little hope of an answer, I said, 'Bevan, who are you working for?'

He squinted at me in the hazy light. 'Work for you, don't I?'

'You know what I mean. All this time together, and you're still a mystery to me.'

'What you see is what I am.'

I sighed. 'Can I trust you?'

He cracked a pink bubble of gum. 'Never let you down yet, have I?'

'It's important for me to believe you're on my side.'

The gum squelched between his teeth. 'I've told you before – I've got a lot of time for you.'

'How gracious you are! Am I supposed to feel flattered?'

'Take it as you please. But if you've got to have a reason, then you can say I still owe you. You kept me out of it when Mad Mash found the disk. So I'm keeping you in the know about anything that crops us.'

As always, there was no sense at all that he was being deferential to my status. He treated everyone the same. I had grown to admire him for that, even when I found him blunt to the point of rudeness.

'This installation, as you call it. Do you think it's important?'

'I reckon the fact they want to keep it under wraps speaks for itself.'

'Then why run the risk of letting Richard marry in the palace, so close to it?'

'Popular sentiment,' he said emphatically. 'It's what he wants, and everyone's behind him at the moment. They'd risk drawing more attention to the place by refusing, wouldn't they? It'll be crawling with guards, no doubt, and you'll be lucky if you get a look in. But you stand a better chance than anyone else. It's worth a shot, if you're up for it.'

'And if I find anything interesting, what am I supposed to do? Report back to you?'

He pulled a string of gum out from between his teeth.

'Wouldn't do any harm, would it?'

Richard and Xochinenen were married in the central transept of the Crystal Palace at noon on a bright autumn morning; the wedding march was played on the great organ, a relic of Victorian days. I was seated at the front of the congregation with Extepan and his new bride. Earlier I had briefly been introduced to Precious Cloud, whom Extepan had christened Chalchi. She seemed rather overawed by the occasion, but friendly enough. Extepan kept her close to his side and paid solicitous attention to everything she said.

The ceremony was conducted by the Archbishop of Canterbury. In the weeks leading up to the wedding there had been considerable debate over whether the Aztecs would allow the primate of the Church of England to conduct the marriage of a Roman Catholic princess; but the controversy never came to a head since Xochinenen indicated that she and all her family were perfectly happy with an Anglican ceremony. Pope Leo, himself a Mexican, also gave his blessing.

The transept was thronged with guests, a sea of faces framed and compartmentalized by the freshly painted wrought-iron pillars and balustrades of Joseph Paxton's great creation. The palace had miraculously survived several fires since it was first built. It was now fully air-conditioned, and solar generators had been mounted atop its two water towers, providing constant power for heating, lighting and humidity. I had to admit it was a perfectly splendid place for a wedding.

Despite this, I sat through the service in a state of distraction, outwardly attentive but secretly wishing I were elsewhere. I think my years in hiding had given me less tolerance of state occasions than I once possessed, and it was hard to feel confident about Richard's future happiness while I remained convinced that his bride was simply an instrument in the political ambitions of Motecuhzoma's dynasty.

The ceremony was carried live on all six domestic channels, and the galleries were crammed with cameras, sound recording equipment and all the other paraphernalia of modern television. Foreign film crews from all the major nations were also covering the event, and I wondered if the *tlatoani* himself was watching from some private room in Chapultepec Castle at the very heart of the empire.

As I had expected, there was a heavy security presence, discreet within the palace itself but obvious outside, with armoured personnel carriers patrolling the environs and jet-copters hovering over the formal gardens which led down from the palace. I had no idea how I was going to attempt to locate Bevan's mysterious installation; but I was determined to try if the opportunity presented itself.

Despite all my cynicism, I must admit that Richard and Xochinenen looked a happy and well-matched couple, Richard the perfect model soldier in his Royal Guards' uniform, Xochinenen prettily petite in a traditional white English wedding dress. When the rings were exchanged and they finally kissed, the entire transept blazed with flashing lights, and I remember wondering if it was possibly the most photographed instant in history.

Because of the clement weather, a last-minute decision had been made to hold the reception outside on the terraces, and hordes of waiters served cold dishes and drinks while the guests mingled and made small talk among the lawns and flowerbeds. I was introduced to admirals, diplomats, members of the nobility from France and Germany, relatives of Xochinenen and Precious Cloud, financiers, businessmen, cinema celebrities – it went on and on. Very few of the most eminent British citizens and aristocrats were familiar to me from my father's days; those that had resisted the invasion had been purged by Nauhyotl after the conquest, and the new breed thrived precisely because they accepted Aztec rule.

And so the afternoon progressed in a wearying tide of pleasantries and platitudes while I gazed at the golden sunlight burnishing the curved glass panes of the palace, my mind entirely elsewhere. I remember that I was in conversation with the Chief Quipucamayoc of Peru when an Aztec guard came to my elbow and said, 'Excuse me, ma'am.'

I turned. It was Zacatlatoa.

'Please forgive me, Your Highness. Could you spare me a few moments? There's something that requires your attention.'

Under ordinary circumstances I would have needed no prompting to escape any further discussion of the potato harvest, but Zacatlatoa's arrival made it imperative. I immediately excused myself and followed him down the stone stairways towards one of the ornamental lakes. Beyond, numerous floaters were parked.

He turned to face me. 'I believe you requested a tour of the park. I understand you felt unwell and needed some air, an escape from the crowds. You asked me to take you on a brief flight around the park so that you could recover yourself.'

I blinked at him.

'Yes,' I said. 'Yes, that's right.'

He was a tall, sharp-nosed Aztec, hair greying at his temples. He spoke English excellently.

'I remember, when I was a child,' I heard myself saying, 'our nannies used to bring us here to see the stone dinosaurs and creatures around the lake. I wonder – are they still there?'

'Now would be a good time to see,' he replied, indicating one of the floaters.

There was a certain urgency in his voice. I knew Maxixca was overseeing the security arrangements in the park, and I hastily glanced around. But there was no sign of him. Guests still thronged the terraces, munching canapés and earnestly exchanging small-talk. There were thousands in sight, but it was as if Zacatlatoa and I were alone.

I nodded and climbed into the floater beside him, heedless of my fine dress. But then he paused, checking his wristwatch.

'What are we waiting for?' I asked.

'You will see.'

The words were hardly out when the tranquil day was shattered by a thunderous explosion. The whole of the central transept erupted, the force of the blast swiftly carrying a hot wind into our faces. Zacatlatoa was already taking off, turning the floater away as the crowds began to scream and retreat in panic from the rain of jagged glass and tangled metal. The transept was an inferno of flame and smoke.

'Wait!' I cried. 'Richard, the others—'

'Do you think this is a game?' He was looking dead ahead, steering the craft low over fountains and yew hedges, dropping down the brow of the hill. 'The King and his bride will have already left. The others must fend for themselves. There is no time for scruples now! We need your help.'

Desperately I strained back and saw the revellers streaming away as the fire raged higher and the skeletal structure began to cave in. Then we dropped down the brow of the hill and everything was lost from sight except for the billowing clouds of oily smoke.

'There,' Zacatlatoa said abruptly.

We were flying towards the Maze, in which I had got lost as a child. Beyond the ring of Lombardy poplars which enclosed it, half hidden by oak and sycamore near the Sydenham entrance to the park, I glimpsed an odd-looking conical tower rising from a cylindrical bunker-like building.

Zacatlatoa brought the floater down behind a dense stand of rhododendron. The towered building stood in front of a small lake, surrounded by electrified fencing. A pair of soldiers were on guard outside the gate, and just inside it was an armoured riot-wagon, two more soldiers scrambling across its slanting nose and into the cockpit. The gates swung open, and the riot-wagon sped off up the hill.

'Are we going in there?' I asked.

'Just wait,' he said fiercely.

He had a strong chin and high cheekbones, was too tall and rangy to be a Central Mexican.

'What's your interest in this?' I asked him.

'I'm Comanche,' he said simply.

It was answer enough. At the turn of the century, his people, a fiercely independent race who lived in Western Texas, had risen up against the rule of Motecuhzoma's grandfather, Xaltemoc. The emperor had responded by exterminating most of them, to the everlasting enmity of those who remained.

The moment the riot-wagon went out of sight, Zacatlatoa drove the floater down towards the gate. The guards were in position, their automatics at the ready. I began to feel frightened, ridiculously out of place in my expensive dress.

'Just follow my lead,' Zacatlatoa said to me as we pulled up outside the gate.

We clambered out.

'There's been an explosion at the palace,' Zacatlatoa told the guards in Nahuatl. 'I was ordered to take the Princess Catherine to a place of safety. You must evacuate the building immediately. There may be further devices.'

He spoke so urgently that the guards, already rattled, took him at his word. One of them raced inside, and soon half a dozen Aztecs, all in civilian clothes, emerged. They climbed into a transporter and drove away, obviously in great fear of their lives.

Now only the two guards at the gate remained. Zacatlatoa began to demand that they escort me to safety. This was too much for one of them, who insisted that they could not leave the installation unguarded. Zacatlatoa pulled his pistol from his holster and shot both men through the head.

I froze with horror. The pistol had sounded like a toy, but both guards slumped to the ground. They lay face down, their heads a mass of blood. Gore and brains had splattered Zacatlatoa's emerald uniform.

'Quickly,' he said. 'We have little time.'

He seized my wrist and hurried me up the path towards the entrance. Sickened and dazed, I had no power to resist him. One minute I had been exchanging inconsequentialities at my brother's wedding, the next I was witnessing two peremptory killings.

The building had a semi-circular entrance like a gaping mouth. It was decorated with concrete mouldings of wind and star and serpent reliefs, pagan images from prefabricated materials. Many were traditional symbols of Quetzalcoatl, the Aztec god of learning, others of his dark alter ego, Tezcatlipoca.

Zacatlatoa wrenched open the heavy doors. I scrambled after him up the steps, knowing he had needed me to gain access to the building but feeling that my trust had been rewarded with butchery.

Inside, it was cool and dim, recessed lights providing only a pale illumination as we hurried down a short corridor. The air felt still yet also alive. Soon I could hear a humming – the sound of power being generated.

The corridor opened out into a circular chamber, lit by a shaft of crystalline light from a window at the top of the tower. The walls were crammed with electronic equipment, power lines snaking from them to a dais at the centre of the chamber, upon which stood something unlike anything I had ever seen before.

Cautiously I climbed the steps of the dais, aware that the electric hum was growing louder with each step I took. In front of me stood a big upright concave mirror made of black glass or obsidian, surrounded by a bronzed frame embellished with more ancient motifs. Electric cables and fibre optics were embedded in its base. The atmosphere was resonantly still, and I had the strange feeling of being in a church devoted to the worship of some high technology which I could not hope to understand.

I moved closer to the mirror – or what I took to be a mirror. I could see no reflection in it but rather an absence of anything, as if it were a space, a *void*, rather than a surface. The nearer I drew and the harder I stared, the more it seemed that its centre, the very heart of its darkness, receded from me. I had the vertiginous feeling that if I went too close, crossed some threshold, it would suck me in, swallow me up, and I would be lost for ever. More frightened than I could say, I backed away from the mirror and stumbled down the steps.

'What is this place?' I asked.

Zacatlatoa had taken a miniature camera from his tunic and was busily taking photographs.

'Motecuhzoma's most prized and secret project,' he replied, still clicking away with the camera, pointing it at everything in sight. 'We want you to pass on these photographs to the Russians. I'll explain everything later.'

It was then we heard the sound of a jetcopter.

'Quickly!' I cried, panic rising in me.

Already I was moving towards the corridor, eager to be out of the place. Zacatlatoa followed hesitantly, still furiously taking photographs.

'Come on!' I shouted.

Still he continued photographing. I fled down the corridor.

The jetcopter was directly overhead as I ran towards the gates, so low that its exhaust tore at my hair and dress. Because I was immediately underneath it, its crew did not apparently see me as I darted across the road and up the bank, scrambling for the safety of the bushes.

Crouched low, I peered through the shrubbery. Zacatlatoa was hurrying down the driveway, but the copter had turned, spotted him. He paused outside the gate and raised his hands, as if in a wave. The copter unleashed a gout of *xihautl*, the fireball consuming him where he stood.

I reeled back from the heat of the blast. Then, in a mad panic, I scurried away through the undergrowth, branches and brambles lacerating my dress, dirt and leaf debris smearing my hands and knees.

I kept to the shrubbery, making sure that there was plenty of foliage to hide me from the still circling jetcopter. I felt sick with horror and fright. Gradually the sound of the copter grew more distant. Then I was out of the undergrowth and teetering across a grassy space towards one of the lower rose gardens. Suddenly I was caught up in the disorderly retreat of the wedding guests from the still-blazing palace on the top of the hill.

Bevan brought a dish of beef consommé to my table in the garden. I had been ordered to rest in bed for a few days but had suffered only scratches.

I had already given Bevan a detailed account of the conical building, which I called the Quetzalcoatl structure for want of a better description. He claimed to know nothing of Zacatlatoa and to be as mystified as I about the building's purpose.

Bevan looked unusually sombre as he set the tray down on the table.

'Is something wrong?' I asked.

'Governor's here to see you,' he replied.

Extepan was already standing on the path. He approached and drew up a chair opposite me while Bevan retreated inside.

'Forgive my unannounced visit,' he said, taking my hand and kissing it. 'I hope you are feeling better.'

'Much better,' I told him.

He appeared to have readily accepted my explanation that I had been caught up in the flight from the burning palace and thrown into the bushes. No one had apparently seen me leave the reception with Zacatlatoa, and there had been no mention of the killing of the guards and the break-in at the Quetzalcoatl structure. I could hardly believe I had been so lucky, given the grim circumstances. Three men were dead, yet I had escaped practically unscathed.

'How is Maxixca?' I asked.

I could not keep a certain relish out of my voice. Remarkably, no one had died in the fire at the palace, but Maxixca had been knocked down a stairway by a high-pressure hose while supervising the fire-fighting operations.

'Recovering,' Extepan told me. 'I think the worst injury was to his dignity.'

I smiled at this. 'We were all very lucky. Is the palace completely destroyed?'

'It's too soon to say whether reconstruction will be feasible.'

'Have you arrested the culprits?'

He eyed me curiously, then said, 'We have certain leads which we are following.'

'Would you mind if I ate my soup while we talk? I so hate it when it goes cold.'

Extepan motioned for me to carry on.

He was silent for a while. I gave him another smile, as if to say I sympathized with all his problems. It is usually when we feel most smug that nemesis strikes.

'There is something else,' Extepan said.

'Oh?'

'I came to see you not only to find out how you were, but also because I have some rather grave news.'

I put my spoon down.

'You have a family connection, so I thought it better that you heard the news directly from me.'

'What news?'

'You're aware that for some time we have been in dispute with the Russian government over the precise extent of its borders.'

I went cold.

'Königsburg, Moldavia, Georgia – all these have proved problematical. In recent months our allies have suffered numerous frontier violations by Soviet troops, and last night border posts in Brest-Litovsk and the Caucasus were fired upon—'

'Spare me the propaganda, Extepan. What are you trying to say?'

'An ultimatum was given. It has been ignored. Consequently, one hour ago our armies under Chimalcoyotl launched an attack on Russia.'

PART THREE

The Serpent of Fire

One

The November fog was lifting as Mia and Chicomeztli led Adamant and Archimedes out of the stables. I mounted Archimedes while they helped Precious Cloud up into Adamant's saddle, both taking care not to put pressure on the swell of her belly.

While Mia checked Adamant's bridle one last time, Chicomeztli scuttled over to me and muttered, 'Forgive me, but is this wise?'

'Is what wise?' I asked.

'Riding. In her condition.'

'She's been riding most days for the last year or so.'

'She has only a month left of her term.'

I shrugged. 'It's what she wants. It raises her spirits.'

'Extepan is concerned.'

'So he should be. She hasn't been happy.'

It was quite unlike Chicomeztli to be so fretful, but he had been mindful of Precious Cloud ever since she became pregnant. During much of her term, Extepan had been away, visiting Channel and North Sea ports both in Britain and on the Continent to ensure that supply convoys departed promptly for the Baltic. The northern group of the Aztec armies had been besieging St Petersburg for the past six months.

I led Archimedes over to Precious Cloud.

'Are you ready?' I asked.

She nodded, smiling for the first time that morning.

The mist had risen, leaving the grass drenched with dew. There was a cool, washed smell to the air, and I could see that Adamant was frisky. Precious Cloud touched her heels to his side, and he was off, leaving me to hurry Archimedes after them.

I had no fears for the princess's safety. Precious Cloud was an even more expert rider than Victoria, and I had readily agreed to exchange Adamant for Archimedes as my mount. She continually spoke to the horse in Dakota and French as we rode, soothing him and making him utterly compliant. When I first suggested the idea of going riding together, she had seized on the opportunity; since her arrival in London, and especially since she became pregnant, she had seemed lonely. I suspected she was homesick.

We rode around the perimeter of the park, jumping low beech hedges, leaping narrow ornamental ponds, and generally treating the place as our own private preserve – which it had in effect become.

We slowed to a trot along the Embankment bridleway. The Thames was filled with motorboats and minesweepers, and the Aztec cruiser *Cacama* was moored downriver just beyond the complex, its great winter-camouflaged bulk festooned with radar dishes and rocket launchers. Military floaters and jetcopters traversed the sky.

Precious Cloud and I paused near the park gates. Beyond the railings, a gaggle of Mayan tourists were taking photographs of the derelict Big Ben, its hands stopped at seven-twenty-five, an inverted V for victory.

Precious Cloud untied her fur cloak. There was a keen breeze off the river, but she was used to far colder winters in her homeland.

'It's so good to ride,' she remarked. 'I feel as if I'm escaping everything then.'

She looked painfully unhappy. I remarked on the fact.

'I feel trapped here,' she admitted. 'I'm bored, Catherine. I miss my people.'

It was the first time she had spoken directly about her feelings. She seemed small and young to me then, a child forced to have surrendered the comforts of home too swiftly.

'Why don't you suggest to Extepan that you both visit your father?' I said.

'I asked him that,' she replied. 'But he's too busy with the war.'

I wasn't entirely surprised. Though possessing superior equipment and firepower, the Aztecs had found the Russian Empire far from easy to subdue. The climate, terrain and sheer weight of forces which Tsar Mikhail could muster had slowed their advance on the European front so that they had failed to take Moscow and St Petersburg before the onset of winter. Only in the south-east had they made progress, thrusting through the Ukraine towards the Volga, where Chimalcoyotl was hoping to link his armies with those of Ixtlilpopoca, who had invaded from China and Tibet, sweeping through Siberia over the past year. Though I knew Margaret was safe in Moscow, I had received no direct word from her since the invasion began, and I feared greatly for her continuing safety.

Adamant was restless. Precious Cloud tugged on his rein, turning him full circle until she was facing me again.

'It's unfortunate the war is distracting him,' I said. 'I know he's concerned for your welfare.'

'Is he?' She almost pouted. 'I'm not so sure. Can he care so much for me when he still keeps that other woman at his side?'

I peered at her. 'Do you mean Mia?'

She seemed to shiver. 'I cannot fathom her. She is so distant and cold.'

She had never referred to Mia before, although she spent more time with her than anyone else. Mia was in attendance wherever she went.

'She was his consort before he married me, wasn't she?'

I had always presumed as much, without ever asking anyone. Housekeeper? Companion? *Auianime?* Mia seemed to combine all these roles.

'I'm sure there's nothing between them now,' I said. 'Extepan is the kind of man who would take his marriage vows seriously.'

I think I believed this, even though the Aztec nobility in general were quite polygamous, none more so than the *tlatoani* himself, who had fathered two dozen children by his subsidiary wives. The Papacy had been encouraged to sanctify the status of these wives forty years before; and yet Extepan had made a point of specifying in his marriage ceremony that he eschewed all intimate relations with other women. His mother had always been a strictly orthodox Catholic, I knew, refusing to accept the status of Motecuhzoma's subsidiary wives after they were married; his own monogamy would be a tribute to her.

'I feel she watches me all the time,' Precious Cloud said. 'She watches me but says nothing.'

'I'm sure she's not spying on you. She's just used to serving in silence.'

'Did you know they were close as children?'

I nodded.

'Then there must be things between them that I will never know.'

Her face was drawn with anxiety, and I began to wonder if this was more than a simple case of low spirits. I tried to put myself in her place – young, unused to the pressures of the court, unhappy in a crowded country filled with strangers, attended by an aloof housemaid who had a prior relationship, perhaps even intimacy, with her absentee husband.

'Try not to worry,' I said softly. 'I'll have a word with Mia—'

'No! I don't want her to know any of this. I feel she tries to read my mind enough as it is.'

Ponderously she shifted her position in the saddle. Her bulge was prominent, making the rest of her body look wasted in comparison.

'Come,' she said, turning Adamant. 'Let's ride.'

Bevan was in his apartment, watching television. On the screen, tanks were rolling across a muddy landscape and a commentator was announcing that Aztec armies under Ixtlilpopoca had just taken Astrakhan on the Volga delta and would soon link up with those in the Western Front, dealing a final crushing blow to their enemies.

'Looks like it's all up for the Russians,' Bevan remarked.

I was angered by the casualness of his tone. Sharply I said, 'Have you been sitting here all morning?'

Slouched in his armchair, he turned his head in my direction, looking both quizzical and wary.

Immediately I relented. 'I'm sorry. But I can't contemplate the war without thinking about Margaret and her children.'

The commentator began a panegyric about the bravery and

steadfastness of the Mexican armies and the nobility of their cause. Bevan levelled the remote and blanked the picture.

'Excuse my manners,' he said, for once sounding genuinely regretful. 'For what it's worth, I'm not exactly thrilled at the prospect neither.'

He got up and went off to fetch my lunch.

Over the past year, there had been little friction between us and no hint of skulduggery on his part. Since the war in Russia had begun, security at home had been tightened, and everyone seemed to be lying low. Bevan's contacts with the underground appeared to have lapsed, and we had made no progress in discovering the purpose of the Quetzalcoatl structure. Bevan claimed to have been as surprised as I by the bomb at the Crystal Palace, and he continued to insist that he had never had any contact with Zacatlatoa or any other pro-English Aztecs at the complex. In the complex itself, everyone was preoccupied with the invasion, and domestic concerns took second place, at least on the surface.

Yet I continued to wonder about the building in the park. Why the religious motifs, when inside it had an obviously technological function? Were they mere ornamentation, or did they have some more sinister meaning? To me, the Aztecs, courteous and correct though they usually were, seemed to retain a secret life which was hidden from outsiders. How much devotion did they retain to their pre-Christian heritage, with all its horrific trappings?

Of course it was hard to imagine diabolic rituals taking place in secret at Richard's court: there was no evidence of it whatsoever. It was the same in the countryside at large. While there were occasional reports from fearful locals about night-time ceremonies at Aztec garrisons, no specific details ever emerged – or if they did, they proved innocuous: a drunken birthday, the feast of a saint, victory for the Mexican football team in the Columbus Cup. Typically Aztec soldiers held Catholic services in sequestered churches or in chapels at their barracks, so their religious observances were to a large degree private. There was nothing but rumour and hearsay about less Christian behaviour, and informed opinion dismissed such stories as the febrile inventions of popular superstition.

In fact, though it pained me in some ways to admit it, the country was generally tranquil, despite the upheavals elsewhere. Extepan's governorship continued to be characterized by moderation and restraint. Local civil courts had been re-established, the police force was once again fully operational, and the occupying Aztec armies tended to keep themselves aloof from all affairs that did not involve military or security matters. The province – for that is what it had become – was settled, and people seemed accepting of the new order.

I viewed all these developments with a resigned dismay. I continued to miss Victoria greatly – my friendship with Precious Cloud was an obvious substitute – but I tried to busy myself in what work I could accomplish. That previous summer I had toured Scotland. Deprivation was rife there in the aftermath of Maxixca's onslaught, but Extepan accepted many of my proposals for emergency action, and even went further than I had expected by agreeing to establish a Scottish Assembly to oversee the reconstruction of the country. Though I knew there was a sense in which my involvement only added further legitimacy to Aztec rule, I felt it was the only thing I could do.

Meanwhile, across the Irish Sea, while the rest of the world was focused on the Aztec invasion of Russia, Maxixca had moved swiftly from Ulster to complete a summer's conquest of the whole of Ireland, hitherto a neutral power. He was promptly installed as governor, and proceeded to impose his authority with uncompromising force, suppressing all forms of dissent with such violence that the Primate of All Ireland actually appealed to the Pope for clemency. Needless to say, his protests were ignored, enabling Maxixca to boost his reputation as a military leader with an authoritative style of governance which was certain to appeal to conservative opinion in Tenochtitlan. Though the Irish people had my deepest sympathies, I was relieved he was gone from London.

Extepan's new second-in-command was a Caucasoid Aztec from the Louisiana province of Greater Mexico called Iztacaxayauh. He had British ancestry on his mother's side and declared himself an anglophile. As acting governor during Extepan's absences, he proved himself Extepan's man, continuing the policies of social reform and minimal Aztec interference in domestic affairs of state.

Under any other circumstances, the conquest of Ireland would have dominated the attentions of the media, but it was treated as a mere sideshow to the campaigns in Russia. Tsar Mikhail's empire, which had once stretched from the Balkans to the Aleutian Islands, was now reduced to the heartland of the Russian peoples west of the Urals. True, this was where most of the empire's industrial and military power was still concentrated, and the Russian armies had shown great resilience in fighting back after several major defeats; but it was hard to imagine the empire surviving much longer. And if it fell, there was little to stand in the way of global Aztec domination.

That evening there was a formal dinner at the complex to welcome the new Japanese ambassador to Britain. Japan, long a vassal state of the Aztecs, was important strategically and economically as a producer of high-quality electronic equipment for the empire. But I chose to attend the dinner less for diplomatic reasons than for the opportunity to talk informally with Extepan, whom I seldom saw these days.

Richard and Xochinenen were also present at the dinner, though not Precious Cloud, whom Extepan announced was suffering from fatigue and confined to her bed. Richard and Xochinenen continued to give every appearance of being happy together, though rumours persisted that the marriage had not been consummated. Over the past year, Xochinenen had grown from being a girl into a young woman. She favoured European dress, had mastered English and remained popular with the British public, as did Richard, whose lack of pomp and circumstance endeared him to everyone.

I bided my time until the dinner was over and we retired for coffee and cognac. It was Extepan who approached me, complimenting me on my dress and saying it had been too long since we had last spoken.

'I need to talk to you now,' I said bluntly.

He allowed me to draw him aside so that no one else could overhear.

'I'm worried about Precious Cloud,' I told him.

'Ah,' he said, staring into his brandy glass. 'Everyone seems concerned about her these days.'

'Aren't you?'

'Of course. I know she's been unhappy. I think the burden of carrying our child has weighed very heavily on her. Her doctors are monitoring her condition very closely.'

'Doctors can only do so much. She needs help from *you* most of all. You've got to support her, encourage her, make her feel . . .' I searched for a suitable word, '. . . cherished.'

He looked at me. 'Don't you think I've been trying to do these things, Catherine?'

'She's lonely,' I told him. 'Homesick. She needs reassurance. She needs to see her family. You should try to take her away for a while after the baby's born.'

'I'm well aware of that. I assure you I've been doing what I can. But the campaign in Russia – it takes up so much of my time. I wish it were otherwise, but I have obligations which go beyond those of a husband.'

It was easier to talk candidly to him now we saw less of one another, now that he had Precious Cloud.

'She's also concerned about Mia,' I said.

A frown.

'She asked me not to say anything, but I feel I must. She thinks Mia's spying on her.' I paused. 'She thinks there's still something between you two.'

'That's ridiculous,' he said immediately. 'I've been completely faithful to her.'

Feeling disingenuous, I said, 'I'm sure you have. But I don't think she's comfortable with the fact that you retained Mia in your household.'

He looked perplexed. 'I'm her patron. Should I tell her to leave because I've taken a wife? That isn't our way, Catherine.'

'I know that. You don't have to justify it to me. But perhaps you should try to explain it to Precious Cloud. She's young, Extepan, insecure. She needs to feel she's not isolated from you.'

He shook his head somewhat wistfully. 'Ah, my Chalchi. She's such a delicate flower.'

'She also hates that name. She told me today, when we were

riding together. It's a Nahuatl name, not hers. It just makes her feel that her life isn't her own any longer.'

'I had no idea. She never spoke of it.'

'That's why I'm telling you now.'

He was silent for a while. We were standing alone, and he put his face close to mine and said quietly: 'Do you know what I wish, Catherine? I wish she had just a little of your spirit.'

With this, he crossed the room to speak to the ambassador's Mexican wife.

I was conscious of meddling in matters that were strictly no business of mine. But Precious Cloud's vulnerability reminded me of Victoria, and I was by nature meddlesome. I think also I relished any opportunity to let Extepan know I still intended to make my presence felt. I wanted to continue to make an impression on him.

I stood near the french windows. It was raining outside, and rivulets of water snaked down the glass. If I focused beyond it, I could see London lit up in the wet darkness, a city continuing with its business despite the tide of war in the east; focusing on the glass itself, I saw the reflections of all the people in the room, well groomed and impeccably mannered, engrossed at that moment in their individual social exchanges. Everything descended in the end to the personal and the private: that was what shaped history, and things to come.

Extepan stood near the door, still talking to the ambassador's wife, serious and handsome, intent on her every word. It was impossible to dislike him, harder still not to admire what he had achieved under the circumstances. I tried to imagine a world in which we had met in a different way, in different roles entirely.

Behind him, a terminal stood in an alcove, its screen blank. I could no longer see one without thinking of ALEX and wondering what had gone wrong. He had been categorical that there was to be no Aztec invasion of Russia, and yet it had happened. Bevan had suggested that the Aztecs may have managed to infiltrate ALEX and plant false information. I couldn't accept this. It was hard to explain why, but I was sure I would have *known* somehow if ALEX had been subverted. Something in his manner would have told me.

Mindful of my social obligations, I turned away from the window. To my dismay, I saw Kenneth Parkhouse approaching.

I had managed to avoid him over dinner, but now he seemed intent on engaging me in conversation. But at that moment Chicomeztli arrived, looking positively alarmed. He spoke urgently to Extepan, whose expression grew grave. Immediately I detached myself from Parkhouse and went over to them.

'Not now, Catherine,' Extepan said sharply, waving me away.

'What is it?' I said. 'Is it Precious Cloud?'

'No, no,' he replied. 'It's nothing to do with her. I can't discuss it at the moment.'

He proceeded to announce his apologies to everyone.

'A serious situation has arisen which requires my immediate attention,' he informed us. 'You must excuse me.'

He exited hurriedly, leaving us all wondering what the emergency could possibly be. Then Kenneth Parkhouse sidled up to me.

'I believe I know what's happened,' he said in a whisper which seemed to imply a ghastly camaraderie between us.

I couldn't bring myself to express curiosity; but he was determined to be the bearer of the news.

'It's most serious,' he said. 'The details are rather sparse at present, but I gather Mexican forces have suffered a severe reversal in the east.'

I was forced to look at him. He pursed his lips, apparently in concern. But I was certain he relished being the bearer of grim tidings.

'Apparently there's been a massive retaliation by the Russians on the Volga. They appear to have exploded a new kind of bomb.'

His bespectacled eyes twinkled; I had never found him more odious.

'What sort of bomb?'

'A bomb powerful enough to obliterate a whole city, by all accounts. Of course, the news is only just trickling in, and the situation is quite confused. It seems to have been dropped on Tsaritsyn, annihilating the Mexican armies there. I understand the Russians timed it to coincide with a victory parade at which both commanders were present.'

'Chimalcoyotl and Ixtlilpopoca?'
Parkhouse nodded gravely.
'They're dead?'
'If they were in the city, it seems likely they were vaporized.'

Two

The woman was pale, dressed in an olive-green gaberdine that had seen better days. She sat down at the table, murmuring her thanks to me for seeing her, already apologizing for taking up my time.

'It's perfectly all right,' I assured her. 'That's why I'm here. To try to help.'

'It seems trivial, bringing this to a princess.'

I met her faltering gaze. 'What?'

She began rummaging in her battered leather shoulder bag. 'It's my youngest son, you see. Richard. We named him after your brother, the King. My husband was a great royalist—'

'Was?'

'He got killed on Salisbury Plain in the fighting. Near Stonehenge, they told me.'

One of the main battles during the invasion had taken place there, the Aztecs annihilating our southern armies.

The woman had a Liverpudlian accent. I wondered if her husband had been in the army but did not ask in case of embarrassment, having posed similar questions on other occasions only to find that the deceased were innocent civilians, conscientious objectors or even collaborators shot by our own people.

I saw from her notes that her name was Cynthia and that she had four children, the youngest twelve years old.

'Did you come to London today?'

'Oh, no. We've lived in Ealing these last twenty years or more.'

'Are you managing? Financially, I mean.'

'We get by.' She pushed a hand through her straw-blonde

hair. 'John was over-age, but he insisted on doing something, so they put him in the medical corps because things were desperate. He was hit by shrapnel, friendly fire they said. The army was very good about it. I got a pension, and my eldest son's working part-time. But I'm worried about what my youngest's being taught in school.'

She had produced an exercise book which she opened in front of me. 'See? This is the sort of thing they're learning them these days.'

There was a history essay entitled 'The Decline of the British Empire', written in a sprawling adolescent hand. I read it through. The boy, obviously under this teacher's guidance, had enumerated ten reasons for the collapse of British power in the 1930s and 1940s. These ranged from racist policies towards the Boers in South Africa and the Muslims in India to the enlightened support for freedom fighters provided by the Mexican government in areas under British control. Aztec armies had been 'invited' into these regions by nationalist movements to supplant the hated British rule.

'If you ask me,' Cynthia was saying, 'it's a load of old twaddle. They're indoctrinating him, making out we were rubbish and them like knights on white chargers. That's not what I learnt in school.'

One of my assistants came up and asked her if she wanted a cup of tea.

'Please,' she said eagerly. 'Milk and two sugars.'

It was hot in the crowded hall, and there were plenty of people still waiting their turn. The central office of the Aid Centre was located in the complex but we had set up a clinic in a defunct cinema near Marble Arch. I visited it twice a week, sitting at a long table on the stage with various advisers and helpers while our petitioners occupied the stalls. Chicomeztli had also set up a soup kitchen in the foyer, and this attracted the most crowds, passersby often walking in simply to avail themselves of the free fare provided by such commercial outfits as MexTaco, obviously as a public-relations exercise.

On most accounts I felt compromised and ineffectual at the clinic. More people came during my visits, many simply to gawp or talk with 'a Royal', relatively few with serious complaints. In addition, security was always very tight when I was present, armed guards and private detectives creating an atmosphere of tension and suspicion by searching people before they were allowed near me. None of my protests had any effect, Extepan insisting that it was essential I be protected from lunatics or zealots. It was plain to me that my attempts to have a normal dialogue with the citizens of the country would be frustrated either by the security forces or by the people themselves. I was a prisoner of my status.

This, however, was a real and serious complaint by a woman who was not prepared to let her awe of me get the better of her. It was not the first example of Aztec interference in the school curriculum I had encountered, the general thrust of the new history syllabus apparently being to eliminate any sort of criticism of their role in world affairs.

'Even the teachers reckon it's rubbish,' Cynthia was saying, 'but they have to do as they're told. I don't think it's right.'

'I agree,' I said, reaching for my pen and notepad. 'Perhaps you can give me full details, including your name and the address of your son's school.'

But before she could speak, all the sounds in the hall were drowned by a huge explosion outside.

The stalls swiftly emptied as people hurried towards the exit. Escorted by my guards and murmuring my apologies to Cynthia, I followed them.

It was the Excelsior Hotel at the end of Piccadilly that was ablaze. One half of its baroque façade had collapsed, and people were screaming and fleeing in disorder from the smoke and flames. Policemen and Aztec soldiers were vainly attempting to marshal the surging crowds as traffic began to pile up on both sides of the street.

The Excelsior was a favourite haunt of visiting Aztecs and had recently undergone a refurbishment to suit their tastes, steambaths and, doubtless, *auianime* having been installed there. But as the air filled with the sound of fire engine and ambulance sirens, it was shoppers and hotel staff whom I saw being carried dead or maimed from the carnage.

I rushed across and did what I could to help. This mostly entailed giving orders to my escort to help with crowd control or stretcher-bearing while I myself was continually kept away from the more gruesome aspects of the carnage. A princess of the realm cannot be allowed to bloody her hands and muck in with the common folk, even if all her instincts tell her she must.

I managed to arrange for the less seriously wounded to be temporarily housed in the cinema, and I was allowed to linger among the wreckage and blood until the press had arrived and taken suitable photographs of me at the scene. Then I was hurriedly shepherded to safety. As my Rolls was driven away, I glimpsed Cynthia, standing alone and bewildered in the middle of the rubble-strewn street, her son's exercise book still clutched in her hand.

At breakfast the following morning, Bevan put a batch of newspapers down in front of me. My photograph was on the front page of all the tabloids, and there were headlines such as KATE AT THE CARNAGE, PRINCESS OF PERIL, CATHERINE THE GREAT!

'This is embarrassing,' I said, scanning the lurid stories accompanying the pictures.

'You're the heroine of the hour,' Bevan remarked drily.

'I didn't do anything much. They wouldn't let me.'

'You mean to say you didn't single-handedly save the day?'

I ignored his sarcasm, my attention already drawn by the weightier reports in the broadsheets.

'What's this?' I remarked. 'They're claiming the Excelsior was destroyed by a Russian missile.'

'Know different, do you?'

Bevan was slurping a mug of tea and leafing through the *News Chronicle*.

'It was a bomb, Bevan, I'm sure it was. The whole frontage of the hotel had caved in, but I couldn't see any damage to the roof. A missile would have hit it from the top, surely?'

'Sounds reasonable.'

'Then why pretend otherwise?'

He turned a page. 'It would suit them, wouldn't it? Make the Russians into everybody's enemies, not just theirs.'

I switched on the television. Here the story was even more elaborate. The Russians had launched not one but several long-range missiles at London, the others having been shot down by

Aztec defensive systems over the North Sea. It was fortunate the missile that had hit carried only conventional explosives.

'I don't believe a word of this,' I said. 'It's propaganda of the basest sort. The Excelsior was destroyed by a bomb that was probably planted by English partisans.'

I was watching Bevan as I spoke, seeing if he knew anything. But, as usual, his face gave nothing away.

'What do you think?' I asked him.

'I think you'd better eat up those crumpets before they go cold.'

Extepan was ensconced with his staff in a briefing room, and I was surprised when he came out to see me.

I began to complain about the media coverage of the Excelsior's destruction, but I could see he was preoccupied. I had not forgotten that he had lost both his elder brothers at Tsaritsyn – a disaster given only minimal coverage in the press – so I paused.

'Catherine,' he said, 'I'm afraid I have more urgent matters to attend to. Shortly, I shall be leaving London.'

I think I had half anticipated this.

'For Russia?'

He nodded. 'The Revered Speaker has ordered me to take command of our armies there. I leave at dawn tomorrow.'

Three

Three weeks before Christmas, at ten o'clock in the morning, Precious Cloud went into labour. Chicomeztli arrived in haste at my suite to announce the news and also to ask if I would attend the birth.

'Me?' I said. 'What use would I be? I'm no midwife.'

'She wants you. She begged me to ask you to come.'

I accompanied him to the hospital, which was on a lower floor of the complex. Precious Cloud lay in a large private room, surrounded by all the paraphernalia of modern medicine – ECGs, drips, oxygen cylinders, a contour bed which was supposed to shape itself to her every movement and so provide constant back support. Extepan's personal physician, a grey-haired Otomi called Yeipanitl, was overseeing her labour, along with three nurses and Mia, who stood at her shoulder, stroking her forehead with slender fingers. The contrast between Precious Cloud's look of panic and Mia's total impassiveness made me think that perhaps Precious Cloud was right and that what I had always assumed was a serenity in Mia was simply an absence of feeling.

Precious Cloud, already wide-eyed and frightened even though her contractions had only just begun, gripped me fiercely by the wrist and said, 'Catherine, I thought you wouldn't come!'

I took her hand in mine. 'Don't worry. Everything's going to be all right.'

Not surprisingly, my platitudes did nothing to dispel her anxiety. I thought of the baby I had lost – a baby I scarcely knew I was carrying before it was gone for ever. This was not going to be easy for me.

'Please,' Precious Cloud said. 'Ask them all to go.'

'They can't,' I said soothingly. 'Someone qualified has to be here to help you.'

'Just for a while. I need to talk with you alone.'

I looked at Yeipanitl.

'No problem,' he said in English. 'You can have a little time together – it's early days yet. But naturally it's important we closely monitor her throughout her labour.'

'Of course,' I said.

Mia showed no reaction to Precious Cloud's request. She withdrew with the others, closing the door behind her.

'They talk as if I'm not here,' Precious Cloud said. 'I think the baby is all that matters to them.'

'Of course it isn't,' I assured her.

She gripped my wrist again. 'Make her go away, Catherine. I want you here, not her.'

I knew she meant Mia.

'I think she's only trying to help. She doesn't have to be here.'

'Then send her away. She's watching me! All the time she's watching me. I think she's hoping something will go wrong. I can't bear it!'

The bed bulged outwards as she arched her back. I put my arms around her. She had begun to sob, and I waited until she was calmer.

'It's all right,' I said softly. 'Don't worry. I'll see to it.'

She cried out as another contraction came. I held both her hands, and she pushed against them. Afterwards, she slumped back and closed her eyes. For the moment, she seemed calmer. I rose and went to the door.

'You will come back, won't you?' she said from the bed.

'As soon as I can,' I promised.

Outside, I spoke privately to Yeipanitl. 'Is she going to be all right?'

'All the vital signs are normal,' he replied. 'She's young and fit. I don't anticipate any problems.'

'She's asked me to stay with her.'

'I think that would be a good idea, if it doesn't inconvenience you.'

'Not at all. Just get ready to catch me if I pass out when it gets gruesome.'

He smiled at this, then returned to Precious Cloud's room.

I stopped Mia at the doorway from following the nurses in.

'Can I have a word with you?' I said in Nahuatl.

She merely blinked at me; but she allowed me to lead her a short distance along the corridor. Then she surprised me by saying, 'She doesn't want me there, does she?'

'She's very vulnerable at the moment,' I replied.

'Of course,' she said matter-of-factly. 'I have many other duties to attend to.'

She made to move away; I caught her by the arm.

'Mia . . .' I began, unsure what I was going to say. 'I think perhaps she's a little bit afraid – or rather, in awe, of you.'

I suppose I was hoping for some sort of real human reaction to this, something which would allow me to gauge her feelings. But again nothing was visible on the surface.

'I find that hard to imagine,' she replied in the same flat tone as before. 'She's a princess. I'm merely trying to serve her. What reason would she have to fear me?'

I wondered what to say. 'I think perhaps she needs friends more than servants at the moment.'

I meant to suggest that she herself might try to show a warmer side to Precious Cloud, but she took it quite differently.

'I understand,' she said. 'I don't wish to do anything to make her uncomfortable. Perhaps you could inform me when the child is born.'

Again she made to move away. I hastily decided that indiscretion was the better part of valour.

'Mia, did Extepan ever ask you to marry him?'

She closed her eyes in a slow blink, as if wishing me vanished. Very reluctantly, she said, 'That would not have been appropriate.'

'Do you wish he had?'

She turned her head away from me without moving any other part of her body. Obviously she did not want to talk about it, but at the same time she was too dutiful to refuse to answer.

'It's always been my role to serve him in whatever way he wishes. I've never expected anything more than this.'

'I find that hard to believe.'

'As Your Highness wishes. I do not feel it's correct that we should be discussing this when his wife is soon to give birth to his child.'

'You're not his slave. You must have needs and desires of your own.'

She looked through me. 'My duties have always been honourable ones. They have accorded my family high status.'

'I wasn't suggesting otherwise. But that can't be the whole of your life, existing merely to attend Extepan. This is the twentieth century. I can't believe that anyone would willingly devote themselves utterly to another person's life without thought or feeling for their own.'

Again the slow blink, like that of a teacher who could not credit a child's stupidity. Of course I was overstating the case, in the hope of breaching the wall of her reserve.

'Your Highness will excuse the impertinence,' she said, 'but possibly that shows how little you understand us.'

Precious Cloud gave birth to a son at two thirty in the afternoon, Yeipanitl having decided to cut short her labour and perform a Caesarian after drugs failed to blunt her agitation. The baby promptly emptied his bladder in the lap of one of the nurses, to the amusement of everyone present. He weighed eight and a half pounds, and looked strong and healthy.

Precious Cloud woke from her drug-induced sleep soon afterwards. The baby, swathed in white linen, was immediately placed in the crook of her arm. She began talking to him in Dakota, and he promptly fell asleep.

Precious Cloud looked exhausted but delighted. I smiled and said, 'I think it was worth it in the end, don't you? He's marvellous.'

She nodded. 'I wonder when Extepan will see him.'

Both Extepan and Maxixca had been dispatched to the Russian front soon after the disaster at Tsaritsyn, Maxixca as Extepan's second-in-command. A total news black-out on the war had prevailed since the disaster, and we had received no word of him.

'I'm sure they'll make it a priority to see he gets to hear about it,' I said. 'What are you going to call him?'

She drew the child closer to her. 'Extepan wants Cuauhtemoc.'

It was a popular royal name which meant 'Descending Eagle'.

The first Cuauhtemoc, a *tlatoani* in the sixteenth century, had been greatly instrumental in establishing the basis of a modern state by defeating the last of the conquistador armies while at the same time giving freedom of entry to missionaries so that his people could profit from European knowledge. The empire owed as much to the civilizing effects of Spanish culture as it did to Aztec prowess at war.

Precious Cloud began to stroke the baby's cheek with her forefinger.

'I'm going to give him a name too,' she said. 'A secret name, for myself and him alone.'

She was peering rapturously at the baby now, and it seemed as if she wanted to exclude everyone else from their closeness.

Yeipanitl came to my side and said, 'I think perhaps we should leave them both to sleep.'

I nodded.

'I have to go,' I said to Precious Cloud.

She was intent on the baby and did not reply.

I withdrew, and found Chicomeztli waiting for me outside the door.

'Word has come from Extepan,' he announced.

'Oh?' I said. 'How is he?'

'There was no personal news of him. The message was relayed through military channels. He has asked that we evacuate the complex and leave London. In case of enemy attack.'

Four

Each morning the frost-rimed grass looked like peppermint icing as I rode Archimedes or Adamant around the grounds of the estate. Sometimes I was accompanied by Richard and Xochinenen, who stayed with us for a few days before they left to spend Christmas at Balmoral, where Xochinenen was hoping for a festive fall of snow.

The horses were unsettled by the move from London, and Archimedes was still recovering from a swollen tendon, so I rode him gently. We were staying at Ambarrow Cottages on the edge of the Wellington College estate in Berkshire. The 'cottages' were actually nothing of the sort, but rather a large rambling modern building, equipped with its own generator and indoor swimming pool. Its design showed obvious Aztec influences in its square-pillared entrance and balconies. It had been built immediately after the invasion as a summer residence for Nauhyotl, the New Lake at its rear created so that the governor could indulge his fondness for tropical fish. Until his assassination, the waters had been constantly heated to a blood-warm temperature; now it was host only to hardy goldfish, dormant under its frozen surface.

I had only agreed to occupy the house because it was urgent we leave London – not only for our own safety but also to give Precious Cloud the chance to recuperate. I wanted to be reasonably close to London in case of emergency but far enough away so that Precious Cloud could benefit from a little rural tranquillity. I visited her every day in her room which looked out over the college, now an Aztec barracks, as was Sandhurst to the south. She was still confined to bed, and the peacefulness of our new surroundings did not seem to help her condition. She continued to be distracted, and there was a haunted look in her eyes. Our conversations grew increasingly strained and strange.

A week after the birth I arrived to find her sitting cross-legged at the centre of her bed with the sheets and pillows arranged in a nest at her side. Cuauhtemoc was asleep in his cot, and Precious Cloud was arranging his soother and fluffy rattlesnake inside her pillows. She did not look up as I entered.

I approached the bed. She continued with her arrangement, swapping objects, then swapping them back again, adjusting and readjusting their positions constantly.

After a while I said softly, 'What are you doing?'

Only now did she look up. Her eyes were as black as pools of tar.

'They were wrong,' she informed me. And then she resumed her ordering of the toys, head bowed, shoulders hunched, as if it were the most important and vital task in the world.

'Wrong about what?' I asked.

'They thought they'd emptied me out. They thought I was hollow.'

Cautiously I drew closer.

'What do you mean?'

'The baby, of course!' she responded sharply. 'The baby!'

I glanced across at Cuauhtemoc, who was still sleeping soundly. She had not looked at him once since my arrival.

'What about the baby?'

'I'm making a cot for her, can't you see?'

I hesitated before saying, 'But hasn't he already got one?'

'Not him!' she said, waving an arm in Cuauhtemoc's direction. 'This is for the other one.'

'Other one?'

'My daughter, of course! The one they didn't know about. The one that's still inside me. She's going to be born soon.'

I swallowed. Casually I asked, 'Has Yeipanitl seen you?'

'I sent him away! I sent them all away. This time I'm going to do it myself, on my own.'

The room was a mess, splatters of food on the bedlinen and carpets, clothes spilling out of her wardrobe, the curtains tied in knots at their ends. Precious Cloud looked like a castaway, shipwrecked in a sea of sheets.

'I haven't been eating,' she announced. 'Mia's trying to poison my food.'

'Mia isn't here,' I said, as calmly as I was able. 'She's gone home to visit her family.'

This had been at my suggestion, Mia departing for Tenochtitlan on the same day we left the complex. But Precious Cloud took no notice of my words.

'Catherine, do you sleep?'

Now she was picking at her fingernails. Before I could reply, she went on, 'It would be good to sleep, just for a little while. But the baby has to come first, doesn't it? We always have to look after the baby.'

I retreated hurriedly to the adjoining room, where a nurse was stationed at a monitor screen. She was middle-aged, English. She rose, bobbed.

'Where's Yeipanitl?' I demanded. 'Why isn't someone attending Precious Cloud?'

'She doesn't want us in there,' the nurse replied. 'But we're watching her all the time.'

She indicated the screen. Precious Cloud was framed at its centre, looking more a prisoner than the object of everyone's concern.

'Can't you see what a state she's in?' I said.

'We're aware of her condition, Your Highness. We need to give her a powerful tranquillizer as part of her treatment, to help her sleep. There've been problems with supplies, because of the war in Russia. Yeipanitl went to London yesterday evening to fetch them himself.'

'When will he be back?'

'He's due any time now.'

She was obviously embarrassed by my angry tone, and there was no point in badgering her. Returning to Precious Cloud's room, I sat with her. My presence seemed to do her little good because she remained obsessed with the phantom child in her womb and the evil intentions of Mia towards her; but at least she tolerated me. I tried to get her to relax and sleep, but this was impossible. When Cuauhtemoc woke and began crying for his feed, she continued to ignore him, and this was a final confirmation to me that her condition was critical. The wet-nurse was summoned, and, under my instructions, she took Cuauhtemoc into another room. Precious Cloud did not appear to notice.

I remained as calm as I could, though I felt both desperately anxious and helpless. Then, to my great relief, Yeipanitl arrived. He had succeeded in obtaining sufficient supplies of the tranquillizer to proceed with a course of treatment. Unfortunately, the drug had to be administered intravenously, and when Yeipanitl produced the hypodermic, Precious Cloud began shrieking in terror and refused to let him near her. Nothing I could do would calm her, and eventually I was ushered from the room on the arrival of several nurses whom I knew would have forcibly to hold her down. Her screams followed me along the corridor as I fled in shame.

For two days, no one but the doctor and his staff was allowed to see her. Early on the morning of the third day, Chicomeztli arrived and said that Precious Cloud had asked for me.

I arrived to find her not only out of bed but dressed in black jeans and a suede waistcoat over a denim shirt. She looked much brighter, her hair washed and plaited, her face made up. The wet-nurse sat in one corner, Cuauhtemoc asleep in her arms. Yeipanitl was also in attendance.

Precious Cloud greeted me with a gentle hug and a kiss on the cheek.

'You look more rested,' I observed.

'I've been sleeping at nights,' she replied with a smile. 'It was something I thought I'd forgotten how to do.'

'I'm so glad.'

'Catherine, can we go riding together this morning?'

I looked at Yeipanitl. It was plain from his face that he did not approve of the idea.

'Perhaps it would be better to wait a few more days.'

'Please, Catherine! I've been so cooped up. Just for half an hour, just you and me.'

I deliberated, unsure what was best. I could see that Chicomeztli didn't like the idea either.

'We don't have to race the horses. Just a trot. I need to get out.'

'A walk would be better at this stage,' Yeipanitl said.

She ignored him. 'Please, Catherine.'

I smiled at her. 'All right.'

I went off to see that the horses were readied. Yeipanitl joined me in the stable.

'I don't think this is wise.'

'I'll take care of her,' I assured him.

'She's still quite weak and far from fully recovered.'

'I'm aware of that. I'll keep a close eye on her.'

'It's vital she doesn't do anything too strenuous at this stage.'

'She needs to be allowed to do something *she* wants to. I think it's important we let her.'

It was another cold morning, and Precious Cloud was bundled up in a sheepskin coat and fur hat when we went outside. She mounted Adamant quite effortlessly, as ever disdaining the stirrups. Chicomeztli fussed around as his own mount was made ready. Although Precious Cloud had wanted to ride with me alone, we had agreed a compromise by which he would accompany us.

Precious Cloud tweaked Adamant's reins, and he trotted off. I spurred Archimedes until we were abreast of her, while Chicomeztli kept pace a few yards behind.

It was a clear, windless morning, the sun casting stark tree shadows on the edges of the grass, smoke rising from a distant field where the last of the autumn leaves was being burned. I could hear Precious Cloud inhaling deeply the sharp air. I assumed she wanted to talk privately with me, but we rode in silence for a while, following the path of the railway line towards Crowthorne station. I watched a hawk hovering high above the embankment.

'It's so good to be outside,' she said at last. 'I thought I'd never escape.'

Cautiously I said, 'Escape from what?'

She shrugged. 'From the attentions of others. Before I came here, I used to ride nearly every day, alone. Sailing the seas of grass, my father used to call it. He always preferred to drive the freeways in his Cadillacs.'

'He's not dead, you know. You can still go and visit him.'

'Sometimes I'd be gone for hours, half a day or more. Prairie or cornfields, it didn't matter to me – I'd just ride. Often the farmers complained to my father that I was ruining their crops, but he never did anything. I enjoyed being on my own.'

'It's very difficult to be alone here,' I said, with some sympathy.

'Oh, no. It's very easy, Catherine. Solitude is what's difficult.'

She spurred Adamant to a faster trot. He looked frisky, nostrils twitching in the crisp air. We were approaching the railway station when Precious Cloud wheeled him around.

'Race you back to the house!' she said suddenly, and with a whack of the reins, galloped off before I could reply.

I turned Archimedes and we hurried off in pursuit, Chicomeztli also following. Precious Cloud was already fifty yards ahead of me, and the gap began to lengthen as she kicked hard against Adamant's flanks, frost flurries erupting from his hoofs as he raced across the frozen ground.

I could feel Archimedes labouring on his bandaged leg, and I knew we had no chance of catching her. Chicomeztli, on a horse that was little more than a pony, was even further back. I saw Precious Cloud gallop through the gates of the house before she was lost to sight behind its walls.

I was certain she would be quite safe now, but I did not tarry. As fast as I was able, I galloped to the gates.

The stables were in sight, but there was no sign of her there. Then I saw her, still riding hard, disappearing around the rear of the house.

It could only have been a matter of minutes, but by the time I caught sight of Adamant again he was riderless, standing beside the New Lake, twitching his head. And in the lake itself, there was a jagged dark hole in the ice.

If only I had known that we could have saved her even then. But both Chicomeztli and I leapt to the obvious conclusion – as she must have wanted us to – that she had thrown herself into the lake. And so we wasted a precious hour summoning help and smashing the ice and trawling the shallow waters until we realized she was not there at all. Only then did we notice that Adamant's reins were gone, only then did one of the maids-in-waiting stumble upon the lambskin coat cast off near the edge of the woods beyond the lake.

It was one of the soldiers from the barracks who found her,

hanging naked from the bough of a tree, the reins forming a crude noose which had broken her neck when she jumped off. In her waistcoat we found a note, addressed to me, which said, 'Tell Extepan to forgive me. Please look after my son.' And that was all.

The next day Bevan arrived from London with the news that there had been a spate of arson attacks on military installations in London and a botched attempt to assassinate Iztacaxayauh by a woman variously described as mad, a feminist anarchist and a member of the New Crusade, a fundamentalist Protestant sect.

I was hardly interested in this, despite having asked Bevan to come so that he could bring me up to date with recent developments. By then I had already reached a decision.

'Extepan must receive the news personally,' I told Chicomeztli. 'I'm going to the front.'

He immediately protested that this was quite impossible, there were no civilian flights to the war zone, *any* flight at all would be highly dangerous, and he could not possibly allow me to risk it. I refused to brook any objections. He tried to compromise by suggesting that someone else be sent in my stead, but I insisted on going myself.

Finally he could see that I would not be moved. He raised both palms as if surrendering.

'It would have to be done unofficially. I could never get authorization at the highest level.'

'I don't care how you manage it, as long as you do.'

'It's madness.'

I merely stared at him. Finally he turned and went out.

Throughout our verbal tussle, I was aware of Bevan watching me dispassionately.

'I feel responsible,' I said to him. 'I took her riding against her doctor's advice. It's partly my fault.'

'You were a friend to her. Without you, she'd have probably done it sooner.'

'That may be true. But it still doesn't alter the fact that she managed to kill herself while I was supposed to be looking after her.'

'So you're going off to the enemy front line.'

'I *have* to, Bevan. It's a question of honour, duty.'

He smiled, looking unconvinced. 'Curious, are you? To see what it's like?'

'In my position, you often have to do things you might not wish to do.'

He gave this the scorn it deserved. 'Even when everyone with a bit of sense advises against it?'

In truth, I could not fully explain my compulsion to go to the front. The reasons I had given were sincere but not exactly sufficient.

'Are you saying I shouldn't go?'

'Bit of a gamble, if you ask me. For a woman of your position.'

'I might pick up some useful intelligence.'

He knew I was vainly striving to find additional justification.

'I have to find out what's going on. I hate feeling useless, being on the sidelines.'

'Want me to come with you?'

The offer surprised me. I was quite touched.

'Thank you,' I said, 'but no. I need to go alone.'

'Don't forget who the enemy is, will you?'

Chicomeztli came to my suite early the following morning.

'There is a troop carrier leaving Harwich at noon,' he informed me. 'That is all we can manage. Otherwise, there will be nothing for several days.'

I think he believed I would refuse. It would be a rush to make the flight, but I had already packed a bag.

'That will be fine,' I said.

'There will not be time to make special arrangements for you. They will just be informed you are joining them.'

'Fine,' I said again.

'We can fly you there by jetcopter. The commander is called Huemac. You will need to report to him.'

'I can be ready to leave in half an hour.'

'Pick warm clothing,' he said.

'I've already done so.'

Unexpectedly, he reached up and hugged me.

'Please look after yourself,' he said.

Five

The carrier hold was brightly lit and packed with warm human bodies, but I stared out of the window at a bleak world of white and grey. The swirling snow melted as it hit the glass, turning into a clear slime which gathered at the base of the window. Far below, I could see a frosted surface – a frozen sea.

I turned and said in Nahuatl to Huemac: 'Is that the Baltic?'

All around me the troopers had removed their snowsuits, but they looked cold, huddled into their padded uniforms. Huemac was adjusting the straps on his boots.

'I asked you a question,' I said.

'Pardon me?' he replied in English.

'I said, is that the Baltic?'

He did not get up. 'If there's a sea below, then that's what it is.'

Soon afterwards I saw the coast. The snow had thinned so that it was possible to make out dark clusters of trees among the white fields. Small villages dotted the landscape, ribbons of roads, isolated farm buildings; but we did not pass over any large settlements. The sky remained clear apart from the snow – no escorts, no sign of any enemy craft. We were probably crossing one of the Baltic provinces.

Crew-women in drab green coveralls doled out mugs of steaming *chocolatl* and rolled *tlaxcalli* filled with mince and tomatoes. The troopers warmed their hands on the mugs and savoured the rolls like men under siege.

'Do you find it cold in here?' I asked Huemac. He looked perfectly at ease himself, and was drinking mineral water rather than *chocolatl*.

'They were transferred from Cyrenaica,' he said, telling me what I wanted to know.

Obviously this was an indication of the seriousness of the situation. To thrust troops from the heat of North Africa into the depths of a Russian winter had to be a measure of desperation, or at least great urgency. Why had there been no word of Extepan or Maxixca for almost a month? I was impatient to find out.

I had no appetite and left my rations uneaten. Darkness began to gather outside the window, and matt-black flaps slid out to cover the wings, blotting out any traces of light. There was no change in the pitch of the engines: they whined on and on, carrying us deeper into the heartland of Mother Russia.

The troopers, true to their Aztec characters, were mostly silent. They played cards or dice, dozed or fingered crucifixes; some puffed on slender clay tubes packed with aromatic tobacco. When they talked, it was quietly, and I could make out none of the words. I sensed Huemac watching me discreetly. I was sure he resented my presence on the flight.

Some time later I was woken from a doze by a change in the sound of the engines. The craft began to tilt and bank.

'Strap yourself in,' Huemac said.

'Are we landing?'

'Soon.'

He was taller than most Aztecs, with rugged features. His hair was still soot-black, but his face was lined. He was forty, forty-five, an experienced commander.

'Where are we landing?' I asked.

'Velikiye-Luki.'

I had never heard of it.

'It's on the road to Moscow,' he told me.

Ten minutes later the carrier touched down at a military landing strip with a soft bump and a wheeze. The flaps were drawn back, and the dimming golden wings were shrouded with steam. Snow had stopped falling some time before, but it lay heavy on the ground and had been piled high on both sides of the runway. Of Velikiye-Luki – a small city, according to Huemac – I could see nothing except for the prefabricated buildings of the landing strip, black under a clear night sky.

'Wait here,' Huemac said. 'I won't be long.'

The troopers were struggling into their camouflaged snowsuits, pulling up hoods, tugging on fat mittens and padded overboots: they resembled morose and grubby polar bears. Soon they began disembarking, slinging their heavy packs over their shoulders and carrying their Xiuhmitl automatics in their hands as they went down the central corridor to the hatch at the rear. Freezing air wafted into the hold, and ice crystallized on the outside of my window.

I quickly donned my own protective clothing. A big caterpillared troop-carrier rolled up, and the soldiers began climbing into its humped back. They were orderly, disciplined, unhurried.

Huemac returned, his suit zipped up and his hood drawn tight over his head. A younger Aztec officer accompanied him, an automatic tucked under his arm.

'Are you ready?' Huemac asked.

I nodded, tugging on my mittens.

Huemac led me towards the hatch at the front of the craft. Even before we stepped outside, the cold air assailed us like something palpable. There was a brisk wind, and the stars shone diamond-bright between tattered ribbons of moonlit cloud.

My feet crunched on a layer of brittle snow. The smell of smoke was in the air, and reddish glows lit the horizon. A sleek black glidecar was waiting nearby, its engine thrumming. The driver sat rigid, head swathed in a peaked cap with the ear-flaps buttoned down.

I followed the young Aztec officer into the back of the vehicle, steadying myself as it rocked on its air cushion. Huemac pulled the door shut behind him, and the car promptly sped off across the runway, throwing up plumes of snow from its flanks.

We passed through a checkpoint without delay, the guards waving us on as if eager to get back to the shelter of their sentry cabins. And who could blame them on such a bitter night?

The glidecar thrummed onwards, soon entering a ruined landscape which was lunar-like in the darkness. Snow-covered rubble lined both sides of the road, electric cables dangled from broken posts, and a wrecked Russian missile launcher was lodged

in a wide storefront window like a huge beast being swallowed
by an enormous black mouth. I could see the imperial eagle on
its flank, blistered and charred. Now tall buildings with orderly
ranks of windows began to rise around us, many gutted or in
ruins. Their concrete façades were decorated with wheatsheafs
and electricity pylons in the monumental imperial collectivist
style.

Huemac and the young Aztec began a quiet conversation
across me. They each spoke Nahuatl with very different accents.
We turned into a broad avenue. Foot patrols passed by, the
troopers crouched against the wind. Fires flickered and smoked
behind skeletal walls, and a burst water-main spread rippled
waves of ice across the road. Here and there emergency arc-lights
had been mounted on solar platforms, their magnesium glare
revealing Aztec soldiers burning wood fires under the engines of
captured diesel trucks. A dog sniffed at a snow-covered mound
which I was sure comprised frozen corpses. Scouters floated by
overhead – artificial moons in purposeful orbit above the shattered city.

'You two aren't Mexica,' I remarked to Huemac in Nahuatl.

'I'm from Peru,' the young officer said immediately.

'Quechua?'

'Aymara.'

'And you?' I asked Huemac.

He had turned away to squint through the window.

'Apache,' he replied.

He managed to convey both pride and solidarity in the word.
The second Motecuhzoma and his successors as *tlatoani* had
succeeded in uniting the warring tribes of Central Mexico after
the Spanish had been repulsed. Later, as the empire extended
into the great continental landmasses to the north and south,
native peoples from both regions had readily accepted Aztec
overlordship in order to repel the European invaders. A true
imperial ideal had arisen as a result, and many non-Mexica, like
Huemac, adopted Nahuatl names.

The glidecar turned into a tree-lined square which held a
statue at its centre. Here the snow was sparse. Ground-cars were
parked everywhere.

We drew up outside a small mansion, its colonnaded front

painted ochre and white. It was illuminated by arc-lights set in a low hedge. Steps led up to a big front door.

The young officer climbed out and retrieved my travel-bag from the rear compartment. I followed Huemac up the steps. Armed guards flanked the doorway, breath smoking from their noses. The wide door was already open, spilling out warm yellow light. Two more guards and a squat elderly woman in a thick black cardigan stood just inside. The woman kept her eyes lowered as we entered.

Huemac led me through a polished marble hallway into a room crammed with antique furniture and tall bookcases. An open coal fire blazed in a large hearth, and in front of it stood a young Aztec in the buff uniform of a non-combatant officer. His dark hair gleamed with oil.

'This is Pachtli,' Huemac said without preamble. 'Extepan's adjutant. He can tell you all you need to know.'

My travel-bag was set down just inside the door, and with a nod Huemac dismissed the young officer. He was about to leave himself, but I said, 'Wait.'

He halted.

I wasn't sure what I wanted to say to him. 'What is this place?'

'Extepan's headquarters.'

'I thought he was in the Ukraine.'

'He has requested you wait here for him,' Pachtli said, giving a white smile. 'I also speak English, you see.'

He spoke it with a very broad Mexican accent, lisping his r's and making 'English' sound like 'Eengleesh'.

'He knows I've arrived?'

'A message has been sent to him,' Pachtli said, still smiling. 'You bring good news?'

'I bring important news.'

'Will he have cause for celebration?'

I disliked his persistence. 'There's good news and bad. Which *I* intend to give to him. Where is he?'

Pachtli's gaze flickered to Huemac. Something told me there was little love lost between them.

'He knows you're here,' the Aztec commander said. 'He'll come as soon as possible.'

'The news I bring is most urgent.'

'We're aware of that,' Huemac said. 'It seems unlikely you would have undertaken this journey if it weren't. But military considerations take precedence here. This applies whether you are a footsoldier or a princess.'

I accepted the rebuke, feeling a little shamefaced.

'Of course,' I said. 'Thank you for bringing me safely here.'

'You must excuse me,' Huemac said. 'My men will be waiting.'

This time I did not attempt to detain him.

'Your flight was a pleasant one?' Pachtli asked.

'Hardly,' I replied, tugging off my mittens and flinging them on a chair. 'I came in a troop carrier. The important thing is I'm here.'

'This is a very pleasant house, comfortable for your stay. The mayor lived here.'

'Did he?' I struggled out of my suit. 'And where is he now?'

'Dead,' Pachtli replied, as if it should have been obvious. 'The battle was hard for this city, but now it is ours.'

'What's left of it.'

'Soon we will march into Moscow.'

'You sound very confident, given what's happened in Tsaritsyn.'

He took the snowsuit from me. 'You've heard of that?'

'Of course I have.' I wasn't going to admit that I didn't know exactly what had happened. 'Why do you assume I wouldn't have done?'

'We have a weapon more mighty than theirs. It will strike down all our enemies, wherever they are.'

'Indeed?' I warmed my hands at the fire. 'And what weapon would that be?'

I glanced at him, and his smile faltered. 'Ah, but I must not speak of these matters. You will be wanting some food and a warm drink, yes? It is cold, this winter Russia. That is one thing I do not like about it.'

He went out, taking the snowsuit with him.

I dragged an armchair up to the fireside, kicked off my boots and warmed my feet. Coals collapsed in the hearth, and sparks fled up the soot-black chimney.

The heat from the fire was very comforting. I stared around

the room, at the lace curtains on the long shuttered windows, the crystal chandelier which hung from the ceiling, the massed ranks of books with indecipherable Cyrillic titles on their spines. Above the mantelpiece hung a reproduction of the famous Dali canvas showing the assassination of the right-wing Prime Minister Dzhugashvili in the Duma in 1939, a key event in modern Russian history which had led to the establishment of the collectivist federation under the progressive patronage of Tsar Nikolai II. Now, fifty years of egalitarian progress were threatened by the Aztec onslaught.

Pachtli returned, carrying a silver tray with a crystal-glass decanter and two short-stemmed glasses.

'Dinner will be soon,' he said. 'But first, something to warm us against the cold, yes?'

He set the tray down on a chessboard table which he then placed in front of the fire. Drawing up an armchair opposite me, he filled the glasses with a brownish liquor, then offered me one.

'What is it?'

'French brandy,' he said, swallowing a large mouthful.

I guessed him to be no more than twenty-five. He was handsome but somehow pampered-looking. He reclined expansively in the armchair, soon draining his glass. I sipped at my drink. I had never much cared for brandy, though tonight its warmth was welcome.

'How long have you been Extepan's adjutant?' I asked.

'Since he came here to Russia. But we have known one another many years.'

'Oh?'

'At the *calmecac* in Tenochtitlan. Both of us studied there. I served him then, as I do now. He can rely on my loyalty and discretion, absolutely.' He poured himself another brandy. 'My father, Apanecatl, he is one of Motecuhzoma's high councillors.'

The name was unfamiliar, and I knew he was not a member of the *tlatocan*, the emperor's inner council. Evidently Pachtli was eager to impress. I was surprised to learn that Extepan had been educated in the *calmecac*, where traditionally the emphasis was on a religious training, rather than the *telpochcalli*, where the sons of nobles usually received a thorough grounding in military skills.

'More brandy?' Pachtli asked.

I shook my head. 'I'd like a bath before I eat.'

Without meeting my eyes, he said, 'I do not think that will be possible.'

'Not possible?'

He shrugged, almost as if an explanation would be too tiresome. I was angered by his insouciance.

'See to it,' I said sharply.

Evidently there were problems with the hot water supply, because the old woman had to carry metal buckets of hot water upstairs to the bathroom. She was also cooking us dinner at the same time. Ashamed to have inflicted this extra burden on her, I insisted on carrying the buckets up the stairs myself, which only increased her discomfiture. I settled for a bath that was tepid rather than hot, and I did not linger long in the water.

My bedroom was just across the landing. The bed was broad and sturdily framed with carved posts of dark wood, the mattress piled high with flower-patterned eiderdowns. A balconied window overlooked the square, and I could see that the statue was of a man holding something in his hand. Beyond it stood a white building with a broken tower at its centre. Its long windows were shuttered, and the wall above the arched entrance was blackened where the door had been burnt down.

One of the household guards had placed my travel-bag at the foot of the bed. I unpacked it, hanging up my clothes in a voluminous mahogany wardrobe which smelt of mothballs. After some deliberation, I selected a black gown in fine angora wool, wondering if Extepan would arrive in time for dinner.

We ate in a large room hung with gilt-framed mirrors. Pachtli and I sat at opposite ends of a walnut table, while the old woman silently served us a thick fish and vegetable soup, followed by coarse sausages and black bread. There was even a bowl of oranges at the centre of the table, and I wondered where they had come from. I entertained visions of the ordinary citizens of Velikiye-Luki starving in the snow even as I ate, hidden away from my eyes. The old woman was the only Russian I had seen since my arrival. I tried to indicate my gratitude for the food to her, but she simply nodded vigorously, then hurried back to the kitchen, as if I had given her an order.

'She's a Ukrainian,' Pachtli told me. 'She was glad to be liberated by us.'

I found this hard to credit, since all the constituent states of the Russian empire had benefited considerably from the Duma's enlightened regional policies over the past half century.

'What about the rest of the people in the city?' I asked. 'What's happened to them?'

'They fled.' He swallowed a mouthful of sausage. 'When our armies drew near, they ran away to the east, taking all they could with them. Only soldiers were here to defend the city when we arrived.'

I also doubted that this was true, given that the mayor had apparently stayed behind. The more Pachtli told me, the less I believed; the more he smiled, the less I liked him. There was a bottle of red wine on the table, and he took pleasure in announcing that it had come from a well-stocked cellar in the house. I did not drink any of it, but he quickly emptied the bottle before calling one of the guards to fetch him another.

The old woman served me strong lemon tea. Pachtli announced that his mother was a Zapotec princess, that both his parents had royal blood. I caught my reflection in one of the mirrors as he prattled and swallowed wine. I looked perfectly miserable.

The guard returned with another bottle of wine, already uncorked. Pachtli filled his glass.

'That is a pretty dress,' he remarked.

His pupils were dilated, his smile slack. I pushed back my chair and rose. 'I'm tired. I'm going to bed.'

'But the wine. We have more.'

'I'm sure you'll have no difficulty with it. I'd like to be informed the moment Extepan arrives.'

I lay in the darkness, snug but unable to sleep. The wind had dropped, so I had left the curtains open; I could see the arc of the moon outside. Voices muttering in Nahuatl drifted up from downstairs: it sounded as if Pachtli was now entertaining the guards in the dining room. No doubt they were availing themselves of more wine from the cellar. Outside a scouter went by, the thin whine of its engine rapidly fading. Sleep had deserted me.

I rose, donned my nightgown, and went out into the carpeted corridor. It was silent and empty, lined on both sides with doors. I crept along it.

The first door I tried opened on a storeroom piled high with furniture draped in white sheets. The second door was also unlocked, opening on a bedroom.

It was in darkness, unoccupied. A black-and-white robe was draped across a four-poster bed. I recognized it as Extepan's.

I edged into the room, peering around. Everything was in its place, clean, dusted, the dark-wooded dressers and wardrobes gleaming in the soft light from the corridor. Apart from the gown, there was no other evidence of Extepan's presence. And no sign that he was sharing the room with anyone else.

A side door led to an adjoining room. It was unfurnished apart from a desk. I switched on the desk-lamp. There were military papers everywhere, a display screen, a leather-bound copy of Cortes's *Advice to the Mexica Nation*. More than any other foreigner, the turncoat Spaniard was still revered by the Aztecs.

Above the desk a large map of the Russian Confederation was pinned to the wall. A physical map in greens and browns, its surface was plastered with golden arrows showing Aztec advances and red ones indicating Russian counter-attacks. A dotted line marked the extent of the advance on all fronts.

Much of it I already knew. In the north, St Petersburg was still under siege, while the advance of the armies in the centre had stopped just east of Velikiye-Luki itself. Which meant that I was now very close to the front-line, as I had suspected. In the south, the armies under Ixtlilpopoca had swept through the southern Asian states to link up with those of Chimalcoyotl in the Ukraine just south of Tsaritsyn. The two great golden arrows converged but then terminated abruptly in a black sunburst at Tsaritsyn itself.

Hundreds of thousands had died in the explosion, it was rumoured, and the city had been flattened. Clusters of red arrows on the east bank of the Volga seemed to suggest that the Russians were massing for a huge counter-attack.

I thought I heard a sound outside, and I immediately switched off the lamp. I waited in the darkness, listening, listening. Everything was quiet.

I crept to the door and peered out. All was quiet.

Safely back in my bedroom, with the door shut behind me, I cursed the lack of a key for the lock. I felt like a prisoner in the house, but at the same time I was defenceless – against what? Pachtli wouldn't try anything with me, knowing that Extepan would soon be returning. It was ridiculous. But I didn't trust him. If he had drunk enough wine, he might be capable of anything.

A sudden noise. Like a distant, muffled scream.

It had come from across the square. I went to the window and peered out. For a moment I could see nothing, but then I noticed a faint flickering light through one of the empty windows of the white building. Presently several snowsuited figures crept out of the doorway. There were six of them. Aztec soldiers. They hurried across the square.

I backed away from the window. Quickly I began dressing, putting on my padded suit and mittens. Opening the door very carefully, I went quietly down the wide stairway.

The doors to the library and dining room were closed, and there were no guards anywhere. Silence and stillness filled the cavernous spaces of the hallway.

The front door was bolted and locked from inside, but a big brass key hung on a hook. Removing my mittens, I eased the bolts out of their brackets, slid the key into the lock. Turned it.

Again the cold air assailed me as I opened the door. There was no sign of the guards who had been on duty outside, no sign of life anywhere. Only the arc-lights still burned under the hedge. Carefully I went down the steps and headed straight across the square.

Of course this was sheer stupidity on my part, venturing out at night in a front-line town. Even now, I can't justify or explain it except to say that I have always been impetuous and that my insatiable curiosity overcame all caution. We also seek what we most fear.

The statue showed a man, half-crouched but defiant, a sickle in his hand. A noble Russian, defending the soil against the enemy. The sickle as harvester and weapon, exemplifying two of the major themes of Russian history. The figure had been cast in bronze, and on its base were the dates 1198, 1581 and 1611, surrounded by Cyrillic script. Neither the script nor the dates meant anything to me.

I climbed the steps to the gutted door of the white building. Nothing could be seen inside. I hesitated, then went in.

A church, as I had known all along. Moonlight filtered down through a large hole in the ceiling, providing just enough light for me to make out its arches and frescoed walls. Ammunition boxes had been piled against them, and empty cartridge cases littered the mosaic floor. Icons of haloed saints and archbishops hung everywhere, and there was a terrible stench in the air.

I moved towards a screen behind which a light was flickering. Rubble and patches of dirty snow lay on the floor, chairs had been stacked against square pillars, the smell was petrol and burnt meat. Silence, a terrifying silence except for the scrunch of my feet on grit and rubble.

Behind the screen a candle burned in a golden holder, and I gasped. A body had been spread across the ammunition box, its arms and legs splayed out, its chest dark and steaming. The face was slack, mouth and eyes open, dead white eyes which saw nothing, felt nothing. Almond eyes, broad nose, black hair – an Aztec soldier. But no, because the heavy brown greatcoat which hung from the body was that of a Russian Army officer, and the boots were Russian, too. An Asian Russian, bloodied from his neck to his belly.

Buttons were missing from his coat where it had been torn open. His uniform and vests had been slit up the middle, his chest bared. There had been no finesse about the ceremony, a gaping wound curving under his left breast. The blood, now blackened and beginning to freeze, had drained over his shoulders and throat, and tendrils of steam still rose from the warm innards.

The candlelit screen bore an icon of the Virgin. In front of it was a small, crudely carved figurine in soap. It had the hunched head and the squat body characteristic of traditional Aztec religious statuary. Beside it, an upturned Russian Army helmet held the charred remains of the offering. Petrol had been poured on it to make sure it would burn.

I backed out of the church and fled across the square. Near the statue I slipped and fell, but I scrambled up again and hurried on. As I neared the house, several hooded figures seemed to materialize out of nowhere.

'Keep away from me!' I screamed. And then I bolted towards the open door of the mansion, scurrying up the steps into the warm light of the hall.

I was leaning against a marble pillar, panting, when Pachtli walked in, the other guards following him.

'Where have you been?' he asked, throwing back his hood. 'We went looking for you. What has happened?'

I was still too breathless and terrified to answer him immediately. He and the other guards were all carrying automatics, and they looked perfectly sober. In the square I had mistaken them for the soldiers who had carried out the sacrifice, but I felt little relief at the sight of them. They waited, standing motionless, watching me.

'The front door was unlocked,' Pachtli said. 'We searched the house and found you gone.'

Had they seen me coming out of the church? I tried to gather my wits, gambling that they hadn't.

'I went for a walk,' I managed to say.

'A walk?'

'I couldn't sleep. I wanted some fresh air.'

He gave a smile to indicate his disbelief. There was a long silence. Then he turned to the other guards and told them in Nahuatl that they were no longer needed.

As soon as we were alone, he said, 'I was concerned. If something should happen to you, my lord Extepan, he would not forgive me.'

He was smiling and fingering the trigger of his rifle. 'There is a curfew. You could have been shot.'

'If I'd known that, then obviously I wouldn't have gone out.'

'There are always curfews in a war zone.'

I said nothing.

'It is a cold night for a walk.'

Only now was I recovering my equilibrium. 'That's why I wore boots and mittens.'

'Something upset you, yes?'

'I got lost. But, as you saw, I found my way back. You startled me when you came upon me in the square, that's all.'

Patently he did not believe me. 'Did you think we might shoot you? It might have happened. In these suits, and in darkness, we all look the same. It is hard to tell friend from enemy.'

I unzipped the front of my suit. 'You must excuse me. I'm really quite exhausted.'

'A little brandy will help you sleep.'

'That won't be necessary.'

I turned and walked up the stairway without looking back. Only when I had closed the door behind me did I let out a breath of sheer relief.

I drew the curtains on the windows, blotting out the night and all its horrors, then removed my snowsuit. Without undressing further, I climbed beneath the eiderdowns and switched on the bedside lamp.

I lay back and tried to calm myself. But my thoughts were racing, and suddenly I began to wonder if I had been wilfully blind and stupid. What if I hadn't been wrong in my first split-second assumption that the soldiers who had appeared in the square were the same ones who had carried out the sacrifice? I'd imagined that they had melted into the night, but what if they had simply returned to the house? All too easily I could imagine Pachtli acting as the chief priest, wielding the knife and reaching into the chest to twist the palpitating heart from its moorings. That was how it was done, with a deft turn of the wrist. A sacrifice to Huitzilopochtli, or some other unforgiving deity of the old Aztec pantheon.

Had I had my wits about me, I might have checked their snowsuits for splatterings of blood; or I might have registered the stench of petrol and burnt flesh. But I had been in no state to notice anything of the sort. Yet this meant nothing in itself – they might have easily changed their clothing on returning to the house immediately after the sacrifice, and before Pachtli discovered I was gone.

I contemplated trying to wedge the wardrobe or the dresser

against my door, but this seemed melodramatic. I would lie there instead and wait until morning, staying awake. Surely they wouldn't dare try anything with me, even if they knew I had discovered the corpse in the church? Huemac had delivered me safely to the mansion, and he, at least, seemed an honourable man who would be no part of any cover-up should I be disposed of. But what if he secretly worshipped the same Aztec gods as they? What if they *all* did?

Awake. I would stay awake. Fight the exhaustion I felt. They wouldn't harm me, I was sure, but I had to remain vigilant. There couldn't be too many hours left before dawn, so I didn't have long to wait. If anyone tried to enter, I would jump up, scream, fight them with all the power I possessed. Awake. I would stay awake. That was my protection.

Six

'Good morning.'

I surfaced abruptly from a deep sleep. Pachtli was standing over me.

'Here is some tea,' he said, putting a silver tray down on the bedside table.

I sat up, still groggy with sleep. Pachtli switched off the lamp and threw open the curtains. Bright winter sunlight flooded in through the window.

'It is a very pleasant morning,' he remarked.

I kept the bedclothes drawn up to my neck; beneath them I was fully dressed.

'Is Extepan here?' I asked.

'He arrived an hour ago.'

'Why didn't you wake me immediately?'

'I explained to him that you were late in sleeping. He said that it was better to leave you for a while. He has been consulting with his generals.'

I was quietly angry. I wondered just how much he had told Extepan.

'Where is he now?'

'In the breakfast room, eating.'

'What time is it?'

'Almost ten o'clock.'

He made to pour the tea, but I said, 'Leave it.'

As soon as he was gone, I rose and washed in the handbasin next to the bed. Changing into a roll-necked lambswool sweater and thick corduroys, I went downstairs.

Two guards were on duty at the breakfast-room door, but they let me through without a word. Extepan sat alone at a table in front of the french windows, his back to me. His rust-coloured uniform had five eagle-heads on the epaulettes. He now held Chimalcoyotl's former rank of *tlacateccatl*, 'he who commands the warriors'.

I approached the table and said quietly in Nahuatl: 'Good morning.'

He looked up from his omelette.

'Catherine.'

A somewhat grave smile. He rose and embraced me formally.

'How good it is to see you,' he said in English. 'A civilized face in an uncivilized world.'

A place had been laid opposite him. He motioned, and I sat down in it. A display screen stood in an alcove next to the table, showing bar charts and columns of data, all of a military nature. Extepan had a small control panel on his side plate.

The old woman entered and put an omelette down in front of me. There was a large plate of sliced ham at the centre of the table, garnished with chopped onions and beetroot.

'I'm pleased you came,' Extepan said. 'Do you bring good news?'

Something told me he already knew of his son's birth and Precious Cloud's death.

'You have a healthy baby boy,' I said. 'He was born ten days ago – no, eleven now.'

Extepan smiled. 'And do we know if it was an auspicious day?'

'Apparently so. According to the *tonalamatl* he's destined to become a rich man.'

His smile became wry, and he nodded. 'That is most encouraging. Even when we profess not to believe in them, good omens are as reassuring as bad ones are troubling.'

He speared a piece of ham and put it on his plate. There was grime under his fingernails, split skin on his knuckles. It was hard to look him in the face, to confront his candid eyes.

I babbled off the details of Cuauhtemoc's weight, and of how he had announced his arrival in the world by urinating over a nurse. Extepan continued eating, glancing occasionally at the screen; but I knew his attention was fully engaged on what I was saying. I spoke of Precious Cloud's labour, and of her wish to have me present during it.

I sensed him waiting until I had run dry. I hurried on. 'Precious Cloud was delighted with Cuauhtemoc. But she wasn't able to sleep after the birth.'

I allowed a pause. Finally he filled it. 'And?'

'She became distraught. She fell ill.'

He put his fork down.

'Tell me,' he said.

'Everyone did what they could. She was tranquillized, and she seemed to improve. I took her riding one morning on Adamant. She galloped off unexpectedly, and I lost her. We found her hanging from a tree.' I swallowed hard. 'Your son is safe and well, but Precious Cloud is dead.'

He was silent for a long time. Although his expression did not alter, I knew he felt genuine sorrow. I was also certain he had already received the news.

'I'm terribly sorry,' I said. 'I took her riding against Yeipanitl's advice. I feel it's my fault.'

He shook his head, slowly but emphatically. At the same time, his gaze was distant, as if I had faded out of both his sight and consciousness.

'Of course you warned me,' he said at length. 'I should have taken better care of her. She was never happy in London.'

I made to say something, but he silenced me by raising a hand.

'It was my responsibility, and I failed her.' He sighed. 'I never loved her, you see. But then you knew that, Catherine, didn't you? My father says the best marriages are arranged on Earth rather than made in heaven, but he married my mother for love as well as diplomacy. Perhaps I would have been a better husband if I had been able to do the same.'

He was staring at the monitor as he spoke. After a silence, he said, 'Who's looking after my son?'

'He's with a wet-nurse. He's very healthy.'

'That's welcome news, at least.' He looked forlorn. 'Thank you, Catherine. Thank you for coming all this way to bring the news personally. I attach no blame to anyone but myself.'

Unexpectedly, he put his hand on mine across the table. I almost flinched. I had been looking forward to seeing him until last night. Finding the corpse had changed everything.

The french windows looked out on a walled garden with fruit trees standing in ranks and an ice-locked ornamental pool.

'Cherry trees,' Extepan said. 'Do you know Chekhov? I imagine the garden looks pretty when they flower. We tried to save as much of the city as possible, but it wasn't easy.'

He was talking to cover his feelings, I knew.

'Was the fighting fierce here?'

'It's been fierce everywhere. The Russians have proved formidable enemies. I'm beginning to understand what Wellington felt like during his march on Moscow.'

'London's rife with rumours. Particularly about Tsaritsyn. What does a black star mean?'

He gave me a questioning look.

'I found your rooms last night,' I admitted. 'There was a map. With a black star over Tsaritsyn.'

He gazed out of the window. 'Indeed. A black star, indeed.'

'It's common knowledge that something terrible happened there. But what?'

'The Russians deployed a new weapon on the city.'

'That's also common knowledge. But what sort of weapon?'

He sighed. 'A weapon of enormous destructive power. Two of our armies were wiped out at a stroke.'

The old woman approached. Extepan waved her away.

'We tested a similar weapon ourselves many years ago,' he went on. 'Would you like to see the results?'

He pressed a sequence of buttons on the control panel. The screen went blank, then came alive again. It showed a grainy picture of a scrubby desert with a settlement of low whitewashed buildings at its centre. Extepan told me that the desert lay in the Cochimi Peninsula, whose long arm stretched down the Pacific Coast of north-west Mexico. A mock-up of a small city had been built there for the express purpose of testing the weapon and recording the results.

'What sort of weapon is it?' I asked again.

'A bomb,' he said simply. 'Watch.'

Nothing happened on the screen at first. Only a long-winged bird drifted by overhead: there was no other movement. Then the whole desert erupted. The landscape bulged as if the earth had shrugged its sun-baked back, and a ball of fire and smoke blossomed outwards and upwards, swallowing the buildings. There was a roar unlike any I had ever heard before.

The camera had been placed some distance from the explosion, but distance only emphasized its scale. The dome-shaped fireball swiftly rose upwards into a column which opened out so that it took on the appearance of a monstrous flat-topped tree. Massive dust clouds surrounded it, streaks of lightning flashed above it in the blue sky, and the whole picture flickered and rippled, as if the very fabric of landscape and sky was about to warp into something else. The settlement had been consumed within seconds by the fireball, and the terrible roaring went on and on like the rage of an awesome god who was the very apotheosis of destruction.

Abruptly Extepan blanked the screen. Everything went silent, but I could still hear the roar. I looked down at my untouched breakfast. For long moments the very idea of eating – of anything remotely involving the everyday behaviour of ordinary individuals – seemed fatuous in the face of what I had seen on the screen.

'Tsaritsyn was destroyed by such a bomb,' Extepan said softly. 'Its power comes from the breakdown of unstable atoms. As you have seen, enormous amounts of energy are released as a result. The Russians used a small missile to carry their bomb to its target. Our armies had just taken the city, and they were annihilated – over three hundred thousand men. My brothers Chimalcoyotl and Ixtlilpopoca were among them.'

I wanted to say something, but nothing seemed adequate.

'Not everyone died immediately in the blast,' he went on. 'It is a particular feature of such bombs that they release radiation which is invisible to the eye but lethal to the body. It rots the internal organs, causing a more lingering death, hours, days or even months later, and it can poison the earth for years.'

Everything about the bomb was already beyond my power to imagine. The sacrifice in the church seemed like a minor breach of etiquette by comparison.

'The Russians have made it clear that they intend to use several more such bombs on cities in Western Europe unless we accept an immediate ceasefire on their terms. They have long-range missiles which could reach London.'

'But you've tested similar bombs yourselves.'

'As long ago as 1945.'

'Then why haven't you ever used them?'

'Motecuhzoma forbade it. He and the *tlatocan* agreed that they were a dishonourable means of waging war, allowing the enemy no opportunity to display his valour and making territory uninhabitable.'

This was typically Aztec. Though they were technologically the most advanced nation on earth, their codes of conduct for warfare bordered on the quaint, harking back to the ritual imperatives of pre-Christian days.

'Then surely the war in Russia is lost,' I said. 'Your armies can't hope to prevail against weapons of that magnitude.'

'That presumes we don't have a weapon of similar effectiveness.'

In the garden, birds were hopping among the cherry trees. Drab brown sparrows, but the sight of them pleased me enormously.

'We haven't been idle in the intervening years,' Extepan said. 'Motecuhzoma anticipated the eventual development of the bomb by other nations, and he was concerned to see a weapon developed which could counter it. A weapon of similar destructive power, but without any lingering after-effects. Something that would kill quickly but cleanly. We've had such a weapon for several years.'

Evidently this was the 'weapon more mighty than theirs' to which Pachtli had referred. But I still didn't understand.

'Then why haven't you used it before now?'

'For the same reasons we didn't use the bomb. It's always been our principle to match ourselves with our enemies as equally as possible. What virtue is there in using a mountain to crush an ant? But the Russians have shown no reluctance to use their most powerful weapon, so now we may do the same.'

'I can't imagine anything as terrible.'

'That's because you can only think in terms of a bomb. Our weapon is equally effective but more accurate.'

'Can it destroy a city at a stroke?'

He nodded. 'But cleanly, and just as swiftly. Instant death, or none at all. For the moment, I can't tell you any more about it.'

'And you'll be giving the order to use it?'

'I have no choice. The *tlatoani* appointed me to lead our armies here. The order has come directly from his palace.'

His new rank of *tlacateccatl* meant that he was now answerable only to Motecuhzoma or Tetzahuitl for his actions. Yet it seemed as if he was asking my approval. I couldn't possibly give it.

'The alternative,' he said, 'is to allow the Russians to destroy other cities with their bomb. In the end, they might turn the whole of Europe into a wasteland where nothing could live.'

'When? When are you going to use it?'

'This very day. Soon I shall be leaving for the front line.'

Despite what he had told me, I suspected the Aztecs had only recently readied their weapon and were making a last-ditch attempt to save the situation.

'I want to come with you.'

I didn't know what made me say this. It seemed like madness, a wilful desire to become an accomplice to an enormous crime.

Extepan wiped his mouth with his napkin and rose.

'You will need to be ready within an hour,' he said.

A glidecar escorted by four low-flying scouters took us through the ruined city until we came to a turreted grey stone building with a wide entranceway. Snowsuited soldiers were everywhere – crack troops, Extepan informed me, from the Alaska province of Greater Mexico.

The building was a railway station, tracks converging from many directions. Pigeons fluttered under the red-roofed platforms, their droppings streaking ornate iron pillars. Several burnt-out carriages sat in a siding, but the station itself looked undamaged. Soldiers milled about on the main platform, some guarding men in charcoal overalls, whom I guessed were Russian mechanics.

Faintly at first, then more loudly, I heard a regular, rhythmic hissing. Gouts of thick white steam came rolling down the platform and spiralled up towards the roof. They brought with them the smell of soot. Everyone stepped back from the edge of the platform.

It was an old steam train, the engine gleaming black and

bottle-green, a vision from another age. It came grinding to a halt with a metallic screech and a great exhalation.

I waited for the steam to clear. The matching carriages were trimmed with gold, their windows hung with embroidered curtains. The engine had a big black snow-plough at its front and cattle-catchers on its flanks. The driver – a Russian, by the look of him – was guarded by two Aztec soldiers, all of them bundled up against the cold.

'We found it in a shed,' Extepan remarked to me. 'It's been quite excellently maintained.'

'We're travelling to the front in it?'

'Of course. Let's get aboard.'

Pachtli accompanied us into the front carriage. Various Aztec generals and other high-ranking officers were also boarding. I thought they looked disgruntled, as if they deemed it absurd to travel in such an antique when a fast-flying transporter would take them to the front in a fraction of the time. But Extepan's insistence on using the train was typical of the whimsical side of his character.

The carriages were carpeted, with upholstered seats, and tables draped with white cloths. It was easier to imagine we were going on a sightseeing tour rather than to use a weapon of unimaginable destructive power.

Soon afterwards the train jolted and began moving out of the station. It quickly gathered speed, steam billowing past my window, wheels settling into a steady *trocketa-trocketa* rhythm on the rails. Extepan began explaining some of the difficulties involved in keeping a steam engine operational in such bitter weather: he had obviously been talking to the driver or his mechanics. Meanwhile Velikiye-Luki slid by the carriage windows. By day, the snow which had covered the city since the battle had softened its shattered appearance, ruined towers and gutted apartment blocks rising like amorphous sculptures and lattices out of a frozen white sea.

A waiter appeared and asked if we wanted drinks. He was a European, though his accented Nahuatl was fluent. A Pole, perhaps, or a German. Extepan and I requested orange juice, Pachtli a glass of red wine.

Presently Extepan departed to check on the comfort of his

generals. I had avoided speaking to Pachtli since rising, and I felt uneasy in his company. Now we faced one another across the table, alone. His reflection in the window was smiling at me.

'This is a good way to travel, yes?'

'Yes.'

'I have never been on such a train before. Did you sleep well last night?'

I looked at him. There was nothing in his face to indicate that the question was anything other than a pleasantry.

The waiter arrived with our drinks. He had no sooner set them down on the table than Extepan returned, much to my relief.

'You will require lunch soon?' the waiter asked.

'Whenever it's ready,' Extepan told him.

I suddenly realized how hungry I was. I had eaten nothing since dinner the night before.

The train was now passing through open countryside, a flat white landscape broken by lines of bare trees and dark stands of pine. A road ran in parallel to the railway, posts holding electric cables marching beside it. The sky had clouded over to a uniform grey, and a pale haze dimmed the horizon.

'Are you going to use the weapon on Moscow?' I asked in English.

Extepan looked surprised. He shook his head. 'We wouldn't destroy any capital unless it was unavoidable. No, a smaller demonstration may suffice. Yesterday a message was sent to the commander of the Russian forces in the city of Rzhev, which lies in the direct route of our advance on Moscow. The message advised him to evacuate the city and all his troops before dawn today. We have clearly indicated that we intend to unleash a major new weapon there and that thousands of lives will be lost unless it's evacuated. Let's hope he sees fit to heed the warning.'

'What if the Russians decide to strike first with another of their bombs?'

'Information received from our *quimichtin* suggests that they won't have further bombs ready for launch for some days. By then we will have destroyed a dozen Russian cities, if necessary.'

The literal meaning of *quimichtin* was 'mice', but it had long been applied to undercover agents and spies.

I glanced down at the pistol in Extepan's belt. It would be a simple matter to snatch it out and shoot him through the heart.

But it would make no difference, I knew that. Someone worse like Maxixca would take command of the empire's armies, and the weapon would be used as planned. What sort of weapon could be as deadly as the bomb – that enormous thunderhead of fire and smoke with its cataclysmic power? It still defeated my imagination. But I knew Extepan better than to imagine he would make empty threats.

The train sped on through a town of wooden houses and drab prefabricated huts. It looked undamaged by the war, but it was deserted, no smoke rising from the chimneys, many doors open to the snow and wind.

We were served pancakes with smoked salmon, followed by thick slices of gâteau. The meal seemed an obscene luxury, but I ate every morsel of it. Pachtli drank his way through a whole bottle of wine. I caught Extepan glancing at him with unmistakable disapproval. He asked Pachtli to leave us, and the adjutant lurched off down the corridor.

'I didn't choose him,' Extepan remarked to me in English.

'Pachtli?'

'His father once saved my brother Ixtlilpopoca from falling into a ravine when he was a small boy. Motecuhzoma was thus bound by a debt of honour to his family. Pachtli is the least worthy of his sons – a *mamiqui*. But he has the protection and patronage of the *tlatoani*.'

Mamiqui meant 'idler'. I watched Extepan's reflection in the window, preferring not to look directly at him. 'He told me you both went to the same *calmecac* in Tenochtitlan.'

'That's true.'

'You were trained to be a priest?'

He gave me an incredulous look. 'No more than you would be trained to be a nun if you went to a convent school.'

'So you didn't have any formal religious training?'

'I thought you had once been a student of our culture.' He waited until I looked directly at him. 'I think, Catherine, that too often people persist in thinking of we Mexica and our world as it was centuries ago.'

'So what happens at the *calmecac*?' I persisted.

'You know quite well what happens. We are educated there, in all areas of knowledge, not just the religion of our Revered Mother. It's hundreds of years since the *calmecac* were schools for the instruction of priests. They educate the sons and daughters of the ruling ranks, as the *telpochcalli* serve the children of all other citizens.'

The train rushed on, over culverts and bridges, through woodland and bare white plain. It was hard to believe that a ferocious war had been raging over these very lands. It was hard to believe that human beings lived here at all.

'There's still a stone in your mouth,' Extepan said. 'Spit it out.'

His shadowy reflection in the window highlighted the angular, un-Mexica aspect of his features. He was less reserved, more approachable than most Aztecs I knew. And yet . . . Was there an unbridgeable gulf between us? The only way to find out was to speak the truth.

'Did Pachtli tell you I went out last night?' I said.

'He mentioned it. That was foolish of you, Catherine.'

'Did he say any more?'

'Only that he had gone searching for you and found you in the square.'

'Nothing more?'

'What is it you wish to say?'

He was impatient, perhaps angry with me, but still restraining himself. He always spoke calmly, was always ready to listen. This had once been reassuring; now it was unnerving.

'I went into the church across the square,' I said.

As plainly and as bluntly as possible, I told him about the steaming corpse and the unmistakable evidence of a ritual sacrifice according to the old Aztec customs. Extepan listened intently, his face giving nothing away. The only thing I held back from him was my suspicion that the six soldiers who had carried out the sacrifice were Pachtli and the household guard.

'Pachtli thought you were trying to escape but were deterred by the snow,' Extepan said.

'Escape? To where? And why should I want to escape?'

'Why indeed?'

'Are you saying you don't believe me?'

'Not at all. I'm rather relieved to learn that it was curiosity rather than a desire to join our enemies that made you leave the house.'

For a moment I was dumbfounded. 'Do you understand what I'm saying? Your soldiers are performing human sacrifices. Am I to take it that this is something you condone?'

It was Extepan's turn to gaze out of the window. The train hurried on, *trocketa-trocketa*, passing through the deserted station of yet another ghost-town. I felt as if I had done something irrevocable, as if I had forced him into the position of having to admit that, yes, it was true what the enemies of the Aztecs had always claimed: the old gods were still secretly worshipped under the veneer of Christianity, and that the bloodthirsty rituals designed to appease them were still practised.

'As a boy,' Extepan remarked, 'I was always asking my father to tell me stories about his military exploits. I remember the first one he told. As a young man he served in India. In 1930 our forces suffered a defeat at Karachi, and he led the counter-attack. When the city was taken, the bodies of over three thousand Mexica officers were found. They had been buried up to their necks, then had their heads smashed to pulp with cudgels. The commanding officer in the city was British.'

The waiter appeared with a jug of black coffee. Extepan waited until he was gone.

'During the invasion of Japan,' he went on, 'captured Mexica were staked to the ground and had boiling oil poured over them. In Cape Colony their limbs and genitals were cut off and they were left to be eaten by scavengers. During the fighting in the Midlands of England, Mexica prisoners were executed by slow disembowelment. This took the form of slashing a crucifix in their abdomens, then tearing back the skin—'

'What are you trying to say?'

'Under the extremes of war, every atrocity is possible, and any race may be the perpetrators. Many killings are supposedly done in the name of religion, but usually that's simply a rationalization for barbarity. Do you think the British soldiers who disembowelled their prisoners with the sign of the cross were true Christians?'

I was silent.

'I'm not condoning what those soldiers did in the church, and I'll see to it that an investigation is carried out to try to discover who was responsible. But I'm not surprised that it happened. The war has been bitter here, and atrocities have been committed by both sides.'

'They tore his heart out and burnt it in a helmet. It was a sacrifice to Huitzilopochtli.'

Extepan sighed, his patience threadbare. 'I'm very well aware that most of our enemies believe that we still practise human sacrifice, cannibalism and doubtless other barbaric rites that I have no inkling of. It's the nature of war to see one's enemies as devils, and rational argument is powerless against such superstitions. We aren't devils, Catherine. We're human beings like any other.'

'Yours is the only nation that's made a religion of war. It's obvious to everyone that the Aztecs are intent on swallowing up the whole world.'

For once he did not take me to task for using the blanket term 'Aztec' rather than 'Mexica'. Instead he simply said, 'We are no more belligerent than you British were when your empire was expanding. We fight to protect our interests, as you did. There's not so much to choose between us, except that we are the victors and you're the losers. I can't say I care for your hypocrisy.'

I decided to match his anger with my own insistence.

'I want to know,' I said. 'Are such sacrifices commonplace?'

'No,' he snapped. 'They're not.'

'Will you give me your word of honour?'

For a moment I thought he might erupt with rage. He rose.

'If it's necessary, then I give it. You will excuse me. There is much to be done before we reach the front line.'

He went off to join his generals.

Pachtli returned soon afterwards, and I steeled myself for the worst. But he looked sullen, and I wondered if Extepan had said anything to him about the sacrifice. He slumped in the seat opposite me, and, to my relief, folded his arms across his chest and went to sleep.

Onwards, deeper and deeper into Russia. I had never seen such flatness, such wildness and desolation. Despite the ample evidence of human habitation – the fields, grain silos like fat

rockets, huddled villages and towns, distant apartment blocks of
community-farm workers – despite all this, the landscape seemed
raw and empty, the works of humans dwarfed by the scale of the
natural world, the immense snow-laden sky, the wind gusting
down from the polar regions, the massed ranks of black pines
like Nature's armies awaiting mobilization.

At length I began to notice moving dots in the sky – aircraft –
and then fields whose snow had been churned by caterpillar
treads or blown into telltale arcs by hovership skirts. I saw a bare
plain littered with the black hulks of Russian tanks, too many to
count. There were hundreds of smaller dark mounds in the
snow. The train veered away, rushing through another town.
Here, many of the buildings had been destroyed. There was a
lurch, and the sound of the wheels on the rails changed subtly.
The train turned down a siding which looked newly constructed.
In the near distance was a dense stand of bare trees and numerous
vehicles and men.

Extepan returned. He had donned his snowsuit. Shaking
Pachtli awake, he ordered him to fetch my luggage.

'We'll soon be there,' he said to me. 'Please get dressed.'

He was stiff, formal, not deigning to look at me. I reached for
my jacket.

'I'm glad I decided to bring you with me,' he said. 'It's one
thing to talk about war, quite another to see it for yourself.'

An hour later I stood surrounded by a cluster of snowsuited
Aztec generals on a low rise at the edge of the stand of trees.

We were looking east, and I could just make out the road and
railway line crossing one another in the distance. Rzhev, apparently less than ten miles away, was just over the horizon. No one
was able – or willing – to tell me whether or not the Russians
had evacuated it.

Dusk was beginning to gather, and the clouds had started to
empty their burden of snow. The fat flakes gusted down, coating
the heads and shoulders of the military élite. They stamped their
feet in the snow, slapped their mittened hands together, but
mostly they were still and silent, awaiting the activation of the
weapon without impatience.

I had expected to find a giant missile launcher or cannon

pointing east, but there was nothing on the ridge except for a long cylindrical trailer, a single gold sunburst on its flank. Extepan had taken me inside the trailer after we disembarked from the train. It was packed with flickering viewscreens, bristling with electronics. Aztec technicians attended the equipment, supervised by none other than Maxixca, his squat figure buttoned up in the uniform of the *tlacochcalcatl*.

On seeing me, Maxixca made no effort to hide his surprise and irritation. But he recovered sufficiently to salute his half-brother. Evidently Extepan remained in overall command of the campaign, though Maxixca now technically equalled him in rank, a development which I found ominous. Both would have seats on the *tlatocan* and a vote in the most important decisions affecting the empire.

'All is ready,' Maxixca said briskly in Nahuatl.

'Is the target in range?' Extepan asked.

Maxixca nodded. 'We've been ready to fire for the past half-hour, awaiting only your arrival. We have another twenty minutes, perhaps. No more.'

'Any reports of troop movements in the area?'

'None. Our intelligence suggests that defensive units have been withdrawn from the outskirts of the town.'

'And the town itself? Has it been evacuated?'

'We have no information on that.'

'And still no response to our ultimatum?'

'None.'

'What about your spy satellites?' I said. 'I thought they were supposed to see all.'

Maxixca glared at me.

'What is she doing here?' he said angrily to Extepan. 'She's a civilian.'

'She brought me good news from London,' Extepan said evenly. 'I have a son.'

Maxixca remembered the formalities of rank and etiquette. He gave a deep bow, then straightened.

'My congratulations. May he grow strong and brave. Do we proceed with the activation of the beam?'

'When I give the order.'

Without further ado, he led me back outside.

'Beam?' I said. 'What sort of beam?'

'You'll soon see for yourself,' he told me.

Now I stood beside him as he scanned the horizon with night-seeing binoculars. I thought it unlikely that he could make out anything in the snow-thick dusk; perhaps it was just a ploy to keep Maxixca waiting.

At length he looked back towards the trailer. It was back-dropped by the silver-and-black trunks of birches, and the whole scene was like a study in monochrome except for the golden sunburst in the trailer's flank and the illuminated wedge-shaped screen at its front. Maxixca was framed in it.

Extepan gave an emphatic nod. Maxixca scuttled from sight.

All eyes turned upwards rather than to the east. Nothing could be seen except the snow swirling down out of the darkening grey sky. Long seconds passed, filled only with the sound of the wind and the soft battering of snowflakes on my face.

I was about to look away when the sky flashed alight. Seamless and sinuous, a rippling bolt of orange-red light split the gloom like a fiery rope held between heaven and earth and shaken by an invisible hand. Wavering and dancing, a brilliant blood-orange, it was the only colour and brightness in a world of grey, the only thing that seemed alive. Yes, it was a living thing, a celestial snake striking down at the earth with all the ferocity it could muster. I became aware of a distant fierce crackling, then a low rumble, as of thunder.

The beam flashed out as abruptly as it had come, leaving a golden after-image in my eyes. The crackling sound had also ceased, but I could still hear the rumbling, and I knew it meant utter destruction.

Even through the snow and the darkness I could see a red glow lighting up the eastern horizon.

Moments later, Maxixca emerged from the trailer.

He marched over to Extepan and saluted.

'Direct hit,' he announced proudly. 'Rzhev no longer exists.'

Seven

On Christmas Day, I entered Moscow with Extepan at the head of a column which crossed a wide bridge over the frozen Moscow river. I was appropriately dressed in black.

Extepan had originally hoped to receive the surrender from Tsar Mikhail himself, but there was only an assemblage of grim-faced generals and a few representatives of the Duma waiting for us in Red Square. The Aztec ultimatum had been rejected after the destruction of Rzhev, and Extepan's attempts to arrange a temporary truce so that negotiations could continue were thwarted because of the threat that the Russians might launch their bombs on targets in Western Europe. Apparently Maxixca, who favoured further action, had appealed directly to Tenochtitlan, and orders were received from the imperial palace that the war should continue until there was an unconditional surrender. And so the beam weapon, fired from an orbiting satellite, had been used on a second Russian city, Ekaterinberg in the Urals, to which the Tsar and his government had removed some weeks before. My cousin Margaret and their three children were also with him.

The weapon was capable of delivering a concentrated burst of solar energy over a radius of several miles for up to twenty seconds. Nothing – bricks, concrete or metal – could withstand the blast, and deep craters were all that remained afterwards, the bedrock fused to a magma which would take months to cool. Margaret and her family were annihilated in an instant.

It was a grey, bitter day, and even the gaudy onion domes of St Basil's Cathedral could do nothing to dispel the bleakness of the occasion. I remember wondering if what I had seen inside the Quetzalcoatl structure was in any way connected with the beam weapon. Perhaps the obsidian mirror had been a prototype, perhaps some sort of lens to focus the sun's rays – a thing of utter blackness to turn light into fiery death. The grim symmetry seemed appropriate.

I found it impossible to blame Extepan for what had happened; on the contrary, I felt a curious kinship with him. We were both united in grief at the loss of someone close to us, Precious Cloud and Margaret, both dead before their time. Only Maxixca looked properly triumphant, as well he might. Moscow, and the rest of Russia, had surrendered without further resistance after the destruction of Ekaterinberg, and now the Aztecs controlled Eurasia from Portugal to the Alaskan Strait.

PART FOUR

He Who Speaks

One

The February wind drove banks of cloud out over the North Sea. Damp with drizzle, it tugged at the collar of my raincoat and tossed my hair about my face. With Extepan beside me, I crunched along the pebble beach.

A few yards behind us, Mia followed, Cuauhtemoc tucked inside her cloak, securely held in a papoose. Down at the sea, Richard and Xochinenen were hurling pebbles into the ragged waves.

'It's good to get away,' Extepan remarked in English. 'I am glad we came here.'

'Despite the weather?' I said.

'*Because* of it,' he replied. 'Compared to Russia, this is nothing. I like your English wind and rain. It blusters and dampens, but there is no real malice in it.'

'I wouldn't be too sure of that. Ever hear of pneumonia?'

He looked at me. 'Do you want to turn back?'

'No, no, I'm fine.'

Dipping and rising in the wind, a floater passed by overhead. Guards patrolled the foreshore and the wooded dunes beyond the beach, ensuring that no one disturbed us.

It was only a fortnight since Extepan had returned from Moscow, leaving Maxixca in charge of mopping-up operations there. Chicomeztli had suggested a long weekend at Sandringham as a break from his duties, and Extepan already looked more rested. We had come to the beach at Richard's insistence.

'Look at those two,' I remarked.

Down at the sea's edge, Xochinenen was retreating from Richard's attempts to splash her.

'I think Richard is proud he is to be a father,' Extepan observed.

Xochinenen had borne her father's death with great fortitude and seemed closer than ever to Richard. She had announced her pregnancy on Extepan's return from Moscow. Richard himself was thrilled, as was the populace at large. In a curious way, the public announcement of the pregnancy had severed my final ties of responsibility towards him. As a prospective father, he was now his own man, and even if he could never be expected to act as a fully mature adult, I knew I had to let him make his own decisions, as far as he was able, for better or worse.

The drizzle intensified, and Extepan motioned for a guard to come forward with an umbrella for Mia. She had returned from Tenochtitlan soon after Precious Cloud's death, and had immediately taken over the care of Cuauhtemoc. It was as if she had never been away, as if Precious Cloud had never existed, and Cuauhtemoc was her own and Extepan's.

Quickening his stride, Extepan headed towards the wooded dunes to seek shelter from the rain. I kept abreast of him, sensing that he wanted to speak privately with me. We drew ahead of the others.

'Catherine,' he said, the moment we were out of earshot, 'I've been intending to talk to you about the immediate future.'

I scrambled up the dunes in his wake. 'Oh?'

'I shall have to leave London soon,' he announced. 'My father has summoned me to Tenochtitlan, and afterwards there will be new duties for me elsewhere. I shall not be returning.'

Although I had anticipated this since his success in Russia, it was still a surprise to hear it. A surprise and something of a disappointment.

'Iztacaxayauh will be appointed to my post here,' he said. 'He's a good man and he will look after the interests of your people.'

I had no quibble with this: Iztacaxayauh struck me as a moderate, and he was infinitely preferable to someone like Maxixca.

'When will you be leaving?' I asked.

'Soon. Chicomeztli, Mia and, of course, my son will be accompanying me. I'd like you to come too.'

He had paused under the shelter of a tree. I peered at him, then turned away.

'My father has asked to meet you. He says it would be a great honour for him. I would very much like you to meet him.'

Below us, Mia and the guards were climbing the dunes. In a minute, they would join us, and I had the urgent sense of having to make a decision that instant, while Extepan and I were still alone. I thought of Motecuhzoma, whose image I had seen countless times on film and television, a man more than any other who had shaped our times. I thought of Tenochtitlan, city on the lake, the heart of the Aztec empire, a distant place of power and exotic dreams. I confess I was flattered to hear that the great *tlatoani*, He Who Speaks, wished to meet me, even though I was the daughter of a king.

I walked off down a brambled path, forcing Extepan to follow. I allowed him to catch up with me.

'Did you ever find out who sacrificed the Russian soldier?' I asked.

He tugged the hem of his cloak free from a briar.

'Nothing was found in the church,' he told me. 'There was no body and no evidence of the . . . *act* you described to me.'

Branches gusted overhead, showering us with water. How convenient – and inevitable – that all signs of the sacrifice had been cleared away. I was now more certain than ever that Pachtli had been involved, and I wished I had insisted that Extepan accompany me to the church the next day. Probably, though, it would have made no difference, the body taken away during the night, the place scrubbed clean of blood.

'It happened,' I insisted.

'I'm sure it did. But without proof, we had no means of proceeding with further enquiries.'

'You do believe me?'

'Catherine, I have never had any reason to disbelieve you.'

I walked on again, descending the dunes back towards the beach, uncaring of the rain. Richard was crouched at the waterline, building a wall of pebbles in front of the waves while Xochinenen looked on under a big black umbrella. In that unguarded moment, her face expressed the sadness which she must have felt; her father would never see the child she was carrying.

Extepan drew abreast of me. 'I think you might be pleased to hear that Pachtli has been transferred to a position of lesser responsibility. Enquiries revealed that he had been selling commandeered wines and spirits to our infantry. He is now in charge of military supplies in Godthaab.'

Did Extepan have the same suspicions as me? Even if he did, the punishment was woefully inadequate.

'So justice has been done,' I said with heavy irony.

Extepan took my arm. 'Catherine, visit Mexico with me.'

He held me close, black hair plastered to his forehead by the rain.

Before I could say anything, there was a rising whine, and a jetcopter appeared over the trees. It banked above our heads, then descended, enveloping us in warm exhaust gases, sending pebbles scurrying as it landed.

'Time for us to be getting back,' I said.

Chicomeztli had arrived sooner than we had expected. When he emerged from the copter, he whispered urgently to Extepan. I knew something was wrong.

'What's going on?' I asked.

'We must return to London immediately,' Extepan told me. 'There has been an explosion. The Prime Minister and many of his cabinet are dead.'

Two

After the memorial service at Westminster Abbey, we were driven back to the complex in a heavily armed motorcade. The crowds were kept well back.

Only one pyramid of the complex had been damaged in the explosion, and this was now swathed in canvas and scaffolding. The repair work was proceeding rapidly, although the bomb had blown out much of the two lower floors, including the cabinet room where Kenneth Parkhouse and his ministers were meeting. He, and seven others, were killed instantly by two kilos of Aztec-manufactured Texcem plastic explosive, carried in a briefcase by a private secretary whom the media described as 'a fanatical member of a small terrorist organization, the English Liberation Army'.

Later, watching the television coverage in my suite with Bevan, I saw Richard and Xochinenen walking among the crowds outside the Abbey, shaking hands and accepting wreaths and sympathy. People interviewed on the street expressed only outrage at the killings. Iztacaxayauh came on screen to announce that the investigation of the case was being put into the hands of the police's anti-terrorist squad, who were treating it as a criminal rather than political affair. He was followed by the new Prime Minister, a strident woman in a dark blue suit, who told the nation that she had already formed a new cabinet, that Parliament would continue to represent the people and would never surrender to common murderers.

The camera panned over the crowd, who held banners saying GOD SAVE THE KING, STOP THE SLAUGHTER and GIVE PEACE A CHANCE. A commentator revealed the results of a poll showing that ninety per cent of the public wanted stability under Aztec governorship and an end to all subversive activities.

'If this is stage-managed,' I remarked, 'it's quite convincing.'

'Sign of the times,' Bevan responded. 'People are fed up with bombs and assassinations and all the rest of it.'

'Oh? Have you been canvassing opinion yourself?'

He sat amply in an armchair, stockinged feet up on the coffee table.

'Written all over their faces, it is. Everybody's had enough of killings, especially after Russia.'

'*Ninety* per cent in favour of Aztec rule? I don't believe it.'

My Citizens Aid office had been gutted in the explosion, and I realized I felt no inclination to start it up again. In recent months, regional centres had been established throughout the country, staffed by local people and including barristers who could bring civil actions against Aztecs if necessary. They would be well equipped to continue the work I had started.

'Something on your mind?' Bevan asked.

He had obviously noticed that I was preoccupied.

'Extepan's asked me to visit Mexico,' I told him.

'Has he now?'

'Apparently Motecuhzoma wants to meet me. Or so he says.'

He grinned. 'I reckon he's more than a bit fond of you, that one.'

To my surprise, I found myself blushing.

'I turned him down,' I said hastily. 'If I went there, it would seem like I was capitulating to Aztec rule over us.'

Bevan looked dubious. 'I doubt it'd make much difference, myself. It's all over bar the shouting any road.'

I was surprised by this. 'I never thought I'd hear you sounding defeatist. I always thought you were a radical. An anarchist, even.'

He shrugged. 'Not going to blind myself to the facts, am I?'

'So you've given up?'

'I'm watching and waiting. See what happens next.'

Now there was a report that the remaining members of the English Liberation Army had been rounded up. A group of dowdy figures were shown being bundled into the back of a riot-wagon. This was followed by a potted celebration of Kenneth Parkhouse. He was portrayed as a man 'whose patriotism showed itself in his constant efforts to provide stable government for his people.'

I made a contemptuous noise. 'Next they'll be telling us he was a martyr to British democracy.'

'There's some would say he was.'

'What?'

Bevan pulled off a sock and began inspecting it for holes.

'Do you think I'm being too hard on him?'

'Depends. Speaking for myself, I always thought he was a toad. But there's talk.'

'Talk?'

'You know. The usual sort.'

'What sort, Bevan?'

His forefinger protruded from a hole in the toe. 'Some are saying the whole thing was rigged by the Aztecs.'

I wrenched the sock from his hands.

'What do you mean?'

He pretended to look cowed. 'They reckon Parkie had contacts. With groups like the ELA. That he was secretly working with the underground.'

'That's absurd.'

'Hard to credit, I agree.'

'He was a careerist, a trimmer. A traitor.'

'Spoke highly of you, though.'

I was angered by the idea. 'Are you trying to tell me the *Aztecs* had him killed? That *they* planted the bomb?'

'I'm only saying that's what some are claiming.'

'I don't believe it.'

'Don't see it myself, neither. But then again, give a dog a bad name . . .'

'Bevan, do you know something?'

He crossed himself. 'Word of honour. You know how it is. Conspiracy theories. Next they'll be claiming you had a hand in it.'

On the screen, Parkhouse was shown outside the complex on the day of his election as Prime Minister. He was waving to the crowds, his wife and two teenage daughters at his side.

'Be a joke, though, wouldn't it?' Bevan was saying. 'If Parkie really was on the side of the angels?' His expression was almost mischievous. 'Any chance of my sock?'

*

Extepan was up on the landing pad, supervising the loading of a luxury Ilhuicamina-class carrier which would be taking him and his retinue to Tenochtitlan tomorrow.

It was sleeting, and we stood together in the lee of the lift shaft. The sickle wings of the carrier glowed bronze in the murky evening light.

'I expect you're pleased to be going home at last,' I remarked.

'In some ways,' he admitted. 'Though I would have been quite happy to stay if my father had wished it. There are many things I like about your country, Catherine.'

'I bet the weather isn't top of the list.'

He smiled. 'I really don't mind it. But it will be good to return to the sun. And good to see my father also.'

Fork-lift trucks whirred back and forth, depositing crates in the carrier's hold.

'There's something I wanted to ask you before you left,' I said.

He gave me a knowing glance. 'I thought as much. It's not like you to make social calls without a purpose.'

I ignored the rebuke. 'There are rumours about the bomb that killed the Prime Minister and his cabinet.'

His attention had returned to the loading operation. He said nothing.

'Some people are claiming your administration was responsible. They say you wanted to get rid of Parkhouse because he had links with the resistance.'

Extepan shouted, and I recoiled. But he was simply calling to two handlers, telling them to be careful with a crate of chinaware.

'I'd like to know if there's any truth in this,' I said.

Only then did he turn to face me.

'Do you have evidence?'

'It's just a rumour. Is it true?'

A gust of wind made me huddle further under the concrete overhang. Extepan suddenly looked intense.

'Ever since the explosion,' he said softly, 'your newspapers and television have been filled with coverage and analysis of the incident. We have given your reporters full access to all the information available. Nothing has been withheld.'

I made to say something, but he was not to be interrupted.

'There has been much dwelling on the pain and suffering of

the families of those who were killed. There have been photographs of these families and the eight dead men, lengthy and respectful obituaries. All this is as it should be. All this is right and proper. Yet almost nothing has been said of the seventeen Mexicans who were also killed in the explosion. They were just anonymous clerical staff, functionaries who oiled the wheels of your government's machinery. But they had families and lives just like the others.'

The calm and care with which he spoke only emphasized how much he was containing his anger. He stood close, and I had the feeling he would have liked to take hold of me and shake me.

'We expected that little account would be taken of them. We do not even demand it, given the circumstances of the occupation and the delicate nature of national sensibilities. But when you come to me and suggest that *we* might have murdered them, it is not unreasonable that I should feel insulted. Is it, Catherine? Do you think we are such creatures that we would cold-bloodedly kill our own people?'

I wanted to argue that it was perfectly possible he had no knowledge of the plot, that it could have been perpetrated by more ruthless and xenophobic Aztecs in the colonial hierarchy. But that would have been to add outrage to insult.

'Bring me evidence, Catherine, and I shall act. Bring me proof that we are *Tzitzimime* and I shall reveal my fangs and claws.'

The *Tzitzimime* were the monsters of twilight in ancient Aztec mythology who would appear at the destruction of the world and destroy any survivors. And the strange thing was, in his anger with his face half lit by the radiance of the carrier's wings, Extepan did, at that moment, look a little demonic.

'I am very busy,' he said, turning away from me. 'I do not propose to discuss this matter further. You must follow it up with Iztacaxayauh, if you wish. He is governor now.'

I caught his arm. 'Extepan, you can't blame me for asking. I intended no insult. I only want the truth.'

'Truth?' he said harshly. 'Truth, Catherine, is whatever you cannot help yourself believing.'

He pulled free and walked away.

Three

'Catherine.'

Extepan's voice woke me from my doze. I stretched in my seat, yawning, and heard Extepan say, 'You asked to be told when we came in sight of Tenochtitlan. There it is.'

He was pointing through the window. It had been dark when I fell asleep, but now dawn was breaking. The carrier had banked over the Valley of Mexico, and there below us, sitting on a lake that was the colour of blood in the gathering light, rose the city.

I stared in silence for long minutes. Tenochtitlan looked like a vast intricate sculpture of many colours, its towers, spires and pyramids rising from a network of lower buildings in which I could discern gardens, courtyards and swimming pools. The city was divided into wedges and trapezoids, cut and crossed at innumerable points by canals which gave access to the wider waters of Lake Texcoco on all sides.

During my honeymoon, I had visited Venice with Alex and been suitably impressed by this city built on water, but at that moment Tenochtitlan seemed even more marvellous. Less than twenty years before, it had been a sprawling metropolis like many others, sitting on a lake bed that was almost entirely dry. But then a major earthquake had struck, killing thousands and making hundreds of thousands homeless. Only the old central quarters of the city, built on the ancient island, had survived without extensive damage. It was then that Motecuhzoma had decided on a radical plan to reshape the city in its former image. The surrounding suburbs had been levelled, their populations transferred to satellite towns around the edges of the valley. Then the lake had been restored by a prodigious feat of engineering which only an autocratic will and the economic power of an empire could have made possible. Using old plans, Motecuhzoma's architects had re-created the ancient heart of the city with as much fidelity as possible. Modern materials and construction methods were used to restore the palaces and houses of the nobles, while the pre-Christian temples were repaired and repainted in their garish pagan colours. They dotted the city at regular intervals, the main ceremonial centre an extensive complex at its very heart.

'Well?' said Extepan.

'It's breathtaking,' I replied.

In the seat behind me, Bevan was taking photographs, while opposite Richard had his nose pressed to the window as Xochinenen provided a commentary.

'Wait until you have a chance to travel around,' Extepan said to me. 'It's even better then.'

There was unashamed pride in his voice. He had recovered his good humour immediately I had made a last-minute decision to accompany him to Mexico. It occurred to me that in his youth he must have seen the city rising anew, ancient yet modern, from the ruins of the old.

Why had I changed my mind and decided to visit Mexico? If I am honest, I believe I was worn down by my ineffectual efforts to resist Aztec hegemony; and I had co-operated with Extepan's administration on too many occasions to maintain the pretence that I was not compromised. I think I had also begun to accept the fact of the occupation, as did the vast majority of my countryfolk. I no longer had the capacity to see the Aztecs as my enemies except on some abstract level which seemed increasingly remote from the daily lives of myself and others around me. Even Bevan seemed fatalistic about the situation and had readily agreed to accompany me to Tenochtitlan. Familiarity breeds not contempt but acceptance. Of course, this doesn't mean that I went without qualms: I think I secretly knew that I was surrendering my last hope of maintaining my integrity; and it was Extepan who had masterminded this.

Soon afterwards, we landed at a private airfield in Azcapotzalco, formerly a suburb of the city, now a large town on the western shore of the lake. It was warm when we emerged, the sun rising in a rosy haze over the mountains. I could see snow on the twin peaks of Popocatepetl and Itzaccihuatl to the south-east.

We were ushered aboard a floater for the short flight to Motecuhzoma's palace on Chapultepec. The palace, undamaged by the earthquake, had been the residence of every *tlatoani* since the sixteenth century, and it sprawled across the hill which overlooked the lake, a rambling, white-stuccoed fortress combining elements of pre-Christian, Renaissance Spanish and modern Aztec architecture. Corbelled towers jostled with chevroned battlements, ornate cupolas with sculpted square entranceways, all combining to a fairytale castle effect; yet at the same time it bristled with aerials and satellite dishes. Within and beyond it, stretched tiered rock gardens ablaze with shrubs and flowers.

The floater descended on to a landing pad which jutted from the battlements. Richard could scarcely wait to get out of his seat. He and Xochinenen were staying a few days to pay their respects to the emperor before flying on to Hawaii for a holiday.

A lift whisked us down into the heart of the building, and we walked through marble hallways decorated with Aztec frescoes and *objets d'art* from all over the world. The frescoes, illustrating ancient battles in bright polychrome, were unsparing of the mutilations and degradations of war: the severed limbs, the burning temples, the prostrations of the vanquished.

Chicomeztli took Richard and Xochinenen off to their suite, while Extepan led Bevan and me into an apartment whose sweeping balcony looked out over the hill. Again I had another view of the city, now stirring as morning advanced. Boats and solar barges were cutting swathes through the lake, raising flocks of white birds from the waters; traffic was moving slowly along the elevated motorway linking the city with the suburb towns on the western shore. The still air was heavy with the scent of flowers.

'I think you'll be comfortable here,' Extepan remarked.

The apartment was airy and spacious, simply furnished with white walls and ochre floor-tiles. The furniture was sturdy Canadian Colonial, even down to the four-poster bed. On the balcony was a private swimming pool.

'I'm sure I shall,' I replied.

Extepan took Bevan through an adjoining door into a smaller

apartment. As at the complex, the lock was on my side. The Aztecs always accommodated him without question, and I had often wondered if Extepan considered I had the same ties of obligation towards Bevan as he did to Mia. And perhaps, in some ways, he was right.

Extepan returned and indicated a desk console which included a telephone.

'If you require anything,' he said, 'just lift the receiver. Chicomeztli or someone else will be at the other end of the line. Now, I must see that Richard and Xochinenen are comfortable.'

I accompanied him to the door. There he paused.

'Catherine, I am so glad you decided to come.'

'So am I,' I replied.

We were standing close. He hesitated, then said, 'I shall show you round later,' before briskly marching off.

I turned. Bevan was standing in the doorway between our apartments.

'Well,' he said. 'Here we are, then.'

'I'm still surprised you decided to come,' I said.

He grinned. 'Wouldn't have missed it for the world, would I?'

We were served a light lunch of salad and beans in our rooms, and afterwards Tetzahuitl visited. He had his own residence in Coyoacan, to the south of the city, but he was frequently to be found in Motecuhzoma's palace, where the *tlatocan* met regularly and all important decisions affecting the empire were taken. He was dressed traditionally in dark green robes over a tunic embroidered with a butterfly motif. Crimson-feathered head-bands adorned his hair.

He presented me with a bouquet of turquoise roses. We sat on the balcony while a servant brought us iced sorrel water, a brilliant red tea.

'The *tlatoani* will receive you tomorrow,' he told me. 'We are greatly honoured you were able to come.'

'The honour is mine,' I replied. 'I never imagined I would visit Tenochtitlan.'

'I hope you will have the opportunity to see much of the city. There are many sights.'

'That would be most gratifying.'

We sipped the crimson tea, the formal conversational exchanges satisfactorily completed. Tetzahuitl regarded me.

'I hear much of your bravery,' he remarked. 'You visited Extepan at the Russian front, is that not so?'

'I don't think that was bravery,' I replied. 'I felt partly responsible for Precious Cloud's death, and I thought it was important that Extepan heard about what had happened from someone who was there rather than get the news through a dispatch.'

'That was considerate of you. Nevertheless, you took a great risk.'

'Perhaps. Though I felt that I would be quite safe travelling under the protection of your armies.'

He smiled at this. 'It was unfortunate the Tsarina Margaret was a casualty of the war. We did not intend that the Tsar and his family should perish. You have my sympathies.'

I looked away. 'Somehow, I knew that when the war started I would never see her again.'

This was true, though it was the first time I had articulated it to myself. I was growing superstitious that everyone I was close to was gradually being lost to me.

Tetzahuitl seemed aware of the drift of my thoughts because he said, 'I think you are a survivor.'

His tone remained dry, so there was no means of telling whether it was meant as encouragement or as a simple statement.

'I think I have some way to go before I can match you,' I remarked.

He was silent for a moment. Then he said, 'Indeed you do. Indeed you do.'

He rose, drawing his robes around him.

'I shall leave you now. No doubt you will wish to sleep. May no monsters disturb your slumber.'

With this rather chilling valediction, he departed.

I fell soundly asleep soon afterwards, and woke to find that it was night. Going out on to the balcony, I looked towards the city, which shone with lights in the darkness. It looked more exotic than ever, its reflection twinkling and shimmering in the dark waters, a fairytale place made real.

The night air was cool, but I stripped off and plunged into the pool. Afterwards, towelled and clad in a robe, I heard Bevan moving about in his room.

I tapped on the door. 'Are you up?'

'I'm making some tea,' he called. 'Fancy a cup?'

We sat out on the balcony to drink it, watching boats move about on the dark waters and identifying neon signs in the coastal towns, advertising the Culhua Bank, Tijuana Film, the ubiquitous MexTaco with its arching golden M. Bevan dunked Jaffa Cakes in his tea, complaining that the milk in Tenochtitlan wasn't the same as at home. He had brought a box of teabags and several packets of biscuits from London.

Next day, Extepan took us on a tour of the gardens. The Aztec passion for flowers was demonstrated in the huge variety on display. Rare tropical orchids were bedded with alpine gentians, rainforest shrubs with poppies from the Atacama Desert, all biomodified to thrive in the climate of the Valley of Mexico. There were lakes and rockeries, a cactus garden and even a refrigerated tundra stocked with flowering mosses. Some areas had been set aside so that wild animals could roam free on the terraces, and there was a special reserve for the big cats. Selective breeding methods had produced striped lions and leopards with dark fur and tawny spots; they were commercially farmed, their skins highly valued for costumes and upholstery. The gardens were used for leisure by the palace staff, many of whom were close relatives of the emperor himself. Two of Extepan's half-sisters accompanied us on the tour, and Extepan himself was more relaxed than I had ever seen him.

Afterwards I returned to my suite to take a nap. Then Chicomeztli arrived with half a dozen female retainers, who proceeded to dress me for my audience with Motecuhzoma. I did not welcome their attentions, deferential though they were, never having liked household staff fussing around me, even as a child. By the time Extepan arrived, I was not in the most gracious of humours.

As soon as we were left alone, he began to instruct me on the etiquette of the occasion. The *tlatoani* would be seated, and I was expected to approach him with my head bowed, not looking at him until he had spoken to me. I would then be told where to sit, and could afterwards proceed in a naturalistic manner, as the conversation dictated.

'Is that all?' I said acidly. 'You mean I won't have to prostrate myself and swear undying fealty to his magnificence?'

Extepan looked a little abashed. 'He's our ruler, Catherine. It's simply our custom, the way we show him our respect. Richard has already seen him. He raised no objections. And he was treated with all the courtesies of his position.'

'Richard will do whatever you tell him. He would have kissed his feet if you had demanded it of him.'

'A bow is a token of honour, not submission.'

'That's a matter of opinion.'

Extepan looked exasperated. 'You agreed to come here. If these formalities are beyond you . . .'

I was being bloody-minded just for the sake of it. I relented with a smile. 'Don't worry. I'll behave myself.'

A sigh. 'You're impossible!'

'It's part of my charm.'

I was dressed in a gown of burgundy velvet and cream silk, adorned with the diamond jewellery which had once been my mother's. Extepan wore the *tlacateccatl*'s uniform. An Eagle Star medal was pinned to his left breast. It was the empire's highest military decoration, but Extepan was almost dismissive when I drew attention to it.

'I was awarded it after the surrender of Moscow,' he told me.

'You sound as if you feel you don't deserve it.'

'There were others in our armies who had a braver war than I. But my father expects us to wear our decorations with pride. Shall we go?'

He offered his arm. I took it.

We walked along the spacious corridors of the palace, finally entering a wide hallway whose ceilings were decorated with representations of *tlalocan*, the heavenly preserve of warriors killed in battle. A green obsidian fountain at the centre of the hall held a figure which spewed water from its mouth and ears. It was the goddess Chalchihuitlicue.

Motecuhzoma's palace within a palace could only be reached by an escalator flanked with guards. Extepan told me his father preferred a stairway to an elevator, which made him prone to vertigo. He had long been known for his dislike of flying, tolerating it as a young man but later refusing to travel any distance by air.

At the top of the escalator was a big mirrored doorway flanked by more guards. Extepan paused and said, 'You look beautiful, Catherine.'

Our reflections were perfectly captured in the centre of the mirror. It was a clever device, giving prospective visitors one final view of themselves before they entered the inner sanctum of the greatest ruler of all time. No doubt they were meant to reflect on their own inadequacy.

Immaculately prepared in my splendid new gown, my glittering necklace and earrings, I looked like a stranger to myself. Extepan was the very model of military dash beside me.

The guards moved to open the door. We entered.

Inside, a matronly Aztec woman in a tasselled skirt and *huipil* was waiting for us. She wore gold seashell earrings and a gold noseplug with a blood-red stone at its centre. Extepan introduced her to me as Cocomicihuatl, the emperor's principal wife for the past twenty years. Dark-skinned and broad-nosed, she greeted me soberly and without expression. I immediately saw the familial resemblance: she was Maxixca's mother.

Without further ceremony, Cocomicihuatl led us through a series of low-ceilinged rooms furnished quite simply with native tapestries and squat upholstered mahogany furniture. There was no grandiloquence here, but rather a cosy, almost rustic atmosphere, as if in his private life the emperor preferred the simple trappings of native Mexican culture to displays of wealth and power. Dusk was falling, and the rooms were illuminated by big smoky globe lamps.

Cocomicihuatl led us towards a patio bathed in a pale golden light. Immediately I saw that the light came from the surrounding roof garden, from rank upon rank of luminous sunflowers.

I was so in awe of the sight that I scarcely noticed we had already entered the *tlatoani*'s presence. Cocomicihuatl was already retreating inside and Extepan was leading me forward. He jerked my arm to gain my full attention, and I bowed my head instinctively, catching only a glimpse of a small man who sat in a large white *icpalli*.

'My Lord Emperor,' Extepan said in Nahuatl, 'it gladdens my heart that I am able to visit you again. Allow me to introduce my great friend and respected adversary, Her Highness, the Princess Catherine, sister of King Richard of the House of Marlborough, Sovereign of the United Kingdom.'

The appellation 'adversary' startled me, but I maintained my composure, bowing even lower.

'You are both most welcome,' a throaty voice said.

Slowly, following Extepan's lead, I straightened. And there before me, ruler of over half the earth, conqueror of lands he had never seen, sat the great *tlatoani* Motecuhzoma Xohueyacatzin, the tenth of his line to bear the illustrious name.

I couldn't stop myself from staring. For a legendary emperor, and a man whose second name meant 'Old Long Foot', he was positively diminutive in stature, but I had expected this. He looked swamped in his big white *icpalli*, which hovered inches above the tiled floor. A striped blanket was wrapped around the lower half of his body, and an ancient hand rested on a control panel set into one of the arms of the chair. The chair itself, of moulded plastic and chrome, was purely functional, having no ornamentation or emblems to display his status. It made him look like an invalid.

'Please,' he said with a wave of his free hand, 'seat yourselves.'

There were more conventional armchairs on either side of him. I allowed Extepan to seat me on Motecuhzoma's right.

The *tlatoani* looked aged and frail, but his eyes were alert and the many lines on his face somehow spoke of all his achievements, as if each one had been etched there by all the momentous events which had shaped the history of his fifty-two-year reign, an Aztec century. Here was the man who, more than any other before him, had brought about a transformation of the entire world.

'You are younger than I had imagined,' he said briskly, leaning forward to address me, as if his hoarse voice would not otherwise carry. 'My son always forgets to inform me of such telling details as a person's age.'

This was said good-naturedly, and I was sure it was simply a conversational pleasantry; Motecuhzoma had the reputation of being scrupulously well informed about anyone he met.

'I would have liked to have visited your country,' he went on. 'Your father once invited me to London when I was a much younger man, but diplomatic conditions did not permit it. This has always been a source of regret to me.'

Trying to keep any hint of sarcasm out of my voice, I said, 'It would be perfectly possible for you to visit now.'

He waved the bent fingers of his hand. 'I'm too old, and my legs no longer work as well as they once did. I have to sit here in this contraption – ' he slapped the arm of his chair with his palm ' – for hours on end, resting them. Rest, rest. All my doctors ever tell me to do is rest.'

He wore a plain white tunic beneath a quilted cotton cardigan in the imperial turquoise. His ash-grey hair, cropped short all over his head, was unadorned, confirming the rumour that he, unlike many of his countrymen, disliked headdresses and seldom wore his crown.

'I gather Extepan's been showing you around my gardens. What do you think of them?'

I stared again at the luminous sunflowers.

'They're magnificent,' I said.

'A useful trick, eh? Sunflowers that really shine. I had them put in so that I could read outside here in the evenings.'

I noticed papers in a recess in one of the arms of the chair. As he moved, the chair adjusted itself, and gusts of air blew about my ankles. Conflicting stories had circulated about his state of health for many years. It was known that he suffered from arthritis of the hips and found walking any distance painful, but other rumours had him near death of heart failure, a liver disorder, leukaemia. To me, he looked reasonably fit for a man of his age, despite his lack of mobility. His movements were brisk and purposeful, and his eyes constantly caught the light of his garden. Extepan had inherited their almond shape, along with his high cheekbones and wedge-shaped jaw.

'I've brought you a small gift,' I said, reaching into the folds of my gown and removing a small rectangular package. It was long and thin, wrapped in dark blue crêpe paper.

He took it from me and removed the wrapping before opening

the lid of a small box. Inside it was a brown-and-gold tortoiseshell Chamberlain fountain pen.

'It was my father's,' I told him. 'His favourite pen. He used it for signing official documents, including, I believe, the surrender of India to you in 1951. I thought you should have it.'

There was a frozen moment of silence, and I could almost feel Extepan going rigid with apprehension. He had not known about the gift, and was doubtless afraid that his father would regard it as an insult. And in truth, I intended it to be an ambiguous present, at once a concession and a challenge.

Motecuhzoma held the pen in his hand as if it were a dart which he was about to throw. As a young man, he had been renowned for his temper, ordering savage reprisals against those who brooked him or insulted his honour.

For long moments, the only sound was the faint hum of his chair. Then he leaned back in it, giving a smile.

'Thank you,' he said softly. 'I accept it in the spirit in which it is offered.'

Cocomicihuatl reappeared, pushing a trolley which held drinks and confectioneries. Motecuhzoma took a glass of lime juice along with a bowl of honeyed nougat which he placed on his lap. There were wines and spirits on the trolley, but Extepan and I both opted for mineral water in deference to the *tlatoani* having renounced alcohol in his later years.

Cocomicihuatl withdrew. She had not uttered a word to any of us, and Motecuhzoma had paid her no attention whatsoever.

'Doesn't your wife wish to join us?' I said pointedly.

'She likes nothing better than to be left in peace,' he responded. 'I'm afraid she finds foreigners an irritation, no matter how high-born.'

I was firmly put in my place. We sat in silence for a short while as Motecuhzoma ate a piece of nougat. I caught Extepan's eye, and he gave me a rather sheepish smile.

'Tell me,' Motecuhzoma said presently, 'what do you think of Extepan here? How has he served your country?'

It was plain that Extepan was unprepared for this; he looked distinctly uncomfortable.

I said, 'Given that I would have preferred him not to have

been there at all, I think he acquitted himself quite well. We might have had a worse master.'

'Indeed? Were you thinking of anyone in particular?'

I wasn't going to fall into the trap of mentioning Maxixca.

'I'm speaking generally,' I said. 'He carried out his duties honourably, in the circumstances. I believe he fulfilled what you asked of him, while always trying to take into account the wishes and concerns of those he governed.'

'High praise indeed,' Motecuhzoma said, 'from so stern a critic of our rule.'

They were practically the same words that Tetzahuitl had used in Kew Gardens. How much of this audience was a ritual, a game, with everything pre-ordained?

Motecuhzoma put another piece of nougat into his mouth and licked his fingers. Plainly, he was enjoying himself.

'You can't expect me to be pleased that my country was occupied by your armies,' I said sharply. 'You'll forgive me if I sound angry, but I didn't expect to be discussing the merits of colonialism.'

'No, no,' Motecuhzoma said swiftly, 'the fault is mine. I shouldn't have raised the subject. Old age makes me forget my manners. You are our guest here, our honoured guest. I don't want to open old wounds. I'm simply concerned to make the correct decisions regarding Extepan's future. Having recently lost two sons, I have no desire to throw away the lives of those that are left to me.'

'I understand,' I said tersely.

'I hope your stay in Tenochtitlan will be a lengthy one. Everything will be arranged for your convenience, you have my personal guarantee. Whatever you require, we'll endeavour to provide it.'

I was not swayed by this newly accommodating tone, but it had given me an opening.

'There is something,' I said.

'Ask.'

'It wasn't directly connected with my visit here.'

'Nevertheless . . .'

'It's about my sister. Princess Victoria.'

He waited.

'She's been in exile for two years now, and I've heard nothing from her. If she can't be released, then it would be good to know where she is, to hear from her.'

Motecuhzoma stroked the underside of his chin with a forefinger, as if in contemplation. He turned to Extepan. 'Where did we send her?'

Extepan was silent for a moment. 'Beijing, I believe.'

'Ah, yes. You can be assured she's being well looked after. Of course, I can't authorize her release from custody, given the seriousness of her actions . . .'

He allowed a pause, as if to give me room to protest her innocence. But I didn't do so, even though I believed as firmly as ever that she had never confessed.

'. . . but it may be possible to arrange some kind of communication, so you may be satisfied that she is safe and well. Would that do?'

'It would be something.'

'Good. Then leave the matter in my hands, and we'll arrange it. Now, was there anything else?'

'I can't think of anything at the moment.'

'Then shall we take a walk around my garden? Of course, I use the term "walk" in a figurative sense in my case.'

A hoarse chuckle. He put the bowl of nougat back on the tray.

Extepan and I rose. The *tlatoani*'s hand was on the control panel. The chair abruptly jerked forward, then began to move at quite a moderate speed towards the path which wound through the sunflower beds. The flowers shone brighter now that the darkness had deepened, and it was easy to understand why even an emperor would be proud of them.

Extepan grasped my hand briefly and squeezed it, as if to congratulate me on passing a test. We hurried off after the diminutive figure in the weaving white chair.

Four

The next day was sweltering, and I spent much of the morning dozing. In the afternoon I visited the steam baths at the palace, sitting in a humid cubicle filled with the scents of resinous wood. That evening, dancers from Chiapas performed a mime for us, all feathers and swirling mantles, their story symbolizing the acceptance of Christianity as the official religion of the empire by the *tlatoani* Tezozomoc in the seventeenth century.

I sat with Richard and Xochinenen, who were flying on to Honolulu the following day. Richard was thrilled at the prospect of going surfing, his latest passion. In a quiet moment I whispered in Nahuatl to Xochinenen, 'Will you be returning to London after Hawaii?'

'Of course,' she replied. 'Richard wants our son to be born in England. He's certain it's going to be a boy.'

I think I must have had some foreboding that a lengthy separation was imminent.

'You will look after him, won't you?'

She knew immediately I was referring to Richard rather than the child. He was clapping his hands to the music which accompanied the mime, completely engrossed in the performance.

'You mustn't worry,' she said, putting a hand on my wrist. 'I would never do anything to hurt him. Do you know he's been teaching me how to speak English correctly?' She paused, licking her scarlet lips. '"How now brown cow".' Her accent was thick, the Os ostentatiously rounded. '"The rain in Spain falls mainly on the plain".'

She giggled. I couldn't help smiling.

*

Later the following morning Chicomeztli came to my apartment to tell me that a message from Victoria had arrived. I was drinking coffee with Bevan, and we waited while Chicomeztli went to the keyboard of the console. Though the telephone and domestic television channels on the unit were operational, there was a security lock on its other functions. Evidently Victoria's message was being transmitted on a private channel.

Presently the screen lit up, showing a still image of Victoria. She sat at a table in a wood-panelled room, dressed in a plain cream kimono-like blouse. She looked healthy enough but rather drawn: lines bracketed her mouth and radiated from her eyes.

'The message was recorded earlier this morning,' Chicomeztli informed me.

'I'd like to watch it alone, if you don't mind,' I said.

'Of course.'

He promptly withdrew. But when Bevan made to leave, I put a hand on his arm and said, 'Stay.'

I went to the console and pressed the PLAY button. For several moments Victoria's fixed expression did not alter. Then abruptly she came alive.

'Catherine,' she began, staring straight out of the screen. 'It's good to be able to talk to you after such a long time. I'm sorry I can't speak to you face-to-face, but they wouldn't allow it. I'm well, as you can see – as well as can be expected, anyway, under the circumstances. How are you? They tell me you're visiting Tenochtitlan. I wish I was there with you. Beijing's pretty enough, but I mustn't leave the palace and it gets very cold here in winter. I miss you terribly.

'How's Richard? I'm told he'll soon be a father – that was quite a surprise. As you can tell, I'm not completely isolated from the outside world, they do let me have some news from time to time. But it's not the same as being there with you all. I've made a few friends here, but not many people speak English and I'm perfectly hopeless at learning Mandarin. I miss so many things – I can't begin to tell you.

'How are Archimedes and Adamant? Have you mastered Adamant yet? There's no opportunity to ride here, but I swim most days. They have a heated pool outside.' She paused, nibbling her lower lip. 'I'm sorry this is so hasty and rambling. I haven't really got any news to report – not much happens here, and if it did I probably wouldn't be allowed to tell you about it.' An empty laugh. 'I hope you're still battling on . . . you always were a fighter, not like me.'

She paused again, looking off-screen, looking pained. 'This is difficult for me. Can I go now?' There was a pause, a muffled voice in the background, a foreign voice speaking English. Then Victoria turned back to the camera. 'I'm sorry, Kate. I don't know what to say. Do take care of yourself, won't you? I think of you often.'

I saw her rising from her chair. Then the image blanked.

I did not move for some time but simply stared at the flickering lines on the screen.

It was Bevan who rose and pressed the STOP button.

'What do you think?' I said to him.

'Very interesting,' he replied.

'She sounded as if she had been told what to say.'

'I reckon that's a fair bet.'

Bevan went out on to the balcony to smoke a cigarette. I followed him.

'What is it?' I said.

He broke a match between his fingers. 'Maybe we can do some checking.'

'Checking?'

'Might be possible to get into the networks here.'

'What?'

A sly grin. 'Watched him, didn't I? He used the network code.'

'You can remember it?'

'Piece of cake.' He tapped his gleaming forehead. 'All in here, it is.'

I put my face in front of his. 'What are you saying? That we might be able to find out more about Victoria?'

'Worth a try. We could root around in the system, see what we can come up with. Who knows, we might even be lucky enough to find her phone number.'

Though I knew he was half-joking, I was excited by the idea.

'We could use the terminal here?'

He nodded. 'Like we did in London. Sniff about at night.'

I was smiling. 'Just like old times.'

'Want to give it a go, then?'

'Yes,' I said emphatically. 'But first I'm going to see Extepan.'

I was not surprised when my request to send a return message to Victoria was turned down. Extepan was apologetic but firm.

'There's nothing I can do,' he told me. 'As an exile, she isn't permitted any unofficial communication from outside. Her message to you was a special favour from the *tlatoani*, but he made it clear to me that this was the extent of his concession.'

I had expected as much. Not for the first time, I demanded to know how long Victoria was to be kept in exile.

'At the moment it's indefinite. You must remember she confessed to serious charges. As far as we are concerned, she's an enemy of the state. But circumstances may change.'

'The charges were false.'

'Catherine, please. I don't want us to argue about this. At least you know she's safe and well.'

We were in his apartment, and Mia sat on a sofa, feeding Cuauhtemoc, watching us in silence. I had come to feel uneasy in her presence.

'I hope you've packed a bag,' Extepan said.

'What?'

'I'm taking you sightseeing this afternoon.'

I returned immediately to my apartment. There I found a scrawled note from Bevan to say that he and Chicomeztli had gone to a football match at the Anahuac stadium and would not be back until late. I wrote a note of my own, explaining that I would be away for a few days and instructing him to feel free to use the facilities in my apartment during my absence. I left the adjoining door unlocked, hoping he would understand what I meant.

After a late lunch, Extepan and I took a hydrofoil across the lake. We spent the afternoon in Tlatelolco Market, its endless stalls piled with fruit and vegetables, its traders selling clothing, jewellery and bric-à-brac from every corner of the world. We walked unhindered among the crowd, I marvelling at their orderliness, my senses swamped by bolts of bright-patterned cloth, iridescent glassware, tiers of fruits in every colour, shape and rich, elusive aroma. This was the commercial heart of the empire.

Heading north across the lake to Tepeyacac, we visited the old Hispanic church of Our Lady of Citlaltepec, a cool stone building commemorating the native woman who had had a vision of the Holy Virgin four hundred years before. It was one of the first Christian churches to be built in Mexico with Aztec approval, and it remained one of their holiest places.

As dusk began to fall, we returned again to Tenochtitlan, entering the broad canal which led to the very heart of the city. We were finally going to visit the place which fascinated me most of all – the ancient temple precinct.

Already the city was largely quiet, its few residents ensconced in their own homes, whose windows and courtyards faced inwards so that only blank walls were presented to the passing traveller. We moved swiftly down the globelamp-silvered water-way. Despite our escort, I felt that Extepan and I were alone.

The shadows of the pyramids loomed ahead of us. We disembarked from the hydrofoil to stand at the main entrance to the precinct. It was a low pillared structure guarded by soldiers in *ocelotl* skins and feathered headdresses. The sight of them unnerved me.

Surrounded by canals and the palaces of ancient rulers, the precinct stood on the very site where Tenochtitlan had been founded, the only dry land in a swampy lake, over six centuries before. Then, the Aztecs had been a despised nomadic tribe, scarcely civilized. It was remarkable to contemplate how far they had come since then. The precinct had withstood earthquakes, floods and the subtler devastations of progress, secure behind its Serpent Wall.

Extepan took my arm as we stood there on the threshold. Beyond, the precinct was deserted, bathed in harsh magnesium light. It looked sterile yet eerie, a place of history and silence, filled with ghosts from former times – rulers, frantic priests, the flailing bodies of innumerable sacrificial victims.

'Shall we go in?' Extepan said in a whisper.

Numbly, I nodded. The guards moved aside to let us through. Night had fallen abruptly, a moonless night which, against the glare of the lights, looked utterly black.

I stayed close to Extepan as we entered, telling myself that my fears were entirely irrational, that the precinct was an architectural museum, with no one even being allowed into it these days except for privileged visitors like myself. All the structures had been restored to perfection, painted gold and turquoise, scarlet and white, their decorative motifs pristine. They were immaculate sculptural edifices rather than still-functioning buildings – or so I kept assuring myself.

Extepan was talking, pointing out the ball court, the palace of Axayacatl, the skull rack . . .

Grass grew thick in the ball court, the skull rack was empty, there was no one here but us and our guards and the enveloping night . . .

'Catherine?'

Something small and dark flitted past overhead. Instinctively, I cringed.

'It's only a bat,' Extepan said with some amusement. 'Do you want to go up to the top?'

Two broad balustraded stairways rose sharply in front of us, climbing the main pyramid to the shrines of Huitzilopochtli and Tlaloc. One shrine was decorated with white skulls on a red background, the other white banded with blue. No blood soaked the steps, no black-skinned priests pranced with obsidian blades, no bodies lay piled at the foot of the steps with gaping chests . . .

I shook my head. 'It's too steep.'

'You can see right over the city from the top.'

'No.'

'Catherine, what's the matter?'

I was still staring around me, looking for shadows, or movement, or evidence, I didn't know what. When I turned, Extepan's face was close to mine. He looked genuinely anxious.

'I'm sorry,' I said. 'It's all so . . . overwhelming. Why is it closed to the public?'

Extepan smiled. 'Did you know that Venice is slowly sinking? Under the weight of its tourists? My father is determined that the same thing will not happen here.'

Directly opposite us stood the Quetzalcoatl temple, its rounded stairs and painted conical tower unlike the others, its entrance a monstrous dark mouth. It inevitably made me recall the building in Crystal Palace Park, and this was also a reminder that the Aztecs certainly did have secrets which I knew nothing about.

'Tell me something,' I said to Extepan. 'What do you think of when you come here?'

'I think of history,' he said promptly. 'Of the past, and sometimes the future.'

'The future?'

'That's where the road from the past leads, isn't it?'

I could see more bats now, three or four, constantly fleeing into the darkness the moment I glimpsed them, as if they were creatures who could only inhabit the periphery of vision.

'I feel uneasy here,' I said. 'This place unnerves me.'

He laughed, but not mockingly. 'It shouldn't do. This is what we *were*, Catherine, not what we *are*.'

'Can we leave now?'

'If you wish. Are you sure there's nothing else you want to see?'

I merely looked at him.

He took my arm again and led me from the place.

We stayed overnight at one of Motecuhzoma's houses near the Tlacopan Causeway. The next day Extepan took me around some of the big department stores off Tlatelolco Square, which were closed to the public that day. The stores sold everything from Simreal electronic games to death masks fashioned from real human skulls and adorned with semi-precious stones.

Later that day, we took the hydrofoil south and visited the floating gardens of Xochimilco, where farmers grew cereals and vegetables to feed the Valley. It was tranquil here, the canals flanking green *chinampas* with their tall poplars and cypresses and their neat rows of maize, squashes and potatoes. We slept in a palace belonging to one of Extepan's uncles in the ancient city of Culhuacan. Next morning we flew on to Texcoco and the great Nezahualcoyotl University, where Extepan himself had studied. This was the intellectual centre of Mexico, whose scholars and philosophers had done so much to unite the many different peoples of the region under a single cultural and political ideal. The university was housed in the palace of the pre-Christian monarch whose name it celebrated, and the tiered gardens which surrounded it were the equal of those on Chapultepec.

The following day we flew north-east to the even more ancient site of Teotihuacan, built by an earlier civilization which the Aztecs still revered. It had once been a great cultural centre, but now its great temple-pyramids stood dusty and deserted. Extepan had obviously arranged for all other tourists to be turned away that day.

I felt more comfortable here than in the temple precinct. It was more spacious, more securely dead and historic; and, of course, we had come during daylight.

This time I did agree to accompany Extepan to the top of the enormous Pyramid of the Sun. We zig-zagged slowly up the great stone steps under the fierce morning heat, a climb I found exhausting and terrifying. It was hard to get my breath in the thin air, and I had to pause frequently on the vertiginous terraces.

Finally we reached the top and looked out over a dry landscape already blurred with heat-haze. My heart was still pounding from the climb.

Presently Extepan said, 'I've enjoyed these days we have had together, Catherine. Alas, tomorrow I must return to my duties.'

There had been no mention of me returning to London, but I thought perhaps he was suggesting that the time had come. I said as much.

'No, no,' he insisted, 'there's no need for you to go. I have to leave Tenochtitlan, but I hope to be gone only a short time. My father wishes me to visit Precious Cloud's family and pay my respects to her father. Understandably, he is grieved at her death, and we may have lost the confidence of his peoples. This could have repercussions for our northern frontier.'

I sensed he was trying to say something else. On an instinct, I said, 'Do you want me to go with you?'

He took my hands in his, smiling and shaking his head. 'No. As much as I would like that, it would not be appropriate.' He paused. 'But there is another proposal I would like to make to you.'

I already knew what he was going to say.

'I ask you again to consider becoming my wife.'

I was still giddy from the climb, still drained and powerless, wanting, yet not wanting, to turn away from him.

'This hardly seems the time . . .'

'It's just the right time, Catherine. My father wants me married, and Cuauhtemoc needs a mother. But those aren't the main reasons. You were always my first choice.'

'Because I'm Richard's sister?'

'Of course not. You know it's not that.'

He held my hands tightly. I was frantically searching my mind for evasions, excuses.

'What about Mia?'

'Mia?'

'She's been at your side for years. She's caring for Cuauhtemoc. You've always been close. I think she would be more than happy to marry you.'

'It wouldn't be possible, even if I wanted it.'

'Why not?'

'She's not from the nobility. It wouldn't be acceptable to our people.'

'Surely it's in Motecuhzoma's power to ennoble her? Some of his ancestors married the daughters of slaves and commoners, didn't they?'

'Not as their principal wives. And I do not intend to take more than one.'

'You'd prefer to keep her as your mistress, perhaps?'

This was cheap of me, I knew. Extepan looked hurt rather than angry.

'You must be very fond of her,' I said hastily. 'You've kept her in your household for so long.'

'You seem equally attached to Bevan.'

'Bevan?'

'Don't you think there have not been rumours? He, the only member of your household staff? With his own door to your apartments? The private conversations you always have?'

It was a measure of my *naïveté* that I had never considered this.

'That's ridiculous,' I said. 'There's nothing like that between us.'

'I'm prepared to believe you,' he replied. 'Perhaps you will also allow me the same courtesy of believing that I have never wanted Mia as my wife. I have asked *you*. For the second time.'

In the distant fields beyond the ruins, farmers were harvesting maguey plants, just as Mexicans had done for centuries, long before Europeans discovered the New World. Some facts of life were unchanging, inescapable.

'If you refuse me this time,' Extepan said calmly, 'I shall never ask you again. But you must believe that it is you, and not your status, that I want.'

'Am I to take it that you've discussed this with your father?'

'I told him I was intending to ask you again. That was one of the reasons why he wanted to meet you. He likes you, Catherine. He approves of you. He's given my proposal his blessing.'

My mind was reeling. Extepan was at his most earnest, and he would not let go of my hands. Atop the pyramid we were isolated, and I knew he had chosen his moment very carefully, giving me no easy opportunity for physical escape. But I was determined to balk him.

'It would hardly go well for you with Matogee if you arrived there newly betrothed.'

He merely held me closer. 'That is why it would have to remain secret until my negotiations were complete. But I needed to ask you now, before I went. I need an answer to take away with me, Catherine, for better or worse.'

A breeze had sprung up, bringing some respite to the relentless midday heat. All around me were dust and ruins and hazy mountains. I felt as if much of my former life had been stripped away, that I stood there without obligations or burdens except those I chose myself. It seemed to me then that I had grown towards Extepan, that perhaps our lives had been on this very collision course ever since we first met.

Looking into his eyes, I said, 'Very well.'

It was a second before he said, 'Is that an answer? Are you saying yes?'

'On one condition. No, two.'

'Tell me what they are.'

'I'd like Victoria to be freed from exile.'

He let his hands fall from mine.

'I can't promise that.'

'I'd accept it as a possibility. As something you'd try to achieve.'

His eyes were narrowed against the glare of the sun. 'If it's possible, I'll do what I can. But this cannot be a condition of our betrothal.'

He was quietly adamant. Suddenly I was anxious that, if I pressed him, he might easily withdraw his proposal altogether. How swiftly the tables were turned.

'That's all I ask,' I said.

'What else? You mentioned two conditions.'

Again I hesitated. Could I risk it? I had no choice. If we were to be married, I wanted no secrets between us.

I stepped back, giving myself space. Then I proceeded to tell him about my encounter with Zacatlatoa on the day of Richard's wedding and our investigation of the Quetzalcoatl structure in Crystal Palace Park. I omitted nothing except for Bevan's indirect involvement in the affair.

I couldn't tell whether he was shocked or already suspected I had links with anti-Aztec forces: his expression gave away nothing. I told him precisely what I had seen and felt inside the building, and then finally I said, 'I'd like to know what it is. What it's for.'

There was another long silence, but he did not take his eyes off my face. At last he said, 'You have my word of honour that when we are married, I'll tell you everything about it. I swear it. When we're married. But not before.'

Once again I felt he had gained the upper hand. I had asked for information, and he had given me a promise. Was this enough? Perhaps it was. Perhaps it was unreasonable of me to expect more, given his position and my past record as an opponent of Aztec power. Perhaps he still mistrusted me a little. Perhaps he was right to do so.

'Very well,' I said again. 'I accept your proposal and also your promise.'

He looked almost startled, as if he hadn't really believed I would ever say yes. He smiled, then raised my hands and touched my knuckles to his lips. Finally he leaned forward and kissed me once, very delicately, on the cheek. Taking my hand again, he led me forward to the edge of the temple's precipitous steps.

'Please be careful,' he said softly. 'It is much harder going down.'

Five

On our return to Chapultepec, Extepan escorted me to my apartment. He left me at the door, saying he would call early the following morning so that we could present ourselves to his father. His manner was very correct, as it had been ever since I had agreed to marry him.

I had no sooner gone inside than Bevan appeared from his room. He was wearing a maize-coloured sombrero with a navy sash carrying the words VIVA CUEPOPAN in white.

'What do you think?' he said.

'Very elegant,' I replied.

'They slaughtered Chalco four–nil. It was a grudge match, according to Chicomeztli. He was over the moon.'

I was tired after my travels, preoccupied with the decision I had made.

'Have a nice time, did you?'

I put my travelling bag on the bed. 'Are you sneering?'

'Not me. Extepan been showing you the sights, has he?'

'That's right.'

'Very nice of him.'

Against my better instincts, I said, 'We slept in separate rooms, in case you're interested.'

Bevan eyed me from under his hat. Now he no longer looked jaunty but quite serious.

'Fancy a breath of air?'

'I'm tired,' I said. 'Can it wait?'

Bevan took off his sombrero. He was still watching me.

'This is important.'

I gave a weary sigh. 'I really am tired. Surely it can wait until the morning?'

Bevan played with his hat. 'Thing is, I'm off again tomorrow. Crack of dawn. Chicomeztli's organized a jaunt to Tehuantepec.'

'Oh?'

'Seven-a-side tournament. Lots of local colour.'

'You and he are thick as thieves all of a sudden.'

He made light of it. 'Gives me something to do, I'll be gone a few days. Maybe a week.'

'I didn't know you were such a football fan.'

He spun the sombrero in his hand. 'Don't play rugby around here, do they?'

Was he making fun of me again? I was too exhausted to care.

'That all right with you, then?'

'Of course. You enjoy yourself.'

I opened my travelling bag, hoping he would take the hint. He didn't move.

'We need to have a chat before I go,' he persisted.

There was an ominous emphasis in his voice, and it made me quail inwardly. I couldn't look up at him, couldn't bear to face something unexpected or revelatory now. Only six hours before I had made a commitment that was going to change my life dramatically.

Very cautiously I asked, 'Is it about Extepan?'

'Not exactly.'

'Then it will have to wait.'

'You need to hear this.'

I rounded on him. 'Bevan, I'm exhausted! Write it down for me if it's so important. Leave me a note! All I want now is a hot bath and an early night.'

He stood motionless, staring at me as if I were mad, as if he could not credit my stupidity. Then he shrugged.

'Have it your way.'

He went off to his apartment without another word.

I sat in the bath for an hour or so, feeling guilty, knowing that my acceptance of Extepan's proposal was my final surrender. I tried to pretend that I had sound strategic reasons for doing so: with Chimalcoyotl and Ixtlilpopoca dead, Extepan was now Motecuhzoma's eldest son, with a good chance of succeeding his father when he died. Wouldn't marriage to him put me in a position where I would be able to undermine the Aztec cause far more effectively in future? What better hiding place for an enemy than in the very heart of their empire?

But I knew this was a spurious rationalization. When Extepan had asked me to marry him, all that had been in my mind at that instant was his face, his eyes, his hands holding mine, the *frisson* of finally surrendering to the forbidden. Only Richard was likely to be pleased; it would be impossible to explain to anyone at home without feeling like a traitor.

Extepan led me through into the council chamber.

It was a large room of carved cedar pillars and terracotta walls, hung with portraits in gilt frames of Aztec rulers and military leaders. Sunlight lanced in through crystalline louvres set in the sloping ceiling, throwing bands of light on the big oval mahogany table at its centre.

All the high-backed chairs around the table were empty. Only Motecuhzoma sat in his white *icpalli* at the head of the table, with Tetzahuitl standing at his shoulder.

Motecuhzoma was dressed as informally as when I had previously met him, though Tetzahuitl wore a dark green cloak with a border of wind jewels. His headdress was a coronet of scarlet macaw feathers.

I was led forward, and Extepan and I bowed as one before the *tlatoani* and the *cihuacoatl*.

'What is your petition?' Motecuhzoma said.

'Yesterday I made Princess Catherine a proposal of marriage,' Extepan replied formally. 'I am honoured to say she has accepted. We ask your blessing and approval for the union.'

There seemed to be a long silence. I fought the urge to look up.

'It is granted. Rise.'

We straightened. Tetzahuitl took my left hand and put it into Extepan's right. He pressed our fingers together, his palm as dry as paper against the back of my hand.

Motecuhzoma was gazing straight at me, a half-smile on his face. Then he looked serious.

'I trust you freely agreed to my son's proposal?'

It seemed an odd thing to say, having already given his blessing.

I nodded. 'I would not be here otherwise.'

'Then I'm greatly pleased for you both. Do you have gifts to exchange?'

'We do,' Extepan said.

He had already prepared me for this, a standard ritual of betrothal. I had chosen an amber ring which I had originally bought in Tlatelolco as a keepsake. Extepan gave me a bead necklace of obsidian and jade. The presents were meant to be simple, symbolizing a promise and the potential fruitfulness of marriage.

I wondered what Motecuhzoma and the ever-impassive Tetzahuitl were thinking. Only the four of us were apparently to know about the betrothal, for the time being at least. I was happy with this; it gave me more room for manoeuvre should I change my mind.

Once all the formalities were complete, Motecuhzoma asked Extepan and Tetzahuitl to leave so that he could talk briefly to me alone.

'In our lives there are always choices to be made,' he remarked to me when they were gone. 'And these choices assume a greater significance when one sits close to the centre of power.'

He steered his chair around the table, coming closer to me.

'Did Extepan tell you I've nominated him as my successor?'

I was surprised both by the fact and its admission.

'I asked him not to, of course. But I didn't demand it of him.'

'He didn't mention it, I promise you.'

He was now so close I could smell the odour which clung to him – a sweet, medicinal odour, the odour of invalidity and age. It seemed strange to me at that moment that he should be reduced to this, a wizened figure wrapped in woollen blankets, a man who bestrode the world yet could scarcely rise from his chair.

'It matters neither way,' he went on. 'In any case, the succession isn't guaranteed. When the time comes, it will be Tetzahuitl and the *tlatocan* who will decide the issue. I will just be a ghost, a memory.'

'Assuming Tetzahuitl outlives you,' I remarked.

'Ah, yes,' he said, almost lightly. 'Assuming that.'

'Does Extepan have many serious rivals?'

'There are always rivals when a succession isn't guaranteed by strict rules of descent. Maxixca, of course.' He mentioned several other names, cousins of Extepan, prominent members of the *tlatocan*, even one of his sons by an *auianime* who had married a Hispaniolan princess.

'If he outlives you,' I said, 'then perhaps Tetzahuitl will set a precedent by becoming *tlatoani*.'

Motecuhzoma smiled at this. No *cihuacoatl* in the past had ever ascended to the Turquoise Throne, both positions of power operating as separate but parallel dynasties which had worked together with remarkable cohesion for hundreds of years. But with Tetzahuitl being the last of his line, he might be tempted to seize the opportunity to become sovereign.

'I think not,' Motecuhzoma said. 'We're both old men now. My reign has been a long one, and when it ends young blood will be needed at the helm – young blood tempered, of course, with wisdom. Tetzahuitl understands this. He's always worked for the interests of Mexico as a whole.'

I wasn't sure I shared his faith in the *cihuacoatl*, but I didn't contradict him.

'Would you say Extepan has his share of wisdom?'

'More so than some of his rivals,' I replied, again pointedly refraining from mentioning Maxixca by name. 'My father always used to tell us that co-operation and restraint were the hand-maidens of firmness. I think it's a principle Extepan understands.'

Again the *tlatoani* smiled. 'It's a good maxim, and one your father followed in his own lifetime. I've tried to do the same, though turning the other cheek or offering the hand of friendship didn't come easy to me as a young man. Of course, age mellows us all.'

I had the sense that he was leading up to something, and I waited.

'You will need to protect his interests as well as your own,' he said. 'Be prudent. Be careful. When I married Doña Maria, there was great opposition from many of my people. They disliked the idea of a European becoming my consort – they felt that it set a precedent which would lead to the dilution of our race with the blood of foreigners. As if that was a *bad* thing! As if races are so pure!' He shook his head. 'There are many who still hold to that view. You must beware of them. They won't take kindly to your presence here, even as Extepan's wife.'

'Are you saying that my life might be in danger?'

He mopped his mouth with a crumpled handkerchief. 'Hardly. You are a princess. Expect difficulties, that's all I'm saying. Don't imagine that every courtesy means liking or even acceptance.'

I was thinking of Maxixca, Tetzahuitl, and even Mia and Cocomicihuatl, none of whom had any reason to be favourably disposed towards me. It was a warning I barely needed.

'Enough,' said Motecuhzoma. 'I mustn't sour the atmosphere of this occasion by hedging it with uncertainties. There is much for us all to celebrate. Let us rejoin your future husband.'

That evening, I accompanied Extepan to Azcapotzalco for his flight north. He was due to meet with Matogee and other leaders at the Sioux capital the following day.

'How long do you think you'll be away?' I asked him.

'A week. No more than two, I hope. The negotiations will be delicate. There are fences to be mended. The New English and the Canadians would like to see them torn down.'

'It's strange,' I said, 'I feel like a traitor, wanting you to succeed. Canada and New England used to be our colonies, and their peoples still have many ties with my country.'

Paradoxically, it was the Aztecs who had assisted both in their wars of independence from Britain, doubtless hoping eventually to subsume the two states in their own empire. The confederation between the two was a loose one, but the Aztecs had been unable to undermine it. Economically prosperous and independent in their foreign policies, they were now the only real impediment to worldwide Aztec domination.

'They aren't my enemies,' Extepan said to me. 'We want peace above all else. But it would be foolish to allow unstable conditions on our longest frontier. That was Rome's mistake.'

I was startled by this. But he was smiling.

'My father's words,' he told me. 'He often quotes the examples of past empires.'

'Does he see himself as another Augustus?'

Extepan kept smiling. 'Well, he certainly doesn't expect – or want – to be deified after his death. But there are lessons in history for all of us. The past illuminates the present, he always says.'

I was silent. Extepan obviously sensed my unease.

'He's just a man, Catherine. A man of remarkable achievements, it's true, but flesh and blood like you and me. In his heart, he's quite humble. Didn't you feel that when you talked to him?'

'Yes,' I said quickly. 'It's all right.'

It was my way of telling him I didn't want to dwell on the subject. He grasped this immediately. He drew me to him and kissed me full on the lips.

It was our first real kiss, devoid of hesitancy or decorum. He smelt of sandalwood and his freshly laundered uniform; his cheeks were smooth against mine. I responded fully, putting my arms around his waist. He felt solid and real and human against me.

Extepan's escort stood nearby, discreetly waiting for him. For a moment, we had both forgotten their presence. Would our secret now be out? It didn't seem to matter at that moment.

Extepan's ship, a fast-flying carrier, stood ready on the landing strip. Reluctantly he disengaged himself from me.

'Take care,' I said.

'I shall.' A final squeeze of my hand. 'You must do the same.'

Extepan had obviously left intructions that I be kept occupied during his absence, because the next day I was flown to Acapulco in the company of Mia, Cuauhtemoc and Extepan's eldest sister, Citlalxauhqui. We stayed for two days, visiting the set of a new epic movie, *Aztec Century*, which was being made to celebrate Motecuhzoma's reign. We were shown rushes and went on location near Coyuca to see preparations for the restaging of the battle of Jerusalem in 1967.

I was ill at ease during the visit, not simply because the studio executives carefully refrained from mentioning that the *tlatoani*'s armies had crushingly defeated British and pan-Arab forces in the battle; the picture offended me in a more general sense, being a blatant farrago of historical truth which simplified and glamorized, making pageantry out of blood and death. I was also uncomfortable with Mia. Her oceanic calmness made matters worse, especially since Extepan had asked that I pay some attention to Cuauhtemoc, whose care I would assume when we married. Each time I asked to hold him, Mia surrendered him without protest, but I thought I detected suspicion and curiosity in her silence. Had she somehow divined that I was betrothed to her master?

Cuauhtemoc himself was a delight by comparison. Strong-limbed yet placid, he proved an excellent traveller and happily nestled in my arms without a murmur. Of course, I kept thinking of my own lost child, and of others I might have with Extepan. How would children of my own affect my feelings towards this, his first-born? Already the complications of my decision were multiplying.

We flew on from Acapulco to California, chasing the setting sun westwards on the last leg of the flight across the Mojave Desert. The desert was green with ripening corn, a veritable ocean of grass.

In California, descendants of English and Spanish settlers had become full Mexican citizens after the province was annexed by the Aztecs in the nineteenth century. For three days we visited vineyards and citrus plantations and coastal waters which shimmered at night with shallow plantations of *tonatiuhacatl*, the 'sun reeds' which were the very basis of Aztec technological superiority. Half plant, half optical fibre, the reeds could be spun into fabrics, embedded in high-performance alloys, fashioned like paper into sheets which stored and could re-emit the energy of the sun with up to eighty per cent efficiency.

North again, to Zanhuanxico, with its pneumatic carriages and its great Aztec bridge spanning the bay. It was while staying there that we received the news which prompted an immediate return to Tenochtitlan.

I was woken early one morning by Citlalxauhqui, who announced that Chicomeztli was on the telephone.

As soon as I sat down at the screen, I saw the anxious look on his face.

'What's happened?' I asked.

'There is news from the north,' he told me.

'Extepan?' I said immediately. 'Is he all right?'

'He will not be able to return as soon as he intended. His negotiations were not successful, and there has been another development.'

'What?'

'The New English have occupied Potomac.'

I understood only too clearly what this meant. Mexico and New England had signed a treaty many years before guaranteeing the city's independence. Breaking it was tantamount to a declaration of war.

'It appears the Canadians are intending to support their action,' Chicomeztli told me. 'We are mobilizing our armies in the north. Extepan will command them.'

We arrived back in Tenochtitlan after midnight. The city already seemed asleep, as if nothing had disturbed its usual placid rhythms. But Motecuhzoma was ensconced with Tetzahuitl and the other members of the *tlatocan* in his council chamber.

I switched on the television in my apartment. There were fifteen channels, and it was a simple matter to find one which carried news of the crisis. Pictures were being shown of a heavy military build-up in Virginia and Ohio, the most north-easterly provinces of Greater Mexico. Tanks and missile launchers were massed near the border with New England, and squadrons of jetcopters and interceptors filled the skies. Crack units of Eagle and Ocelotl commandos had been mobilized, we were told, ready to repel any further New English aggression.

The entire report had the expected jingoistic flavour, with Tetzahuitl appearing on the screen to condemn the illegal occupation of the city and demand that the New English withdrew. This is rich, I thought, from a man who had helped orchestrate the invasions of half the sovereign territories of the world. Motecuhzoma himself did not appear, though his name was frequently invoked in support of Mexican efforts. There was no mention of Extepan.

I searched the channels, looking for different slants on the story. Gradually it emerged that New English troops had entered Potomac at the request of the city's rulers, who were promptly condemned as traitors to their own people. It was difficult to winnow any truth from the propagandizing, but I began to wonder if the Aztecs had precipitated the crisis as a pretext for invasion. Was Extepan himself personally responsible for engineering the situation?

Over the next few days, events moved swiftly to an inexorable climax. The Aztecs issued an ultimatum for the New English to withdraw. They refused, with the full backing of the Canadians, claiming that they had been asked to defend the city from Aztec aggression – this was not actually said in the commentaries, but it was easy to read between the lines. Extepan, celebrated as Motecuhzoma's eldest son and victor of Russia, was shown in battle gear, consulting with his chiefs-of-staff. He seemed infinitely remote, in another world entirely from mine. A second ultimatum was rejected, and all Mexican citizens were ordered to evacuate the city. A third and final ultimatum was ignored. At dawn the next day, the invasion of New England began.

I followed the progress of the war from my apartment, with Chicomeztli often at my side. Bevan had taken himself off marlin-fishing in the Caribbean during my absence, and his return was delayed by the outbreak of the war. I had a suspicion he was also sulking.

The war began promisingly for the Mexicans, with Extepan's armies making rapid gains after striking eastwards from Ohio rather than attacking as expected from the south. But Canadian forces were massing across the border, and the Sioux Confederacy joined them. They struck more swiftly than expected, sweeping down towards the Ohio river and endangering Extepan's supply lines. With the New English stiffening their resistance in the east, within days a danger developed that Extepan's armies might be cut off between both forces and destroyed. None of this was reported on television, but Chicomeztli daily brought me the latest intelligence, sparing no details. Motecuhzoma and Tetzahuitl remained incommunicado, a measure of the seriousness of the situation.

Chicomeztli obviously sensed my concern for Extepan, and I felt a growing need to unburden myself to him. He had always been a friend to me, and in some ways I trusted him more than anyone else.

Only a week after the war had begun, Chicomeztli informed

me that the Caucasian provinces of Ohio and Kentucky had revolted and declared for the New English. Extepan's armies were in retreat, fighting their way southwards towards Potomac.

I didn't attempt to hide my surprise.

'I don't understand,' I said. 'The Empire has more troops and equipment than all theirs put together. Why isn't Extepan getting the support he needs?'

'It is not so easy to move armies swiftly across a whole continent,' he replied.

'But he's the *tlatoani*'s son. And he's in danger.' I hesitated. 'And you have the beam weapon.'

He smiled at this. 'Ah, yes. That is true.'

'Then why hasn't it been used? Surely that would end the war swiftly, just like in Russia.'

He agreed. 'But there is honour at stake.'

'Honour?'

'Both we and our enemies are contesting a point of international principle. There would be no contest if they were forced to surrender immediately.'

I could hardly believe what I was hearing. In the background, the TV featured a bombastic report about the Mexican naval blockade of New York and Philadelphia. It seemed a farce, a pantomime.

'I don't understand,' I said again. 'You could have probably avoided the war altogether, just by threatening to use it.'

It was not that I wanted the beam to be used – far from it. I was simply trying to understand the mentality of a nation that had such a powerful weapon yet refused to employ it.

Chicomeztli's smile was almost condescending. 'There would be great shame for our enemies if they were forced to surrender before they had the opportunity to defend their positions.'

I glanced around the apartment. We were surrounded by the products of the most sophisticated civilization on earth, yet it seemed to me that the sentiments which Chicomeztli was expressing were entirely primitive. In Russia, they had waited until two armies were obliterated before using the beam. 'Are you telling me this war is being waged to satisfy not just your own honour but that of the New English, too? Even if the emperor risks losing another of his sons in the process?'

His skewed eye darted in its socket. He shrugged. 'It's our way.'

By now, I was thoroughly bemused by the conduct of the war, which had brought home to me how superficially I had always understood the Aztec character. In pre-Christian times, the Aztecs often pursued the *xochiyaoyotl*, or flowery war, whose chief purpose was to secure prisoners for sacrifice rather than conquer enemies or acquire new lands. Over the past four hundred years, they had waged war for territorial gain, but it seemed as if the underlying ideal of war as an end in itself, war as a ritual vital to their race, remained. Of course, Extepan had said as much when I visited him in Russia, but I hadn't quite believed him. Now, with his own life possibly in the balance, I saw too clearly that the Aztecs were indeed prepared to put death before dishonour.

By now, even Mexican television was reporting the reversals in the north, and when a still picture of Extepan was shown on the screen, my emotions were close to the surface. Naturally, Chicomeztli noticed immediately.

'You care greatly for him,' he observed.

'We were betrothed before he left,' I admitted.

Chicomeztli beamed. He got up from his chair and hugged me.

'I am so sorry. And so happy for you both. It will all be well in the end, you will see.'

'It has to be kept secret,' I stressed. 'Especially now. Only Motecuhzoma and Tetzahuitl know. It might endanger Extepan's position even further if the news were made public.'

'Of course.' He seemed to wink at me. 'Mum is the word.'

Next day, Chicomeztli brought me more welcome news: Bevan was returning.

I had not seen him in almost a month, and when I learnt that he would be landing at Cuauhtitlan Airport that afternoon, I decided to go and meet him. I needed to get away from the palace and the war, if only for a short while. I also felt that friendly overtures were necessary, in case he was still aggrieved with me.

Arrangements were made for a glidecar to bring him direct

from the airport to a private mooring where I was waiting for him aboard a long low-slung motorboat. I intended to ferry him leisurely across the lake to Chapultepec, giving us time to be alone and renew our acquaintance.

As his glidecar drew up on the jetty, I was as expectant as any child anticipating a reunion with a rapscallion but good-hearted uncle.

When Bevan emerged from the car, I saw that his face and arms were brick-red from the sun. He wore a floppy white hat with navy flannels and a holiday shirt on which parrots and toucans disported themselves in radiant colour. His bulging travelling bag was slung over his shoulder.

He eyed me curiously as he was escorted aboard the boat.

'Welcome back,' I said with a smile.

I received only a grunt in reply.

'Did you have a good time?'

'Good enough, I reckon.'

He moved to the bow of the boat, dumping his bag on one of the seats.

'Catch any fish?' I asked.

He took off his hat and mopped his forehead with it. 'Spent most of my time drinking Marley's and eating seafood salads.'

He let out a burp as if in emphasis. I sat down beside him as the boat was unmoored and we headed out into the lake.

'I missed you,' I said.

'That a fact?'

He was making it difficult for me. I was determined to remain cheerful.

'Do you like the launch? It was modelled after the old Aztec canoes.'

'Executive barge, is it?'

'Bevan!'

Only now did he look me straight in the face.

'I'm sorry,' I said. 'I don't want there to be any friction beween us. Especially now.'

He was silent for a moment. 'Been having problems, have you?'

I shook my head. 'It's just . . . you know, all the fighting in New England.'

One of the escort brought us a jug of iced lemonade. Our boat was heading south, shadowed by two motor launches. The escort were congregated at the stern with the pilot, out of earshot of us.

'Do you know what's been happening in the north?' I asked.

Bevan stroked his misted glass. 'I've got the gist of it. Number One Son in big trouble, is he?'

I didn't know what to say to this. Bevan was obviously enjoying my discomfort. He swallowed his drink then proceeded to take off his sandals and socks. Rolling his trousers up to his knees, he perched himself on the edge of the boat and dangled his feet in the water.

The afternoon was bright and still, the lake tranquil.

'Watch the *ahuitzotl* doesn't eat your toenails,' I remarked.

'Missing him, are you?'

This threw me completely. 'What?'

'The man of the hour. Your favourite Mexican.'

I hid my face behind my drink. But Bevan wasn't even watching me: he was staring out over the lake. We were hugging the western shore, and herons were congregated in the coastal marshes.

'He proposed marriage to me,' I said.

'Did he now?'

'I accepted.'

He flattened his sunhat on his head, tugging at the droopy brow.

'That's a turn-up for the book.'

'Do you think I'm a traitor?'

His smile was like a sneer. 'I think you don't know the half of it.'

'What's that supposed to mean?'

He swung his feet out of the water. 'Ever heard of Quauhnahuac?'

'Of course,' I said. 'It's a city. To the south of here.'

'Your sister's there.'

I just stared at him.

'They never sent her to China.'

'What?'

'I got into the networks here, like you asked. They brought her here. To Mexico. It's where she's been all the time.'

I was staggered by this. 'Are you sure?'

'I'm sure, all right. It was all on file – dates, flights, even her address. They've put her up in an old Spaniard's retirement home.'

It was not just the rocking motion of the boat which made me steady myself.

'There must be some mistake.'

'There's no mistake.'

'Was that what you were trying to tell me?'

He took a battered pack of cigarettes from his shirt pocket and lit one. They were Kingston Clouds, their smoke resinous and aromatic.

'Wasn't going to leave you a note about it, was I? Besides, I could tell something else had happened. You weren't ready for it.'

Something in his face made me say, 'Is there more?'

He nodded. 'You sure you want to hear this?'

'Tell me.'

'Not on her own there, is she? She's shacked up with somebody you know.'

Six

'Why have we come here?' Chicomeztli asked, not for the first time, as we disembarked from the transporter.

I led him down the street, an armed escort accompanying us.

'There's a place I need to see,' I said.

We had arrived in the full heat of the day, and Quauhnahuac had closed its doors and shutters against the sun. The only person in evidence was a municipal worker, thrumming by in the shadows on a street-sweeper.

'Your Highness is being very mysterious,' Chicomeztli persisted, hastening to keep up with me as I hurried down the street.

'Just be patient,' I said, leading him down a broad avenue which debouched into the tree-lined central square of the city.

Directly across the square was the palace. It was smaller than I had imagined, Aztec in design but with Spanish features such as elaborate Isabelline balcony windows and a broad pilastered front doorway. I knew from Bevan that it had once been a residence of Hernan Cortes, whom the *tlatoani* Motecuhzoma Xocoyotzin had installed there in recognition of his services to the Aztecs. It looked as much a fortress as a palace.

'Do you know who's living there?' I asked Chicomeztli.

He looked at the palace, then at me. He frowned.

'It is an historical place, not a public building.'

I was testing him, trying to find out how much he knew. He had readily arranged a flight to Quauhnahuac when I had urgently demanded one, even though I had not specified why. The truth was, I had no clear idea what to do now that we were in the city. Bevan's revelations needed confirmation, but I was uncertain how best to go about this. I was urgent to know the truth, but I didn't want to play my hand too soon.

It was hot in the square, and I suggested we retire to a bar nearby for drinks. Chicomeztli roused the sleeping owner, who readily obliged us with beers and soft drinks when he saw who we were: my arrival in Tenochtitlan had been widely publicized on Mexican television.

From where we sat under the awning of the bar, I had a clear view of the front of the palace. Its arched doorway faced directly out on the square, no walls or railings surrounding it. The windows were all shuttered.

Chicomeztli was beginning to grow restless when I had a stroke of good fortune. A glidecar pulled up outside the palace – a sleek black Xicotencatl limousine with tinted windows. The main door of the palace opened, and two guards emerged, escorting a woman, tall and slim, in a fringed Mexican-style dress of summer blue. Her blonde hair was short, her skin tanned.

While one guard put a big leather shoulder bag into the back seat of the limousine, the other climbed into the driver's seat. Victoria spoke to him in a light yet businesslike manner. I could have rushed to her then, despite all my suspicions. But at that moment a balcony window opened and a man stepped out, a Caucasian. He was a tall figure, dressed in a stylish Aztec tunic of oatmeal and black. He waved at Victoria as she got into the back of the car with a second guard. She barely acknowledged him.

The limousine glided away, out of sight. If I knew Victoria, she was going on a shopping expedition. I was trying to remain calm, despite my shock at seeing the other figure, despite my expectation of finding him here. He withdrew, closing the shutters behind him.

Chicomeztli noticed nothing; he was sitting with his back to the palace, a situation I had deliberately engineered. I sipped my drink for several minutes, all the while thinking with an Arctic calm. Then I decided what I was going to do.

'I'm going to need your full co-operation,' I said to Chicomeztli, keeping my voice low so that the escort could not hear me. 'You have to trust me. I need to visit someone. Someone in the palace. Alone.'

He looked alarmed. Then he shook his head. 'I can't possibly allow that.'

'You must,' I insisted. 'You must. Believe me, I'm acting on Extepan's orders. He gave me instructions before he left for the north. There's a European living there, a British citizen. I have to speak to him.'

Chicomeztli swivelled his head around to look at the palace. It was quiet outside, only a plump black-and-white dog lying in the shade of its balcony.

'I don't understand,' he said. 'Why was nothing said to me?'

I kept my voice low. 'Extepan couldn't tell you anything. You're the only one who knows about our betrothal apart from Motecuhzoma and Tetzahuitl.' I had no intention of confessing that I had also told Bevan. 'There's no danger for me in there, I assure you. Do you think Extepan would let me take the risk if there was?'

He was in a quandary, wrestling with his loyalty to Extepan and his duty to me.

'Who is this person you have to see?'

'I can't tell you that at the moment. You have to trust me. Extepan and I are betrothed. Our interests are the same now. All I need is half an hour, perhaps not even that. If I'm not out by then, you can come looking for me.'

He still looked alarmed. 'This is foolishness.'

And, in a way, it was, given what I had decided.

'It's vital,' I said. 'There's nothing else for it. If you go against my wishes now, you might destroy Extepan. It's as important as that.'

I had never seen him look so torn.

'Have I ever asked for your help before and let you down?'

'Do I have your word of honour that you will be safe? That there is no other alternative to this?'

'You do.'

'You swear to me there is no danger?'

'None.'

I was beyond shame or conscience now. But still he was vacillating. I decided to bolster my case with a confidence. Very quietly I said, 'Motecuhzoma has nominated Extepan as his successor.'

He beamed. 'This was my cherished hope.'

'But there are other contenders, as I'm sure you're well aware. It's by no means certain he'll be the next *tlatoani*, even if he survives the fighting in the north. That's why we have to move with extreme caution in this matter. That's why you have to trust me implicitly.'

I could tell that I had finally won him over. It amazed me that I could remain so calm, so devious, when my mind was in turmoil, when I had suffered a greater betrayal than I could ever have imagined. But I was determined that I would be the deceiver and manipulator from now on.

'Very well,' Chicomeztli said softly.

I did not delay. While Chicomeztli spoke to the escort, I visited the washroom and splashed cold water on my face before primping and prettifying myself as best I could. I was dressed in an embroidered satin jumpsuit by the fashionable Mexican designer Iztli, a functional but suitably decorous outfit. I regarded myself in the mirror with a mixture of venom and determination. I was about to embark on a course of action which was almost certain to bring my entire world crashing down around me. I felt no hesitation whatsoever.

'Please take the greatest care,' Chicomeztli said when I emerged.

'I shall,' I replied. 'Have faith in me.'

Then I walked out into the heat of the day.

I crossed the square to the palace door. The knocker was fashioned in a representation of Xilonen, a goddess of fertility. She held a brass ring in her cupped hands. Disdaining the electric bell, I rapped it hard against the door.

It was not long before the door opened. I was confronted by a stout and venerable female housekeeper, her grey hair tied up in a bun. She squinted at me.

'I must speak to your master,' I said in Nahuatl.

I made myself look and sound as imperious as I could. The woman continued to squint, craning her head forward, her back bowed. She was a pure-blood Mexican. Did she recognize me? Could she even see me clearly?

'He's taking a nap,' she said, somewhat tentatively.

'Then wake him,' I replied, pushing past her into the house. 'It's extremely important.'

I stood in a big white hallway dominated by the famous Rivera mural *The Triumph of Mexico*. A broad marble stairway with wrought-iron banisters curved upwards.

The old woman looked flustered and unsure of herself.

'Is he expecting you?' she asked.

'We're old friends,' I said. 'I want it to be a surprise.'

She was still peering at me. 'Who shall I say is calling?'

I smiled, surprised but pleased she hadn't recognized me. It wouldn't have mattered if she had, but it meant I could retain the advantage of anonymity to the last possible moment.

'Just fetch him. He'll know who I am.'

She was obviously at a loss. For a moment she did not move. Then she slowly turned and began shuffling up the stairs.

I was so impatient I was tempted to rush past her and do the deed myself. But I had to be controlled. Now was not the time for hasty action.

At the top of the stairs, she turned along a balcony, finally disappearing from view. I retreated into an alcove, where anyone coming down the stairs would not immediately see me.

The palace was silent around me, its tiled floor adorned with the heraldic devices of old Spain. It was said that Cortes had betrayed his country for the love of his Aztec mistress, Malinalli, but that he had surrounded himself with memories of his homeland in the later years of his life.

It was not long afterwards that he appeared at the top of the stairs. He was still clad in his tunic, his chestnut hair ruffled from sleep. In the two and a half years since I had seen him last, he had shaved off his beard but grown a healthy paunch.

He could not see me, but he slowly began descending the stairs, one hand on the curlicued rails, looking back over his shoulder to say in Nahuatl to the old woman: 'There's no one here.'

'Yes, there is,' I said, stepping out of the shadows.

He was almost at the bottom of the stairs. He froze, staring at me with utter astonishment.

'Kate,' he said. 'Good God Almighty.'

I made myself smile with great joy.

'Hello, Alex.'

Then I rushed forward and flung my arms around him.

For a moment he stood rigid. Then slowly his arms came up and closed around my back as I buried my head in his chest.

'How did you know I was here?' I heard him say in a voice that sounded broken.

'Motecuhzoma told me. I'm so relieved you aren't dead. I thought they'd killed you. I only learnt the other day that they'd put you here in exile instead. You can't imagine how happy I was.'

I kept my face close to his chest, giving him every opportunity to recover his composure. He smelt of old cologne, sleep and Mexican cigarettes.

'I thought I'd lost you,' I blubbered. 'I thought you were gone for ever. Did they tell you about Victoria?'

'Victoria?'

He couldn't disguise the quaver in his voice.

'She's in exile. In China. I haven't seen her for almost two years.'

Now there was a palpable decrease in the tension of his body. It was only then that I truly knew he had betrayed me.

'Kate,' he said. 'I can't believe you're here. It's like a dream. So much has happened . . . They brought me here after I was captured . . . I – I didn't know whether you knew I was alive or not.'

Now I did look up at him. He was an adaptable liar, this long-lost husband of mine, seizing each opportunity I gave him. But he remained cautious.

'How did . . . Did they let you come here?'

I beamed at him. 'Motecuhzoma's going to declare an amnesty for all political prisoners. You're going to be released.' I paused, and then, with the grisly satisfaction of an assassin sliding home a knife, added, 'We can be together again.'

An instant of shock, quickly hidden. Then a smile came to his lips.

'That's marvellous. I can hardly believe it. I've been a prisoner so long here I thought I'd never be free. It's like a dream come true.'

What an effort those words must have cost! But I was far from finished with him.

'They had our marriage annulled,' I said on instinct. 'Until just recently I thought I was a widow. They wanted me to think that.'

A broken-backed nod. 'They told me about the annulment. I tried to plead with them, but there was nothing I could do.'

'Motecuhzoma says the annulment carried no legal weight because your death was faked. Do you know they showed me a dead body that looked just like you? It even had an appendix scar in the right place.'

He swallowed. 'They're very good at that sort of thing. It must have been terrible for you.'

'It's all over now. We can be man and wife again.'

The smile remained fixed. 'It's incredible news.'

'Unless,' I said slowly, 'you've found someone else.'

Fear snaked behind his eyes. I affected not to notice it.

'Just teasing,' I said lightly. 'They told me you've been living alone here.'

The smile broadened again, blissful with relief at his luck. He stepped back, holding me out in front of him. 'You look marvellous, Kate.'

He drew me to him again. I knew he was about to kiss me, to bury his feelings in that kiss, to hide his lies. I put a hand on his chest, indicating that he look over his shoulder.

The old woman stood at the top of the stairs, peering down at us.

'Don't worry,' Alex whispered. 'She's half blind.'

It was a blithe demonstration of his contempt for others. In the past, I might have taken it as daring.

'Can't we be alone?' I pleaded. 'There's so much I want to tell you.'

Again it was obvious he felt that fortune was favouring him.

'Matlalli,' he called to the old woman, 'that's all for now. And tell the other servants we're not to be disturbed.'

He took me into one of the rooms off the hall. It was furnished with Regency armchairs and a chesterfield. Striped fish floated in a big green-lit tank above the open hearth. On the wall was a Hockney hologram of Bradford Town Hall. Alex had been born on one of his father's estates near Bingley, though he had never lived in the north. It was the sentiment of the exile again.

'Your Nahuatl has improved,' I remarked; formerly he had been hardly able to speak it at all.

'I had to learn it,' he replied. 'No one here spoke English. They made me dress Mexican-fashion, too.'

How easily the lies tripped off his lips! How easily I was able to identify them now.

'Motecuhzoma told me they captured you and faked your death in the hope of marrying me off to one of their princes. Is it true?'

This was mere supposition on my part, and Alex's response was to half squirm, half shrug.

'They never told me why,' he said hastily. 'I was just brought here, told I'd never be able to see you again.'

'I don't understand why they went to all the trouble of faking your death. I'm surprised they didn't simply kill you.'

He had no answer for this, and I could see I was in danger of throwing him completely off-balance by being too cold-blooded and rational. I had to give him more time to recover his composure if I was to revenge myself on him – and on Extepan – to the full.

I surveyed the room. 'At least they made you comfortable.'

He took my arm, seated me beside him on the chesterfield, 'It looks like it,' he said, 'but no amount of comfort can replace freedom and having those you love beside you.'

This deserved a suitably withering riposte, but I did not rise to it. The more he talked, the easier I found it to despise him.

'I don't think Victoria's going to be released,' I said. 'Do you know she was accused of trying to kill Tetzahuitl and others with a bomb? It's ridiculous, but they say she confessed. She's still regarded as an enemy of the state. I can't believe she had any part in it.'

Without his beard, it was easier to read the expressions on his face. He looked somehow naked, no longer the cavalier of old. Every mention of Victoria seemed to make him writhe inwardly.

'It sounds quite unlike her,' he managed to say.

'I think they're going to keep her in exile for some time yet.'

He hesitated. 'Where is she?'

'In China, of course. Beijing.'

He was struggling to maintain an appearance of equanimity. He rose, taking out a pack of Xitli Golds.

'Forgive me,' he said, lighting one. 'Having you here . . . so unexpectedly. I still can't believe it.'

I proceeded to smother the situation with gossip, telling him about Richard's marriage, Precious Cloud's suicide, and all the other things that had happened since his 'death'. Of course, I was sure he was fully informed about them, but I wanted to give him more time to recover, to understand – or think he did – his current situation. I wasn't ready to tell him the real truth yet; I wanted to see how far he would go in his duplicity.

Alex was dutifully attentive, chain-smoking Xitlis and squeezing my hand from time to time, as if to say he still couldn't quite believe my joyous return to his life. The old charm was beginning to reassert itself, the self-confidence and sheer well-heeled nerve which had fooled me so often in the past. He clearly thought he might, even yet, extricate himself from this extraordinary situation. No doubt he imagined I knew only partial truths. Perhaps he thought that Victoria might indeed be discreetly got out of the way by Motecuhzoma's agents so that he could resume his life with me. Or perhaps he was simply paralysed and was going along with me because he didn't know what else to do.

I myself knew no more than what Bevan had gleaned from the network. Alex had been transferred to Mexico only a matter of months after our capture, and he had been living in Quauhnahuac ever since. Victoria was sent to join him there when she was 'exiled'. Her message was a fake in the sense that she had pretended she was in Beijing, whereas I now knew she had never set foot in China. Of course, she may have been forced to lie by the Aztecs, but I doubted this. I was now certain they were not only lovers, but had been so ever since those long-ago days of Ty Trist.

How I had deluded myself about Alex from the very start! My father had never really approved of him, I knew. Though he had not once said anything specific to me, I had always felt that he considered Alex charming but untrustworthy, a user who would do anything to elevate his status. And what better way than by marriage to me? I could never have accepted that at the time, and my father must have agreed to the marriage because he knew I was in love with him. He had been prepared to surrender me to a man he considered worthless because to do otherwise would have ruined my happiness. And Alex had turned out to be more despicable than even he imagined.

Despite all this, I continued talking, telling Alex about my life over the two and a half years of our 'separation'. I wondered how much he already knew. According to Bevan's information, he and Victoria had never been prisoners in Quauhnahuac, although there were apparently certain restrictions on their movement. I talked to maintain my grip on the situation, to keep him guessing.

At length I said, 'Did you know Extepan wanted to marry me?'

His mouth opened, but I rushed on.

'I think that's why he arranged to get you out of the way. But Motecuhzoma told me you were alive. He realized he couldn't let his son marry me under false pretences. Urgent action was needed, which is why he told me the truth and sent me here. Now he wants to see you, but of course things are rather tricky with Extepan still believing he's going to marry me. We have to go back secretly to the palace, sneak you in. Motecuhzoma doesn't want Extepan to know anything about it until he's had a chance to speak to you.'

Alex looked suitably cautious at this farrago. 'Isn't he in New England? Extepan, I mean. The war's been all over the television.'

'He has his own men at the palace. As you can imagine, there's a lot of intrigue at the moment, and Motecuhzoma wants to do what's best for us. I think he's going to try to get us out of the country as quickly as possible and back to England.'

Alex was in a corner, but he came out fighting.

'Kate, do you realize how risky all this sounds? Have you any more reason to trust Motecuhzoma than any other Mexican?'

'I have the best reason. He doesn't want his son – who might be the next *tlatoani* – to marry me.'

He stroked my hand in his paternal way. 'I understand that. But how do you know we're not being set up? It all sounds very underhand and suspicious.'

'Of course it is. The emperor wants as few people to know as possible. Do you think I would have been told about you and allowed to come here if he didn't?'

Alex nodded sagely. 'Nevertheless, I think you should let me check. I've established one or two useful contacts since I was here, people I know I can trust. I'll make a few phone calls.'

He was on his feet. I jumped up. 'Alex, we have to leave immediately. There's an escort waiting for us outside.'

'It'll only take a few minutes, Kate.'

'We don't have the time.'

He was obviously surprised by my vehemence. In the past, I had always been the one to give way in the face of his wishes. He hesitated, still unsure, but perhaps concerned that Victoria might at any time return from her shopping and ruin everything.

'At least allow me to pack a bag,' he said.

'Alex, we have to go *now*.' I couldn't allow him out of my sight. 'Don't worry, we can arrange for everything to be shipped on to us if necessary. It's imperative we get you to the palace.'

Still he was cautious. 'What about the servants?'

'They don't need to know anything. We'll just leave. We have to maintain the utmost secrecy until your audience with the *tlatoani*. It's better if they don't even know you're gone.'

Naturally my story was muddled and filled with inconsistencies, but Alex was in no position to argue. He could only refuse by telling me the truth: this was the challenge I had set him.

'Are you absolutely sure about this, Kate?'

I noticed a pair of Victoria's shoes under an armchair.

'Of course,' I assured him. 'Who can you trust if you can't trust me?'

Reluctantly, he let me lead him out of the palace and across the square to Chicomeztli. Already I was thinking ahead. I warned Alex not to speak of either our discussion or our true relationship, telling him that the escort knew nothing and that he had to maintain his anonymity. I was acting for the *tlatoani*, and him alone.

To my surprise, Alex raised no protest. Suddenly his confidence seemed to have evaporated, and what I saw in its place was bewilderment and even fear.

Chicomeztli came out from under the awning to meet us. I was already confident that he would not know who Alex was because he hadn't been aware that he was living in the palace. And so it proved.

'We have to take this man back to Chapultepec,' I told him.

Chicomeztli scrutinized Alex, then took me aside.

'Who is he?'

'I can't tell you that at the moment, and he's under instructions to say nothing. He's a friend of Extepan's, that's all I can say. An important friend.'

'If he was a friend, then I would know of it.'

'Please, you *have* to trust me. We must get him into my apartment without anyone else knowing. And without further delay.'

'This is a great trust you are asking of me.'

'I know. I know. Please help me.'

Chicomeztli glanced at Alex, who looked unnerved by our whispering. I indicated to him that he had to keep silent, that I knew what I was doing.

Chicomeztli's erratic gaze darted between the two of us. I felt ashamed because he was an innocent whose loyalty I was betraying. But it was too late for conscience now.

'We *must* leave immediately,' I insisted.

'Do you understand what you're asking?'

'I'm asking you to do as I say without explanation. For my sake. And for Extepan's.'

'And what then?'

'Then you go back to your normal duties, and wait. When the time's ripe, everything will be explained. That's all I can tell you now.'

I had stretched his good faith to the limit, and I was sure he was going to refuse me.

But I was wrong. He turned to the escort and informed them we were leaving.

Seven

Throughout the flight back to Tenochtitlan, I made sure that Alex and Chicomeztli had little opportunity to speak to one another. We sat together like strangers, and I was aware of playing a multiplicity of roles: one for Alex, another for Chicomeztli, still another for myself. I had no justification for using Chicomeztli in this way. The fact that he did not know Alex merely emphasized that he had had no part in any of the subterfuges which had been played on me. But I had to use him to gain my revenge.

The Valley towns were asleep under neon-lit darkness when we landed at a private airfield in Tlatelolco. We took a hydrofoil across the lake to the palace, and Chicomeztli had us admitted through a side entrance, Alex and I bundled up in hooded cloaks at my request. It was all suitably melodramatic, but I was relieved that Chicomeztli seemed prepared to play his part to the full.

Though there were guards on duty, they did not stop us or ask for identification. It was obvious that the palace was more preoccupied with events in New England, and our comings and goings were of no great concern to them at that moment. Besides, Chicomeztli was a trusted servant of the empire.

He accompanied Alex and me to my apartment. At the door I took him aside and said, 'It's better if you leave us now.'

He eyed Alex again. 'Are you intending to keep him in your rooms?'

'I'll lodge him with Bevan for the night,' I lied. 'He'll be safe there.'

Again the look of uncertainty. Alex himself was too disorientated to question my whisperings to Chicomeztli; either that, or he was obeying my instructions to the last word.

'And in the morning?' Chicomeztli said.

'Arrangements will be made. I can't say any more than that at present.'

He looked stiff, unconvinced. Because he was so small, it was easy to make the assumption that he could be treated like a child. I knew better than that.

'And what am I to do in the meantime?'

'Nothing. Do nothing. Just keep your head down and wait. Remember, this is in Extepan's interests.'

'I greatly hope so,' he said. 'I've placed every trust in you.'

'You have my undying gratitude. And Extepan's.'

For a moment he hesitated. Then he marched off to his own quarters.

I led Alex inside. He was like a lamb. The first thing I did was to creep across to the adjoining door. There was no sound from beyond. I checked that the door was securely locked, then removed the key and dropped it in a vase.

Alex was still standing there in the centre of the room. He looked fearful, unsure of himself.

'It's all right,' I whispered. 'You're safe here. Motecuhzoma will see you in the morning.'

'I've never met him,' he remarked.

It was obviously a source of regret on his part. I wondered if this was what had finally persuaded him to accompany me – the opportunity, at last, to meet the emperor himself.

'He's kind,' I said. 'More considerate than I'd ever imagined.'

He was eager to agree with me. 'They're not such bad people, Kate.'

'I know he'll be happy to see us reunited again.'

What pleasure I took in seeing him squirm! I went forward and put my arms around him. He responded as a husband might.

'Alex,' I breathed, 'I'm so happy to have you back. Nothing else matters.'

He smiled. I think he was pleased that I was so rewarded by his presence. The old vanity. Again he leaned down to kiss me on the lips, and this time I did not stop him.

I responded as fully as I might have done in the past, feeling the unfamiliar abrasion of his shaven face, the strength of his arms enfolding me, his sheer bulk – even more ample now. Inside I remained cold, unrelenting, determined to avenge myself on him.

Alex had always been easily aroused, and quite soon I could feel him responding, an obligatory kiss giving way to a familiar need which I knew he would want to satisfy, despite the uncertainties of the situation. And I was not going to deny him: in fact, this was what I intended – the final consummation of my betrayal. I had pledged myself to Extepan, but he would never have me now.

'We've got all night to ourselves,' I said softly into his ear. 'No one will disturb us here.'

His eyes were filled with desire. It was lust rather than love that had always made him want me, I knew that now. But I was ready for it, ready to make a calculating submission to him. He could have me one last time if it meant his damnation.

'The bedroom,' I murmured. 'It's through there.'

The door was already ajar. As he had done so many times in the past, he lifted me up and carried me through.

When it was over, I lay in silence while Alex smoked a Xitli and told me how he had survived after the attack on Ty Trist by hiding out in deserted towns and villages further down the valley until he was finally picked up by the Aztecs. I was certain it was a lie, just as I was certain that all his expressions of pleasure at our reunion were fake. I gazed idly around the room, wondering whether anyone was watching us even now through a hidden camera. Of course I had no concrete evidence that my apartment was under surveillance, but it was unlikely that foreign guests would be allowed complete privacy in the very heart of the empire.

Who would come to arrest us? Chicomeztli, possibly – I was certain he would check my story as soon as he was able – or, more likely, some anonymous minion of the empire. It didn't matter to me either way; I no longer cared about destroying myself if I brought disgrace on those who had betrayed me.

I thought of all the mornings, in exile in Wales, when I had looked into Victoria's room and seen tousled sheets and smelt

312   *Christopher Evans*

body heat. Alex was up early most mornings. I thought of how solicitous he had always been to Victoria, taking her bilberry-picking in summer, visiting her when she was confined to her room with a migraine – just pretexts, I saw now, for adultery. I had wilfully blinded myself to all this, unable to credit not simply that he would seduce my sister but that she would let him, perhaps even encourage him.

There was much I still didn't know about the circumstances of his 'death'. Who had organized it? And had Victoria known all the time? Was her supposed part in the bomb plot simply a ruse to ensure that she could be reunited with Alex in Mexico? Somehow I found this hard to credit. It was easy to imagine them as illicit lovers, harder, with Alex's fickleness and Victoria's lack of moral fibre, to imagine them in a long-term partnership. But it was possible. It was possible they had fallen in love so deeply with one another they had indeed risked everything.

I let Alex murmur his endearments and promises, soothing him with my own platitudes in return. He looked drained by the day's events, and eventually he fell asleep. I smiled, satisfied that for once I had played the game far better than he.

But then he began to snore. It was a sound I had always found endearing in the past, but it was louder, more raucous than I remembered, and in my bitterness it became positively irritating to the point where I would have liked to press a pillow to his face, to end it all, then and there, by suffocating him. Of course, this was not practicable, and besides, I had already committed my crime. Now I simply had to wait and let the consequences unfold.

After a while I crept from bed and put on a pair of jeans and a cotton blouse. Then I returned to bed, pulling the sheets up to my neck. I wanted to be ready to face my accusers. Beside me, Alex slept on, satiated, cheek pressed to the pillow. His mouth was slack and his incipient double chin sagged. I began to long for the soldiers to come, to burst in and arrest us. But nothing happens quite as we plan it, and as the quiet night wore on, with no hint of disturbance, I, too, exhausted, slept.

In the morning I woke to a room filled with sunlight. Alex was still profoundly asleep beside me, as if he had not moved at all throughout the night. I was surprised to find that I felt no shame but was simply amazed that both he and I had slept without interruption.

Then I rolled over and saw Maxixca standing at the foot of the bed.

He wore full uniform, and there were four armed guards with him. He was smiling, of course, a broad, satisfied smile.

Slowly I sat up, letting him see I was fully clothed.

'How good to see you again,' I said.

In his hand he held a small device, a tape recorder, which he promptly switched on.

Alex had always been a demonstrative lover, but I had also ensured that there could be no doubt about my willing part in the seduction. Every intimate sound was perfectly captured, so that even if we had not been found in bed together, there could have been no mistake about what had happened.

Maxixca plainly relished playing the tape in front of us. He turned the volume up until Alex stirred and sat up blearily. When he realized what was happening, he was horrorstruck.

I smiled sweetly at him and sat back.

It was true I hadn't expected Maxixca, whom I assumed was still in Russia. But somehow he was perfect, though I admit I was now more frightened than I had anticipated. When the tape finally fell silent, he switched it off with a contemptuous flourish.

Alex looked like a cornered animal. He was too terrified to say anything. I also remained silent.

'Just like your sister,' Maxixca remarked.

I manufactured a smile. 'Is it normally your habit to burst into the bedroom of a husband and wife?'

'The marriage is null and void,' he replied instantly. 'Perhaps you weren't aware that the good duke has been living here in Mexico with your own sister for almost two years.'

'Oh, yes,' I replied. 'I was aware of it.'

Alex recoiled at this, gazing incredulously at me. A mixture of raw emotions flooded across his face – shame, guilt, anger, but, above all, fear.

'I came here in good faith,' he announced to Maxixca in his halting Nahuatl. 'The *tlatoani* wants to see me.'

'Get dressed,' Maxixca told him in English.

'I must protest. This is outrageous treatment—'

Maxixca pulled a pistol from his holster. 'If you do not get dressed immediately, I will shoot you myself.'

Alex had no option. In full view of everyone, he was forced to stumble around, gathering up his scattered clothes and pulling them on.

I got out of bed and stood up. I was dressed even down to my shoes. Immediately a guard took me by the arm.

I could see Maxixca thinking; he was obviously surprised by my preparedness, yet his dignity would not allow him to enquire further.

We were marched off, Alex doing his best to maintain some shred of dignity. Not once did he look at me.

We were taken down the long corridor which led to the council chamber. As we approached its serpent-decorated doors, I anticipated our final humiliation in front of the entire *tlatocan* with Motecuhzoma presiding. What would they do to us? A real exile this time, no doubt, somewhere truly remote and Spartan. Would Extepan be there? I hoped so. He had deceived me, and I wanted to see his face now that I had betrayed him.

When we entered the chamber, however, only Tetzahuitl was there. Maxixca and his guards led us forward.

'Well,' the *cihuacoatl* said to me. 'An interesting turn of events.'

He wore a charcoal-coloured mantle with a silver scorpion clasp. Clusters of white-tipped crows' feathers hung from his hair.

I found the fact that we were alone with him and Maxixca ominous. In his dark colours, the *cihuacoatl* looked even more fearsome, very much a figure of retribution. I did my best to appear, if not defiant, then at least unintimidated.

It was Alex who spoke. 'You must forgive me if I've offended anyone. I certainly didn't intend it.'

'I brought him here,' I said. 'I fooled Chicomeztli into thinking he was doing it for Extepan. I don't intend to justify my actions, but you must believe me that Chicomeztli is blameless. He thought he was doing his duty.'

'I understood I was coming here to see Motecuhzoma,' Alex

said. 'I was told that my marriage to Catherine had been restored by him.'

Tetzahuitl gave him a withering stare.

'I think I would have known, had that been the case. You were given strict instructions never to come to Tenochtitlan.'

'She came to my home. She told me the *tlatoani* had sent her. What was I to do?'

He sounded firm and forceful, but underneath I could hear his fear. I was determined to do nothing to help him.

'He wasn't aware I knew he's been living with my sister,' I said. 'That arrangement didn't stop him from sharing my bed last night.'

'You bitch!' Alex blurted.

I merely smiled at him. 'That must be the first honest thing you've said to me since I turned up at your door.'

I expected him to bite back again, but something changed in his expression. In place of anger, I saw a final acceptance of his defeat. He was thoroughly compromised, and he knew it. Mustering all his composure, he took a step towards me and laid a hand on my arm.

'Catherine,' he said softly. 'Forgive me. Forgive me for everything.'

I couldn't forgive him, of course, but I had no desire to humiliate him further.

'What are you going to do with us?' I asked Tetzahuitl.

'That remains to be seen,' he replied. 'There's much to consider. You must tell me how you learned about your former husband's whereabouts.'

'Women's intuition,' I said scathingly.

'Surely you see it will make no difference to you now?'

'I won't give you the satisfaction.'

A smile of imperturbable calm. 'Such hatred. From someone we were prepared to take into our hearts.'

He had a chilling way with the most commonplace expressions. I was not going to let him frighten or rile me.

'Does Extepan know?' I asked.

'That would be difficult,' Maxixca interjected. 'He's under siege in Potomac.'

Tetzahuitl glared at him, and he fell silent. He had obviously spoken out of turn, revealing something the *cihuacoatl* preferred me not to know. And there was glee in his voice.

'Under siege?' I repeated.

'The war has not progressed as smoothly as we had hoped,' Tetzahuitl said, smiling.

What did the smile mean? Were they both *glad* that Extepan was in difficulty?

'Are you intending to relieve him?' I aked.

The *cihuacoatl* waved the question aside. 'We're here to discuss your conduct, not that of our armies. I'm intrigued to know – why did you do it?'

'Revenge,' I replied. 'When I'm lied to and betrayed, I strike back.'

'But you've sacrificed yourself in the process.'

I tried to ignore the possibility that he meant this literally.

'What was the alternative? To continue to let myself be manipulated by you?'

Tetzahuitl tut-tutted. 'Would you have expected us to let you into our complete confidence until we were certain of your loyalty?'

'You faked my husband's death. For him to take my sister as his lover. What was in it for you?'

Tetzahuitl glanced briefly at Alex. 'There were reasons. There were reasons. Unfortunately you've gone beyond the point where you might have a proper appreciation of them.'

'What's going to happen to us?' Alex asked.

The *cihuacoatl* seemed loath to address him directly. He contemplated his fingernails. 'You've brought great shame to this household at a time when we have far graver matters to concern us.'

'Are we to be executed?' I asked. 'Sacrificed?'

He gave an incredulous laugh.

'Your fate will be decided in due course. When other matters have resolved themselves.'

I assumed he meant the war, yet somehow he seemed to imply more than this. It was then I recalled that the Aztecs had adopted the European practice of wearing black or dark colours for mourning. Except that they often wore them *during* a person's dying as well as after it. Was Extepan's position already hopeless?

I knew I could expect no answer to such a question. And Extepan was only one of my concerns.

'What about Victoria?' I asked. 'What will be done with her?'

He made a dismissive gesture. 'I'm not here to answer your questions. Take them away.'

As the guards encircled us, Alex made one last attempt to use his old powers of diplomacy to try to soften the blow.

'Please tell the *tlatoani* that neither of us intended any personal insult to him or his family.'

The *cihuacoatl* made a sound like an amused snarl.

'Unless you can speak with ghosts,' he said, 'that will prove difficult. Motecuhzoma died last night.'

We were taken down into the depths of the castle, where a catacomb of cells had been hewn from the bedrock. Before Alex and I were separated, he asked for a moment to speak with me alone. Maxixca, magnanimous in his victory, was ready to allow this.

Alex drew me aside.

'I know I've acted shamelessly, Kate. And no doubt you feel betrayed by Victoria, too. But think a little more kindly of her. *I* asked to have her sent here to be with me.'

I frowned. 'Are you telling me that's why she was exiled? Because of you?'

'I helped them, Kate. It was hopeless, our situation in Wales. They knew where we were all the time.'

'How can you be sure of that?'

'Because they contacted me on the radio. Offered me a deal.'

'A deal?'

'They knew about the disk. It was a prototype, not fully operational. But they saw they might be able to use it. I agreed to collaborate with them. The raid, my escape, it was all arranged beforehand. We made the deal over the radio.'

'But why?'

'Because we were never going to get out of there otherwise. We would have been exiles for the rest of our lives, or at least until they decided to kill us or pick us up. I just couldn't bear it any more. In exchange for my freedom, I agreed to help them use the disk to feed you fake information. That was my treason.'

I stared at him. 'What are you saying? Was it really you I was talking to all the time?'

'The image on the screen was electronic. But it was the real me talking to you. They kept me on call twenty-four hours a day, with computer people on hand to make sure I didn't slip up. You really put me through my paces, Kate.' He shook his head ruefully. 'The programme could have worked if we'd had time to perfect it. It could have been everything I said it was.'

He sounded almost wistful, and I wondered if he was expecting me to compliment him.

'All that,' I said bitterly, 'just to fool the Russians?'

'The disk was extra insurance for them. They used you to gain the Russians' confidence, to make them believe that there really wasn't going to be an attack. Coming from an impeccable source, they hoped it would be convincing.'

'It seems impossibly elaborate.'

'They love intrigue, Kate. And I don't think it was the only trick they were trying. They would have done anything to minimize the risks beforehand. You can't imagine the scale of such an operation, the logistics and manpower involved—'

'I can imagine it. I was there, at the front line.'

He didn't follow this up. 'The disk had lots of potential in other spheres. If it hadn't been destroyed, they would have probably let you continue to use it, but for their own ends.'

'You're a traitor, Alex.'

He did not try to deny it. 'I bargained for everyone's life, I swear to you.'

'It didn't save the others in the house, did it?'

'They asked me to make sure everyone was together, so that they could pick us all up.'

'Is that why you made up the story about the Russian ship?'

He shook his head ruefully. 'That was a mistake. I suppose I wanted to give you a little bit of hope. I did it out of guilt. I thought we'd all be safe, Kate. The officer who fire-bombed the house was acting against orders. They had him court-martialled.'

'So that made everything all right, did it?'

'No, of course not. I'm just telling you what happened, and why.'

I didn't know what to say. Even if I believed his story, it did nothing to soften my feelings towards him.

'And Victoria?' I said bitterly. 'Where does she fit in to all this?'

'I was practically under house arrest when I came here, and I was desperate for some female company. *Her* company.' He swallowed. 'And there were reasons why the Mexica wanted her out of London. So she agreed to join me. It was either that, or real exile. For what it's worth, she didn't do it out of any great love for me.'

My laugh was brittle. 'Then why did she let you sleep with her? It was even happening in Wales, wasn't it?'

He looked me in the eyes, nodded. 'We were together so much, all living in the same house. You know what I'm like – never could resist a pretty face.'

My stony expression made it plain that his roguishness was no longer endearing to me.

'You have to try to forgive her, Kate. Few of us have the same high standards as you.'

'Standards? My standards are no higher than anyone else's. I just had a more highly developed sense of duty. *Had*. Now I find it hard to care about anything.'

'Because I let you down so badly.'

'Don't flatter yourself – it would take more than your grubby philandering to do that. It's simply brought home to me that there was no one I could trust. No one.'

'I'm sorry.'

'Why, Alex? I still don't see why. Was it worth it?'

He shook his head. 'Of course not. I just exchanged one form of exile for another. When Victoria first came to Quauhnahuac, I thought we might recapture a bit of the old magic. But it never worked out that way. We both knew we were prisoners in all but name. We had too much behind us, too much guilt and dishonour, I suppose.'

Maxixca stepped forward.

'That is all,' he said brusquely in English.

As Alex was led away, he called back to me, 'I swear that not a day passed when I didn't think of you.'

With this final lie, he disappeared into the gloom.

Eight

The cell was a drab stone chamber, furnished with two bunk beds, a low table and a pair of padded floor mats. It was lit by a strip of fly-specked neon, the light switch on the wall inside the door. The air was cool but not uncomfortably cold.

I huddled on one of the bunks for the rest of the day, thinking. Did I have any more reason to believe Alex's story than all the other lies I had swallowed over the past few years? No; and yet it smacked of the truth. I saw Alex far more clearly now, all romantic idealizations stripped away. His sophistication now seemed like simple hedonism, his geniality self-interest, his boyish humour an infantile masculinity. It was only too easy to imagine him sacrificing his principles – if he had ever possessed any in the first place – for a secure life in which he could indulge his appetites without conscience. I could never forgive him; but I understood.

Only now, alone and imprisoned, did I begin to regret my decision to compromise myself as well as Alex. While I had expected retribution, I had not seriously imagined we might be executed, or worse; but this now seemed all too probable. Motecuhzoma's death had completely unbalanced the equation. With Maxixca returned to Tenochtitlan, it was obvious he was Tetzahuitl's candidate for the Turquoise Throne. And Cocomicihuatl, whose influence could not be underrated, would naturally favour the succession of her own son. With Extepan so conveniently marooned in Potomac – a circumstance which Tetzahuitl and Maxixca seemed to welcome – there was no other serious rival. All they had to do was wait until Extepan's forces were destroyed in the siege, whereupon Maxixca could be proclaimed Motecuhzoma's successor. No doubt he would then use the beam weapon to win the war in the north dramatically, inaugurating his reign by establishing total Aztec hegemony from the Aleutians to Patagonia.

Though I knew Extepan had betrayed me as much as anyone else, I disliked the idea that he had been outmanoeuvred by his half-brother. I had wanted to wound him personally because he had used me, but I hadn't intended to weaken him politically. Now Tetzahuitl and Maxixca would be able to use my indiscretions to undermine him further in his absence. Indirectly, I might well have helped usher in the reign of a man I considered to be vain, impulsive and xenophobic to a dangerous degree.

I was still wearing my wristwatch and so was able to keep track of the time. At noon a silent guard brought me a dish of bean stew with *tlaxcallis*; at six I was provided with a plate of rice and peppers and bottled Acuecuexatl water. Adjoining the cell was a small washroom, with full toilet facilities. For the moment, my conditions of imprisonment were relatively luxurious, given the gravity of my crime.

I remained calm, even though the hopelessness of my situation was never more obvious. But there were further surprises in store. Late that evening, Maxixca returned.

He brought Victoria with him.

She was ushered into the cell, looking frightened and ashamed. Maxixca, once again relishing the situation, said, 'Sisters should be together, should they not?'

I stared him out, my face expressionless.

'You two deserve one another,' he said fiercely. Then he went out, slamming the door behind him.

I heard the key turn in the lock, the bolts being rammed home. His footsteps, and those of his escort, receded down the stone corridor into silence.

Victoria stood motionless, staring at the floor. She was dressed in a rose-print *huipil* and cream culottes, stylish clothes already crumpled and dust-stained.

I was sitting cross-legged on my bed, and I did not get up. There was a long silence, until at last I said, 'When did they arrest you?'

She kept her head bowed. 'This afternoon. When I came back

from the masseur. They told me you were in prison, and Alex. They said what had happened.'

'I expect you were surprised.'

She nodded. She couldn't bring herself to look at me.

'An eye for an eye. That's what I thought.'

Tears began to trickle down her cheeks.

'Why did you do it?' I asked. 'You're my sister. I thought the world of you.'

Silence except for her crying.

'Alex says you didn't even love him.'

Even more tears. 'They were going to send me away in any case.'

'Why? Were you really involved in the bomb plot?'

An ardent shake of the head. 'I knew nothing about it until it was over. They said it was either that, or public disgrace.'

She didn't elaborate.

'You might as well sit down,' I said quietly.

Slowly she squatted on one of the floor mats, sitting sideways to me.

'Tell me,' I insisted.

She gave a long doleful sigh. 'Going to Alex, at least I'd be with someone I knew. They were determined to get rid of me one way or another.'

'Why?'

Now there were more tears, and she buried her face in her hands. It was so theatrical, I thought, and yet it had always worked in currying my sympathy in the past. I was ready to let her cry until she was drained of tears.

'They had photographs,' she sobbed. 'Photographs and films.'

'Photographs? Of what?'

'Of me. With Huahuantli.' She mentioned other Aztecs, all young members of the court in London.

I was slow to grasp what she was driving at.

'You were sleeping with them?'

'All I wanted was some company. Some fun and life. I didn't intend a scandal, Kate. They took advantage of me. I didn't know they were filming and photographing everything. It was horrible!'

I remembered Tlacahuepan at Windsor Castle, and how I had

automatically taken Victoria's side. She had probably seen me
approaching and pretended he was forcing himself on her to
spare her embarrassment. I had needed no persuading.

'Where were these films and photographs taken?'

She was reluctant to tell me. 'At parties. Sometimes in their
rooms. Or mine.'

'You took them back to your own suite?'

'It sounds so *sordid*, I know! But I never planned it that way,
I swear. I enjoyed their company, and we'd have a few drinks,
and I knew they wanted me. You don't know what it's like,
Kate, feeling so useless, so scared—'

'I know what's it's like,' I said harshly. 'I had to fight to keep
it under control.'

More tears, back heaving, hands clawing her knees.

'So what did they do? With the evidence?'

'They showed it to me. They said I was a disgrace. A scandal.
A royal whore. They couldn't allow me to – what was it? –
undermine the moral fibre of their administration. I was given a
choice. Either I went to Alex, or they'd make everything public
and send me into real exile in disgrace.'

'You knew Alex was alive?'

Only now did she look up at me with bleary eyes. 'I swear I
didn't until then! I thought he was dead, like you did. But they
told me he'd co-operated with them, and that he'd been given a
place to live in Mexico. He was asking for me to be sent there.
What choice did I have, Kate? There was nothing I could do.'

'You could have come to me and told me the truth.'

She shook her head vehemently. 'They made sure there was
no chance of that. They were determined to keep me away from
you. They came for me in the night. That was the first I knew
about it. They kept me away from everyone.'

I had no doubt she was telling me the truth. It all fitted, even
down to the fact that a sister I had always considered a perfect
innocent had proved to be a perfect libertine. How blind I had
been!

'Who arrested you?'

'Maxixca came with his men. I was taken before the *cihuacoatl*.
He scared me, Kate. I was terrified. I knew I had to do what
they said.'

'And Extepan?'

'I didn't see him.'

This gave me pause. Was it possible that Extepan was totally innocent of all this chicanery? I doubted it, but it occurred to me that there was nothing to link him directly with Alex's faked death or Victoria's 'exile'. Had it all been engineered by Maxixca, under Tetzahuitl's instructions? But if so, why?

'You were set up,' I said. 'They let Huahuantli and the others seduce you so that they'd have a hold over you.'

She nodded dejectedly. 'I realize that now.'

I felt no temptation to chide her for her foolishness; I had been naïve enough myself.

'I missed you dreadfully, Kate,' she said softly. 'I know I let you down—'

'Let me down? I think you did rather more than that. You were sleeping with Alex even before we were captured.'

Renewed tears. 'He seduced me.'

I gave a scornful laugh. 'It takes two to sleep together. On a regular basis. He came to you in the mornings, didn't he? Warm from my bed?'

She had no answer for this.

'How did you feel, knowing I was still asleep nearby, suspecting nothing? Did that add to the thrill?'

She affected to look both astonished and saddened at the suggestion.

'It wasn't like that. I promise you, Kate.'

'Oh? What was it like, then?'

'I couldn't stop him.'

'What are you saying? That he raped you? Every morning before breakfast?'

My tone was scathing and she closed her eyes in the face of it. There were no tears now, no attempts to win my pity.

'It didn't occur to you to scream, cry out for help? How lucky for Alex!'

She took out a handkerchief and blew her nose. It seemed to me that the bloom was vanished from her youthful prettiness. She was raddled, coarsened by all that had happened.

'Do you remember the night of my nineteenth birthday, Kate?'

I said nothing.

'It was our first winter in Wales. I got drunk on the Chablis Alex had unearthed from somewhere. He took me up to bed.'

'I remember.'

'That's when it first happened. I was only half conscious, Kate. He was putting me into bed, helping me off with my clothes. Next thing I knew he was kissing me all over. Telling me how much he'd always wanted me.' She paused, looking shame-faced. 'I promise you it's true! Before I knew it, he'd started. I tried to struggle, to get free, but he told me not to cry out or else you'd come and where would we both be then? He told me you'd never believe I hadn't egged him on. I didn't know what to do. I was so confused, so drunk. That's how it happened.'

She was wringing the handkerchief in her fists, as if she could throttle the very memory. Or was desperately fabricating the whole sorry tale as she went along.

'And afterwards?' I said.

'Afterwards he had a hold over me. He threatened to confess everything to you, to shame me in your eyes. I couldn't bear that thought. I *idolized* you, Kate, though I know you'll find that hard to believe now. That's why I went along with him.'

I could see she desperately wanted me to believe her, to have some sympathy for her. But I was satiated with lies and tawdry excuses. We always seek to justify our most shameful acts by portraying ourselves as victims of circumstance.

'So,' I said acidly, 'you repeatedly submitted yourself to this torture in order that I wouldn't think badly of you?'

'It wasn't torture. I . . . I enjoyed it after a while. I'm sorry, Kate, but I have appetites like anyone else. Alex was the first, and he was a . . .' She caught herself, and had the grace to look embarrassed. 'I was flattered by his attentions. It didn't stop me feeling guilty, but it became . . . something to look forward to, I suppose. What else was there in Wales?'

It was plausible, as plausible as anything I had heard. Victoria, weak-willed, insecure, miserable in our Welsh exile, discovering her 'appetites' with Alex, the arch seducer. Hadn't he blinded me with his charms throughout our courtship and marriage?

'I always felt you'd find out in the end,' Victoria said. 'I'm amazed we lasted so long. I think Bevan knew. He caught us alone together once, and although we weren't doing anything, he must have guessed what was going on.'

This also made sense in retrospect. Bevan and Alex's mutual dislike probably arose from this. Alex must have found it intolerable that the Welshman knew his guilty secret, while Bevan's sarcasm concerning Victoria would naturally follow. Yet Bevan had never said anything direct to me. I began to wonder whether he had *always* known more than he revealed, and about more than just the sordid facts of my marriage. Whose side was he really on? It was possible he had also used me throughout, feeding me information only when he chose, when it suited his mysterious purposes. In all our adventures and secret machinations, he had emerged unscathed. Or was he, too, now under arrest, a prisoner in some other cell here? Somehow, it was hard to imagine this.

'There's something else I need to know,' I said to Victoria.

'I'll tell you anything, Kate.'

'When you and Alex were together, alone together, I mean, what did you think about?'

She lowered her head again. 'At first I thought about you all the time. What I was doing to you. I felt wretched. But as time went on . . . well, you simply lose sight of those things, I suppose. That's an awful thing to say, I know. The thing is, it wasn't really Alex that was important – who he was, I mean. I know that probably sounds strange. It probably sounds frightfully immoral, but it's true. I didn't even find him especially attractive.' She swallowed. 'Often when we were together I'd close my eyes and imagine I was with someone else entirely, a made-up lover. That made it easier to bear, easier to forget the . . . shameful side of it.'

'There must have been some excitement in it for you.'

She looked extremely self-conscious.

'I suppose it was that someone wanted me so badly he couldn't resist it, despite the dangers. It didn't matter who the person was. Do you understand?'

'The same sort of excitement you got from Huahuantli and the others?'

She gave me a wounded look. 'Is that so bad, Kate? Does it make me so terrible?'

'I'm the wrong person to ask.'

'I was growing up, Kate. I made the most hideous mistakes, and I'll always regret them. But I'll always love you, no matter what you think of me.'

'Don't talk to me about love.'

There was a waver in my voice, and Victoria sensed an opening. She made to rise, to approach me.

'Sit down!' I said, mustering as much calm as I could. 'I don't want you near me!'

She sat. There was a long silence.

'They must have put us together to torment us,' Victoria said at length. 'Do you think someone's listening?'

'Probably.'

'I don't care any more. I couldn't have gone on much longer.'

'Alex told me he loved you.'

Again she looked awkward. 'He was always telling me things like that. It didn't stop him from having his share of servant girls on the side.'

'Did you love him? At any stage?'

With apparent reluctance, she shook her head. 'I suppose that makes it worse. I suppose it makes me more terrible, doesn't it? I went to him because it was better than being alone.'

'I understand that. You would never have survived without anyone.'

'We didn't have much of a life. They wouldn't let us travel far, and we were always under escort wherever we went. It was as if we were living in a glasshouse, with everyone watching. They never trusted us.'

'Did Alex ever talk to you about why he betrayed us?'

'He always said he knew we had no hope of surviving in Wales. He thought we'd all be killed in the end. So he secretly got in touch with the Aztecs on the radio, and they came to an arrangement.'

'He told them where we were?'

She nodded. 'In exchange for our lives, he said. And the disk he had – that was what they wanted. The Aztecs saw they could use it for their own ends, plant disinformation, I think they called it, for their enemies.'

'Using me?'

Another nod. 'Until they could launch an attack on Russia. It was horrible, Kate. He had to keep feeding you lies.'

Which confirmed Alex's own story. He had carefully ensured he was separated from us in the confusion so that he could be whisked away, perhaps at a later date, by the Aztecs. No doubt he had also helped them prepare a body which matched his own as closely as possible so that I would be certain he had been killed. I could see he would have preferred this arrangement, even down to the elaborate lengths of pretending that he had died in battle in Scotland: better a dead hero than a secret traitor still living with a wife he had betrayed.

'Do you know something?' Victoria said. 'I always wondered, when I knew what he had done, why they kept him alive afterwards. When they no longer had any use for him, I mean. It would have been safer to kill him, wouldn't it? After all, everyone else assumed he was already dead. But he claimed the Mexica – he always called them that – were honourable people. He knew he was a traitor to his country and couldn't expect complete freedom. But he had served them well, and they honoured their obligations in turn.'

This sounded credible: the Aztecs set great store by such things. Equally, they reacted with extreme severity against those who failed them.

Tentatively, Victoria asked, 'How did you find out about us?'

I told her my side of the story, beginning with Bevan's infiltration of the networks. I spared no thought for whether our conversation was being recorded; I also spared Victoria no details. She showed little reaction when I recounted how I had seduced Alex, though I found it strange to view myself as a *femme fatale* when I had been his wife and Victoria his mistress.

'Did you know that our marriage was annulled?' I asked.

'Alex told me when I joined him in Quauhnahuac,' she replied. 'That was another of the conditions he asked for. He wanted to be sure there was no constitutional bar to you remarrying.'

I laughed at this. 'More likely he wanted it annulled so that he could marry you.'

She shook her head. 'You mustn't think him totally selfish, Kate. He did try to think of you, in his way. He wanted to make it as easy as possible for you to build a new life.'

'You'll forgive me if my heart doesn't swell in gratitude at the thought. Alex was self-centred to the core.'

She didn't bother to dispute this.

'Where is he now?' she asked.

'They took him away. I don't know where.'

'What's going to become of us, Kate?'

I remembered her asking the same question when we were first captured. Then she was fearful and dependent; now she sounded merely fatalistic.

'I don't know,' I said. 'Maxixca's always hated me, and I doubt that either Alex or I can expect any mercy if he becomes *tlatoani*. You might be luckier. You're just an innocent in all this – relatively speaking.'

'It would be easier for them if they got rid of us all, at a stroke, wouldn't it?'

I was tempted to fob her off with reassurances, as I had done so many times in the past. But it was ominous that she had been arrested, since, from the Aztec point of view, she had done nothing to compromise them.

'Expect the worst,' I said. 'Then you won't be disappointed.'

'You must hate me.'

'I thought I did,' I replied. 'But it's too strong a word. I'm disappointed, disillusioned. Part of me will never be able to forgive you. But I think you were more a fool than a real schemer. And you're still my sister.'

Very slowly, she rose and came tentatively forward. She squatted in front of me, head bowed, a sinner expecting absolution. When I did nothing, she laid her hands gently on my knees.

'I think I'm prepared for anything now,' she said. 'I'm just glad I'm with you at last. Honest, Kate, I've always loved you best, despite what I did.'

I reached out and almost absently began stroking her hair. I did it to avoid speaking, as a gesture to the past which carried little of the sisterly affection of old. Declarations of love and affection are always devalued when tendered in the coinage of remorse. Yet her need for me was sincere, I was certain; she had no one else.

'It's late,' I said. 'We should try to sleep.'

'Can we be together tonight, Kate? I need someone close.'

'There's hardly room.'

'Please.'

The bunk bed was narrow, but I moved across to give her room. She snuggled up close, head on my breast, an arm draped across my waist. I continued stroking her hair, determined that I wouldn't allow myself to return to our relationship of old. Yet to all outward appearances, it was just like before.

After a time I remarked, 'I've forgotten to turn off the light.'

Silence; she was already asleep.

Nine

Over the next few days, we talked a great deal, largely because there was nothing else to do. Guards brought us food and drink three times a day, plain fare, but sufficient to keep our stomachs satisfied. We saw no one else. We spoke mostly about that part of the past which was safe from recriminations – our childhood and adolescence, the uncomplicated days before the invasion, before our whole world changed. We spoke of Father, and of Richard, speculating on his future now that we were both in disgrace. I thought it likely he would continue to prosper with Xochinenen at his side: he was popular with everyone, and a Mexican stake in the succession would be guaranteed when his child was born. I had a feeling he would scarcely miss us.

We avoided further mention of Alex, except in passing relation to other things. I asked Victoria about Bevan, hoping that she would know more than I did about his true motivations. She could tell me nothing I didn't already know. Whatever his true loyalties, Bevan had kept them well hidden from everyone around him.

The more we talked, the more the familiar patterns of old re-established themselves, the simple ease of communication between sisters who had spent most of their lives together. And, of course, there is always great comradeship in adversity. We needed chatter to smother our fears.

On the fourth day, we went without supper, and the following morning we received no breakfast. Neither of us made a great issue of this, though we had doubtless begun to think the same thing: they were going to starve us to death. But late in the afternoon, a guard opened the door briefly to push two plates inside. The door was immediately closed again.

A slow starvation then, I thought as I spooned a mash of sweet potato and green beans into my mouth; perhaps they intend to let us die by degrees.

There was no further food that day, which tended to confirm my worst suspicions. But then, at ten o'clock that night, we heard footsteps approaching outside.

The door opened, and in marched an Aztec officer I had never seen before, accompanied by an escort. He surprised me by saluting.

'Please come with us,' he said in perfect English.

It sounded like a request rather than a command, though I didn't seriously imagine we could refuse him.

He took us down a long corridor. As far as I could see in the gloom, all the other cells were empty, their doors open.

We were ushered into a lift, and carried downwards rather than up. At the bottom, a monorail carriage was waiting. A lighted tunnel carrying the rail stretched off into the distance to vanishing point. I knew we had to be deep underground.

Victoria sat close to me, and her hand found mine. The carriage slid away, rapidly building up speed.

After a ten-minute subterranean journey, we reached another terminus. There were no signs or anything to say where it was. We entered another lift, which took us upward.

We emerged into a narrow carpeted corridor with pale blue walls and a frieze of crocodiles. The officer led us to a door and opened it.

Inside was a well-appointed bathroom.

'Perhaps you would like to refresh yourselves,' the officer said.

'Why?' I responded. 'Are we meeting someone important?'

He smiled indulgently. 'We're simply thinking of your own comfort. You will have complete privacy, I assure you.'

I led Victoria inside without further comment, closing the door behind us. There was lemon-scented soap, perfumed towels, a shower and a shell-shaped corner bath. Water came out of the mouths of golden taps shaped like squatting frogs.

Were they simply toying with us, delaying the inevitable moment of our punishment? I told myself it didn't matter, at least not for the moment. Though Victoria and I had washed twice daily in our cell, we both felt grubby.

'Come on,' I said. 'Let's make the most of it!'

We spent over an hour in the bathroom, soaking in hot water saturated with bath crystals, washing and conditioning our hair, applying moisturizing lotions to our skins. We dried ourselves slowly, at our ease.

The clothes we had been wearing were dirty and stale. On a heated rail were draped long dresses of plain white cotton. There were no undergarments.

Victoria looked at me. I shrugged, trying to make light of the fact that the dresses would only emphasize our lack of status. I reached for one and slipped it over my shoulders.

The Aztec officer was still waiting patiently outside the door with the escort. He smiled at us, as if to say that he had expected to be kept waiting, then led us without a word to another door at the end of the corridor.

The room inside was small and windowless, hung with patterned curtains. The only furniture was a Victorian-style dining table and two matching chairs. They looked out of place, as if they had been brought to the room specifically for this occasion.

The table was laden with hot food, and as soon as the smell of cooked meat reached my nostrils, I began to salivate. Two places had been set with white napkins and shining cutlery. There was a pair of wine bottles in a silver cooler.

'No doubt you are hungry,' the officer said. 'This is for you. Please feel free to eat.'

I turned to him. 'What is this? The condemned women's last meal?'

Another smile. 'I don't believe it's a tradition we follow.'

'Perhaps it's poisoned, then. Is that it? Is that how you plan to be rid of us?'

'I assure you there's nothing here to endanger your life. Would you like me to taste it for you?'

I said nothing.

'You aren't forced to eat it. It's there if you want it. Now we shall leave you alone.'

He withdrew with his men before I had a chance to argue.

After the door was closed, I heard them marching away. I went to the door and turned the handle. It was locked.

On the further side of the room was a second door. It, too, was locked.

Victoria and I inspected the food on the table. There were meat dishes with mushrooms and chillis, plates of sautéed vegetables and pulses in rich sauces, multicoloured maize-cobs drenched in garlic butter. The food was still hot, its aromas assailing us. My stomach felt like a yearning void and my mouth was drenched.

'What should we do?' Victoria asked.

She was just as ravenous as I. The idea of dying by poisoned food held little appeal, even though it was preferable to some forms of death. But I doubted they intended to kill us this way: it was somehow too blatant. We had been left alone, which suggested they weren't yet ready to pass final judgement. I had a feeling that a very public example would be made of us.

'We've nothing to lose,' I said. 'Let's eat.'

Cautiously at first, then with increasing abandon, we spooned food on to our plates. Most of the dishes were white meats such as pork or turkey, heavily spiced and quite delicious. We were so hungry that almost anything would have tasted wonderful, poisoned or not. I shared a bottle of Zaachila Chardonnay with Victoria, drinking as freely as she, hoping the alcohol would blunt any terrors to come. It was to prove a futile hope.

Were we being watched as we ate? Probably, and yet the room had a hermetic feel, encouraging the sense that we were totally alone. I was unused to wine in any quantity, but when the first bottle was emptied, we took the second from the cooler and uncorked it.

There were persimmons in honey for dessert, with vanilla ice cream from a refrigerated bowl. Victoria and I sated ourselves, conscious that this was probably the last time we would be allowed any luxury. And so it was to prove.

I began to feel light-headed, frivolous, even. Victoria and I started making jokes about our predicament; we started to giggle, to whisper pretended secrets, as if playing to our unseen audience. The room was dimly lit with wall lights, and I began to imagine shadows moving at the periphery of my vision while at the same time remaining certain no one was there. The wall lights seemed to give off a soft prismatic play of colours which entranced me. I grew hot, and had to resist the urge to loosen my dress. Victoria had no such inhibitions: she untied the thong at her neck.

I can't remember what we talked about, but we kept chattering blithely. My voice sounded distant, as if someone else were using it. I continued to chase the shadows at the edges of my gaze. Victoria was sharply in focus across the table, but her own speech also had a remote yet hypnotic quality so that what I reacted to was not what she said but rather the sound and cadence of her voice.

I don't know how long it was before I realized that someone had entered the room. The light seemed to have dimmed at this point so that I felt as if I was viewing everything through an amber haze. The figure was in shadow at first, but as he stepped forward into the light, I gasped.

It was Extepan.

He was dressed in a similar fashion to us, in a simple tunic of white cotton. His feet were bare except for gold circlets around his ankles, and his hair had been cropped to a stubble. He looked like a prisoner, a sacrificial victim just like ourselves. Behind him stood two other Aztecs, both in ceremonial costumes with cloaks, ear pendants, coiled serpent staffs of black wood.

Extepan held out both his hands and said, 'Come.'

His two companions raised Victoria and me from our chairs. I felt detached from what was happening, as if the core of my consciousness had retreated to a private place that was inside me yet not part of me. As if I had become an observer, a watcher and a listener, in my own actions.

We were led up a long stairway into another room, where Teztahuitl and numerous other Aztecs were waiting. All wore traditional costume, a plethora of feathered ornaments, richly patterned cloaks and gold jewellery which shone in the flickering light of torches in brackets on the bare stone walls. The light entranced me, making shadows loom and ripple. Voices were distant yet occasional sounds sharp and distinct: the rustling of a fabric, the chink of metal on stone, a cough.

Extepan went forward and stood before Tetzahuitl, who promptly lifted the cotton tunic from his body, leaving him standing naked before us, light gleaming on his body. Then the *cihuacoatl* draped a mantle around him. It was turquoise, the imperial colour.

The other figures seemed to retreat, to dissolve into the shadows, so that now there were only the four of us, Victoria and I facing Extepan and the *cihuacoatl*.

'I thought you were in Potomac,' I heard myself say.

It was Tetzahuitl who spoke: 'The siege was ended. We have destroyed the enemy's capital. The New English have sued for peace.'

I could feel my tongue, rough and bloated, in my mouth. It was hard to speak.

'Where's Maxixca?' I asked.

'He's been sent to accept the surrender,' Tetzahuitl replied.

I laboured with my tortuous thoughts, with the effort of speaking Nahuatl.

'I thought you were going to make him *tlatoani*.'

He smiled at this. 'What gave you that idea?' His face rushed at me, then sank back as swiftly. 'He's an able soldier, but he lacks the finer instincts necessary for a ruler. We already have a successor.'

Extepan stood motionless, expressionless, his gaze on me. He was now wearing a headdress of precious stones and quetzal feathers.

'You betrayed him,' Tetzahuitl said.

The stone room was cool, a wide pillared doorway opening to the night.

'What did you expect?' I said. 'You all lied to me. Used me.'

Extepan raised a hand as if to silence any further discussion.

Then a voice said: 'I was worthless. I never honoured you.'

Victoria and I both turned. There, sitting in the shadows on an *icpalli*, was Alex. He was naked, and there was something wrong with him, something utterly wrong. In the dimness, it was hard to see, but his face looked a travesty of the real thing, eyes sunk in blackness, skin slack, his shape all wrong.

'At this time of the year,' I heard Extepan saying, 'our ancestors celebrated the feast of Xipe Totec . . .'

Even as he spoke, 'Alex' rose and began capering grotesquely towards us, waving his arms, genitals flapping, face like a mask.

Victoria's fingernails clawed into my wrist, and my whole body crawled. His skin sagged, then fell away entirely, crumpling to the floor to reveal the prancing, black-painted figure that had been wearing it.

Xipe Totec, the Flayed One . . .

Victoria's screams were long, ululating shrieks of terror and loathing. They went on and on, unearthly in their intensity, drowning out everything else. Within myself I remember wondering how I remained so calm. I simply stood there, revolted and petrified, it was true, yet at the same time I had a sense of finally confronting what I had always feared.

The torches kept flickering on the walls, and my eyes were drawn to the flames, the restless, changing patterns and colours. Dimly I was aware of Victoria's screams diminishing, but only because she was being led away. Tears were flooding from my eyes, unaccompanied by any feelings of sorrow. Then I seemed to be alone with Extepan, who was raising me from a kneeling position.

'Why?' I said. 'Why?'

His face was close to mine, familiar yet completely strange in its frame of feathers.

'You loved him, didn't you?' he said softly in English. 'Even at the end.'

'Why did you use me? I believed in you.'

'You never believed I truly wanted you for yourself. Did you, Catherine? Did you?'

Only in his eyes did his rage show. He held me by the upper arms, very tightly.

'He was a traitor and a coward. I would have honoured you, made you everything my mother was.'

The lights of the torches behind him danced. I began lolling in his hands, but he raised me roughly upright. His robe had fallen open, and I was certain he was going to revenge himself by raping me.

'You killed him,' I said, aware that I was sobbing. 'You had him flayed alive.'

'I gave you what you wanted.'

He let me go, and I slumped to the cold stone floor.

Blood rushed and swirled in my head, filling my ears with a roaring. I tried to sit up, but the walls of the chamber seemed to pulse around me, as if I were trapped within a stone heart. There were muttered exchanges, sandalled feet passed close by my face. Then snakes rose up my throat and gushed out of my mouth in a teeming mass, leaving only the acid reek of bile.

After a time I was raised up again. A mountain lion and a man-sized eagle reared their faces at me. I was dragged out through the doorway, past squatting stone soldiers with braziers in their laps. The bright comma of the moon punctuated the dark night sky, and a host of Aztec nobles waited with jewelled costumes and feathered banners.

We were on top of the Great Pyramid in the Temple Precinct: I had been brought out of one of the shrines. The thick night air was filled with smoke and incense, and ranks of whitewashed skulls leered down at me from a blood-red background on Huitzilopochtli's crowning glory. Extepan sat on a raised throne with Tetzahuitl at his side.

The sky was filled with shooting stars. Fascinated, I traced their paths with my eyes, after-images lingering. Those assembled were murmuring and chanting, a vast communal sound like the pulse and ebb of life itself. I swam in and out of awareness, my mind adrift, unharnessed, accepting of everything. I saw Tetzahuitl raise the imperial diadem and place it on Extepan's head; I heard him announce that the new *tlatoani* had taken the name of Xiuhcoatl. I saw Extepan rise and receive the humble obeisances of the nobles, who came forward, crouching, heads bowed, not daring to look him in the face. Was that Chicomeztli in the crowd? I could not be sure. Mia stood close to the throne, holding Cuauhtemoc, placid and joyous, fulfilling her desires at last beside the man she loved. I was certain she would become his queen now, and foreign women would be expunged from the heart of the empire. Xiuhcoatl, the Serpent of Fire, weapon of Huitzilopochtli, the instrument which he used to destroy all his enemies.

Now everything slowed, as if all the figures were moving through water. Torchlight spilled across the stone like melted butter. Black-skinned figures with Medusa hair moved on the edges of the darkness, and the pristine sacrificial stone awaited me. I had a vision of Extepan looming over me with a long obsidian knife, naked except for his golden body ornaments. As the black blade sliced through my breast, he mounted me, penetrated me to the core, and as my heart was torn out, I died in a flurry of release.

When some semblance of consciousness returned, I found myself being led into the Quetzalcoatl temple, through the great gaping mouth.

Still wearing his royal diadem, Extepan stood in front of an obsidian mirror just like the one in Crystal Palace Park. I was brought before it. I searched for my reflection but saw only an opaque blackness that nevertheless had depth. I was certain that if the guards pushed me forward, I would plunge down into a pit of nothingness.

'You betrayed your vows to me,' Extepan said, 'but I intend to honour one of mine to you. Come forward.'

The guards' hands fell away. Extepan was standing right next to the mirror. I teetered, steadied myself. Took a step towards him. He caught me by the hand.

Figures watched from the shadows around us. My lips were numb, my mouth parched.

'Once we Mexica believed the world was destroyed and renewed four times,' Extepan said. 'Now we know that it has countless existences, all occurring together but apart from one another, like multiple reflections in a mirror.' His smile was like a leer. 'Did you know we've found another world similar to our own, Catherine? A different Earth, recognizable yet changed in many important respects from our own. We know it's there because this – ' he gestured at the mirror ' – is a doorway into it.'

My ears were filled with a buzzing, and I couldn't tell whether it came from outside or within me.

'That is what you found in England,' he said. 'A doorway. A passage to another place. My father had several built at different locations so that we could send our people through to explore. They return with fascinating stories, Catherine, of people and places so like yet unlike the ones we know.' He paused. 'Of course, they travel secretly, a few at a time, disguising themselves. For the moment.'

I wanted to sleep, to flee into darkness and oblivion. But he held me up, drew me close to him. To the mirror.

'Perhaps you still imagine I intend to have you killed?' Slowly he shook his head. 'Not so, Catherine. Not so. I'm sending you into exile, your sister, too. Somewhere very far away.'

I barely heard him; I felt myself slipping away. Then he put a hand under my chin, raising my head. At first I thought he intended to kiss me, but my jaw opened under the continued pressure of his fingers, and a figure stepped forward to press something into my mouth, something crumbly and sweet which dissolved on my tongue.

The small crowd in the shadows loomed close, and it was as if I saw them through a fish-eye lens, grinning down at me. As I fell forward, plunging into blackness, I was almost certain that one of them, at the very last, was Bevan.

Epilogue

In my dreams, I dreamt of Aztecs, lighting New Fires on mountain tops to celebrate the rebirth of the world, offering human hearts in sacrifice to the sun, aloft in huge solar fleets which flew over vast uncharted landscapes, hungry for conquest.

I dreamt vividly, and at great length.

I remember waking, yet not waking, because my eyes were still closed. I couldn't move or speak. An Aztec-accented voice was talking in persuasive, hypnotic tones, telling me that Victoria and I had been taken to another Earth, where we were unknown and would lead a simple life of anonymity. All the essentials had been provided for us: a place to live, new identities, a fixed income which would allow us to survive with a modicum of comfort. We were banished utterly, with no hope of returning to our old world. There would be no contact with it, nothing.

The voice was quietly insistent, and I was in a receptive, accepting state of mind. I listened calmly and carefully, absorbing everything. At length the voice fell silent, and I sank back down into sleep again.

When I next awoke, it was to a bright morning. I was lying in a bed in an eggshell green room, flower-patterned curtains drawn back at the window.

I sat up sharply, feeling fragile and brittle but very clear-headed. The room was warm, though a veil of condensation hung on the lower pane of the window. Victoria lay asleep in a bed next to mine.

I rose and went over to her. She was breathing slowly and regularly, her face tranquil.

A cream towelling robe hung on the back of the door. It fitted perfectly. I turned the tortoiseshell handle of the door, opened it very slowly.

A narrow landing gave access to a bathroom and a second bedroom. Both had a newly decorated look, and they had not been used. Very gingerly, I descended the stone stairway.

Downstairs was a furnished living room with a television and a Welsh dresser stacked with crockery. There was a book-lined study, and a new fitted kitchen with oak-panelled cupboards and a wall-clock that said eight twenty. A pristine water boiler thrummed and swished high on one wall.

The windows looked out across a valley which I immediately knew to be the same one where we had spent our years in hiding. And yet it was not the same: where the Ty Trist colliery had stood were flat-topped landscaped mounds, one of them with a football pitch on top.

Cautiously I opened the door and went outside into a neglected garden whose lawn had, nevertheless, recently been mown. The valley was the same yet different, trees and fields wrongly placed, all the contours of the land subtly or starkly changed. A car passed by on the road which wound up the valley to Tredegar – a petrol-driven car of a design that looked old-fashioned to my eyes. Farms, houses, even the russet stretches of bracken – they were not as I remembered them.

Though the sun was shining, the spring air was chill. I went back inside, opening the kitchen cupboards and finding them stocked with food. I inspected the cartons and tins and jars. Their labels were unfamiliar to me, though they looked just like products that might have existed in my own world. The fridge hummed away in one corner, eggs and several cartons of UHT milk inside. There were two sliced loaves in the freezer, another one in the breadbin. I squeezed it; it was fresh.

The whole place was spotless, and yet it had an unoccupied feel, as if we were newly arrived. I plugged the television into its primitive socket and switched it on. Two presenters, a man and a woman, were talking to a British movie star whom I had never seen or heard of before. Then there was a brief report about a phenomenon called the Greenhouse Effect. A plump, smiling man came on screen with astrological forecasts. Then a relentlessly jovial woman began doing exercises.

On the wall above the fireplace was a print of an oil painting showing a vase of sunflowers.

I heard Victoria scream.

I raced upstairs and found her cowering in the corner of her bed, knees up to her chest, bedclothes drawn around her. She looked terrified. I went to her and she clung tightly to me, whimpering uncontrollably and making inarticulate sounds.

'It's all right,' I said, feeling as if I was living a dream.

I began to stroke her hair while she trembled in my arms. For a long time I did nothing else. I thought then that she was merely suffering a shock reaction to the strangeness of her surroundings and all the terrors which had preceded it. I thought that she would eventually calm down and that we would be able to talk about what happened, to draw comfort and reassurance from one another, to face our bizarre new circumstances together. But I was wrong. Downstairs, the television blared unfamiliar theme music and advertisements for products I felt I should have known, yet didn't. When at length Victoria seemed calm enough to speak, when I raised her head from my breast, it was damp with the saliva which had been drooling from her mouth. She gazed at me with eyes that had hugely dilated pupils. There was nothing behind them.

Victoria was broken, her mind finally destroyed by what had been done to Alex. I realized this when she emptied her bladder on the bed and had to be led into the bathroom and undressed like a child. After that first shock reaction, she became docile, but, though I tried, I could not get her to utter a single word. She watched my mouth as I spoke, as a young baby might, but never reacted to what I was saying. I didn't even know if she understood me.

There was soap and fresh towels in the bathroom. The wardrobes were stocked with clean sheets and clothing for both of us, well-tailored but undemonstrative fashions, manufactured in London, Paris and Milan rather than Amecameca or Potomac or Shanghai. The brand names were entirely unfamiliar.

I got Victoria downstairs and sat her in an armchair. The cottage was centrally heated, but I wrapped a blanket around her for extra comfort. I was extremely hungry, and presumed that she was too, though she gave no sign. But before I set to preparing us a meal, I quickly scouted the spacious surroundings of the cottage, looking for any lurking figures, hoping to find whoever had brought us here hovering nearby, keeping us under surveillance. The cottage stood alone, surrounded by fields, with a terrace of houses and a redbrick school on the hillside above us. There was no one in sight.

I heated some tomato soup, then opened a can of curried vegetables, which we ate with rice. Since arriving here I haven't eaten meat or served it to Victoria. I remember only too well our final supper, and I think of Alex, and of the pre-Christian Aztec ceremonial rite which reputedly included the eating of the flesh of the sacrificial victim. Human flesh is said to resemble pork in flavour, and rich sauces make many meats indistinguishable from one another. It does not bear dwelling on.

Victoria was ravenous, gulping her soup and ripping slices of bread apart to cram into her mouth. I continued to feel a kind of inner brightness and stillness which I suspected were the after-effects of whatever drugs had been fed to us in our last meal. The Aztecs were expert in the use of hallucinogenics, and it would have been easy for them to incorporate fungi and other narcotic plants into the dishes we had eaten – *peyotl*, probably, and *ololiuhqui*, and the sacred fungus *teonanacatl*. No doubt there were others, carefully chosen to keep us stupefied yet distracted with visions. I found it impossible to separate what had really happened from what were products of my own drugged imaginings. Everything I could remember seemed slightly unreal.

For the first three days I did nothing except remain in the cottage with Victoria, learning to care for her and attempting to get my bearings. Victoria required little attention except at mealtimes; she soon learned how to use the bathroom, to wash and dress herself, and she sat contentedly in front of the television for hours, watching whatever programmes were showing with a faint, vacant smile. Though she began to respond to me and seemed to understand simple instructions, she never spoke.

The study held a wall of books, some old, some new. There was an atlas and a gazetteer, guides to South Wales and Gwent, a one-volume history of the world, big coffee-table books on literature, the cinema and popular art. And, of course, there

were titles on Mexico and the Aztecs, at least two dozen of them.
These, and the sunflower painting, were not-so-subtle forms of
Aztec mockery, I was certain. The painting, famous in this
world, I later discovered, was unknown in mine.

I scouted the area around the cottage whenever I was able,
avoiding contact with the locals. One of the guidebooks told me
that the terrace of houses was the village of Troedrhiwgair, again
unknown in my world. The people were Welsh, but English-
speaking, dressed in a recognizable style of clothing, while the
television revealed the manners and mores and means of speaking
in this Britain as no different from the one I had left.

It was March here, as on our world, and I was able to calculate
that two days had passed beween Extepan's coronation and my
waking up in the cottage. Two whole days of nothing except the
sound of the Aztec voice in my waking sleep, telling me what I
could expect. Yet nothing could have prepared me for the
actuality.

It rained for the rest of the week, and I spent much of my time
sitting with Victoria, watching news reports and current affairs
programmes, perusing book after book, studying their illus-
trations and photographs minutely, fascinated and dislocated by
every fact, small or large, which forced me to accept that we had
indeed been cast adrift on a different Earth.

And how different! How mundanely yet stunningly different.
Its landscapes and histories echo my own, there are places and
names and people which are familiar; yet nothing is quite the
same. It is as if our destinies are separate but linked, like ghost
reflections of one another, so that some people and places are
famous in both – often for different reasons – others not at all.
Of course, I was startled to discover that here the Aztecs are but
a memory, their nascent empire destroyed by the very man who
set them on the path to future greatness in my world. There is a
British royal family that stems from a line of the ruling house
extinguished on my Earth. Here, my great-grandfather was never
born and our house at Marlborough does not exist. I feel like a
ghost. What could be more cruel than to inhabit a world which
knows nothing of you? Extepan chose his revenge well.

There were days, especially early on, when I believed my
knowledge that I was but a fiction would drive me into the same

kind of madness as Victoria. Imagine, just try to imagine, living in a world that seems an invention, a parody of reality. It's little wonder that I have become intensely mistrustful to the point of paranoia and seldom like leaving the cottage. Even less do I like having to meet people, however ordinary-looking or prosaic their concerns. A chance encounter fills me with dread; a simple 'Good morning' is enough to make me want to flee for fear that I might be forced into a conversation that will swiftly reveal the depths of my ignorance of this world, exposing me as a fake, an intruder, an anomaly. What could be worse than living in a place where every mundanity is an attack on memory and belief, a threat to one's already fragile sense of self?

Yet if I thought that oblivion in this world was punishment enough, I did not realize that Extepan had reserved the subtlest cruelty for last. At the end of the first week, a maroon van came jolting down the rutted driveway to the cottage. Stomach churning with anxiety, I rushed outside as it pulled up. A man got out and smiled at me.

I went immobile with shock.

I watched him walk around to the back of the van, open the door and remove a large cardboard box filled with groceries.

It was Bevan.

He wasn't the Bevan of my world, I knew that immediately, because he was slimmer, balder, and wore a greying beard. He carried himself differently, was less slovenly dressed, wearing blue jeans and a sweatshirt, the kind of clothing which my Bevan had never favoured. But their faces were the same – the prominent jaw and ears, the small mouth – and they were the same age. They could have been twins.

He brought the box up to me, still smiling.

'Not a bad morning, is it? They said you wanted this.'

The smile was more open, less devious, than the one I knew. He wasn't the same man, yet it was him, it was him.

'You're down for weekly deliveries, that's right, isn't it?'

I made to speak, but first had to clear my throat.

'Who arranged this?'

He looked a little put-out. 'Got a call from a bloke in London, didn't I? He said you and your sister had just moved in and wanted a regular delivery. Run the local store I do, see.'

Again I found it hard to speak, and even harder to think clearly.

'Did they say who they were?'

Now he was distinctly unsure of me. 'Someone from your bank, it was. They've opened an account for you with me, so it's all paid for. All right, is it?'

I looked at the box. It held bread, milk, tinned goods and washing powder. It was hard not to stare at him.

'There's another one in the back of the van,' he said. 'Where'd you want me to put it?'

I was still numb. 'In the kitchen,' I said, moving aside, indicating. 'It's in there.'

I followed him inside. He put the box down, then went out again, but not before saying, 'Bit of rain we've been having.'

I couldn't answer. He returned promptly with a second box, holding fresh vegetables and fruit.

Victoria was still asleep upstairs, and I was grateful, in case the sight of him sent her into another screaming frenzy. Everything about his manner suggested he was entirely innocent of who we really were and where we had come from, but his very appearance had thrown me into the throes of suspicion and unease. I wanted him to be gone, but at the same time I needed to find out what he knew.

'You said it was paid for,' I remarked.

He nodded blithely. 'There's an account at the local branch. They said you din't want any fuss. Sister's not well, is she?'

My suspicions redoubled. 'Who told you that?'

He was peering around the kitchen. 'Man who phoned. Mentioned that she'd had a breakdown, poor dab, and that you'd come here so she could convalesce. Nice and peaceful spot, isn't it?'

'Did he tell you who we were?'

Off-handedly he said, 'Sisters from London. Got a bit of money behind you, have you?'

'Who said that?'

He obviously found me strange, and perhaps was trying to be casual in response.

'I just assumed. With neither of you working, like.'

Was this simple inquisitiveness? Or an echo of the other Bevan's insolence? Did he really know something?

'Was there someone living here before us?' I asked.

'Headmaster of the school,' he said, obviously referring to the one above us on the hill. 'He moved to Newport when it shut down. It's been empty this past year or more. Pleasant spot, I reckon, with the river close by and no one to bother you.' He sucked on his teeth. 'Well, I'd best be going. See you in a week. If there's anything extra you need, the number's in the book. It's the Gwalia Stores in town. Castle Street, up by the town clock. You can't miss it.'

I followed him out to the door. He climbed into the van and started the engne. I had the impression he was eager to be going.

The driver's window was open. I went up to it as he revved the engine.

'What's your name?' I asked, a tremor in my voice.

But he was already pulling away.

Five months have passed since we first arrived here, and all my efforts to discover some firm evidence of our former lives have failed. Even if I had been so inclined, it would have proved difficult to travel widely because Victoria becomes agitated if we are away from the cottage for any length of time; and I share her tendency to want to huddle there.

Despite this, I did make several forays at first, forcing Victoria to accompany me to Tredegar, where the Gwalia Stores indeed exist. I watched Bevan serving customers inside but did not enter myself. Of course, I'm not certain his name is Bevan because the store front gives no proprietor and I'm afraid to ask any of the locals. I'm afraid to ask them in case they confirm it, or in case they don't. Somehow uncertainty seems preferable, though I can't rationally explain why. I refused even to consult the telephone directory, which might not, in any case, be conclusive. Bevan is a common name in this part of the world, a legacy of the English conquest of Wales, as on my Earth.

On that same visit, I steeled myself to go into the local bank, where it was confirmed that an account had indeed been opened in my name – Catherine Marlborough, the family name my great-grandfather adopted when he ascended the throne. Moneys from a trust fund would pay a net annual income of fifteen thousand pounds a year – more than enough to live on. Why such generosity? I wondered. It would have been far easier, and more cruel, for Extepan to have dumped us here penniless. Was it in deference to our former status? Or was he not yet finished with us?

It was difficult to establish the facts behind the trust fund without revealing my utter ignorance and thus arousing suspicion, but eventually I was allowed to speak by telephone to someone from the parent bank in London. He sounded business-like and very English, and gave every impression of knowing nothing about the Aztecs, of being no part in any duplicity on their behalf. By a tortuous process involving equal measures of dissembling and strategic absent-mindedness, I was able to establish that Victoria and I were supposedly the daughters of a diplomat who had been lost, with his wife, in an aircraft which had disappeared over the Gulf of Mexico – my heart quailed at this – two years before. Victoria was ill through a shock reaction to their deaths, but arrangements had been made in my father's will to provide for us. We had lived much of our lives in the Americas, and had no friends or relatives here.

I did not press the matter. No doubt all the relevant documentation existed, expertly faked and on file. Presumably the Aztecs had been sending their agents into this world for long enough to have built up impeccable identities as well as funds to support their operations. It was possible their agents in London would be British citizens from my world, collaborators with the Aztec Empire who could move with complete confidence through this Britain.

Not a day passed when I didn't look, in my surroundings or in newspapers and television programmes, for evidence of Aztec infiltration. I was certain someone from that world would have been put close by to watch over us. But I could never pinpoint anything. My suspicions tended to focus more and more on our new Bevan, a true native of this world, I was sure, but too much the *alter ego* of his enigmatic and elusive counterpart. Perhaps this Bevan had been recruited by the other one, was serving masters in my world. He called every week with our groceries, and while there was never anything in his manner to suggest this, his very presence and continual off-hand curiosity about us suggested a link. He was the only person I could identify directly with my own world, no matter that he differed from his progenitor. There were times when I wanted to ask him outright, but I could never muster the courage. I was torn between the need to know the truth and a fear of reopening terrible wounds. Victoria, for her part, showed absolutely no reaction when they finally encountered one another. Either something in her flatly refused to recognize him, or the abominations which had wiped away her sanity had also erased all memory of our past life.

So I vacillated, until one day I decided that there might be another means of confirming the truth. One Saturday, with a nervous Victoria in tow, I took a train to Paddington, and from there we travelled by Underground and suburban railway to Crystal Palace. I already knew that the palace in this world had been destroyed by fire decades before our own, but I had not come for that. I led Victoria through the park, down the hill towards the lake where the Quetzalcoatl structure had stood. On our world, it was the staging point for a tunnel into this one. And every entrance has an exit.

As we approached, I heard rhythmic percussive music. It was evening, and a small crowd was sitting on the big grassy bowl fronting the lake, watching a steel band play on a stage which had been built over it.

Behind the stage, there was only a chalet-like building with a black felt roof, too small to house any kind of secret installation. How could this be? Did the tunnel only generate its exit when it was activated? Or did the infiltrators from my world simply blink into existence in this one after transference? But that would allow them no means of getting back, whereas Extepan had told me Aztec agents regularly returned after their explorations.

The building was a drab municipal structure, used for storage and fenced off. I searched the surroundings thoroughly, rooting in the leaf litter under sycamore and holly trees for the smallest piece of evidence, an artifact or item inadvertently dropped, something disposable carelessly thrown away – a cigarette butt, a *tzictli* wrapper, a button or ring or footprint which indisputably came from my Aztec world. Anything would have convinced me. But there was nothing.

Victoria was agitated with the noise of the steel band, unsettled by the disruption and strangeness of London. It was growing dark, and I knew I had to get her home to the cottage that same day. I made one last desperate reconnoitre.

Nothing.

The fruitless visit to London undermined my confidence more than I first imagined. As the weeks turned into months and I remained ensconced in the cottage with Victoria, so our past lives seemed to me to become more like a dream, a mere figment of my own imaginings, while this world pressed its claims as the only true reality simply because we had to live in it day by day, to accept its domesticities and the sheer weight of its own normalcy. I think the after-effects of the Aztec drugs intensified this impression, distancing me from my memories, making them seem surreal.

Perhaps that's why I decided to write this account, to try to restore their legitimacy. Yet sometimes I wonder whether it may have the reverse effect, whether to put things down in words, make a story of them, is to make them fiction. Sometimes I imagine the Bevan of this world as a true innocent. I imagine him coming upon these pages and reading them. What would he think? That they were the deluded ramblings of a lonely woman who has to care for a debilitated sister in a part of the country where she knows no one? That I wrote them as a fantasy to divert and deliver myself from the drab realities of everyday existence? That I am, myself, mad?

Yet I hold to my beliefs, despite my growing doubts. I have to. And there are small victories, affirmations of the past which I cling to. A few days ago, while rummaging in the dressing-table drawer, I came upon a necklace secreted at the back. A bead necklace of jade and obsidian. Extepan's betrothal gift to me.

Every evening, when my work is done and Victoria is safely in bed, I go to the window and stare down the valley. I watch and wait. Extepan hasn't finished with us yet, I'm certain of that, otherwise he wouldn't have provided for us. He wouldn't have put us here, in this place, he wouldn't have left the necklace as a remembrance, he wouldn't have arranged for this other Bevan to be on hand. He hasn't finished with us because he's scarcely started with this world. The Aztecs now rule mine, but they live by conquest. I know it's only a matter of time before they build tunnels big enough to send whole armies through, tunnels which will enable them to extend their empire by conquering another world. Here, things are different, and they will find armies aplenty to test their mettle. But none, ultimately, to resist them. In the end, their onslaught will be irresistible.

I don't know when it will come, but I'm certain it shall. So I sit at the window each evening, turning the necklace in my hands, looking down the valley while Victoria sleeps and the house lies silent around me. I search the skies for points of light which will tell me that at last it has begun, at last it has begun again.

They will come in their shining ships to conquer and destroy, barbarians of gold and feathers and serpents of fire. There are days when I firmly believe this, days when I consider it an absurd delusion. Every evening I watch and wait with fear and longing.